FANTASY

THE BEST OF 2004

KAREN HABER
and JONATHAN STRAHAN
Editors

ibooks
new york
www.ibooks.net

DISTRIBUTED BY SIMON & SCHUSTER, INC.

ACKNOWLEDGMENTS

Our thanks to Robert Silverberg, Marianne Jablon, and Charles N. Brown for services above and beyond the call of duty. We'd also like to thank Justin Ackroyd, John Joseph Adams, Brian Bienkowski, Jennifer Brehl, Laura Cleveland, Bill Congreve, Andy Cox, Jack Dann, Ellen Datlow, Nick Gevers, Gavin J. Grant, Martin H. Greenberg, John Helfers, Rich Horton, Jay Lake, Deborah Layne, Kelly Link, Elizabeth A. Lynn, Robin Pen, Tim Pratt, Larry Segriff, Gordon Van Gelder, Jeff VanderMeer, and Sean Williams for their invaluable assistance with this book.

CONTENTS

INTRODUCTION
  Karen Haber and Jonathan Strahan   ix

FORBIDDEN BRIDES OF THE FACELESS
SLAVES IN THE NAMELESS HOUSE OF
THE NIGHT OF DREAD DESIRE
  Neil Gaiman   1

THE WORD THAT SINGS THE SCYTHYE
  Michael Swanwick   20

THE LITTLE STRANGER
  Gene Wolfe   64

THE FAERY HANDBAG
  Kelly Link   90

QUARRY
  Peter S. Beagle   119

THE ENCHANTED TROUSSEAU
  Deborah Roggie   170

THE SORCERER'S APPRENTICE
  Robert Silverberg   195

THE ANNALS OF
THE EELIN-OK
    Jeffrey Ford   226

PAT MOORE
    Tim Powers   251

THE ANGEL'S DAUGHTER
    Jay Lake   296

THE SILVER DRAGON
    Elizabeth A. Lynn   302

INTRODUCTION

When the estimable critic John Clute undertook the task of defining "fantasy" in his 1995 *Encyclopedia of Fantasy* he described it as a "most extraordinarily porous term," one that essentially covers an area so broad that it resists definition. Still, he assayed the following as a working definition: "A fantasy text is a self-coherent narrative. When set in this world, it tells a story which is impossible in the world as we perceive it; when set in an otherworld, that otherworld will be impossible, though stories set there may be possible in its terms."

That definition, and the difficulty it clearly suggests in readily identifying "fantasy" for a book of this type were very much on our minds when compiling this, the third volume in the *Fantasy: Best of* series, and the first to be published since founding editor Robert Silverberg stepped down and we (founding co-editor Karen Haber and Jonathan Strahan) took up the reins for both this and the companion *Science Fiction: Best of* anthology series. As long-time readers of fantasy, we were eager to assemble a book that represented all of the many wonders of the fantasy genre at the beginning of a new century, one that attempted to give some idea of the incredible richness and diversity of the field today. To us, that meant looking to both acknowledge the excellence to be found in genre fiction—the retelling of fairy tales, the construction of vast epic fantasies and such—as well in the more cross-genre "slipstream" work that has gained so much attention of late.

Of course, attempting to encompass all of the possible sources of fantasy short fiction today is a staggering undertaking. Because of its Clutean porosity, fantasy fiction is as likely to appear in the pages of genre magazines like *The Magazine of Fantasy & Science Fiction*, *Realms of Fantasy* or *Black Gate*, as in the pages of *The New Yorker*, *Conjunctions*, or the latest undertaking from *McSweeney's*. We found ourselves reading magazines, 'zines, chapbooks, anthologies, short story collections, and websites and what we found as we read was that 2004 was an extraordinary year for fantasy. It was certainly an extraordinary year for events and event books. Stephen King concluded Roland the Gunslinger's epic quest for the Dark Tower begun in 1978, while Stephen Donaldson resumed the quest for Thomas Covenant that he had set aside in 1983, both to mixed praise. Meanwhile British writers Susannah Clarke and Steph Swainston produced the two best first fantasies of the year in *Jonathan Strange and Mr Norrell* and *The Year of Our War* to near universal acclaim; Patricia A. McKillip delivered the best traditional fantasy of the year in *Alphabet of Thorn*; Elizabeth Hand managed her best novel to date in *Mortal Love*, and Gene Wolfe stepped in at year's end with the marvelous *The Wizard Knight*.

At shorter lengths, things were equally exciting. 2004 was a wonderful year for anthologies. The ever-reliable Ellen Datlow and Terri Windling produced one of the best fantasy anthologies of the year in *The Faery Reel: Tales of the Midnight Realm*. Aimed at a younger audience, it featured standout material by Kelly Link, Jeffrey Ford, Delia Sherman, and others. The other main contender was Al Sarrantonio's *Flights: Extreme Visions of Fantasy*. Although more uneven than the Datlow/Windling book, and designed for a considerably older audience, it featured excellent stories by Tim Powers, Elizabeth A. Lynn, Gene Wolfe, Robert Silverberg, and others. We were also impressed with Deborah Layne & Jay Lake's *Polyphony 4*, Harry Turtledove & Noreen Doyle's *The First Heroes*, Deborah Noye's *Gothic!*, and F. Brett Cox & Andy Duncan's *Crossroads*. One of the more disappointing anthologies of the year, Michael Chabon's *McSweeney's Enchanted Chamber of Astonishing Stories*, didn't seem to quite achieve what it's editor had hoped, but nonetheless featured fine stories by Stephen King, Peter Straub, Joyce Carole Oates and China Mieville.

It was a good year for fantasy stories in the magazines as well—many featured excellent work. Gordon Van Gelder's *The Magazine of Fantasy & Science Fiction* had a good year, with fine stories by Peter S. Beagle, Gene Wolfe, Robert Reed, and others. The other main genre fantasy magazine, Shawna McCarthy's *Realms of Fantasy* also had a good year, with solid stories from Jay Lake, Gene Wolfe, and David D. Levine, and deserves more acclaim than it seems to get. *Asimov's Science Fiction Magazine*, in its last year under long-time editor Gardner Dozois, published some fine fantasy by Michael Swanwick, Michael McDowell, Gregory Feeley, and others. We were also impressed by work from *The Third Alternative*, *Postscripts*, *Lady Churchill's Rosebud Wristlet*,

Electric Velocipede, and *Black Gate*, among many others.

There were a number of extraordinary short story collections published this year by John Crowley, Joanne Harris, Lucius Shepard, Jeff VanderMeer, Gene Wolfe and others. We were particularly impressed with Margo Lanagan's second collection, *Black Juice*, which was published in her native Australia.

And that, too briefly, is a sketch of the year we saw in reading for this book. Within it you will find dragons and foxes, witches and angels, and a woman who once hid a town in her handbag. All meet John Clute's definition, but more importantly they sparkle with the inescapable evidence of magic. We hope you enjoy reading it, as much as we enjoyed reading for it.

—Karen Haber & Jonathan Strahan
November 2004

Forbidden Brides of the Faceless Slaves in the Nameless House of the Night of Dread Desire

Neil Gaiman

Neil Gaiman was born in England in 1960, and worked as a freelance journalist before co-editing Ghastly Beyond Belief *(with Kim Newman) and writing* Don't Panic: The Official Hitchhiker's Guide to the Galaxy Companion. *He started writing graphic novels and comics with* Violent Cases *in 1987, and with the seventy-five installments of award-winning series* The Sandman *established himself as one of the most important comics writers of his generation. His first novel,* Good Omens *(with Terry Pratchett), appeared in 1991, and was followed by* Neverwhere, Stardust, American Gods, *and* Coraline. *His most recent books are* The Sandman: Endless Nights *and picture book* The Wolves in the Walls *(with long time collaborator Dave McKean). Gaiman's work has won the Hugo, World Fantasy, Bram Stoker, Locus, Geffen,*

1

International Horror Guild, Mythopoeic and Will Eisner Comic Industry awards. Upcoming, among many other projects, is a new novel Anansi Boys. *Gaiman moved to the United States in 1992 with his wife and three children, and currently lives in Minneapolis.*

Gaiman is, first and foremost, a storyteller. Moving with admirable ease from one form to another, he has published everything from poetry and song lyrics to picture books and full-length adult novels. In the tale that follows, he takes a fairly unprepossessing premise, combines it with more than a touch of humor, and produces something very special.

I.

Somewhere in the night, someone was writing.

II.

Her feet scrunched the gravel as she ran, wildly, up the tree-lined drive. Her heart was pounding in her chest, her lungs felt as if they were bursting, heaving breath after breath of the cold night air. Her eyes fixed on the house ahead, the single light in the topmost room drawing her toward it like a moth to a candle flame. Above her, and away in the deep forest behind the house, night-things whooped and skrarked. From the road behind her, she heard something scream, briefly—a small animal, that had been the victim of

2

some beast of prey, she hoped, but could not be certain.

She ran as if the legions of hell were close on her heels, and spared not even a glance behind her until she reached the porch of the old mansion. In the moon's pale light the white pillars seemed skeletal, like the bones of a great beast. She clung to the wooden doorframe, gulping air, staring back down the long driveway, as if she were waiting for something, and then she rapped on the door—timorously at first, and then harder. The rapping echoed through the house. She imagined, from the echo that came back to her that, far away, someone was knocking on another door, muffled and dead.

"Please!" she called. "If there's someone here—anyone—please let me in. I beseech you. I implore you." Her voice sounded strange to her ears.

The flickering light in the topmost room faded and vanished, to reappear in successive descending windows. One person, then, with a candle. The light vanished into the depths of the house. She tried to catch her breath. It seemed like an age passed before she heard footsteps on the other side of the door, and spied a chink of candlelight through a crack in the ill-fitting doorframe.

"Hello?" she said.

The voice, when it spoke, was dry as old bone—a desiccated voice, redolent of crackling parchment and musty grave-hangings. "Who calls?" it said. "Who knocks? Who calls, on this night of all nights?"

The voice gave her no comfort. She looked out at the night that enveloped the house, then pulled herself straight, tossed her raven locks, and said, in a voice that, she hoped, betrayed no fear, "'Tis I, Amelia

Earnshawe, recently orphaned and now on my way to take up a position as a governess to the two small children—a boy, and a girl—of Lord Falconmere, whose cruel glances I found, during our interview in his London residence, both repellent and fascinating, but whose aquiline face haunts my dreams."

"And what do you do here, then, at this house, on this night of all nights? Falconmere Castle lies a good twenty leagues on from here, on the other side of the moors."

"The coachman—an ill-natured fellow, and a mute, or so he pretended to be, for he formed no words, but made his wishes known only by grunts and gobblings—reined in his team a mile or so back down the road, or so I judge, and then he shewed me by gestures that he would go no further, and that I was to alight. When I did refuse to do so, he pushed me roughly from the carriage to the cold earth, then, whipping the poor horses into a frenzy, he clattered off the way he had come, taking my several bags and my trunk with him. I called after him, but he did not return, and it seemed to me that a deeper darkness stirred in the forest gloom behind me. I saw the light in your window and I...I...." She was able to keep up her pretence of bravery no longer, and she began to sob.

"Your father," came the voice from the other side of the door. "Would he have been the Honourable Hubert Earnshawe?"

Amelia choked back her tears. "Yes. Yes, he was."

"And you—you say you are an orphan?"

She thought of her father, of his tweed jacket, as the maelstrom seized him, and whipped him onto the rocks and away from her forever.

"He died trying to save my mother's life. They both were drowned."

She heard the dull chunking of a key being turned in a lock, then twin booms as iron bolts were drawn back. "Welcome, then, Miss Amelia Earnshawe. Welcome to your inheritance, in this house without a name. Aye, welcome—on this night, of all nights." The door opened.

The man held a black tallow candle; its flickering flame illuminated his face from below, giving it an unearthly and eldritch appearance. He could have been a Jack O'Lantern, she thought, or a particularly elderly axe-murderer.

He gestured for her to come in.

"Why do you keep saying that?" she asked.

"Why do I keep saying what?"

"On this night of all nights. You've said it three times so far."

He simply stared at her for a moment. Then he beckoned again, with one bone-coloured finger. As she entered, he thrust the candle close to her face, and stared at her with eyes that were not truly mad, but were still far from sane. He seemed to be examining her, and eventually he grunted, and nodded. "This way," was all he said.

She followed him down a long corridor. The candle-flame threw fantastic shadows about the two of them, and in its light the grandfather clock and the spindly chairs and table danced and capered. The old man fumbled with his keychain, and unlocked a door in the wall, beneath the stairs. A smell came from the darkness beyond, of must and dust and abandonment.

"Where are we going?" she asked.

He nodded, as if he had not understood her. Then

5

he said, "There are some as are what they are. And there are some as aren't what they seem to be. And there are some as only seem to be what they seem to be. Mark my words, and mark them well, Hubert Earnshawe's daughter. Do you understand me?"

She shook her head. He began to walk, and did not look back.

She followed the old man down the stairs.

III.

Far away and far along the young man slammed his quill down upon the manuscript, spattering sepia ink across the ream of paper and the polished table.

"It's no good," he said, despondently. He dabbed at a circle of ink he had just made on the table with a delicate forefinger, smearing the teak a darker brown, then, unthinking, he rubbed the finger against the bridge of his nose. It left a dark smudge.

"No, sir?" The butler had entered almost soundlessly.

"It's happening again, Toombes. Humour creeps in. Self-parody whispers at the edges of things. I find myself guying literary convention and sending up both myself and the whole scrivening profession."

The butler gazed unblinking at his young master. "I believe humour is very highly thought of in certain circles, sir."

The young man rested his head in his hands, rubbing his forehead pensively with his fingertips. He sighed. "That's not the point, Toombes. I'm trying to create a slice of life here, an accurate representation of the world as it is, and of the human condition.

Instead, I find myself indulging, as I write, in school-boy parody of the foibles of my fellows. I make little jokes." He had smeared ink all over his face. "Very little."

From the forbidden room at the top of the house an eerie, ululating cry rang out, echoing through the house. The young man sighed. "You had better feed Aunt Agatha, Toombes."

"Very good, sir."

The young man picked up the quill pen and idly scratched his ear with the tip.

Behind him, in a bad light, hung the portrait of his great-great grandfather. The painted eyes had been cut out most carefully, long ago, and now real eyes stared out of the canvas face, looking down at the writer. The eyes glinted a tawny gold. If the young man had turned around, and remarked upon them, he might have thought them the golden eyes of some great cat or of some misshapen bird of prey, were such a thing possible. These were not eyes that belonged in any human head. But the young man did not turn. Instead, oblivious, he reached for a new sheet of paper, dipped his quill into the glass inkwell, and commenced to write:

IV.

"Aye..." said the old man, putting down the black tallow candle on the silent harmonium. "He is our master, and we are his slaves, though we pretend to ourselves that it is not so. But when the time is right, then he demands what he craves, and it is our duty and our compulsion to provide him with..." he shuddered, and drew a breath. Then he said only, "...with what he needs."

The bat-wing curtains shook and fluttered in the glassless casement as the storm drew closer. Amelia clutched the lace handkerchief to her breast, her father's monogram upwards. "And the gate?" she asked, in a whisper.

"It was locked in your ancestor's time, and he charged, before he vanished, that it should always remain so. But there are still tunnels, folk do say, that link the old crypt with the burial grounds."

"And Sir Frederick's first wife...?"

He shook his head, sadly. "Hopelessly insane, and but a mediocre harpsichord player. He put it about that she was dead, and perhaps some believed him."

She repeated his last four words to herself. Then she looked up at him, a new resolve in her eyes.

"And for myself? Now I have learned why I am here, what do you advise me to do?"

He peered around the empty hall. Then he said, urgently, "Fly from here, Miss Earnshawe. Fly while there is still time. Fly for your life, fly for your immortal aagh."

"My what?" she asked, but even as the words escaped her crimson lips the old man crumpled to the floor. A silver crossbow quarrel protruded from the back of his head.

"He is dead," she said, in shocked wonderment.

"Aye," affirmed a cruel voice from the far end of the hall. "But he was dead before this day, girl. And I do think that he has been dead a monstrous long time."

Under her shocked gaze, the body began to

putresce. The flesh dripped and rotted and liquefied, the bones revealed crumbled and oozed, until there was nothing but a stinking mass of foetor where once there had been a man.

Amelia squatted beside it, then dipped her fingertip into the noxious stuff. She licked her finger with her tongue, and she made a face. "You would appear to be right, sir, whoever you are," she said. "I would estimate that he has been dead for the better part of a hundred years."

V.

"I am endeavouring," said the young man to the chambermaid, "to write a novel that reflects life as it is, mirrors it down to the finest degree. Yet as I write it turns to dross and gross mockery. What should I do? Eh, Ethel? What should I do?"

"I'm sure I don't know, sir," said the chambermaid, who was pretty and young, and had come to the great house in mysterious circumstances several weeks earlier. She gave the bellows several more squeezes, making the heart of the fire glow an orange-white. "Will that be all?"

"Yes. No. Yes," he said. "You may go, Ethel."

The girl picked up the now-empty coal-scuttle and walked at a steady pace across the drawing room.

The young man made no move to return to his writing-desk; instead he stood in thought by the fireplace, staring at the human skull on the mantel, at the twin crossed swords that hung above it upon the wall. The fire crackled and spat as a lump of coal broke in half.

Footsteps, close behind him. The young man turned. "You?"

The man facing him was almost his double—the white streak in the auburn hair proclaimed them of the same blood, if any proof were needed. The stranger's eyes were dark and wild, his mouth petulant yet oddly firm.

"Yes—I! I, your elder brother, whom you thought dead these many years. But I am not dead — or perhaps, I am no longer dead—and I have come back—aye, come back from ways that are best left untravelled—to claim what is truly mine."

The young man's eyebrows raised. "I see. Well, obviously all this is yours—if you can prove that you are who you say you are."

"Proof? I need no proof. I claim birth-right, and blood-right—and death-right!" So saying, he pulled both the swords down from above the fireplace, and passed one, hilt first, to his younger brother. "Now guard you, my brother—and may the best man win."

Steel flashed in the firelight and kissed and clashed and kissed again in an intricate dance of thrust and parry. At times it seemed no more than a dainty minuet, or a courtly and deliberate ritual, while at other times it seemed pure savagery, a wildness that moved faster than the eye could easily follow. Around and around the room they went, and up the steps to the mezzanine, and down the steps to the main hall. They swung from drapes and from chandeliers. They leapt up on tables and down again.

The older brother obviously was more experienced, and, perhaps, was a better swordsman, but the younger man was fresher and he fought like a man possessed, forcing his opponent back and back and back to the roaring fire itself. The older brother reached out with his left hand and grasped the poker. He swung it wildly at the younger, who ducked, and, in one elegant motion, ran his brother through.

"I am done for. I am a dead man."

The younger brother nodded his ink-stained face.

"Perhaps it is better this way. Truly, I did not want the house, or the lands. All I wanted, I think, was peace." He lay there, bleeding crimson onto the grey flagstone. "Brother? Take my hand."

The young man knelt, and clasped a hand that already, it seemed to him, was becoming cold.

"Before I go into that night that none can follow, there are things I must tell you. Firstly, with my death, I truly believe the curse is lifted from our line. The second..." His breath now came in a bubbling wheeze, and he was having difficulty speaking. "The second...is...the...the thing in the abyss...beware the cellars...the rats.... the—*it follows!*"

And with this his head lolled on the stone, and his eyes rolled back and saw nothing, ever again.

Outside the house, the raven cawed thrice. Inside, strange music had begun to skirl up from the crypt, signifying that, for some, the wake had already started.

The younger brother, once more, he hoped, the rightful possessor of his title, picked up a bell and rang for a servant. Toombes the butler was there in the doorway before the last ring had died away.

"Remove this," said the young man. "But treat it well. He died to redeem himself. Perhaps to redeem us both."

Toombes said nothing, merely nodded to show that he had understood.

The young man walked out of the drawing room.

11

He entered the Hall of Mirrors—a hall from which all the mirrors had carefully been removed, leaving irregularly-shaped patches on the paneled walls, and, believing himself alone, he began to muse aloud.

"This is precisely what I was talking about," he said. "Had such a thing happened in one of my tales—and such things happen all the time—I would have felt myself constrained to guy it unmercifully." He slammed a fist against a wall, where once a hexagonal mirror had hung. "What is wrong with me? Wherefore this flaw?"

Strange scuttling things gibbered and cheetled in the black drapes at the end of the room, and high in the gloomy oak beams, and behind the wainscoting, but they made no answer. He had expected none.

He walked up the grand staircase, and along a darkened hall, to enter his study. Someone, he suspected, had been tampering with his papers. He suspected that he would find out who later that evening, after the Gathering.

He sat down at his desk, dipped his quill pen once more, and continued to write.

VI.

Outside the room the ghoul-lords howled with frustration and hunger, and they threw themselves against the door in their ravenous fury, but the locks were stout, and Amelia had every hope that they would hold.

What had the wood-cutter said to her? His words came back to her then, in her time of need, as if he were standing close to her, his manly frame mere inches from her feminine curves, the very scent of his honest labouring body surrounding her like the headiest perfume, and she heard his words as if he were, that moment, whispering them in her ear. "I was not always in the state you see me in now, lassie," he had told her. "Once I had another name, and a destiny unconnected to the hewing of cords of fire-wood from fallen trees. But know you this—in the escritoire, there is a secret compartment, or so my great-uncle claimed, when he was in his cups..."

The escritoire! Of course!

She rushed to the old writing desk. At first she could find no trace of a secret compartment. She pulled out the drawers, one after another, and then perceived that one of them was much shorter than the rest, which seeing she forced her white hand into the space that the drawer had been, and found, at the back, a button. Frantically, she pressed it. Something opened, and she put her hand on a tightly-rolled paper scroll.

Amelia withdrew her hand. The scroll was tied with a dusty black ribbon, and with fumbling fingers she untied the knot, and opened the paper. Then she read, trying to make sense of the antiquated handwriting, of the ancient words. As she did so, a ghastly pallor suffused her handsome face, and even her violet eyes seemed clouded and distracted.

The knockings and the scratchings redoubled. In but a short time they would burst through, she had no doubt. No door could hold them forever. They would burst through, and she would be their prey. Unless, unless...

"Stop!" she called, her voice trembling. "I abjure you, every one of you, and thee most of all, oh Prince

13

of Carrion. In the name of the ancient compact, between thy people and mine."

The sounds stopped. It seemed to the girl that there was shock in that silence. Finally, a cracked voice said, "The compact?" and a dozen voices, as ghastly again, whispered "The compact," in a susurrus of unearthly sound.

"Aye!" called Amelia Earnshawe, her voice no longer unsteady. "The compact."

For the scroll, the long-hidden scroll, had been the compact—the dread agreement between the Lords of the House, and the denizens of the crypt in ages past. It had described and enumerated the nightmarish rituals that had chained them one to another over the centuries—rituals of blood, and of salt, and more.

"If you have read the compact," said a deep voice from beyond the door, "then you know what we need, Hubert Earnshawe's daughter."

"Brides," she said, simply.

"The brides!" came the whisper from beyond the door, and it redoubled and resounded until it seemed to her that the very house itself throbbed and echoed to the beat of those words—two syllables invested with longing, and with love, and with hunger.

Amelia bit her lip. "Aye. The brides. I will bring thee brides. I shall bring brides for all."

She spoke quietly, but they heard her, for there was only silence, a deep and velvet silence, on the other side of the door.

And then one ghoul-voice hissed, "Yes, and do you think we could get her to throw in a side-order of those little bread-roll things?"

VII.

Hot tears stung the young man's eyes. He pushed the papers from him, and flung the quill pen across the room. It spattered its inky load over the bust of his great-great-great grandfather, the brown ink soiling the patient white marble. The occupant of the bust, a large and mournful raven, startled, nearly fell off, and only kept its place by dint of flapping its wings, several times. It turned, then, in an awkward step and hop, to stare with one black bead eye at the young man.

"Oh, this is intolerable!" exclaimed the young man. He was pale and trembling. "I cannot do it, and I shall never do it. I swear now, by..." and he hesitated, casting his mind around for a suitable curse from the extensive family archives.

The raven looked unimpressed. "Before you start cursing, and probably dragging peacefully dead and respectable ancestors back from their well-earned graves, just answer me one question." The voice of the bird was like stone striking against stone.

The young man said nothing, at first. It is not unknown for ravens to talk, but this one had not done so before, and he had not been expecting it to. "Certainly. Ask your question."

The raven tipped its head onto one side. "Do you *like* writing that stuff?"

"Like?"

"That life-as-it-is-stuff you do. I've looked over your shoulder sometimes. I've even read a little here and there. Do you enjoy writing it?"

The young man looked down at the bird. "It's literature," he explained, as if to a child. "Real literature.

Real life. The real world. It's an artist's job to show people the world they live in. We hold up mirrors."

Outside the room lightning clove the sky. The young man glanced out of the window: a jagged streak of blinding fire created warped and ominous silhouettes from the bony trees and the ruined abbey on the hill.

The raven cleared its throat.

"I said, do you enjoy it?"

The young man looked at the bird, then he looked away and, wordlessly, he shook his head.

"That's why you keep trying to pull it apart," said the bird. "It's not the satirist in you that makes you lampoon the commonplace and the humdrum. Merely boredom with the way things are. D'you see?" It paused to preen a stray wingfeather back into place with its beak. Then it looked up at him once more. "Have you ever thought of writing fantasy?" it asked.

The young man laughed. "Fantasy? Listen, I write literature. Fantasy isn't life. Esoteric dreams, written by a minority for a minority, it's—"

"What you'd be writing if you knew what was good for you."

"I'm a classicist," said the young man. He reached out his hand to a shelf of the classics—*Udolpho*, *The Castle of Otranto*, *The Saragossa Manuscript*, *The Monk* and the rest of them. "It's literature."

"Nevermore," said the raven. It was the last word the young man ever heard it speak. It hopped from the bust, spread its wings and glided out of the study door into the waiting darkness.

The young man shivered. He rolled the stock themes of fantasy over in his mind: cars and stockbrokers and commuters, housewives and police, agony columns and commercials for soap, income tax and cheap restaurants, magazines and credit cards and streetlights and computers...

"It is escapism, true," he said, aloud. "But is not the highest impulse in mankind the urge towards freedom, the drive to escape?"

The young man returned to his desk, and he gathered together the pages of his unfinished novel, and dropped them, unceremoniously, in the bottom drawer, amongst the yellowing maps and cryptic testaments and the documents signed in blood. The dust, disturbed, made him cough.

He took up a fresh quill; sliced at its tip with his pen-knife. In five deft strokes and cuts he had a pen. He dipped the tip of it into the glass inkwell. Once more he began to write:

VIII.

Amelia Earnshawe placed the slices of wholewheat bread into the toaster and pushed it down. She set the timer to dark brown, just as George liked it. Amelia preferred her toast barely singed. She liked white bread, as well, even if it didn't have the vitamins. She hadn't eaten white bread for a decade now.

At the breakfast table, George read his paper. He did not look up. He never looked up.

I hate him, she thought, and simply putting the emotion into words surprised her. She said it again in her head. *I hate him.* It was like a song. *I hate him for his toast, and for his bald head, and for the way he chases the office crumpet—girls barely out of school who laugh at him behind his back, and for the way he ignores me whenever he doesn't want to be bothered with me, and for the way he says "What, love?" when I ask him a simple question, as if he's long ago forgotten my name. As if he's forgotten that I even have a name.*

"Scrambled or boiled?" she said aloud.

"What, love?"

George Earnshawe regarded his wife with fond affection, and would have found her hatred of him astonishing. He thought of her in the same way, and with the same emotions, that he thought of anything which had been in the house for ten years and still worked well. The television, for example. Or the lawnmower. He thought it was love.

"You know, *we* ought to go on one of those marches," he said, tapping the newspaper's editorial. "Show we're committed. Eh, love?"

The toaster made a noise to show that it was done. Only one dark brown slice had popped up. She took a knife and fished out the torn second slice with it. The toaster had been a wedding present from her Uncle John. Soon she'd have to buy another, or start cooking toast under the grill, the way her mother had done.

"George? Do you want your eggs scrambled or boiled?" she asked, very quietly, and there was something in her voice that made him look up.

"Any way you like it, love," he said amiably, and could not for the life of him, as he told everyone in the office later that morning, understand why she simply stood there holding her slice of toast, or why she started to cry.

IX.

The quill pen went *scritch scritch* across the paper, and the young man was engrossed in what he was doing. His face was strangely content, and a smile flickered between his eyes and his lips.

He was rapt.

Things scratched and scuttled in the wainscot but he hardly heard them.

High in her attic room Aunt Agatha howled and yowled and rattled her chains. A weird cachinnation came from the ruined abbey: it rent the night air, ascending into a peal of manic glee. In the dark woods beyond the great house, shapeless figures shuffled and loped, and raven-locked young women fled from them in fear.

"Swear!" said Toombes the butler, down in the butler's pantry, to the brave girl who was passing herself off as chambermaid. "Swear to me, Ethel, on your life, that you'll never reveal a word of what I tell you to a living soul…"

There were faces at the windows and words written in blood; deep in the crypt a lonely ghoul crunched on something that might once have been alive; forked lightings slashed the ebony night; the faceless were walking; all was right with the world.

19

The Word That Sings the Scythe
Michael Swanwick

Michael Swanwick's first two short stories were published in 1980, and both appeared on the Nebula ballot that year. One of the major writers working in the field today, he has been nominated for at least one of the field's major awards in almost every successive year (he may have been out of the country in 1983 and 1986), and has won the Hugo, Nebula, World Fantasy, Theodore Sturgeon Memorial, and the Locus awards. He has published six collections of short fiction, six novels—In the Drift, Vacuum Flowers, Stations of the Tide, The Iron Dragon's Daughter, Jack Faust, and Bones of the Earth—and a Hugo Award-winning book-length interview with editor Gardner Dozois. In recent years Swanwick has also established himself as the modern master of the short-short story, publishing several hundred short-shorts, most notably "The Periodic Table of Science Fiction" and "The Sleep of Reason." His most recent book is a short-short collection Cigar Box Faust and Other Miniatures. Upcoming is a second short-short collection, The Periodic Table of Science Fiction.

Last year Swanwick published a fine novelette "King Dragon," the opening section of his next novel. Set during a Vietnam-style war in Faerie, it introduced the novel's protagonist and sent him out into the larger world as a refugee. As Swanwick said in an interview, "He goes off to a much stranger place than his native Faerie, toward adventures I hope will be satisfying to the fantasy reader while at the same time being a subversion of all that is good and decent in fantasy!" The powerful story that follows is the next subversive piece of that tale.

Will's first several days as an outlaw were peaceful ones. He traveled south along the river road and then, where the marshlands rose up, followed that same road eastward and inland Among the farms. Now and then he got a ride on a hay-wain or a tractor, and sometimes a meal or two as well in exchange for work. He fed himself from the land and bathed in starlit ponds. When he could not find a barn or an unlocked utility shed, he burrowed into a haystack, wrapping his cloak about him for a defense against ticks. Such sleights and stratagems were no great burden for a country fey such as himself.

His mood varied wildly. Sometimes he felt elated to have left his old life behind. Other times, he fantasized vengeance, bloody and sweet. It was shameful of him, for the chief architect of his ruin was dead, at his own hand, and the others in the village were as much the war-dragon's victims as he. But he was no master of his own thoughts, and at such moments would bite and claw at his own flesh until the fit passed.

Then one morning the roads were thronged with people. It was like a conjuring trick in which a hand is held out, palm empty, to be briefly covered by a silk handkerchief that, whisked away, reveals a mound of squirming eels. Will had gone to sleep with the roads empty and that night dreamed of the sea. He woke to an odd murmuring and, when he dug his way out of the hay, discovered that it was voices, the weary desultory talk of folk who have come a great distance and have a long way yet to go.

Will stood by the road letting the dust-stained travelers stream past him like a river while his vision grabbed and failed to seize, searching for and not finding a familiar face among their number. Until at last he saw a woman whose bare breasts and green sash marked her as a hag, let slide her knapsack to the ground and wearily sit upon a stone at the verge of the road. He placed himself before her and bowed formally. "Reverend Mistress, your counsel I crave. Who are all these folk? Where are they bound?"

The hag looked up. "The Armies of the Mighty come through the land," she said, "torching the crops and leveling the villages. Terror goes before them and there are none who dare stand up to their puissance, and so perforce all must flee, some into the Old Forest, and others across the border. 'Tis said there are refugee camps there."

"Is it your wisdom," he asked, touching his brow as the formula demanded, "that we should travel thither?"

The young hag looked tired beyond her years. "Whether it is wisdom or not, it is there that I am bound," she said. And without further word, she stood, shouldered her burden, and walked on.

The troubles had emptied out the hills and scoured from their innermost recesses many a creature gener ally thought to be extinct. Downs trolls and albino giants, the latter translucent-skinned, blue-veined, and weak as tapioca pudding, trudged down the road, along with ogres, brown men, selkies, chalkies, and other common types of hobs and feys. After a moment's hesitation, Will joined them.

Thus it was that he became a refugee.

Late that same day, when the sun was high and Will was passing a field of oats, low and golden under a harsh blue sky, he realized he had to take a leak. Far across the field the forest began. He turned his back on the road and in that instant was a carefree vaga-bond once more. Through the oats he strode, singing to himself a harvest song:

"Mowers weary and brown and blithe,
What is the word methinks ye know...."

It was a bonny day, and for all his troubles Will could not help feeling glad to be alive and able to enjoy the rich gold smell that rose from the crops and the fresh green smell that came from the woods and the sudden whirr of grasshoppers through the air.

"What is the word that, over and over,
Sings the Scythe to the flowers and grass?"

Will was thinking of the whitesmith's daughter, who had grown so busty over the winter and had blushed angrily last spring simply for his looking at her, though he hadn't meant a thing by it at the time. Reflecting upon that moment, his thoughts went now where she'd assumed them to be then. He would like to have her here, with a blanket, so they could seek out a low spot in the field where the oats would hide them, and perform those rites which would guaranteed a spectacular harvest.

A little girl came running across the field, arms outstretched, golden braids flying behind her. "Papa! Papa!" she cried.

To his astonishment, Will saw that she was heading toward him. Some distance behind, two stickfellas and a lubin ran after her, as if she had just escaped their custody. Straight to Will the little girl flew and leapt up into his arms. Hugging him tightly, she buried her small face in his shoulder.

"Help me," she whispered. "Please. They want to rape me."

Perhaps there was a drop of the truth-teller's blood in him, for her words went straight to Will's heart and he did not doubt them. Falling immediately into the role she had laid out for him, he spun her around in the air if in great joy, then set her down and, placing his arms on her shoulders, sternly said, "You little imp! You must never run away like that again—never! Do you understand me?"

"Yes, Papa." Eyes downcast, she dug a hole in the dirt with the tip of one shoe.

The girl's pursuers came panting up. "Sir! Sir!" cried the lubin. He was dog-headed, like all his kind, great of belly but with a laborer's arms and shoulders, and wore a wide-brimmed hat with a dirty white plume. He swept off the hat and bowed deeply. "Saligos de Gralloch is my name, sir. My companions and I found your daughter wandering the roads, all by herself, hungry and lost. Thank the Seven we..." He stopped, frowned, tugged at one hairy ear. "You're her *father*, you say?"

"Good sir, my thanks," Will said, as if distracted. He squatted and hugged the child to him again, thinking furiously. "It was kind of you to retrieve her to me."

The lubin gestured, and the stickfellas moved to either side of Will. He himself took a step forward and stared down on Will, black lips curling back to expose yellow canines. "Are you her father? You *can't* be her father. You're too young."

Will felt the dragon-darkness rising up in him, and fought it down. The lubin outweighed him twice over, and the stickfellas might be slight, but their limbs were as fast and hard as staves. Cunning was required here. "She was exposed to black iron as an infant and almost died," he said lightly. "So I sold a decade of my life to Year Eater to buy a cure."

One of the stickfellas froze, like a lifeless tree rooted in the soil, as he tried to parse out the logic of what Will had said. The other skittishly danced backward and forward on his long legs and longer arms. The lubin narrowed his eyes. "That's not how it works," he rumbled. "It can't be. Surely, when you sell a fraction of yourself to that dread power, it makes you older, not younger."

But Will had stalled long enough to scheme and knew now what to do. "My darling daughter," he murmured, placing a thumb to his lips, kissing it, and then touching the thumb to the girl's forehead. All this was theater and distraction. Heart hammering with fear, he fought to look casual as he took her hand, so that the tiny dab of warm spittle touched her fingers. "My dear, sweet little…"

There was a work of minor magic which every lad his age knew. You came upon a sleeping friend and gently slid his hand into a pan of warm water. Whereupon, impelled by who-knew-what thaumaturgic principles, said friend would immediately piss himself. The spittle would do nicely in place of water. Focusing all his thought upon it, Will mumbled, as if it were an endearment, one of his aunt's favorite homeopathic spells—one that was both a diuretic *and* a laxative.

With a barrage of noises astonishing from one so small, the sluice-gates of the girl's body opened. Vast quantities of urine and liquid feces exploded from her nether regions and poured down her legs. *"Oh!"* she shrieked with horror and dismay. "Oh! Oh! Oh!"

Her abductors, meanwhile, drew back in disgust. "Pfaugh!" said one of the stickfellas, waving a twiggish hand before his nose. The other was already heading back toward the road.

"I'm sorry." Will smiled apologetically, straightening. "She has this little problem…." The girl tried to kick him, but he nimbly evaded her. "As you can see, she lacks self-control."

"Oh!"

Only the lubin remained now. He stuck out a blunt forefinger, thumb upward, as if his hand were a gun, and shook it at Will. "You've fooled the others, perhaps, but not me. Cross Saligos once more, and it will be your undoing." He fixed Will with a long stare, then turned and trudged away.

"Look what you *did* to me!" the little girl said angrily, when Saligos was finally out of sight and they were alone. She plucked at the cloth of her dress. It was foul and brown.

Amused, Will said, "It got you out of a fix, didn't it? It got us both out of a fix." He held out his hand. "There's a stream over there in the woods. Come with me, and we'll get you cleaned off."

Carefully keeping the child at arm's length, he led her away.

The girl's name was Esme. While she washed herself in the creek, Will went a little downstream and laundered her clothes, rinsing and wringing them until they were passably clean. He placed them atop some nearby bushes to dry. By the time he was done, Esme had finished too and crouched naked by the edge of the creek, drawing pictures in the mud with a twig. To dry her off, he got out his blanket from the knapsack and wrapped it around her.

Clutching the blanket about her, as if it were the robes of state, Esme broke off a cattail stalk, and with it whacked Will on both shoulders. "I hereby knight thee!" she cried. "Arise, Sir Hero of Grammarie Fields."

Anybody else would have been charmed. But the old familiar darkness had descended upon Will once more, and all he could think of was how to get Esme off his hands. He had neither resources nor prospects and, traveling light as he must, he dared not take on responsibility for the child. "Where are you from?" he asked her.

Esme shrugged.

"How long have you been on the road?"

"I don't remember."

"Where are your parents? What are their names?"

"Dunno."

"You do have parents, don't you?"

"Dunno."

"You don't know much, do you?"

"I can scour a floor, bake a sweet-potato pie, make soap from animal fat and lye and candles from beeswax and wicking, curry a horse, shear a lamb, rebuild a carburetor, and polish shoes until they shine." She let the blanket sag so that it exposed one flat proto-breast and struck a pose. "I can sing the birds down out of the trees."

Involuntarily, Will laughed. "Please don't." Then he sighed. "Well, I'm stuck with you for the nonce, anyway. When your clothes have dried, I'll take you upstream and teach you how to tickle a trout. It'll be a useful addition to your many other skills."

There were armies on the move, and no sensible being lingered in a war zone. Nevertheless they did. By the time the sun went down, they had acquired trout and mushrooms and wild tubers enough to make a good meal, and built a small camp at the verge of the forest. Like most feys, Will was a mongrel. But there was enough woods-elf in his blood that, if it weren't for the war, he could be perfectly comfortable here forever. He built a nest of pine-boughs for Esme and once again wrapped her in his blanket. She demanded of him a song, and then a story, and then another story, and then a lullaby. By degrees she began to blink and yawn, and finally she slid away to the realm of sleep.

She baffled Will. The girl was as much at ease as

if she had lived in this camp all her life. He had expected, after the day's events, that she would fight sleep and suffer nightmares. But here, where it took his utmost efforts to keep them warm and fed, she slept the sleep of the innocent and protected.

Feeling sorely used, Will wrapped his windbreaker about himself and fell asleep as well.

Hours later—or possibly mere minutes—he was wakened from uneasy dreams by the thunder of jets. Will opened his eyes in time to see a flight of dragons pass overhead. Their afterburners scratched thin lines of fire across the sky, dwindling slowly before finally disappearing over the western horizon. He crammed his hand into his mouth and bit the flesh between thumb and forefinger until it bled. How he used to marvel at those dread machines! He had even, in the innocence of his young heart, loved them and imagined himself piloting one someday. Now the sight of them nauseated him.

He got up, sourly noting that Esme slept undisturbed, and threw an armload of wood on the fire. He would not be able to sleep again tonight. Best he were warm while he awaited the dawn.

So it was that he chanced to be awake when a troop of centaurs galloped across the distant moonlit fields, grey as ghosts and silent as so many deer. At the sight of his campfire, their leader gestured and three of them split away from the others. They sped toward him. Will stood at their approach.

The centaurs pulled up with a thunder of hooves and a spatter of kicked- up dirt. "It's a civilian, Sarge," one said. They were all three female and wore red military jackets with gold piping and shakos to match.

FANTASY

"Happy, clueless, and out on a fucking walking-tour of the countryside, apparently."

"It's not aware that there's a gods-be-damned war on, then?"

"Apparently not." To Will, she said, "Don't you know that the Sons of Fire are on their way?"

"I have no idea what you're talking about," Will said shakily. Then, gathering his courage, "Nor whose side you are on."

One centaur snorted in disdain. A second struck the insignia on her chest and cried, "We are the Fifth Amazons—the brood mares of death! Are you a fool, not to have heard of us?"

But the third said, "It does not matter whose side we are on. The rock people come, the dwellers-in-the-depths from the Land of Fire. Even now they climb toward the surface, bringing with them both immense heat and a fearful kinetic energy. When they arrive, the ground will bubble and smoke. All of *this*—" She swept her arm to take in all the land about them—"will be blasted away. Then will the battle begin. And it will be such that all who stand within the circuit of combat, no matter what their allegiance, will die."

"Come away, Althea," said the first, who was older than the other two and, by the tone of authority in her voice, the sergeant. "We were told to clear the land of any lingering noncombatants. Our orders do no require us to rescue idiots."

"What's this?" said the second. She knelt. "A child—and a girl!"

Will started forward, to snatch Esme away from the centaur. But the other two cantered sideways into his path, blocking him. "Look at her, Sergeant Lucasta.

30

The poor little bugger is as weary as a kitten. She doesn't awaken, even when I pick her up." She handed Esme to her superior, who held the sleeping child against her shoulder.

"We've wasted enough time," Sergeant Lucasta said. "Let's go."

"Should we douse the fire?" Anthea asked.

"Let it burn. This time tomorrow, what fucking difference will it make?"

The second centaur packed up Will's gear with startling efficiency, stowed it in leathern hip-bags and started after her commander. Then the youngest of the three seized Will's arm and effortlessly lifted him onto her back. She reared up and hastily he placed his arms around her waist. "My name is Campaspe." She grinned over her shoulder. "Hang on tight, manling. I'm going to give you the ride of your life."

So began their midnight gallop. Up hill and down they sped, past forests and farms. All the world flowed by like a billowing curtain, a thin veil over something vast, naked, and profound. Will tried to imagine what lay beneath and could not. "Will all this really be destroyed?" he asked. "Is it possible?"

"If you'd been through half the shit *I* have," Campaspe replied, "you would not doubt it for an instant. Rest quiet now, it's a long ride." Taking her at her word, Will lay his cheek against Campaspe's back. It was warm. Her muscles moved smoothly beneath him and between his legs. He became acutely aware of the clean stench of her sweat.

"Hey! Sarge! I think the civilian likes me—he's getting hard!"

"He'll need to mount a stump if he expects to stick it to you," the sergeant replied.

31

"At least he won't need any petroleum jelly!" Anthea threw in.

"That was...I didn't..." Will said hastily, as they all laughed.

"Oh, really?" Campaspe's eyes and teeth flashed scornfully. She took his hands from around her waist and placed them firmly on her breasts. "Deny it now!"

Horrified, Will snatched his hands away, almost fell, and seized Campaspe's waist again. "I couldn't! The Nameless Ones forbid it!"

"It would be bestiality for me too, little ape-hips," she laughed. "But what's a war for, if not to loosen a few rules here and there? Eh, Sarge?"

"Only fucking reason I know."

"I knew a gal in the Seventh who liked to do it with dogs," Anthea said. "Big ones, of course. Mastiffs. So one day she..." And she went on to relate a story so crude that Will flushed red as her jacket. The others laughed like horses, first at the story and then at his embarrassment.

For hours they coursed over the countryside, straight as schooners and almost as fast. By slow degrees, Will grew accustomed to Campaspe's badinage. She didn't mean anything by it, he realized. But she was young and in a war, and flirted out of nervousness. Again he lay his cheek against her back, and she reached behind her to scratch his head reassuringly. It was then that he noticed the brass badge on her shoulder, and twisted about so he could read it. An image had been worked into the brass, a fine line of moon-silver that glimmered slim and bright by the light of Selene, showing three sword-wielding arms radiant from a common point, like a three-limbed swastika. Will recognized the symbol as the triskelion of the Armies of the Mighty. And he was in their power! He shuddered in revulsion and fear.

Sergeant Lucasta, galloping near, saw this and shifted the slumbering Esme from one shoulder to the other. "So you've caught on at last," she said. "We're the wicked baby-eating enemy. And yet, oddly enough, we're the ones clearing you away from an extremely dangerous situation, rather than your own fucking army. Kind of makes you think, don't it?"

"It's because he's a civilian, right, Sarge? Not much sport in killing civilians." Campaspe said.

"They can't fight and they can't shoot," Anthea threw in. "They're lucky if they know how to bleed."

"Fortunately, they have us to do all those things for them." Sergeant Lucasta held up a hand, and they slowed to a walk. "We should have joined up with the platoon a long time ago."

"We haven't missed 'em," Anthea said. "I can still see their spoor."

"And smell their droppings," Campaspe added.

They had come to a spinney of aspens. "We'll stop here for a bit and rest," the sergeant said, "while I work this thing through in my head."

Campaspe came to a halt and Will slid gratefully from her back. She took a thermos of coffee from a harness-bag and offered him some.

"I...I have to take a leak," he said.

"Piss away," she said carelessly. "You don't need *my* permission." And then, when he started into the woods, "Hey! Where the fuck do you think you're going?"

Again Will flushed, remembering how casually his

companions had voided themselves during the night, dropping turds behind them even as they conversed. "My kind needs privacy," he said, and plunged into the brush.

Behind him, he heard Campaspe say, "Well, la-de-da!" to the extreme amusement of her comrades.

Deep into the spinney he went, until he could no longer hear the centaurs talking. Then he unzipped and did his business against the side of a pale slim tree. Briefly, he considered slipping away. The woods were his element, even as open terrain favored the centaurs. He could pass swiftly and silently through underbrush that would slow them to a walk and bury himself so cunningly in the fallen leaves of the forest floor that they would never find him. But did he dare leave Esme with them? Centaurs had no bathroom manners to speak of because they were an early creation, like trolls and giants. They were less subtle of thought than most thinking creatures, more primal in emotion. Murder came to them more easily than spite, lust than love, rapture than pity. They were perfectly capable of killing a small child simply out of annoyance with him for evading their grasp.

Esme meant nothing to him. But still, he could not be responsible for her death.

Yet as he approached the spot where he had left their captors, he heard childish laughter. Esme was awake, and apparently having the time of her life. Another few steps brought him out of the aspens, and he saw Sergeant Lucasta sitting in the grass, forelegs neatly tucked under her, playing with Esme as gently as a mother would her own foal. Will could not help but smile. Females were females, whatever their spe-

cies, and whatever their allegiance, Esme was probably as safe with these lady-cavaliers as anywhere.

"Again!" Esme shrieked. "Please, again?"

"Oh, very well." Sergeant Lucasta said fondly. She
lifted her revolver, gave the cylinder a spin, cocked
the hammer, and placed it to the child's forehead.

"*Stop!*" Will screamed. Running forward, he
snatched up Esme into his arms. "What in the name
of sanity do you think you're doing?"

The sergeant flipped open the cylinder, looked
down into the chamber. "There's the bullet. She would
have died if you hadn't stopped me. Lucky."

"I *am*," Esme said. "I *am* lucky!"

The centaur snapped the cylinder shut, gave it a
spin, and all in one motion pointed it at Esme again
and pulled the trigger.

Snap! The hammer fell on an empty chamber.

Esme laughed with delight. "For the sake of the
Seven!" Will cried. "She's only a child!" He noticed
now, as he had not before, that Campaspe and Anthea
were nowhere to be seen. This did not strike him as
a good omen.

"She has the luck of innocence," Sergeant Lucasta
observed, holstering her revolver. "Twenty-three times
I spun the cylinder and fired at her, and every time
the hammer came down on an empty chamber. Do
you know what the odds are against that?"

"I'm not very good at math."

"Neither am I. Pretty fucking unlikely, though, I'm
sure of that."

"I *told* you I was lucky," Esme said. She struggled
out of Will's arms. "Nobody ever listens to me."

"Let me ask you a question, then, and I promise to

listen. Who is *he*—"she jerked a thumb at Will—"to you?"

"My Papa," Esme said confidently.

"And who am I?"

The little girl's brow furrowed in thought. "My...mama?"

"Sleep," said the centaur. She placed a hand on the girl's forehead and drew it down over her eyes. When she removed it, Esme was asleep. Carefully, she laid the child down in the grass. "I've seen this before," she said. "I've seen a lot of things most folks never suspect. She is old, this one, old and far from a child, though she thinks and acts as one. Almost certainly, she's older than the both of us combined."

"How can that be?"

"She's sold her past and her future, her memories and adolescence and maturity, to the Year Eater in exchange for an undying present and the kind of luck it takes for a child to survive on her own in a world like ours."

Will remembered the lie he had told the lubin and experienced a sudden coldness. The tale had come to him out of nowhere. This could not be mere coincidence. Nevertheless, he said, "I don't believe it."

"How did you come to be traveling with her?"

"She was running from some men who wanted to rape her."

"Lucky thing you chanced along." The sergeant patted the pockets of her jacket and extracted a pipe. "There is only a limited amount of luck in this world—perhaps you've noticed this for yourself? There is only so much, and it cannot be increased or decreased by so much as a tittle. This one draws luck from those around her. We should have rejoined our companions hours ago. It was good luck for her to be carried so much further than we intended. It was bad luck for us to do so." She reached into her hip-bags and came out with a tobacco pouch. "The child is a monster—she has no memory. If you walk away from her, she will have forgotten you by morning."

"Are you telling me to abandon her?"

"In a word? Yes."

Will looked down on the sleeping child, so peaceful and so trusting. "I...I cannot."

Sergeant Lucasta shrugged. "Your decision. Now we come to the second part of our little conversation. You noticed that I sent my girls away. That's because they like you. They don't have my objectivity. The small abomination here is not the only one with secrets, I think." All the while she spoke, she was filling her pipe with tobacco and tamping it down. "There's a darkness in you that the rookies can't see. Tell me how you came to be traveling by yourself, without family or companions."

"My village cast me out."

The sergeant stuck a pipe into the corner of her mouth, lit it, and sucked on it meditatively. "You were a collaborator."

"That oversimplifies the matter, and makes it out to be something that was in my power to say yea or nay to. But, yes, I was."

"Go on."

"A...a dragon crawled into our village and declared himself king. It was wounded. Its electrical system was all shot to hell, and it could barely make itself heard. It needed a lieutenant, a mediator between itself and the village. To...give orders. It chose me."

"You did bad things, I suppose. You didn't mean

37

to, at first, but one thing led to another. People dis-
obeyed you, so they had to be punished."

"They hated me! They blamed me for their own
weakness!"

"Oh?"

"They wouldn't obey! I had no choice. If they'd
obeyed, they wouldn't have been punished!"

"Go on."

"Yes, okay, I did things! But if I hadn't, the dragon
would have found out. I would've been punished.
They would've been punished even worse than they
were. I was just trying to protect them." Will was
crying now.

For a long moment the Sergeant was silent. Then
she said, "Kill anyone?"

"One. He was my best friend."

"Well, that's war for you. You're not as bad a sort
as you think you are, I suspect. In any case, you're
neither a spy nor an *agent provocateur,* and that's all
that really concerns me. So I can leave you behind
with a clean conscience."

"I beg your pardon?"

"You're far enough from the epicenter now that you
should be safe. And we'll never rendezvous with our
platoon unless we ditch the luck-eater." She
unholstered her gun and pointed it at the sleeping
child. "Shall we try the monster's luck one last time?
Or should I shoot it up in the air?"

"In the air," Will said tightly. "Please."

She lifted the gun and fired. The report shattered
the night's silence, but did not awaken Esme.

"Lucky again," Sergeant Lucasta said.

Summoned by the gunshot, Campaspe and Anthea trotted back to the spinney's edge. They received the news that the civilians were to be left behind without any visible emotion. But when Will bade them farewell, Campaspe bent, as if to give him a swift peck on the cheek, and then stuck her tongue down his throat and gave his stones a squeeze. Anthea dumped his gear at his feet and playfully swatted him on his aching bum.

The sergeant too leaned down, as if to kiss him. Will stiffened involuntarily. But instead, she said, "Listen to an old campaigner: Trouble will follow you so long as the child is in your care." She straightened. "Keep the lodestar to your left shoulder, and then at dawn walk toward the sun. That will take you east—there are refugee camps just across the Great River. Best not dawdle."

"Thank you."

"Let's go, ladies—this war isn't going to fucking well fight itself!"

The cavaliers cantered off without so much as a backward glance.

Will gently shook Esme awake, shouldered his pack, and took her hand. Eventually they came upon a road and followed it eastward until they found a junk car in a thicket of sumac alongside an abandoned garage. Will made beds for himself and Esme on the front and back seats. When dawn shone through the windshield, he arose. He divided the last of his food into five parts, gave one to Esme, and put the rest in his pack.

Then they started out again.

At noon, the land behind them turned to smoke. Not long after, an enormous blast reverberated across the land, so loud that refugees crouched in the road with their hands over their ears, and no one could hear properly for an hour afterward. All of the western shire was swallowed up in a deep and profound darkness punctuated by transient gouts of flame as farmhouses and silos were engulfed in molten rock and exploded. Those who had lived within eyeshot raised their voices in anguished shrieks. In an instant, all the generations of lives beyond counting that had been written onto the land were erased from it. It was as if they all, the cherished and the forgotten alike, not only were no more but had ceased ever to have been.

The giants that rose up out of the smoke burned bright as the Holy City itself, hotter than the forges of the sunset. By gradual degrees they darkened and cooled, first to a magma glow, then to a grey barely distinguishable from the clouds. There were two of them, and they carried cudgels. They still shone a ruddy red when they began to wheel and turn upon each other. They were great shadowy bulks, lost in the sky, when their cudgels were hauled as far back and high as they would go.

The giants' motions were slow beyond the eye's ability to discern. But if Will looked away for a few minutes and then back, their positions would be subtly altered. Over the long course of the morning, their cudgels swung toward each other. At noon, they connected. For as long as it would take to count to thirty, the silence was absolute. Then the blast rolled across the land. Will saw it coming, like a great wind making the trees bow down before it. He grabbed

Esme and flung them both into a ditch, and so evaded the worst of it.

They walked many miles that day, to the sunset and beyond, though the Great River held itself ever distant and remote. Sometimes they rested, but only briefly. More, Will did not dare. At last, when the first stars were emerging in the sky, Esme began to cry for weariness. Will stooped and, with a grunt, picked her up. His legs did not quite buckle.

Eventually, Esme fell asleep on Will's shoulder. He plodded along for a while, and then a truck driver slowed down and offered to let him sit on the tailgate along with four others, just because Esme looked particularly small and weary. The driver said he was going all the way to the camps, and that with luck they would be there by morning.

So, really, she paid for herself.

Camp Oberon stank of overflowing latrines and pitchpenny magicks. The latter were necessary to compensate for the former. Glamours as fragile as tissue paper were tacked up on almost every tent flap, so that walking down the dirt lanes between canvas dwellings Will caught sudden whiffs of eglantine, beeswax, cinnamon, and wet oak leaves, felt the cold mist of a waterfall, heard the faint strains of faraway elfin music. None of it was real, or even convincing, but each was a momentary distraction from his surroundings. Whitewashed rocks picked out borders to the meager flowerbeds planted about the older tents.

The camp was situated on a windswept ground high above the Aelfwine. Its perimeters were patrolled but it had no fences—where could anybody go?

Thrice daily a contingent of yellow-jackets herded the refugees into mess tents for meals. Between times, the old folks coped with boredom by endlessly reminiscing about lives and villages they would never see again. The younger ones, however, talked politics. "They'll be shipping us East," a kobold said knowingly at one such impromptu discussion, "to the belly of the beast, the very heart of Empire, the Tower of Whores itself. Where we'll each be given a temporary ID card, fifty dollars, a voucher for a month's housing, and the point of their boots in our backsides for putting them to such expense."

"They could of saved themselves a shitload of expense by not destroying our fucking homes in the first place," a dwarf growled. "What's the fucking point?"

"It's their policy. Rather than leaving enemies at their borders, they absorb us into themselves. By the time we've found our feet through pluck and hard work, our loyalties have shifted and we become good, obedient citizens."

"Does this work?" Will asked dubiously.

"Not so far." The kobold got up, unbuttoned the corner flaps of the tent, and took a long piss into the weeds out back. "So far, all it's done is made them into the most contentious and least governable society in existence. Which surely has something to do with their sending their armies here to solve all our problems for us, but fuck if I know what." He turned back, zipping his fly.

"This is just venting," somebody said. "The question is, what should we *do?*"

From the depths of the tent, where it was a darkness floating in darkness, an uneasy shimmer that the eye

42

could perceive but not resolve into an image, a ghast said, "A trip-wire, a bundle of matches, and some sandpaper can set off a coffee can filled with black powder and carpet tacks. A pinch of chopped tiger's whiskers sprinkled into food will cause internal bleeding. A lock of hair tied to an albino toad and buried in a crossroads at midnight with the correct incantation will curse somebody with a slow and lingering death. These skills and more I might be convinced to teach to any interested patriots."

There was an awkward silence, and then several of those present got up and left.

Will joined them.

Outside, the dwarf pulled out a pack of cigarettes. He offered one to Will and stuck a second in the corner of his mouth. "I guess you ain't no fucking patriot either."

Will shrugged. "It's just...I asked myself, if I was running this camp, wouldn't I be sure to have an informer in a group like that?"

The dwarf snorted. He was a red dwarf, with the ginger hair and swarthy complexion of his kind. "You suspect our beloved Commandant of unethical methods? The Legless One would cry in his fucking beer if he could hear you say that."

"I just think he'd have somebody there."

"Ha! There were ten in the tent. In my experience, that means at least two snitches. One for money and the other because he's a shit."

"You're a cynic."

"I've done time. Now that I'm out, I'm gonna keep my asshole clenched and my hand to the axe. Knaw-mean?" He turned away. "See ya, kid."

Will ditched the cigarette—it was his first, and he

43

was certain it was going to be his last as well—and went off in search of Esme.

Esme had adapted to the Displaced Persons Camp with an intense joy that was a marvel to behold. She was the leader of whatever gang of children she fell in with, every adult's pet, and every crone's plaything. She sang songs for the bedridden patients in the infirmary and took part in the amateur theatricals. Strangers gave her scraps of cloth so she could play at dress-up and shooed her back whenever she started down the road that led to the cliffs overlooking the Gorge. She could feed herself, a sweetmeat and a morsel at a time, just by hopping from tent to tent and poking her head in to see how everyone was doing. It made things easier for Will, knowing that she was being lovingly watched over by the entire camp. Now he followed the broken half-shilling he carried always in his pocket, straight to its mate, which he'd hung on a cord about Esme's neck.

He found her playing with a dead rat.

From somewhere, Esme had scrounged up a paramedic's rowan wand that still held a fractional charge of vivifying energy and was trying to bring the rat back to life. Pointing the rod imperiously at the wee corpse, she cried, "Rise! Live!" Its legs twitched and scrabbled spasmodically at the ground.

The apple imp kneeling on the other side of the rat from her gasped. "How did you do that?" His eyes were like saucers.

"What I've done," Esme said, "is to enliven its archipallium or reptilian brain. This is the oldest and most primitive part of the central nervous system and controls muscles, balance, and autonomic functions." She traced a circuit in the air above the rat's head.

Jerkily, like a badly handled marionette, it lurched to its feet. "Now the warmth has spread to its paleopallium, which is concerned with emotions and instincts, fighting, fleeing, and sexual behavior. Note that the rat is physically aroused. Next I will access the amygdala, its fear center. This will..."

"Put that *down*, Esme." It was not Will who spoke. "You don't know where it's been. It might have germs."

The little girl blossomed into a smile and the rat collapsed in the dirt by her knee. "Mom-Mom!"

Mother Griet scowled down from her tent.

There were neighborhoods within the camp, each corresponding roughly to the locale of origin of its inhabitants, the camp officials having long ago given up on their rationalized plans for synthetic social organization. Will and Esme lived in Block G, wherein dwelt all those who belonged nowhere else—misfits and outcasts, loners and those who, like them, had been separated from their own kind. For them, Mother Griet served as a self-appointed mayor, scolding the indolent, praising those who did more than their share, a perpetual font of new projects to improve the common lot. Every third day she held a pie-powders court, where the "dusty footed" could seek justice in such petty grievances as the Commandant deemed beneath his attention.

Now she gestured imperiously with her walking stick. "Get in here. We have things to discuss." Then, addressing Will, "You too, grandchild."

"Me?"

"Not very quick on the uptake, are ye? Yes, you."

He followed her within.

Mother Griet's tent was larger on the inside than

45

it was on the outside, as Will discovered when he stepped through the flap and into its green shadows. At first, there seemed to be impossibly many tent poles. But as his eyes adjusted, the slim shapes revealed themselves to be not poles but the trunks of trees. A bird flew by. Others twittered in the underbrush. High above floated something that could not possibly be the moon.

A trail led them to a clearing.

"Sit," Mother Griet said. She took Esme in her lap. "When was the last time you brushed your hair, child? It's nothing but snarls and snail shells."

"I don't remember."

To Will, Mother Griet said, "So you're Esme's father. A bit younger than might be expected."

"I'm her brother, actually. Esme's easily confused."

"No kidding. I can't get a straight answer out of the brat." She pulled a hairbrush from her purse and applied it vigorously to Esme's hair. "Don't wriggle." Mother Griet turned to Will, her pale blue eyes astonishingly intense. "How old is she?" Then, when he hesitated, "Is she older than you are?"

"She...might be."

"Ah. Then I was right." Mother Griet bowed low over the child's head. The trees around them wavered and the air filled with the smell of hot canvas. Briefly it seemed they were sitting in a tent like any other with a wooden platform floor and six cots with a footlocker resting by each one. Then the forest restored itself. She looked up, tears running down her cheeks. "You're not her brother. Tell me how you met her."

As Will told his tale, Mother Griet dabbed away her tears with a tissue. "Let me tell you a story," she

46

said when he was done. In her lap, Esme flopped over on her back and grinned up at her. The old crone gently stroked her cheek.

"I was born in Corpsecandle Green, a place of no particular distinction, save that it was under a curse. Or so it seemed to me, for nothing there endured. My father died and my mother ran off when I was an infant and so I was raised 'by the village,' as they say. I flitted from house to house, through an ever- changing pageant of inconstant sisters, brothers, torment-ors, protectors, and friends. When I came of age, some of these turned to lovers and husbands, and they were inconstant, too. All was flux: My businesses failed, my pipes burst, creditors repossessed my furniture. The only things I dared hope to hold onto were my children. Oh, such darlings they were! I loved them with every scrap of my being. And how do you imagine they repaid me for it?"

"I don't know."

"The little bastards grew up. Grew up, married, turned into strangers, and moved away. And because their fathers had all wandered into the marshes and died—but that's another story and one I doubt you'll ever hear—I was left alone again, too old to bear another child but wanting one nonetheless.

"So, foolish as I was, I bought a black goat, gilded its horns, and led it deep into the marshlands at midnight. There was a drowning-pool there, and I held it under until it stopped struggling, as a sacrifice to the *genius loci*, begging that puissant sprite for a child that would not treat me as the others had. Such a wail I set up then, in my need and desire, as would have scared away a dire-wolf." She stopped. "Pay attention, boy. There might be a test afterwards."

"I *was* paying attention."

"Yeah, right. Well, exactly at dawn there was a rustling in the reeds and this child emerged, this beautiful child right here." She tickled Esme, who squirmed and laughed. "She didn't know who she belonged to and she'd forgotten her name—not the first time she'd done so, I warrant—so I called her Iria, 'little island.' Do you remember any of this, sweetness?"

"I don't remember anything," Esme said. "Ever. That way I'm always happy."

"She sold her memory to the—"

"Shush!" Mother Griet said fiercely. "I *said* you weren't bright. Never mention any of the Seven indoors." She returned to her brushing. "She was like this then, every dawn her first one ever, every evening moon a new delight. She was my everything."

"Then she's yours," Will said with an unexpected pang of regret.

"Look at me, boy, I could die tomorrow. You don't get free of her that easy. Where was I? Oh, yes. For ten or twenty years, I was happy. What mother wouldn't be? But the neighbors began to mutter. Their luck was never good. Cows dried up and cellars flooded. Crops failed and mice multiplied. Sons were drafted, unwed daughters got knocked up, gaffers fell down the cellar stairs. Refrigerator pumps died and the parts to fix them went out of stock. Scarecrows spontaneously caught fire.

"Suspicion pointed the good village-folk straight at the child. They burned down my house and drove me from Corpsecandle Green, alone and penniless, with no place to go. Iria, with her usual good fortune, had wandered off into the marshes that morning and missed her own lynching. I never saw her again—until, as it turns out, these last few days."

"You must have been heartbroken."

"You're a master of the obvious, aren't ye? But adversity is the forge of wisdom and through my pain I eventually came to realize that loss was not a curse laid down upon me or my village, but simply the way of the world. So be it. Had I the power, the only change I'd make would be to restore Iria-Esme-Whatevershername's memory to her."

Esme pouted. "I don't want it."

"Idiot child. If you remember nothing, you learn nothing. How to gut a fish or operate a gas chromatograph, perhaps, but nothing that *matters*. When death comes to you, he will ask you three questions, and they none of them will have anything to do with fish guts or specimen retention times."

"I'm never going to die."

"Never is a long time, belovedest. Someday the ancient war between the Ocean and the Land will be over, and the Moon will return to her mother's womb. Think you to survive that?" Mother Griet rummaged in her purse. "No, so long as you never die, this happy forgetfulness is a blessing." She rummaged some more. "But nobody lives forever. Nor will you." Her hand emerged triumphant. "You see this ring? Ginarr Gnomesbastard owed me a favor, so I had him make it. Can you read the inscription on the inside?"

Esme brushed the hair out of her eyes. "Yes, but I don't know what it means."

"*Memento mori*. It means 'remember to die.' It's on your list of things to do and if you haven't done it yet, you haven't led a full life. Put the ring on your finger. I whispered my name into it when the silver was molten. Wear it and after I'm gone, whatever else you forget you'll still remember me."

"Will it make me grow up?"

"No, little one. Only you can do that."

"It's not gold," Esme said critically.

"No, it's silver. Silver is the witch-metal. It takes a spell more readily than gold does, and holds it better. It conducts electricity almost as well as gold and since it has a higher melting point, it's far superior for use in electronic circuitry. Also it's cheaper."

"I can repair a radio."

"I bet you can. Go now. Run along and play." She swatted the little girl on the rump and watched her scamper away. Then, to Will, she said, "Your hands are bleeding from a thousand cuts."

He looked down at them.

"It's a figure of speech, ye fool. Each cut is a memory, and the blood is the pain they cause you. You and the child are like Jack and Nora Sprat; she forgets everything, and you remember all. Neither is normal. Or wise. You've got to learn to let go, boy, or you'll bleed yourself to death."

Blood rushed to Will's head and his fists clenched involuntarily. But he bit back the retort that flew to his lips. If he had learned nothing else from dealing with old ladies much like this one in his native village, it was that sassing them back was worse than useless. You had to be polite when you told them to buzz off. He stood. "Thank you for your advice," he said stiffly. "I'm leaving now."

Though it had been a long walk to the clearing, three strides took him out through the tent flap. He stood blinking in the sunlight.

Two yellow-jackets seized his arms.

"Garbage duty," one said. Will had been pressed into such service before. He went unresisting with them to a utility truck. It grumbled through Block G and out of the camp and when the tents were small in the distance, slowed to a halt. One soldier shoved a leather sack over Will's head and upper body. The other wrapped a cord around his waist, lashing him in.

"Hey!"

"Don't struggle. We'd only have to hurt you."

The truck lurched, clashed gears, got up to speed. Soon they were driving uphill. There was only one hill overlooking Camp Oberon, a small, barren one atop which stood the old mansion that had been seized for the Commandant's office. When they got there, Will was prodded through passages that had a musky, reptilian undersmell, as though the house were infested with toads.

Knuckles rapped on wood. "The DP you sent for, sir."

"Bring him in and wait outside."

Will was thrust forward, and the bag untied and whisked from his head. The door closed behind him.

The Commandant wore a short-sleeved khaki shirt with matching tie and no insignia. His head was bald and speckled as a brown egg. His forearms rested, brawny and stiff-haired, on his desk. Casually, he dipped a hand into a bowl of dead rats, picked up one by its tail, tilted his head back, and swallowed it whole. Will thought of Esme's plaything and had to fight down the urge to laugh.

Laughter would have been unwise. The Commandant's body language, the arrogance with which he held himself, told Will all he needed to know about him. Here was a pocket strongman, a manipulator and would-be tyrant, the Dragon Baalthazar writ small. The hairs on the back of Will's neck prickled. Cruelty coupled with petty authority was, as he knew only too well, a dangerous combination.

The Commandant pushed aside some papers and picked up a folder. "This is a report from the Erlking DPC," he said. "That's where your village wound up."

"Did they?"

"They don't speak very highly of you." He read from the report. "Seizure of private property. Intimidation. Sexual harassment. Forced labor. Arson. It says here that you had one citizen executed." He dropped the folder on the desk. "I don't imagine you'd be very popular there, if I had you transferred."

"Transfer me or not, as you like. There's nothing I can do to stop you."

The Commandant sucked his teeth in silence for a long moment. Then he rose up from the desk, so high his head almost touched the ceiling. From the waist down, his body was that of a snake.

Slowly, he slithered forward. Will did not flinch, even when the lamius circled him, leaving him surrounded by loops of body.

"What happened to you, boy? Did it put the needles to you? I see that it did. What did it feel like, sitting in the pilot's couch with the needles in your wrists and that great war-drake slithering around in your mind? They say it changes you. Is that why you won't help us?"

Will looked away.

"You act as if you did something wrong. Hell, you're a hero! If you'd been in the forces, you'd have a medal now. Tell you what. Cooperate, and afterward I'll put you in for officer training. If you do well, there's every chance they'll grandfather you in for the decoration. That's a great deal in return for very little. Do you even know what I want from you?"

Yes, Will thought, I know what you want. You want to put your hand up inside me and manipulate me like a puppet. You want to wiggle your fingers and make me jump. Aloud, he said, "I collaborated once, and it was a mistake. I won't do it again."

"Bold words," the Commandant said, "for somebody who was conspiring with subversives not half an hour ago. You didn't know I had an ear in that meeting, did you?"

"You had two. The ghast and the dwarf."

For a blank instant, the Commandant said nothing. Then he circled Will again, widdershins this time, freeing him from the coils of his body.

"Enough of your defiance. Either you'll do as I ask, or else you'll leave by the front door and without the courtesy of a bag over your head. How long do you think you'll last then? Once word gets out you're friendly with me?"

Will stared down at his feet and shook his head doggedly.

The Commandant slid to the door and opened it. The two yellow-jackets stood there, silent as grimhounds. "You can stand in the foyer while you think it over. Knock hard when you've made up your mind; this thing's mahogany an inch thick." The lamius smiled mirthlessly. "Or, if you like, the other door's unlocked."

The foyer had a scuffed linoleum floor, an oliphauntfoot umbrella stand, and a side-table with short stacks of medical brochures for chlamydia, AIDS, evil eye, and diarrhea. Sunlight slanted through frosted panels to either side of the front door. There were two switches for the overhead and outside lights that made a hollow *bock* noise when he flicked one on or off. And that was it.

He wouldn't become the Commandant's creature. On that point he was sure. But he didn't want to be branded an informant and released to the tender mercies of his fellow refugees either. He'd seen what the camp vigilantes did to those they suspected of harboring insufficient solidarity. Back and forth Will strode, forth and back, feverishly working through his options. Until finally he was certain of his course of action. Simply because there was nothing else he *could* do.

Placing his palms flat on its surface, Will leaned straight-armed against the table. Like every other piece of furniture he had seen here, it was solidly built of dark, heavy wood. He walked his feet as far back as he could manage, until he was leaning over the table almost parallel to its surface. He wasn't at all sure he had the nerve to do this.

He closed his eyes and took a deep breath.

Then, as quickly as he could, Will whipped his hands away from the table and clasped them behind his back. Involuntarily, his head jerked to the side, trying in vain to protect his nose. His face hit the wood hard.

"Cer*nunn*os!" Will staggered to his feet, clutching his broken nose. Blood flowed freely between his fingers and down his shirt. Rage rose up in him like fire. It took a moment or two to calm down.

He left by the front door.

Will walked slowly through Block A, wearing his blood-drenched shirt like a flag or a biker's colors. By the time he got to the infirmary, word that he had been roughed up by the yellow-jackets had passed through the camp like wildfire. He had the bleeding stanched and told the nurse that he'd slipped and broken his nose on the edge of a table. After that, he could have run for camp president, had such an office existed, and won. Backslaps, elbow nudges, and winks showered down on him during his long slog home. There were whispered promises of vengeance and muttered obscenities applied to the camp authorities.

He found himself not liking his allies any better than he did his enemies.

It was a depressing thing to discover. So he went on past his tent to the edge of camp, across the railroad tracks, past a casual refuse dump and some abandoned construction equipment, and down the short road that led to the top of the Gorge. The tents were not visible from that place and, despite its closeness, almost nobody went there. It was his favorite retreat when he needed privacy.

The Gorge extended half a mile down-river from the hydroelectric dam to a sudden drop in the land that freed the Aelfwine to run swift and free across the tidewater toward its confluence with the Great River. The channel it had dug down through the bedrock was so straight and narrow that the cliffs either side were almost perpendicular. The water below was white. Crashing, crushing, tumbling as if possessed by a thousand demons, it was energetic enough to splinter logs and carry boulders along in its current. Anyone trying to climb down the cliffs here would surely fall. But if he ran with all his might and jumped with all his strength, he might conceivably miss the rock and hit the water clean. In which case he would certainly die. Nobody could look down at that raging fury and pretend otherwise.

It was an endlessly fascinating prospect to contemplate: Stone, water, stone. Hardness, turbulence, hardness. Not a single tree, shrub, or flower disturbed the purity of its lifelessness. The water looked cold, endlessly cold.

"Hey, there. Remember me?"

Will spun. Out from behind a rusting bulldozer stepped the lubin who had tried to rape Esme back in Grammarieshire. Saligos de Gralloch. Will remembered him in a flash. Everything about the dog-headed creature was familiar—even, when he sauntered forward, his stench. "I certainly remember *you*, young master. The both of ye."

There was a movement behind Saligos as Esme climbed up into the cab of the bulldozer. She plopped herself down on the seat and began yanking at the steering levers, pretending to drive.

"You've lost your hat," Will said. "And what happened to your stickfellas?"

"We had a falling-out. I had to kill them. Good thing I chanced upon the moppet here—otherwise I'd be all by my lonesome."

"Not chance. You broke a pin or button in two when you first found the child and hid half among her clothes against the chance of her slipping away from you. Then, today, you followed the other half here."

"That's very sharp of you," Saligos said. "I note, however, that you didn't say 'my daughter,' but 'the child.' So you're not her father after all. That's two things I've learned today. The other is that she's a retard. She doesn't remember me at all. Think how convenient that would be for somebody of my particular tastes."

"She's not retarded."

"Then she's something just as good." Casually, Saligos removed his belt. "You got cute with me last time we met. That's an imbalance needs addressing. But first, I'm going to tie your wrists to yon machine. You can watch while I do *her*—" he nodded toward Esme, still preoccupied with the bulldozer's controls—"good and hard."

The dragon-darkness was rising up in Will again but this time, rather than fighting it down, he embraced it, letting it fill his brain, so that its negative radiance shone from his eyes like black flame. Ducking his head to keep the lubin from seeing it, he said, "I don't think I can allow that."

"Oh, you can't, eh? And how exactly do you plan to stop me?"

A thrill stirred Will's body then, such as he had not felt since that night when the dragon had entered him and walked him barefoot through the village streets, leaving footprints of flame in his wake. His fury had burned hot as a bronze idol then, and the heat had gone before him in a great wave, withering plants, charring house-fronts, and setting hair ablaze when some unfortunate did not flee from him quickly enough.

Much of the power had come from the war-drake's presence. But the rage—had not the rage then been his and his alone? Dragon Baalthazar had said as much afterward. Had said as well that though the sentence of death was laid down upon his rebel-friend by the dragon, it had been Will's choice and Will's alone that the death be by crucifixion.

"Esme," he said. "I want you to put your hands over your eyes now, and keep them there. Will you do that for me?"

"Yes, Papa."

The lubin sneered. "That won't do you no—" His words cut off in a gasp as Will reached forward and seized his forearms.

Will squeezed. Bones cracked and splintered under his fingers. "Do you like it now?" he asked. "Do you like it now that it's happening to *you?*"

Saligos de Gralloch squirmed helplessly in his implacable grip. His lips were moving, though Will could not hear him through the rush of blood pounding in his ears. Doubtless he was pleading for mercy. Doubtless he whimpered. Doubtless he whined. That was exactly what he *would* do.

Will knew the type well.

First the dragon-lust turned the world red, as if he were peering out through a scrim of pure rage, and then it turned his vision black. Time passed. When he could see again, Saligos de Gralloch's mangled body lay steaming and lifeless on the ground beside the bulldozer. Will's fingers ached horribly, and his hands were tarred with blood up to his wrists. The lubin stared blindly upward, teeth exposed in a final, hideous grin. Something that might be his heart lay on the ground beside his ruptured chest.

"Papa?" Esme was still sitting in the bulldozer seat, hands neatly folded in her lap. Her eyes were open and had been for he did not know how long. "Are you all right?"

Sick with revulsion, Will turned away and shook his head heavily from side to side. "You should leave," he said. "Flee me. Run!"

"Why?"

"There is something...wrong with me. Something that makes me dangerous."

"That's okay."

Will started down at his hands. Murderer's hands. His head was heavy and his heart was pounding so hard his chest ached. He was surprised he could still stand. "You don't understand. I've done something very, very bad."

"I don't mind." Esme climbed down from the bull-dozer, careful not to step on the corpse. "Bad things don't bother me. That's why I sold myself to the Year Eater."

He turned back and stared long and hard at the child. She looked so innocent. Golden-haired, large-headed, toothpick-legged, skin as brown as a berry. "You don't have any memory," he said. "How do you know about the Year Eater?"

"Everybody thinks I have no memory. That's wrong. I only forget people and things that happen. I remember what's important. You taught me to tickle trout. I remember that. And the contract I made is as clear in my mind as the day I gave up my future for it." She turned her back on what remained of Saligos. "But by this afternoon, I'll have forgotten *him* and what you had to do to him as well."

At Esme's direction, Will rolled the body over the cliff-edge. He did not look away in time to avoid seeing it bounce off the rock below. He kicked the maybe-

59

heart after it. The blood on the dirt looked like that which remained after a deer had been gutted and cleaned. Nobody would think twice about it.

Then Esme led Will to a puddle by the tracks to wash his hands. While he did so, she laundered his shirt, whacking it on a rock until every last trace of gore was gone from it. Wordlessly, she began to sing the tune he had been singing when first he saw her. Despite all that had happened, she was perfectly happy. She was, Will realized then, as damned and twisted a thing as he himself.

In a way, they belonged together.

Mother Griet died a fortnight later not from any neglect or infection but as a final, lingering effect of a curse that she had contracted in her long-forgotten childhood. As a girl, she had surprised the White Ladies in their predawn dance and seen that which none but an initiate was sanctioned to see. In their anger, they had pronounced death upon her at the sound of—*her third crow-caw,* they were going to say but, realizing almost too late her youth and innocence of ill-intent, one of their number had quickly emended the sentence to a-million-and-one. From which moment onward, every passing crow had urged her a breath closer to death.

Such was the story Mother Griet had told Will and so when its fulfillment came he knew it for what it was. That morning she had called to him from a bench before her tent and set him to carding wool with her. Midway through the chore, Mother Griet suddenly smiled and, putting down her work, lifted her ancient face to the sky. "Hark!" she said. "Now, *there's* a familiar sound. The black-fledged Sons of Corrin have followed us here from—"

Gently, then, she toppled over on her side, dead.

The citizens of Block G honored Mother Griet's death with the traditional rites. Three solemn Words were carved upon her brow. Her abdomen was cut open, and her entrails read. In lieu of an aurochs, a stray dog was sacrificed. Then they raised up her corpse on long poles to draw down the sacred feeders, the vultures, from the sky. The camp's sanitary officers tried to tear down the sun-platform, and the ensuing argument spread and engulfed the camp in three days of rioting.

In the wake of which, railroad trains were brought in to take them all away. To far Babylonia, the relief workers said, in Fäerie Minor where they would build new lives for themselves, but no one believed them. All they knew of Babylonia was that the streets of its capitol were bricked of gold and the ziggurats touched the sky. Of one thing they were certain: No villager could thrive in such a place. It was not even certain they could survive. All pledged therefore a solemn oath to stay together, come what may, to defend and protect one another in the unimaginable times ahead. Will mouthed the pledge along with the rest, though he did not believe a word of it.

They were sitting alongside their baggage—Will's knapsack and a gryphon-leather valise Mother Griet had left to Esme—when the first train pulled in. The yellow-jacketed soldiers had set up a labyrinthine arrangement of cattle chutes and were feeding the refugees into it according to a system of numbered cards they had handed out earlier. Will and Esme had high numbers, so they watched the jostling crowds from a distance.

"Do you have everything?" he asked, for the umpteenth time.

"Yes," she replied, as always. Then, suddenly, "No! I don't have my ring, the one that somebody gave me. The silver one that I like so much."

"Little scatterbrain. You took it off when you went to sleep, and it rolled under the bed. That's where I found it, anyway." He dug the bauble out of his pocket. "I've been holding onto it for you for a week."

"Gimme it!" She thrust the ring on her finger.

In that very instant, she began to wail as if her heart were broken.

"What is it?" Will cried in alarm. "What's the matter?"

He took the child in his arms, but she was inconsolable. "She's dead," she said. "Griet is dead." He made hushing noises, but she kept on crying. "I *remember* her!" she insisted. "I remember now."

"That's good." Will groped for the right words to say. "It's good to remember people you care about. And you mustn't be unhappy about her dying. She led a long and productive life, after all."

"No!" she sobbed. "You don't understand. Griet was my daughter."

"What?"

"She was my sweetness, my youngest, my light. Oh, my little Grietchen! She brought me dandelions in her tiny fist. Damn memory! Damn responsibility! Damn time!" Esme tugged off her ring and flung it away from her. "Now I remember why I sold my age in the first place."

She wept into Will's shoulder. He hugged her, rocking back and forth. *"Hush,"* he sang to her, *"hush, ah hush."* It was the song of the scythe on a hot summer's day. *"Hush."*

She was just a child, after all, whatever else she might be.

The Little Stranger
Gene Wolfe

Gene Wolfe was born in New York in 1931, served in the Korean War, and graduated from the University of Houston with a degree in mechanical engineering. He worked as an engineer, before becoming editor of trade journal Plant Engineering. *He came to prominence as a writer in the late '60s with a sequence of short stories—including "The Hero as Werewolf," "Seven American Nights," and "The Island of Doctor Death and Other Stories"—in Damon Knight's* Orbit anthologies. *His early major novels were* The Fifth Head of Cerberus *and* Peace, *but he established his reputation with a sequence of three long multi-volume novels—*The Book of the New Sun *(4 vols)*, The Book of the Long Sun *(4 vols)*, The Book of the Short Sun *(3 vols)—and pendant volume,* The Urth of the New Sun. *Wolfe has published a number of short story collections, including* The Island of Doctor Death and Other Stories and Other Stories, Endangered Species, *and* Strange Travelers. *He has won the Nebula Award and World Fantasy Award twice, the Locus Award four times, the John W. Campbell Memorial Award, the British Fantasy Award, the British SF Award, and is* *the recipient of the World Fantasy Award for Lifetime Achievement. Wolfe's most recent books are collection* Innocents Aboard *and major new fantasy novel* The Wizard Knight. *Upcoming is a new collection of science fiction stories and a new novel.*

*Wolfe has often cast his stories in the form of letters—*The Wizard Knight *is a good recent example—and in the tale that follows an elderly woman writes to a dead relative to tell him about what happened when a car broke down outside her isolated home.*

Dear Cousin Danny:

Please forgive me for troubling you with another letter. I know you understand. You are the only family I have, and as you are dead you probably do not mind. I am lonely, terribly lonely, living alone way out here. Yesterday I drove into town, and at the supermarket Brenda told me how lucky I am. She has to check groceries all day, keep house, and look after three children. I would love to know whether she divorced him or he divorced her, but I do not like to ask. You know how that is.

And why. I would dearly love to know why.

I said I would trade with her if I could stand up to so much work, which I could not, and I would take her children anytime and take care of them for as long as she wanted. They could run through the woods, I said, play Monopoly and Parcheesi, and explore the old road. I should have said only the girls, but I did not think of that in time, Danny. Not that I have anything against you boys, but I don't know much about them or taking care of them.

One time Sally Cusick showed me her husband's fish. There was a big lady fish and a little man fish, very shiny and silvery, and Sally said the man fish just came and went and that was that. I said I thought that was about how people were too, but Sally did not agree and has not had me over since although I have had her twice and invited her three times, one time when she said she could not come because the rain, as if rain ever stopped her from going anywhere. She is my nearest neighbor, and I could ride my bicycle down Miller Road and up the County Road and come anytime.

Brenda gave me the name of a plumber friend of hers. It is Jack C. Swierzbowski. I have called him (phoned), and he says he will come.

Every time I turn on the hot water the whole house moans. I think that when I told you about this before, Danny, I said it yelled but it is really more of a moan. Or bellow, like a cow. It is a big house. I know you must remember my house from when you came as a little boy and we played store and all that. Well, probably you remember it bigger than it really is. But it *is* big. Five big bedrooms and all the other rooms like the big cold dining room. I never eat in there anymore. You and I would eat in my merry little kitchen, in the breakfast nook.

If Brenda really sends her girls to me someday that is where we will eat, all three crowded around the little table in the breakfast nook, and for the first day we will make chicken soup and bake brownies and cookies.

There it goes again, and I am not even running the water. Maybe I left it on somewhere, I will see.

Hugs,
Your cousin Ivy

Dear Cousin Danny:

I do not know whether I ever told you what a relief it is to me to write you like this, but it is. I never write to Mama or Papa because I saw them before they were embalmed and everything, and I went to the funerals. But I feel like you are still alive, so I can do it. I put on a stamp but no return address. That nice Mr. Chen at the Post Office said yesterday it might go to the Dead Letter Office, and I said yes that is where I want it to go. I did not even smile, but it was all I could do to keep from laughing out loud.

Mr. Swierzbowski came and worked for three hours and even got up on the roof, three floors up. Then he turned on the water to show me and it was as quiet as mice. But last night it was doing it again. I do not think I will call him again. It was almost two hundred dollars and I am so afraid he will fall.

I went for a ramble in the woods after he left, Danny, remembering how you and I played there. If Brenda sends her girls to stay with me for a while, they will go out there and talk about it afterward, and I ought to know the places.

So I started learning today. It is sad to see how much was fields and farms back in the colonial times. Now it is woods all over again and the Mohawks would feel right at home, but they are gone. You can still see the square hole where the old Hopkins place stood, but it is filling up. Father used to say that the

Hopkins were the last people around except us. He did not count the Cusicks, because it was too far to see their smoke. When they had a fire in the fireplace, I mean, or burned their leaves. Only I think probably Mr. Swierzbowski could have seen it when he was up on the roof. It is not so far that I could not ride over on my bicycle, Danny, and Sally drives all over.

She does not even feed those fish. Her husband does it.

It might be nicer if I had another cat. I used to have Pussums. She was as nice a cat as ever you saw, a calico and oh so pretty. I did not have her fixed or anything because I thought I would find a nice boy calico for her and they would have pretty kittens. I would give away the ones that were not calicos themselves, but I would keep the calicos and have three or four or even five of them. And then the mice would not come inside in the winter the way they do. It was terrible last winter.

Only Pussums got big and wanted a boy cat, but I had not found one for her yet. And one day she just disappeared. I should have gotten another cat then, I think. I did not because I kept thinking Pussums would come back after she had her little fling. Which she has not done, and it is more than three years.

Hugs,

Your cousin Ivy

Dear Cousin Danny,

Here I am, bothering you again. But a lot has happened since I wrote a week ago, and I really do need to tell somebody.

One night I was lying in bed and I heard the house

moan in the way I have told you about. A few minutes later it did it again, and it did it again a few minutes after that.

Pretty soon I understood why it was so unhappy, Danny. It is just like Pussums. It wants another house. You were a man and would not understand, but I *knew*. It was not from thinking, even if I think a lot and am good at it, my teachers always said. I knew. So I got out of bed and told it as loud as I could that I would get it another house. At first I said a tool shed, but that didn't work, so a house. A little house, but a house.

Well, that is what I am going to do. I am going to talk to people who build houses and have a cottage built right here on my own property. I know they will probably cheat me, but I will have to bear it and keep the cheating as small as I can. I mean to talk to Mr. LaPointe at the bank about it. I know he will advise me, and he is honest.

So that is one thing, but just one. There is another one.

An old truck was going up Miller Road towing a big trailer when it broke down right in front of my house here. There were two men in the truck and two ladies in the trailer, and one lady has a little baby. They are all dark, with curly black hair and big smiles, even the baby.

The older man rang my bell and explained what had happened. He asked if he could pull his truck and the trailer up onto my front lawn until he and the other man could get the truck fixed.

I said all right, but then I thought what if they want to come inside to use the bathroom? Should I let them in? I decided I did not know them well enough to make up my mind about that, but you cannot keep somebody who needs to come inside quickly standing on the porch while you ask questions. I went into the parlor and watched them awhile through the window. They had put the baby on the lawn. The young lady was steering, and the men and the older lady were pushing, because the lawn is higher than Miller Road, and there was the ditch and everything. I could see everyone was working hard, so I made lemonade.

When it was ready they had tied a big chain around the biggest maple. There were zigzag ropes between the chain and their truck, turning and turning around little wheels, and they were pulling on the other end. It was working, too. They had already gotten the front end of their truck up on the grass. I went out and we had lemonade and talked awhile.

The older man is Mr. Zoltan, and the younger one is Johnny. The older lady is Marmar. Or something like that. I cannot say it like they do. She is Mrs. Zoltan. The young lady is Mrs. Johnny, and the baby is hers. Her name is Ivy, just like mine. Her mother's name is Suzette, and she is really quite pretty.

I never said about the bathroom, but I decided if they asked I would let them come in, especially Suzette. Only they never have. I think they are going in the woods. Now I am somewhat scared about going to bed. What if they break in while I am sleeping?

Well, I just went into the parlor and watched them through the window, and both men are working really hard on their truck, with flashlights to see and the engine in pieces. So I do not think they will break in tonight. They will be too tired. I will write to you again really soon, Danny.

Hugs,

Your cousin Ivy

P.S. The house has been quiet as mice ever since they came.

Dear Cousin Danny:

I have such good news! You will not believe how nicely everything is working out. Mr. Zoltan came to breakfast this morning. It was just bacon and eggs and toast, but he liked it. He drinks a lot of coffee. He said they were poor people, and they need parts for their truck. I said I did not have any, which was the truth. Then he asked if they could stay here until they could earn enough to fix their truck. Not in my house, I said. He said they would live in their trailer, like always, but if they parked it someplace without permission the police would make them leave, and they could not leave here so they would go to jail.

That was when I got my wonderful idea. I get many wonderful ideas, Danny, but this was the most wonderful ever. I explained to Mr. Zoltan that I wanted another house built on my property. Not a big house, just a little one. I said that if he and Johnny would build it for me in their spare time, I would let them stay.

Mr. Zoltan looked at me in a worried kind of way, then looked over at the stove. I said if they could fix a truck they could build a house, and would they do it?

He told me all over again how poor they were. He said they would have to earn enough to buy wood and shingles and so forth. They could find some things at the dump, he said, but they would have to buy the rest. It might take a long time.

I said that I would not ask them to buy the material, only to build me a little old-fashioned cottage like the

71

picture I showed him. I would buy the material for them. That made him happy, and he agreed at once. He wanted to know where I wanted it built. I said you look around and decide where you think it ought to be and tell me.

So you see, Danny, why I said I had wonderful news. The Willis Lumber Co. in town will not cheat me more than they cheat everybody, and Mr. Zoltan and Johnny will not cheat me either, because I am not going to give them any money at all.

Hugs,
Your cousin Ivy

Dear Cousin Danny,

I had not planned to pester you with another letter as soon as this, but I just have to tell *somebody* how well my plan is going. Mr. Zoltan came to tell me he had found a foundation in the woods we could use. I knew it was the old Hopkins place, but I asked him questions about it, and it was. Then I told him we could not use it because it was not on my land.

It took all the happiness right out of him. He explained that digging the foundation and building the things to hold the cement were going to be some of the hardest work and would take a long while. The old Hopkins foundation is stone, big stone blocks like tombstones, and he said it was as good as new. So I thought, well, I was going to have to pay for the cement and picks and shovels and all that anyway, so perhaps I could buy the land.

When Mr. Zoltan had left, I called up (phoned) Mr. LaPointe and said I wanted the land where the house had been, and a patch in between so I could get there without going off my property. He said how high are you willing to go?

I thought about that, and looked at my bank books and the checking account and all that. I talked to that foreign woman at Merrill Lynch, too. Finally I called Mr. LaPointe back and said fifty thousand. He said he thought he could get it for me cheaper. By that time my mind was made up. I have a hard time making up my mind about things sometime, Danny, but when I do it is done. I said to buy me as much of the Hopkins property as fifty thousand would get, only to make sure where the old house was, was the part I was buying.

After that Mr. Zoltan came back twice to talk about other places, but I said wait.

Then (this was Tuesday afternoon, I think, Danny) Mr. LaPointe called me. (Phoned.) He was so happy it made me happy for him. He said he had gotten the whole property for thirty-nine thousand five hundred. The whole farm, only it is all woods now. I went right out and told Johnny, who was working on the truck. And that afternoon he and Mr. Zoltan started shoveling the cellar out. I know they did because I went to see, and it is very black soil, good garden soil I would say and mostly rotted leaves. Compost is what the magazines call it.

I showed them pictures of houses like the one they are going to build for me, and they said they would go to the Willis Lumber Company and buy enough lumber to get started as soon as their truck would run again if I would give them the money. I said no, we will go in my car now and the company will deliver it for a little more money.

Which is what we did. You know how bossy I can

be. Suzette needed a ride into town, too, so there were four of us on the drive in. She is opening a shop there to make money. It says "Psychic." I let her out in front of it, and Mr. Zoltan, Johnny, and I went to Willis's. I made them tell me what everything they wanted was and why they wanted it, but I promised that they could keep the scroll saw and the other new tools. We bought a whole keg of nails! And ever so much wood, Danny.

Now I am sitting in the Sun Room to write this, and I can hear their hammers, way off in the woods. If they get quiet before dark, I will go out there and see what the matter is.

Hugs,
Your cousin Ivy

Dear Cousin Danny,

I haven't even mailed that other letter, and here I am writing again. But the envelope is sealed and I do not wish to tear it open. You will get two letters at once, which I hope you will not mind too much.

There are reasons for this, a big one and a little one. I am going to tell you the little one first, so the big one does not squash it flat. It is that the young lady called me (phoned). She has a cell phone. She said she was Yvonne. I said who? She said Yvonne as plain as anything and she was staying with me. (This is what she said, Danny. It is not true.) Then she said I had given her a ride into town that morning, so I knew it was Suzette. She said she was ready to come home now and there was a friend who would drive her, only she called her a client. But she did not know the roads and neither did her friend.

So I gave her directions, how to find the County Road and how you turn on Miller Road and so on. I know you know already, so I will not repeat everything. Then I sat down and thought hard about the young lady. Could I have remembered her name wrong? I know I could not, not as wrong as that.

So she is fooling her friend, and if she will fool her friend she will fool me. I would like to talk with Marmar about her, but I know Marmar will not talk if I just come up and ask. I must think of something, and writing you these letters helps.

It helps more now, because I know that you get them and read them, Danny. That is my big thing. I know it because I saw you last night. You must have thought I was sleeping. I could see you were being very quiet so as not to wake me up.

But I was awake, sitting by the window looking down at the trailer and Mr. Zoltan's truck. I could not sleep. That is how it is with folks my age. We take naps during the day, and then we cannot sleep at night. I think that it is because God is getting us ready for the grave. Is that right? Did He ever tell you?

You went into the woods to look at my new house. I saw you go and sat up waiting for you to come back. The moon was low and bright when you did, and I got to see it right through you, which was very pretty and something I had never seen before at all. You looked at their truck and even went into the trailer without opening the door, which must be very handy when you are carrying a basket of laundry or grocery bags. When you went back into the woods I waited for you to come out for a while. I thought about coming downstairs and saying hello, but I knew you would think you woke me up. You did not, I just did, and it would not have been fair for me to make you feel guilty, as I am sure you would even if I said not to.

But I want you to know that I am often awake, and there is no reason I could not put on a robe and have a nice chat. I could make tea or anything like that which you might like, Danny.

Hugs,

Your cousin Ivy

Dear Cousin Danny,

I have had the nicest time! I must tell you. Yvonne (Suzette) was in town at her shop, and Marmar had ever so much work to do, cooking and cleaning her trailer. So I said I would look after little Ivy for a while. We played peekaboo and had a bottle, and I changed her three times. She is really the dearest little baby in the world! Of course I had to give her back eventually, which I did not like to do. But Mr. Zoltan came and wanted her, and I gave her to him. He looked pale and ill, I thought, and his hands shook. So I did not like to and I am afraid he will give little Ivy something. A really bad cold or the flu. But he is her grandfather, so I did.

Then something very, very odd happened. I cannot explain it and don't even know who to ask. I got to thinking about you, and how much I would like to talk to you. And it came to me that you might not want to come into my house unless you were invited. I know you could walk right through my door like you did into Mr. Zoltan's trailer, but I thought you would probably not want to. I thought of inviting you in this letter, and I do. Just come in anytime, Danny.

What is more, I remembered about the rock. There is this big rock in my flower bed close to the front porch, and I keep it there because it was in Mama's. She had it there because Papa always kept a key under it in case he lost his. Only when he died she took the key away for fear someone would find it and come in.

And I thought, well, I *want* Cousin Danny to come in and talk. So I will just put a key there for him to find, and tell him it is there. I got my extra key from the desk in Papa's study and went outside to put it under the rock.

But when I picked that rock up, there was foreign writing on the bottom. It was yellow chalk, I think, very ugly and new-looking. Just looking at it made me feel sick. I took that rock inside right away and washed it in the sink. It made me feel a lot better, and I think it made the rock feel better too. You know what I mean.

Anyway, that rock is all nice and clean now, Danny, and I have put the key under it as a sign that you are welcome to come in anytime. If you pick up the rock and there is bad writing on the bottom, I did not put it there. I do not even have any yellow chalk. Tell me when you come in, and I will wash it off.

But the main thing was little Ivy. She is the darlingest baby, and I just love her.

Hugs,

Your cousin Ivy

Dear Cousin Danny,

In some ways it has been very nice here today, but in others Not So Nice. Let me begin with one of the nice ones, which is Pusson. I went out to see how my new little house was. I had heard a lot of sawing and hammering that morning, and then it had stopped, and I thought I should see what the trouble was. Well, Danny, you would never guess.

It was a cat. Just a cat, not very big and really quite friendly once he gets to know you. He was up on the plywood that Mr. Zoltan and Johnny are going to nail the shingles on. They were afraid of him. Two big men afraid of a little cat! I thought it was silly and said Pussums, Pussums, Pussums! Which was the way I used to call my old cat, and this nice young cat came right down. I let him smell my fingers, and soon he was rubbing my legs.

Yes, Danny, I took Pusson home with me. I think he is really a calico cat under all the black. Other cats are not so friendly and sweet. I have kept Pussums's cat box all ready in case she ever comes home, and Pusson knows how to use it already. So I think he is calico underneath. Pussums found the boy cat she was looking for, and they had children, and this is her son, coming back to the Old Home Place to see how it was when his mama was young. You will think I am just a silly old woman for writing all that, but it could have happened, and since I want to believe it, why should I not be happy?

Besides there is nobody out here for Pusson to belong to except Sally Cusick and she should not have a cat because of all the fish. So he can live here with me, and if Sally ever comes he can hide under the sofa in the parlor.

The not so nice part is Mr. Cherigate. I did not

know him at all until he pulled up in his big car. He was perfectly friendly and drank my tea and petted Pusson, but he told me very firmly that I cannot have Mr. Zoltan and Johnny put in the pipes and the electric like I had planned. Mr. Cherigate is a Building Inspector for the county. He showed me his badge and gave me his card, which I still have on the nice hallmarked silver tray that used to be Mama's when you were here. I must have a licensed plumber for the pipes and an electrician for the electric. I explained that Mr. LaPointe at the bank did not think I would need a building permit way out here, and he said I did not, but a building that people might live in must pass inspection and ever so much more.

Naturally I called Mr. Swierzbowski (phoned). He will do the plumbing, and he will send his friend Mr. Caminiti for the electric. I am sure it will cost ever so much, but I don't think I will be able to get Mr. Zoltan to pay, although I will try.

I am not sure if this is the worst thing or just a funny thing, Danny. Perhaps I will know tomorrow, and if I do I will tell myself that I should have waited and told you all about it then. But I am going to tell you now and let you decide. While Mr. Cherigate was drinking my tea he asked if I knew I was a witch. I thought about it and said I did not, but if it meant I get to ride through the air on a broom and throw down candy to the boys and girls I might do it. He laughed and said no, a real witch, one that cast spells and sours milk while it is still in the cow.

Of course I said I could not do that and I did not think anybody else could either. Mr. Cherigate said there was a rumor going around town that said that, and I explained that there was nobody rooming with

me except Pusson. I should have said little Ivy sometimes, too, Danny, but I forgot.

But Mr. Cherigate meant *rumor*. So I had made a
silly mistake that I would not have made if it were
not for Yvonne (Suzette) telling people she lived here.
Then Mr. Cherigate said that he had heard it from his
wife, who heard it from a fortune-teller. I said is that
the same as psychic and he said it was. So it was
Suzette after all! I will talk to her about this the first
chance I get, Danny, and I will write you again soon
to tell you what I said and what she said.

Hugs!

Your cousin Ivy

Dear Cousin Danny,

You will not believe what I am going to tell you in
this letter, but it is true, every bit.

When I had finished the letter I wrote yesterday, I
waited for somebody to bring Suzette (Yvonne) home.
Then I went out to the trailer to talk to her. She was
inside, and Marmar said she was nursing little Ivy. I
certainly did not want to interrupt that and perhaps
make little Ivy cry, so I went to my new little house
to see whether Mr. Swierzbowski or Mr. Caminiti had
come.

They had not, but Mr. Zoltan and Johnny were
there sawing fretwork. When Mr. Zoltan saw me, he
got down on his knees. When Johnny saw that, he
did too. They begged me to let them use their truck
again. If they had their truck, they could go to the
dump and find things for me, and buy nails and
shingles whenever they needed them, and bring them
back here in their truck. It was hard for me to under-

stand everything they said, Danny, because Mr. Zoltan's English is not even as good as Mr. Chen's (at the Post Office). And Johnny would not look at me, or talk very loud either. But that was what they wanted, and when I understood I said of course they could use their truck, go right ahead.

They started thanking me then, over and over, and crying. And while they were doing that, we heard a funny noise from the direction of my house. I did not know what it was. You will think it silly of me, Danny, I know. But I did not. Mr. Zoltan and Johnny knew at once and ran toward it. I worried for a minute that someone might come and take the saws and hammers and things they were leaving behind. And I thought, they are not my things, and Johnny and Mr. Zoltan ran right off and left them so why should not I? No one asked me to watch them while they were gone.

By that time even Mr. Zoltan was out of sight. Johnny was out of sight almost before he began to run, because Johnny can run very fast. I did not run. I walked, but I walked fast, carrying Pusson and petting him as I went along. He is very nice for a black cat, Danny, about as nice as any cat that is not calico can be.

When I got back to my big house, Mr. Zoltan's trailer was still there, but Mr. Zoltan's truck was gone. That was when I knew what the noise we heard had been. It was the noise of the engine starting. Mr. Zoltan and Johnny had heard it many times, so they knew what it was. I had not, so I did not know.

Marmar said Suzette (Yvonne) had taken it. She thought she had run away. I said I did not think so, because I think that she needed to visit her little store, and that if Johnny telephoned her there in a few minutes she would be there. Johnny did not think so. Marmar said we would never see her again and little Ivy cried. Zoltan said I could get her back, but he would not say how.

After that, I decided to telephone myself, but I did not tell them that because I did not want them to think I was interfering.

That was when Mr. Swierzbowski came to talk about plumbing for my new little stranger. I made Mr. Zoltan and Johnny go back to it with us, so they could show Mr. Swierzbowski what needed to be done. There were some trees that would have to be cut for the septic tank, and a lot more that would have to be cut so Mr. Swierzbowski could bring in his big digging machine. I do not like trees being cut, so I said Mr. Zoltan and Johnny would dig it with shovels. They looked very despondent when I said this, so I said that if they would I would get their truck back or get them a new one. I said it because I do not think Suzette (Yvonne) has really run away and left her baby.

After that I came back here and Pusson and I called (phoned) Yvonne's store. There was no answer, so I am writing this letter to you instead. As soon I sign it and address your envelope and find a stamp for it, I will try again.

Hugs,
Your cousin Ivy

Dear Cousin Danny:

I have been so busy these past few days that I have not written. I am terribly sorry, but I have not even had a chance to go to the post office to buy Mr. Chen's stamps. Little Ivy is sleeping now. I think that she is more used to me, or perhaps I am more used to her. But she is sleeping like a little angel, with Pusson curled up beside her. I would take a picture if I could only find my camera, which is not in the kitchen cabinet or the library or anywhere.

But I have stopped trying to remember where my camera might be, and started trying to remember what I have told you and what happened after that letter was out in the big tin box, with the flag up. You know that Suzette (Yvonne) took Mr. Zoltan's truck. He is angry about it and so is Johnny. Suzette is not even Mr. Zoltan's daughter, only his daughter-in-law. I have talked to them, and Marmar is Mr. Zoltan's wife, just like I thought. Suzette (Yvonne) is Johnny's wife. But Johnny says was, and says he will beat her for a week. I do not see how he can beat her if he is going to divorce her. He says he will go to the king and get a divorce. Do you think he means George III, Danny? George III is dead, but then you are dead too, so perhaps George III can still divorce people. Johnny is Mr. Zoltan's son, and Marmar's.

It is funny, sometimes, how these things work out. When I had called Suzette's (Yvonne's) store several times and gotten no answer, and talked to Marmar besides Mr. Zoltan and Johnny, and called the store twice more, I felt sure that Suzette had stolen Mr. Zoltan's truck and was not ever going to bring it back.

So she had really stolen my truck because I had promised Mr. Zoltan and Johnny that I would get them a new one if we could not get their old one back. Besides, their trailer was parked in my front yard, and it still is. I like them and they have never asked to use my bathroom, not even once. But I do not want them living in my front yard until I am old and gray, which is now.

So I called the police. I described my truck to the nice policeman, and when he asked about license plates I said it did not have any because I had noticed that before Suzette took it. I said it had just been parked on my property but I had gotten two men to work on it, and as soon as it would run Suzette had run off with it. You can see that I told the nice policeman nothing but the truth, Danny. All that was just as true as I could make it without getting all complicated. I spoke clearly and enunciated plainly, and the nice policeman never argued with me about a thing.

Then he asked me about Suzette. I told him how old she was, and pretty, and black hair. And I explained that she was the wife of one of the men who had been working on my truck and building a new little house for me. That was fine too, Danny, and perhaps I ought to have left it at that, but I did not, and that seemed like it might be a mistake for a while. I told him that her professional name was Yvonne. Which it was.

He became very interested and asked about her store, so I told him where it was and that I had never gone in there to buy anything. He said that there was a Mr. Bunco who would want to hear about Yvonne. I said Mr. Bunco could come out and talk to me anytime and I would tell him all I could, and I told him where I live.

After that I fixed dinner, which was macaroni-and-cheese and salad from my garden with canned salmon in it for me, and more salmon for Pusson. It was very good, too.

Pusson had only just finished saying thank you when we heard a police car. I went outside because I thought I ought to show the policemen where the truck had been, and I was just in time to see Mr. Zoltan and Marmar running into the woods. Johnny was gone already. I know he can run much faster. Little Ivy was crying, so I went into their trailer and picked her up. I rocked her, and she quieted down right away. She is such a good baby, Danny. You would never believe how good she is.

I told the lady who came with the policeman that I had been expecting Mr. Bunco. And she said she was Miz Bunco and that would have to do. But she gave me her card, and she was only fooling. Her name is really Sergeant Lois B. Anderson, unless it was someone else's card. She asked about little Ivy, and I explained that I was taking care of her while Suzette (Yvonne) was away stealing my truck. She said she would tell D.C. and F.S. and they would take her off my hands. I do not know who F.S. is, Danny, but D.C. is the District of Columbia which means the president. He looks like a very nice man, I know. Still, Danny, he is very busy and may not know how to take care of children. So I said that I did not want little Ivy taken off my hands, that I like her and she likes me, which is the truth. Then Miz Anderson said we ought to go inside where I could sit down, and perhaps little Ivy's diaper needed changing.

Miz Anderson held her while I put water on for tea and we had a nice talk. She said the president would put little Ivy in a faster home, and that might not be the best thing for her. Some faster homes were nice and some not so nice, she said. I did not like the idea of little Ivy living in another trailer, and it seems to me that one that went fast would be worse than Mr. Zoltan's, which does not move at all but is terribly crowded and smelly. So I said why not just let me keep her, she will be right here and perhaps Suzette will come back?

Miz Anderson and I agreed that might be better, and Miz Anderson took her card and wrote call at once if Yvonne returns for baby on the back of it.

So little Ivy is mine now, Danny. Another little stranger is what I said to Pusson, who is a little stranger himself and delighted. I have told Marmar that I have to keep her until Suzette (Yvonne) comes back for her. I do not think Marmar likes that very much, but Mr. Zoltan and Johnny are on my side.

Hugs,
Your cousin Ivy

Dear Cousin Danny:

It has been days and days since I wrote last. I have been so busy! My little house is finished now, and some nice children came to see me today. Their names are Hank and Greta, isn't that nice? They are *twins*, and their mother loves old movies. They are ever so cute, and we had a wonderful time together. They have promised to come back and see me again. I made them promise that before they left, Danny, and they did. I am so looking forward to it.

So that is what I wanted to write you about. But I should have written before, because I have ever so much wonderful news. My little house is finished! Isn't that nice? And little Ivy is still with me, which is even nicer. I will give my little stranger back to her mother, of course, if her mother (Suzette) ever comes back. I suppose I'll have to, but I won't like it.

I call her the little stranger, and then I have to remind myself there are really three. That is little Ivy, Pusson, and the first little stranger ever, my new little house. But, Cousin Danny, there are *five* now, because I must include Hank and Greta, who are such sweet little strangers. I could just eat them up!

After Ivy got settled down for her nap this morning, I went to my new little house (it has a name now and I will tell you in a minute) to see if the nice lady from the department store had brought my new furniture yet. And out in front of my new little house were the sweetest children you ever saw, little towheads about seven or eight. I said hello and they said hello, and I asked their names, and they wanted to know if my little house was made of gingerbread.

I explained that there was a lot of gingerbread on it, because that is what you call the lovely old-fashioned woodwork Mr. Zoltan and Johnny made for me. Danny, I had to hold each of them up so they could feel it and see it was not the kind of gingerbread you eat! Can you imagine?

After that we went inside, and I told them all about the nice big Navigator car you got for me from Mr. Cherigate, the building inspector. How hard it was to get him to stand up, and how I promised I would stop the bleeding and walk him out of my cute little Gingerbread House and never tell anyone what happened if he would give me his car for Mr. Zoltan. But I am not breaking my promise by talking about it to you in this letter, because you know already. He was so startled when you and that Hopkins girl joined us that he ran into the pantry and bumped his nose on a shelf trying to get out, remember? I still laugh when I think of it, but it was not really funny at all until I made it stop bleeding. Anyway Mr. Caminiti has come and fixed what he had put in wrong, and there are lights, ever so pretty when they shine out through all the trees.

But I just told Hank and Greta that a nice man had given me a big black car for what I did, bigger than Mr. Zoltan's truck had been. And I had given it to Mr. Zoltan and Johnny for building my house. It was too big for me anyway, and I have my own car. I do not think I could ever drive a big thing like that.

Hank and Greta liked my new little house so much that I have decided to call it Gingerbread House. Now I will never forget them, and I will find somebody to paint a sign saying that and put it on my little house, too.

But I was worried about little Ivy. I do not like to leave her alone for a long time, and the time was getting long. So I made Hank and Greta come back with me to this big house. I showed them little Ivy, and I showed them to little Ivy, too! She liked them and laughed and made all sorts of baby noises. Pusson told me her diaper needed changing, and Greta changed while Hank and I helped. After that, we baked gingerbread men and played with little Ivy, and played checkers with our gingerbread men, too, breaking off heads and things to make them fit on the squares. You could eat the cookies you captured, but if you did you could not use them to crown your kings. Hank ate all his, so Greta beat him. I did too. By that time it was getting dark, so I showed them how I could make fire fly out of Pusson's fur.

Then we went back to Gingerbread House, and Miz Macy had brought the furniture and set it up like she promised, just like magic. The children were amazed and ever so pleased. Hank wanted to know if they could come back on Halloween, and Greta said no, she will be busy then.

So I said I hoped I would be very busy with little trick-or-treaters, but I would save special treats for them. Children never come, Danny, but I did not want Greta to feel badly. So perhaps she and Hank will come then. I hope so. Oh, I do! It has been ever so long since the children came here.

Hugs,

Your cousin Ivy

P.S. Brenda called while I was looking for your envelope. Hank and Greta are hers! And they had come home very late, she said, full of stories about baking cookies with a witch in the woods. Sally Cusick gave her my number and told her I might know something since I lived out this way. Of course I said my goodness there are no witches out here.

Only me.

The Faery Handbag
Kelly Link

*Kelly Link was born in Miami, Florida and grew up
on the East Coast. She attended Columbia University
in New York and the University of North Carolina,
Greensboro. She sold her first story, "Water Off a Black
Dog's Back," just before attending Clarion in 1995.
Her later stories have won and been nominated for
numerous prestigious awards: "Travels With the Snow
Queen" won the James Tiptree Jr. Award, "The Special-
ist's Hat" won the World Fantasy Award, and the
novelette "Louise's Ghost" won a Nebula. Link's stories
have been gathered in chapbook* 4 Stories *and collection* Stranger Things Happen, *both from Small Beer
Press, which she owns with her husband, publisher
Gavin Grant. Link edited the 2003 anthology* Trampo-
line, *co-edits* The Year's Best Fantasy and Horror *with
Grant and Ellen Datlow, and co-edits the 'zine* Lady
Churchill's Rosebud Wristlet *with Grant. They live
in Brooklyn, New York. Upcoming is a new collection,*
Magic for Beginners. *Link is also currently at work on
a novel based on the story that follows.*

I used to go to thrift stores with my friends. We'd take the train into Boston, and go to The Garment District, which is this huge vintage clothing warehouse. Everything is arranged by color, and somehow that makes all of the clothes beautiful. It's kind of like if you went through the wardrobe in the Narnia books, only instead of finding Aslan and the White Witch and horrible Eustace, you found this magic clothing world—instead of talking animals, there were feather boas and wedding dresses and bowling shoes, and paisley shirts and Doc Martens and everything hung up on racks so that first you have black dresses, all together, like the world's largest indoor funeral, and then blue dresses—all the blues you can imagine—and then red dresses and so on. Pink-reds and orangey reds and purple-reds and exit-light reds and candy reds. Sometimes I would close my eyes and Natasha and Natalie and Jake would drag me over to a rack, and rub a dress against my hand. "Guess what color this is."

We had this theory that you could learn how to tell, just by feeling, what color something was. For example, if you're sitting on a lawn, you can tell what color green the grass is, with your eyes closed, depending on how silky-rubbery it feels. With clothing, stretchy velvet stuff always feels red when your eyes are closed, even if it's not red. Natasha was always best at guessing colors, but Natasha is also best at cheating at games and not getting caught.

One time we were looking through kid's T-shirts

and we found a Muppets T-shirt that had belonged to Natalie in third grade. We knew it belonged to her, because it still had her name inside, where her mother had written it in permanent marker, when Natalie went to summer camp. Jake bought it back for her, because he was the only one who had money that weekend. He was the only one who had a job.

Maybe you're wondering what a guy like Jake is doing in The Garment District with a bunch of girls. The thing about Jake is that he always has a good time, no matter what he's doing. He likes everything, and he likes everyone, but he likes me best of all. Wherever he is now, I bet he's having a great time and wondering when I'm going to show up. I'm always running late. But he knows that.

We had this theory that things have life cycles, the way that people do. The life cycle of wedding dresses and feather boas and t-shirts and shoes and handbags involves the Garment District. If clothes are good, or even if they're bad in an interesting way, the Garment District is where they go when they die. You can tell that they're dead, because of the way that they smell. When you buy them, and wash them, and start wearing them again, and they start to smell like you, that's when they reincarnate. But the point is, if you're looking for a particular thing, you just have to keep looking for it. You have to look hard.

Down in the basement at the Garment Factory they sell clothing and beat-up suitcases and teacups by the pound. You can get eight pounds worth of prom dresses—a slinky black dress, a poufy lavender dress, a swirly pink dress, a silvery, starry lamé dress so fine you could pass it through a key ring—for eight dollars.

I go there every week, hunting for Grandmother Zofia's faery handbag.

The faery handbag: It's huge and black and kind of hairy. Even when your eyes are closed, it feels black. As black as black ever gets, like if you touch it, your hand might get stuck in it, like tar or black quicksand or when you stretch out your hand at night, to turn on a light, but all you feel is darkness.

Fairies live inside it. I know what that sounds like, but it's true.

Grandmother Zofia said it was a family heirloom. She said that it was over two hundred years old. She said that when she died, I had to look after it. Be its guardian. She said that it would be my responsibility.

I said that it didn't look that old, and that they didn't have handbag two hundred years ago, but that just made her cross. She said, "So then tell me, Genevieve, darling, where do you think old ladies used to put their reading glasses and their heart medicine and their knitting needles?"

I know that no one is going to believe any of this. That's okay. If I thought you would, then I couldn't tell you. Promise me that you won't believe a word. That's what Zofia used to say to me when she told me stories. At the funeral, my mother said, half-laughing and half-crying, that her mother was the world's best liar. I think she thought maybe Zofia wasn't really dead. But I went up to Zofia's coffin, and I looked her right in the eyes. They were closed. The funeral parlor had made her up with blue eyeshad-

93

ow, and blue eyeliner. She looked like she was going to be a news anchor on Fox television, instead of dead. It was creepy and it made me even sadder than I already was. But I didn't let that distract me.

"Okay, Zofia," I whispered. "I know you're dead, but this is important. You know exactly how important this is. Where's the handbag? What did you do with it? How do I find it? What am I supposed to do now?"

Of course she didn't say a word. She just lay there, this little smile on her face, as if she thought the whole thing—death, blue eyeshadow, Jake, the handbag, faeries, Scrabble, Baldeziwurlekistan, all of it—was a joke. She always did have a weird sense of humor. That's why she and Jake got along so well.

I grew up in a house next door to the house where my mother lived when she was a little girl. Her mother, Zofia Swink, my grandmother, babysat me while my mother and father were at work.

Zofia never looked like a grandmother. She had long black hair which she wore up in little, braided, spiky towers and plaits. She had large blue eyes. She was taller than my father. She looked like a spy or ballerina or a lady pirate or a rock star. She acted like one too. For example, she never drove anywhere. She rode a bike. It drove my mother crazy. "Why can't you act your age?" she'd say, and Zofia would just laugh.

Zofia and I played Scrabble all the time. Zofia always won, even though her English wasn't all that great, because we'd decided that she was allowed to use Baldeziwurleki vocabulary. Baldeziwurlekistan is where Zofia was born, over two hundred years ago. That's what Zofia said. (My grandmother claimed to be over two hundred years old. Or maybe even older. Sometimes she claimed that she'd even met Ghenghis Khan. He was much shorter than her. I probably don't have time to tell that story.) Baldeziwurlekistan is also an incredibly valuable word in Scrabble points, even though it doesn't exactly fit on the board. Zofia put it down the first time we played. I was feeling pretty good because I'd gotten forty-one points for "zippery" on my turn.

Zofia kept rearranging her letters on her tray. Then she looked over at me, as if daring me to stop her, and put down "eziwurlekistan", after "bald." She used "delicious," "zippery," "wishes," "kismet", and "needle," and made "to" into "toe". "Baldeziwurlekistan" went all the way across the board and then trailed off down the righthand side.

I started laughing.

"I used up all my letters," Zofia said. She licked her pencil and started adding up points.

"That's not a word," I said. "Baldeziwurlekistan is not a word. Besides, you can't do that. You can't put an eighteen letter word on a board that's fifteen squares across."

"Why not? It's a country," Zofia said. "It's where I was born, little darling."

"Challenge," I said. I went and got the dictionary and looked it up. "There's no such place."

"Of course there isn't nowadays," Zofia said. "It wasn't a very big place, even when it was a place. But you've heard of Samarkand, and Uzbekistan and the Silk Road and Ghenghis Khan. Haven't I told you about meeting Ghenghis Khan?"

I looked up Samarkand. "Okay," I said. "Samarkand is a real place. A real word. But Baldeziwurlekistan isn't."

"They call it something else now," Zofia said. "But I think it's important to remember where we come from. I think it's only fair that I get to use Baldeziwurleki words. Your English is so much better than me. Promise me something, mouthful of dumpling, a small, small thing. You'll remember its real name. Baldeziwurlekistan. Now when I add it up, I get three hundred and sixty-eight points. Could that be right?"

If you called the faery handbag by its right name, it would be something like "orzipanikanikcz," which means the "bag of skin where the world lives," only Zofia never spelled that word the same way twice. She said you had to spell it a little differently each time. You never wanted to spell it exactly the right way, because that would be dangerous.

I called it the faery handbag because I put "faery" down on the Scrabble board once. Zofia said that you spelled it with an "i," not an "e." She looked it up in the dictionary, and lost a turn.

Zofia said that in Baldeziwurlekistan they used a board and tiles for divination, prognostication, and sometimes even just for fun. She said it was a little like playing Scrabble. That's probably why she turned out to be so good at Scrabble. The Baldeziwurlekistanians used their tiles and board to communicate with the people who lived under the hill. The people who lived under the hill knew the future. The Baldeziwurlekistanians gave them fermented milk and honey, and the young women of the village used to go and lie out on the hill and sleep under the stars. Apparently the people under the hill were pretty cute. The important thing was that you never went down into the hill and spent the night there, no matter how cute the guy from under the hill was. If you did, even if you only spent a single night under the hill, when you came out again a hundred years might have passed. "Remember that," Zofia said to me. "It doesn't matter how cute a guy is. If he wants you to come back to his place, it isn't a good idea. It's okay to fool around, but don't spend the night."

Every once in a while, a woman from under the hill would marry a man from the village, even though it never ended well. The problem was that the women under the hill were terrible cooks. They couldn't get used to the way time worked in the village, which meant that supper always got burnt, or else it wasn't cooked long enough. But they couldn't stand to be criticized. It hurt their feelings. If their village husband complained, or even if he looked like he wanted to complain, that was it. The woman from under the hill went back to her home, and even if her husband went and begged and pleaded and apologized, it might be three years or thirty years or a few generations before she came back out.

Even the best, happiest marriages between the Baldeziwurlekistanians and the people under the hill fell apart when the children got old enough to complain about dinner. But everyone in the village had some hill blood in them.

"It's in you," Zofia said, and kissed me on the nose. "Passed down from my grandmother and her mother. It's why we're so beautiful."

When Zofia was nineteen, the shaman-priestess in her village threw the tiles and discovered that something bad was going to happen. A raiding party was coming. There was no point in fighting them. They would burn down everyone's houses and take the young men and women for slaves. And it was even worse than that. There was going to be an earthquake as well, which was bad news because usually, when raiders showed up, the village went down under the hill for a night and when they came out again the raiders would have been gone for months or decades or even a hundred years. But this earthquake was going to split the hill right open.

The people under the hill were in trouble. Their home would be destroyed, and they would be doomed to roam the face of the earth, weeping and lamenting their fate until the sun blew out and the sky cracked and the seas boiled and the people dried up and turned to dust and blew away. So the shaman-priestess went and divined some more, and the people under the hill told her to kill a black dog and skin it and use the skin to make a purse big enough to hold a chicken, an egg, and a cooking pot. So she did, and then the people under the hill made the inside of the purse big enough to hold all of the village and all of the people under the hill and mountains and forests and seas and rivers and lakes and orchards and a sky and stars and spirits and fabulous monsters and sirens and dragons and dryads and mermaids and beasties and all the little gods that the Baldeziwurlekistanians and the people under the hill worshipped.

"Your purse is made out of dog skin?" I said. "That's disgusting!"

"Little dear pet," Zofia said, looking wistful, "Dog

is delicious. To Baldeziwurlekistanians, dog is a delicacy."

Before the raiding party arrived, the village packed up all of their belongings and moved into the handbag. The clasp was made out of bone. If you opened it one way, then it was just a purse big enough to hold a chicken and an egg and a clay cooking pot, or else a pair of reading glasses and a library book and a pillbox. If you opened the clasp another way, then you found yourself in a little boat floating at the mouth of a river. On either side of you was forest, where the Baldeziwurlekistanian villagers and the people under the hill made their new settlement.

If you opened the handbag the wrong way, though, you found yourself in a dark land that smelled like blood. That's where the guardian of the purse (the dog whose skin had been been sewn into a purse) lived. The guardian had no skin. Its howl made blood come out of your ears and nose. It tore apart anyone who turned the clasp in the opposite direction and opened the purse in the wrong way.

"Here is the wrong way to open the handbag," Zofia said. She twisted the clasp, showing me how she did it. She opened the mouth of the purse, but not very wide and held it up to me. "Go ahead, darling, and listen for a second."

I put my head near the handbag, but not too near. I didn't hear anything. "I don't hear anything," I said.

"The poor dog is probably asleep," Zofia said. "Even nightmares have to sleep now and then."

After he got expelled, everybody at school called Jake Houdini instead of Jake. Everybody except for me.

I'll explain why, but you have to be patient. It's hard work telling everything in the right order.

Jake is smarter and also taller than most of our teachers. Not quite as tall as me. We've known each other since third grade. Jake has always been in love with me. He says he was in love with me even before third grade, even before we ever met. It took me a while to fall in love with Jake.

In third grade, Jake knew everything already, except how to make friends. He used to follow me around all day long. It made me so mad that I kicked him in the knee. When that didn't work, I threw his backpack out of the window of the school bus. That didn't work either, but the next year Jake took some tests and the school decided that he could skip fourth and fifth grade. Even I felt sorry for Jake then. Sixth grade didn't work out. When the sixth graders wouldn't stop flushing his head down the toilet, he went out and caught a skunk and set it loose in the boy's locker room.

The school was going to suspend him for the rest of the year, but instead Jake took two years off while his mother home-schooled him. He learned Latin and Hebrew and Greek, how to write sestinas, how to make sushi, how to play bridge, and even how to knit. He learned fencing and ballroom dancing. He worked in a soup kitchen and made a Super Eight movie about Civil War reenactors who play extreme croquet in full costume instead of firing off cannons. He started learning how to play guitar. He even wrote a novel. I've never read it—he says it was awful.

When he came back two years later, because his mother had cancer for the first time, the school put him back with our year, in seventh grade. He was still way too smart, but he was finally smart enough to figure out how to fit in. Plus he was good at soccer and he was really cute. Did I mention that he played guitar? Every girl in school had a crush on Jake, but he used to come home after school with me and play Scrabble with Zofia and ask her about Baldeziwurlekistan.

Jake's mom was named Cynthia. She collected ceramic frogs and knock-knock jokes. When we were in ninth grade, she had cancer again. When she died, Jake smashed all of her frogs. That was the first funeral I ever went to. A few months later, Jake's father asked Jake's fencing teacher out on a date. They got married right after the school expelled Jake for his AP project on Houdini. That was the first wedding I ever went to. Jake and I stole a bottle of wine and drank it, and I threw up in the swimming pool at the country club. Jake threw up all over my shoes.

So, anyway, the village and the people under the hill lived happily every after for a few weeks in the handbag, which they had tied around a rock in a dry well which the people under the hill had determined would survive the earthquake. But some of the Baldeziwurlekistanians wanted to come out again and see what was going on in the world. Zofia was one of them. It had been summer when they went into the bag, but when they came out again, and climbed out of the well, snow was falling and their village was ruins and crumbly old rubble. They walked through the snow, Zofia carrying the handbag, until they came to another village, one that they'd never seen before. Everyone in that village was packing up their

101

belongings and leaving, which gave Zofia and her friends a bad feeling. It seemed to be just the same as when they went into the handbag.

They followed the refugees, who seemed to know where they were going, and finally everyone came to a city. Zofia had ever seen such a place. There were trains and electric lights and movie theaters, and there were people shooting each other. Bombs were falling. A war going on. Most of the villagers decided to climb right back inside the handbag, but Zofia volunteered to stay in the world and look after the handbag. She had fallen in love with movies and silk stockings and with a young man, a Russian deserter.

Zofia and the Russian deserter married and had many adventures and finally came to America, where my mother was born. Now and then Zofia would consult the tiles and talk to the people who lived in the handbag and they would tell her how best to avoid trouble and how she and her husband could make some money. Every now and then one of the Baldeziwurlekistanians, or one of the people from under the hill came out of the handbag and wanted to go grocery shopping, or to a movie or an amusement park to ride on roller coasters, or to the library.

The more advice Zofia gave her husband, the more money they made. Her husband became curious about Zofia's handbag, because he could see that there was something odd about it, but Zofia told him to mind his own business. He began to spy on Zofia, and saw that strange men and women were coming in and out of the house. He became convinced that either Zofia was a spy for the Communists, or maybe that she was having affairs. They fought and he drank more and more, and finally he threw away her divination tiles.

"Russians make bad husbands," Zofia told me. Finally, one night while Zofia was sleeping, her husband opened the bone clasp and climbed inside the handbag.

"I thought he'd left me," Zofia said. "For almost twenty years I thought he'd left me and your mother and taken off for California. Not that I minded. I was tired of being married and cooking dinners and cleaning house for someone else. It's better to cook what I want to eat, and clean up when I decide to clean up. It was harder on your mother, not having a father. That was the part that I minded most.

"Then it turned out that he hadn't run away after all. He'd spent one night in the handbag and then come out again twenty years later, exactly as handsome as I remembered, and enough time had passed that I had forgiven him all the quarrels. We made up and it was all very romantic and then when we had another fight the next morning, he went and kissed your mother, who had slept right through his visit, on the cheek, and then he climbed right back inside the handbag. I didn't see him again for another twenty years. The last time he showed up, we went to see *Star Wars* and he liked it so much that he went back inside the handbag to tell everyone else about it. In a couple of years they'll all show up and want to see it on video and all of the sequels too."

"Tell them not to bother with the prequels," I said.

The thing about Zofia and libraries is that she's always losing library books. She says that she hasn't lost them, and in fact that they aren't even overdue, really. It's just that even one week inside the faery handbag is a lot longer in library-world time. So what is she supposed to do about it? The librarians all hate Zofia. She's banned from using any of the branches in our area. When I was eight, she got me to go to the library for her and check out a bunch of biographies and science books and some Georgette Heyer romance novels. My mother was livid when she found out, but it was too late. Zofia had already misplaced most of them.

It's really hard to write about somebody as if they're really dead. I still think Zofia must be sitting in her living room, in her house, watching some old horror movie, dropping popcorn into her handbag. She's waiting for me to come over and play Scrabble.

Nobody is ever going to return those library books now.

My mother used to come home from work and roll her eyes. "Have you been telling them your fairy stories?" she'd say. "Genevieve, your grandmother is a horrible liar."

Zofia would fold up the Scrabble board and shrug at me and Jake. "I'm a wonderful liar," she'd say. "I'm the best liar in the world. Promise me you won't believe a single word."

But she wouldn't tell the story of the faery handbag to Jake. Only the old Baldeziwurlekistanian folktales and fairytales about the people under the hill. She told him about how she and her husband made it all the way across Europe, hiding in haystacks and in barns, and how once, when her husband went off to find food, a farmer found her hiding in his chicken coop and tried to rape her. But she opened up the faery handbag in the way she showed me, and the dog came out and ate the farmer and all his chickens too.

She was teaching Jake and me how to curse in Baldeziwurleki. I also know how to say I love you, but I'm not going to ever say it to anyone again, except to Jake, when I find him.

When I was eight, I believed everything Zofia told me. By the time I was thirteen, I didn't believe a single word. When I was fifteen, I saw a man come out of her house and get on Zofia's three-speed bicycle and ride down the street. His clothes looked funny. He was a lot younger than my mother and father, and even though I'd never seen him before, he was familiar. I followed him on my bike, all the way to the grocery store. I waited just past the checkout lanes while he bought peanut butter, Jack Daniels, half a dozen instant cameras, and at least sixty packs of Reeses Peanut Butter Cups, three bags of Hershey's kisses, a handful of Milky Way bars and other stuff from the rack of checkout candy. While the checkout clerk was helping him bag up all of that chocolate, he looked up and saw me. "Genevieve?" he said. "That's your name, right?"

I turned and ran out of the store. He grabbed up the bags and ran after me. I don't even think he got his change back. I was still running away, and then one of the straps on my flip flops popped out of the sole, the way they do, and that made me really angry so I just stopped. I turned around.

"Who are you?" I said.

But I already knew. He looked like he could have

been my mom's younger brother. He was really cute. I could see why Zofia had fallen in love with him.

His name was Rustan. Zofia told my parents that he was an expert in Baldeziwurlekistanian folklore who would be staying with her for a few days. She brought him over for dinner. Jake was there too, and I could tell that Jake knew something was up. Everybody except my dad knew something was going on.

"You mean Baldeziwurlekistan is a real place?" my mother asked Rustan. "My mother is telling the truth?"

I could see that Rustan was having a hard time with that one. He obviously wanted to say that his wife was a horrible liar, but then where would he be? Then he couldn't be the person that he was supposed to be.

There were probably a lot of things that he wanted to say. What he said was, "This is really good pizza."

Rustan took a lot of pictures at dinner. The next day I went with him to get the pictures developed. He'd brought back some film with him, with pictures he'd taken inside the faery handbag, but those didn't come out well. Maybe the film was too old. We got doubles of the pictures from dinner so that I could have some too. There's a great picture of Jake, sitting outside on the porch. He's laughing, and he has his hand up to his mouth, like he's going to catch the laugh. I have that picture up on my computer, and also up on my wall over my bed.

I bought a Cadbury Cream Egg for Rustan. Then we shook hands and he kissed me once on each cheek. "Give one of those kisses to your mother," he said, and I thought about how the next time I saw him, I might be Zofia's age, and he would only be a few days older. The next time I saw him, Zofia would be dead. Jake and I might have kids. That was too weird.

I know Rustan tried to get Zofia to go with him, to live in the handbag, but she wouldn't.

"It makes me dizzy in there," she used to tell me. "And they don't have movie theaters. And I have to look after your mother and you. Maybe when you're old enough to look after the handbag, I'll poke my head inside, just long enough for a little visit."

I didn't fall in love with Jake because he was smart. I'm pretty smart myself. I know that smart doesn't mean nice, or even mean that you have a lot of common sense. Look at all the trouble smart people get themselves into.

I didn't fall in love with Jake because he could make maki rolls and had a black belt in fencing, or whatever it is that you get if you're good in fencing. I didn't fall in love with Jake because he plays guitar. He's a better soccer player than he is a guitar player.

Those were the reasons why I went out on a date with Jake. That, and because he asked me. He asked if I wanted to go see a movie, and I asked if I could bring my grandmother and Natalie and Natasha. He said sure and so all five of us sat and watched "Bring It On" and every once in a while Zofia dropped a couple of milk duds or some popcorn into her purse. I don't know if she was feeding the dog, or if she'd opened the purse the right way, and was throwing food at her husband.

I fell in love with Jake because he told stupid knock-knock jokes to Natalie, and told Natasha that he liked her jeans. I fell in love with Jake when he took me and Zofia home. He walked her up to her front door and then he walked me up to mine. I fell in love with Jake when he didn't try to kiss me. The thing is, I was nervous about the whole kissing thing. Most guys think that they're better at it than they really are. Not that I think I'm a real genius at kissing either, but I don't think kissing should be a competitive sport. It isn't tennis.

Natalie and Natasha and I used to practice kissing with each other. Not that we like each other that way, but just for practice. We got pretty good at it. We could see why kissing was supposed to be fun.

But Jake didn't try to kiss me. Instead he just gave me this really big hug. He put his face in my hair and he sighed. We stood there like that, and then finally I said, "What are you doing?"

"I just wanted to smell your hair," he said.

"Oh," I said. That made me feel weird, but in a good way. I put my nose up to his hair, which is brown and curly, and I smelled it. We stood there and smelled each other's hair, and I felt so good. I felt so happy.

Jake said into my hair, "Do you know that actor John Cusack?"

I said, "Yeah. One of Zofia's favorite movies is 'Better Off Dead.' We watch it all the time."

"So he likes to go up to women and smell their armpits."

"Gross!" I said. "That's such a lie! What are you doing now? That tickles."

"I'm smelling your ear," Jake said.

Jake's hair smelled like iced tea with honey in it, after all the ice has melted.

Kissing Jake is like kissing Natalie or Natasha, except that it isn't just for fun. It feels like something there isn't a word for in Scrabble.

The deal with Houdini is that Jake got interested in him during Advanced Placement American History. He and I were both put in tenth grade history. We were doing biography projects. I was studying Joseph McCarthy. My grandmother had all sorts of stories about McCarthy. She hated him for what he did to Hollywood.

Jake didn't turn in his project—instead he told everyone in our AP class except for Mr. Streep (we call him Meryl) to meet him at the gym on Saturday. When we showed up, Jake reenacted one of Houdini's escapes with a laundry bag, handcuffs, a gym locker, bicycle chains, and the school's swimming pool. It took him three and a half minutes to get free, and this guy named Roger took a bunch of photos and then put the photos online. One of the photos ended up in the Boston Globe, and Jake got expelled. The really ironic thing was that while his mom was in the hospital, Jake had applied to M.I.T. He did it for his mom. He thought that way she'd have to stay alive. She was so excited about M.I.T. A couple of days after he'd been expelled, right after the wedding, while his dad and the fencing instructor were in Bermuda, he got an acceptance letter in the mail and a phone call from this guy in the admissions office who explained why they had to withdraw the acceptance.

My mother wanted to know why I let Jake wrap himself up in bicycle chains and then watched while Peter and Michael pushed him into the deep end of the school pool. I said that Jake had a backup plan. Ten more seconds and we were all going to jump into the pool and open the locker and get him out of there. I was crying when I said that. Even before he got in the locker, I knew how stupid Jake was being. Afterwards, he promised me that he'd never do anything like that again.

That was when I told him about Zofia's husband, Rustan, and about Zofia's handbag. How stupid am I?

So I guess you can figure out what happened next. The problem is that Jake believed me about the handbag. We spent a lot of time over at Zofia's, playing Scrabble. Zofia never let the faery handbag out of her sight. She even took it with her when she went to the bathroom. I think she even slept with it under her pillow.

I didn't tell her that I'd said anything to Jake. I wouldn't ever have told anybody else about it. Not Natasha. Not even Natalie, who is the most respons- ible person in all of the world. Now, of course, if the handbag turns up and Jake still hasn't come back, I'll have to tell Natalie. Somebody has to keep an eye on the stupid thing while I go find Jake.

What worries me is that maybe one of the Baldeziwurlekistanians or one of the people under the hill or maybe even Rustan popped out of the handbag to run an errand and got worried when Zofia wasn't there. Maybe they'll come looking for her and bring it back. Maybe they know I'm supposed to look after it now. Or maybe they took it and hid it some- where. Maybe someone turned it in at the lost-and-found at the library and that stupid librarian called the F.B.I. Maybe scientists at the Pentagon are examining the handbag right now. Testing it. If Jake comes out, they'll think he's a spy or a superweapon or an alien or something. They're not going to just let him go.

Everyone thinks Jake ran away, except for my mother, who is convinced that he was trying out another Houdini escape and is probably lying at the bottom of a lake somewhere. She hasn't said that to me, but I can see her thinking it. She keeps making cookies for me.

What happened is that Jake said, "Can I see that for just a second?"

He said it so casually that I think he caught Zofia off guard. She was reaching into the purse for her wallet. We were standing in the lobby of the movie theater on a Monday morning. Jake was behind the snack counter. He'd gotten a job there. He was wearing this stupid red paper hat and some kind of apron-bib thing. He was supposed to ask us if we wanted to supersize our drinks.

He reached over the counter and took Zofia's handbag right out of her hand. He closed it and then he opened it again. I think he opened it the right way. I don't think he ended up in the dark place. He said to me and Zofia, "I'll be right back." And then he wasn't there anymore. It was just me and Zofia and the handbag, lying there on the counter where he'd dropped it.

If I'd been fast enough, I think I could have followed him. But Zofia had been guardian of the faery handbag for a lot longer. She snatched the bag back and glared at me. "He's a very bad boy," she said. She was absolutely furious. "You're better off without him, Genevieve, I think."

"Give me the handbag," I said. "I have to go get him."

"It isn't a toy, Genevieve," she said. "It isn't a game. This isn't Scrabble. He comes back when he comes back. If he comes back."

"Give me the handbag," I said. "Or I'll take it from you."

She held the handbag up high over her head, so that I couldn't reach it. I hate people who are taller than me. "What are you going to do now," Zofia said. "Are you going to knock me down? Are you going to steal the handbag? Are you going to go away and leave me here to explain to your parents where you've gone? Are you going to say goodbye to your friends? When you come out again, they will have gone to college. They'll have jobs and babies and houses and they won't even recognize you. Your mother will be an old woman and I will be dead."

"I don't care," I said. I sat down on the sticky red carpet in the lobby and started to cry. Someone wearing a little metal nametag came over and asked if we were okay. His name was Missy. Or maybe he was wearing someone else's tag.

"We're fine," Zofia said. "My granddaughter has the flu."

She took my hand and pulled me up. She put her arm around me and we walked out of the theater. We never even got to see the stupid movie. We never even got to see another movie together. I don't ever want to go see another movie. The problem is, I don't want to see unhappy endings. And I don't know if I believe in the happy ones.

"I have a plan," Zofia said. "I will go find Jake. You will stay here and look after the handbag."

"You won't come back either," I said. I cried even harder. Or if you do, I'll be like a hundred years old and Jake will still be sixteen."

"Everything will be okay," Zofia said. I wish I could tell you how beautiful she looked right then. It didn't matter if she was lying or if she actually knew that everything was going to be okay. The important thing was how she looked when she said it. She said, with absolute certainty, or maybe with all the skill of a very skillful liar, "My plan will work. First we go to the library, though. One of the people under the hill just brought back an Agatha Christie mystery, and I need to return it."

"We're going to the library?" I said. "Why don't we just go home and play Scrabble for a while." You probably think I was just being sarcastic here, and I was being sarcastic. But Zofia gave me a sharp look. She knew that if I was being sarcastic that my brain was working again. She knew that I knew she was stalling for time. She knew that I was coming up with my own plan, which was a lot like Zofia's plan, except that I was the one who went into the handbag. *How* was the part I was working on.

"We could do that," she said. "Remember, when you don't know what to do, it never hurts to play Scrabble. It's like reading the I Ching or tea leaves."

"Can we please just hurry?" I said.

Zofia just looked at me. "Genevieve, we have plenty of time. If you're going to look after the handbag, you have to remember that. You have to be patient. Can you be patient?"

"I can try," I told her. I'm trying, Zofia. I'm trying really hard. But it isn't fair. Jake is off having adventures and talking to talking animals, and who knows, learning how to fly and some beautiful three-thousand-year-old girl from under the hill is teaching him how to speak fluent Baldeziwurleki. I bet she lives in a house that runs around on chicken legs, and she tells Jake that she'd love to hear him play something on the guitar. Maybe you'll kiss her, Jake, because she's put a spell on you. But whatever you do, don't go up into her house. Don't fall asleep in her bed. Come back soon, Jake, and bring the handbag with you.

I hate those movies, those books, where some guy gets to go off and have adventures and meanwhile the girl has to stay home and wait. I'm a feminist. I subscribe to *Bust* magazine, and I watch *Buffy* reruns. I don't believe in that kind of shit.

We hadn't been in the library for five minutes before Zofia picked up a biography of Carl Sagan and dropped it in her purse. She was definitely stalling for time. She was trying to come up with a plan that would counteract the plan that she knew I was planning. I wondered what she thought I was planning. It was probably much better than anything I'd come up with.

"Don't do that!" I said.

"Don't worry," Zofia said. "Nobody was watching."

"I don't care if nobody saw! What if Jake's sitting

there in the boat, or what if he was coming back and you just dropped it on his head!"

"It doesn't work that way," Zofia said. Then she said, "It would serve him right, anyway."

That was when the librarian came up to us. She had a nametag on as well. I was so sick of people and their stupid nametags. I'm not even going to tell you what her name was. "I saw that," the librarian said.

"Saw what?" Zofia said. She smiled down at the librarian, like she was Queen of the Library, and the librarian were a petitioner.

The librarian stared hard at her. "I know you," she said, almost sounding awed, like she was a weekend birdwatcher who just seen Bigfoot. "We have your picture on the office wall. You're Ms. Swinks. You aren't allowed to check out books here."

"That's ridiculous," Zofia said. She was at least two feet taller than the librarian. I felt a bit sorry for the librarian. After all, Zofia had just stolen a seven-day book. She probably wouldn't return it for a hundred years. My mother has always made it clear that it's my job to protect other people from Zofia. I guess I was Zofia's guardian before I became the guardian of the handbag.

The librarian reached up and grabbed Zofia's handbag. She was small but she was strong. She jerked the handbag and Zofia stumbled and fell back against a work desk. I couldn't believe it. Everyone except for me was getting a look at Zofia's handbag. What kind of guardian was I going to be?

"Genevieve," Zofia said. She held my hand very tightly, and I looked at her. She looked wobbly and pale. She said, "I feel very bad about all of this. Tell your mother I said so."

Then she said one last thing, but I think it was in Baldeziwurleki.

The librarian said, "I saw you put a book in here. Right here." She opened the handbag and peered inside. Out of the handbag came a long, lonely, ferocious, utterly hopeless scream of rage. I don't ever want to hear that noise again. Everyone in the library looked up. The librarian made a choking noise and threw Zofia's handbag away from her. A little trickle of blood came out of her nose and a drop fell on the floor. What I thought at first was that it was just plain luck that the handbag was closed when it landed. Later on I was trying to figure out what Zofia said. My Baldeziwurleki isn't very good, but I think she was saying something like "Figures. Stupid librarian. I have to go take care of that damn dog." So maybe that's what happened. Maybe Zofia sent part of herself in there with the skinless dog. Maybe she fought it and won and closed the handbag. Maybe she made friends with it. I mean, she used to feed it popcorn at the movies. Maybe she's still in there.

What happened in the library was Zofia sighed a little and closed her eyes. I helped her sit down in a chair, but I don't think she was really there any more. I rode with her in the ambulance, when the ambulance finally showed up, and I swear I didn't even think about the handbag until my mother showed up. I didn't say a word. I just left her there in the hospital with Zofia, who was on a respirator, and I ran all the way back to the library. But it was closed. So I ran all the way back again, to the hospital, but you already know what happened, right? Zofia died. I hate writing that. My tall, funny, beautiful, book-stealing, Scrabble-playing, story-telling grandmother died.

But you never met her. You're probably wondering about the handbag. What happened to it. I put up signs all over town, like Zofia's handbag was some kind of lost dog, but nobody ever called.

So that's the story so far. Not that I expect you to believe any of it. Last night Natalie and Natasha came over and we played Scrabble. They don't really like Scrabble, but they feel like it's their job to cheer me up. I won. After they went home, I flipped all the tiles upside-down and then I started picking them up in groups of seven. I tried to ask a question, but it was hard to pick just one. The words I got weren't so great either, so I decided that they weren't English words. They were Baldeziwurleki words.

Once I decided that, everything became perfectly clear. First I put down "kirif" which means "happy news", and then I got a "b," an "o," an "l," an "e," a "f," another "i," an "s," and a "z." So then I could make "kirif" into "bolekirifisz," which could mean "the happy result of a combination of diligent effort and patience."

I would find the faery handbag. The tiles said so. I would work the clasp and go into the handbag and have my own adventures and would rescue Jake. Hardly any time would have gone by before we came back out of the handbag. Maybe I'd even make friends with that poor dog and get to say goodbye, for real, to Zofia. Rustan would show up again and be really sorry that he'd missed Zofia's funeral and this time he would be brave enough to tell my mother the whole story. He would tell her that he was her father.

Not that she would believe him. Not that you should believe this story. Promise me that you won't believe a word.

Quarry

Peter S. Beagle

*Peter S. Beagle was born in New York in April 1939.
He studied at the University of Pittsburgh and gradu-
ated with a degree in creative writing in 1959. Beagle
won a* Seventeen Magazine *short story contest in his
sophomore year, but really began his writing career
with his first novel,* A Fine and Private Place, *in 1960.
It was followed by non-fiction travelogue* I See By My
Outfit, *in 1961 and by his best known work, the
modern fantasy classic* The Last Unicorn *in 1968.
Beagle's other books include novels* The Folk of the
Air *and* The Innkeeper's Song, *story collections* The
Fantasy Worlds of Peter S. Beagle *and* The Rhinoceros
Who Quoted Nietzsche and Other Odd Acquaint-
ances, *several non-fiction books and a number of
screenplays and teleplays. Upcoming is a new novel
and a new short story collection.*

*In the complex and richly detailed story that follows
a man attempts to escape a mysterious and evil fate.*

I never went back to my room that night. I knew I

had an hour at most before they would have guards on the door. What was on my back, at my belt, and in my pockets was all I took—that, and all the *tilgit* the cook could scrape together and cram into my pouch. We had been friends since the day I arrived at *that place,* a scrawny, stubborn child, ready to die rather than ever admit my terror and my pain. "So," she said, as I burst into her kitchen, "Running you came to me, twenty years gone, blood all over you, and running you leave. Tell me nothing, just drink this." I have no idea what was in that bottle she fetched from under her skirts and made me empty on the spot, but it kept me warm on my way all that night, and the *tilgit*—disgusting dried marshweed as it is—lasted me three days.

Looking back, I shiver to think how little I understood, not only the peril I was in, but the true extent of the power I fled. I did know better than to make for Sumildene, where a stranger stands out like a sailor in a convent; but if I had had the brains of a bedbug, I'd never have tried to cut through the marshes toward the Queen's Road. In the first place, that grand highway is laced with tollbridges, manned by toll-collectors, every four or five miles; in the second, the Queen's Road is so well-banked and pruned and well-maintained that should you be caught out there by daylight, there's no cover, nowhere to run—no rutted smuggler's alley to duck into, not so much as a proper tree to climb. But I didn't know that then, among other things.

What I did understand, beyond doubt, was that they could not afford to let me leave. I do not say *escape,* because they would never have thought of it in such a way. To their minds, they had offered me their greatest honor, never before granted one so young, and I had not only rejected it, but lied in their clever, clever faces, accepting so humbly, falteringly telling them again and again of my bewildered gratitude, unworthy peasant that I was. And even then I did know that they were not deceived for a single moment, and they knew I knew, and blessed me, one after the other, to let me know. I dream that twilight chamber still—the tall chairs, the cold stone table, the tiny green *tintan* birds murmuring themselves to sleep in the vines outside the window, those smiling, wise, gentle eyes on me—and each time I wake between sweated sheets, my mouth wrenched with pleas for my life. Old as I am, and still.

If I were to leave, and it became known that I had done so, and without any retribution, others would go too, in time. Not very many—there were as yet only a few who shared my disquiet and my growing suspicions—but even one unpunished deserter was more than they could afford to tolerate.

I had no doubt at all that they would grieve my death. They were not unkind people, for monsters.

The cook hid me in the scullery, covering me with aprons and dishrags. It was not yet full dark when I left, but she felt it risky for me to wait longer. When we said farewell, she shoved one of her paring knives into my belt, gave me a swift, light buffet on the ear, said, "So. On your way then," pushed me out of a hidden half-door into the dusk, and slapped it shut behind me. I felt lonelier in that moment, blinking around me with the crickets chirping and the breeze turning chill, and that great house filling half the evening sky, than I ever have again.

As I say, I made straight for the marshes, not only

meaning to strike the Queen's Road, but confident that the boggy ground would hide my footprints. It might indeed have concealed them from the eyes of ordinary trackers, but not from those who were after me within another hour. I knew little of them, the Hunters, though over twenty years I had occasionally heard this whisper or that behind this or that slightly trembling hand. Just once, not long after I came to *that place*, I was sent to the woods to gather kindling, and there I did glimpse two small brown-clad persons in a tree. They must have seen me, but they moved neither foot or finger, nor turned their heads, but kept sitting there like a pair of dull brown birds, half-curled, half-crouched, gazing back toward the great house, waiting for something, waiting for someone. I never saw them again, nor any like them; not until they came for me.

Not those two, of course—or maybe they were the same ones; it is hard to be sure of any Hunter's age or face or identity. For all I know, they do not truly exist most of the time, but bide in their nowhere until *that place* summons them into being to pursue some runaway like me. What I do know, better than most, is that they never give up. You have to kill them.

I had killed once before—in my ignorance, I supposed the cook was the only one who knew—but I had no skill in it, and no weapon with me but the cook's little knife: nothing to daunt those who now followed. I knew the small start I had was meaningless, and I went plunging through the marshes, increasingly indifferent to how much noise I made, or to the animals and undergrowth I disturbed. Strong I was, yes, and swift enough, but also brainless with panic and hamstrung by inexperience. A child could have tracked me, let alone a Hunter.

That I was not taken that first night had nothing to do with any craft or wiliness of mine. What happened was that I slipped on a straggling *tilgit* frond (wild, the stuff is as slimy-slick as any snail-road), took a shattering tumble down a slope I never saw, and finished by cracking my head open against a mossy, jagged rock. Amazingly, I did not lose consciousness then, but managed to crawl off into a sort of shallow half-burrow at the base of the hill. There I scraped every bit of rotting vegetation within reach over myself, having a dazed notion of smothering my scent. I vaguely recall packing handfuls of leaves and spiderwebs against my bleeding wound, and making some sort of effort to cover the betraying stains, before I fainted away.

I woke in the late afternoon of the next day, frantically hungry, but so weak and sick that I could not manage so much as a mouthful of the *tilgit*. The bleeding had stopped—though I dared not remove my ragged, mushy poultice for another full day—and after a time I was able to stand up and stay on my feet, just barely. I lurched from my earthen shroud and stood for some while, lightheaded yet, but steadily more lucid, sniffing and staring for any sign of my shadows. Not that I was in the best shape to spy them out—giddy as I was, they could likely have walked straight up to me and disemboweled me with their empty hands, as they can do. But they were nowhere to be seen or sensed.

I drank from a mucky trickle I found slipping by under the leaves, then grubbed my way back into my poor nest again and slept until nightfall. For all my panicky blundering, I knew by the stars that I was headed in the general direction of the Queen's Road, which I continued to believe meant sanctuary and the start of my new and blessedly ordinary life among ordinary folk.

I covered more distance than I expected that night, for all my lingering faintness and my new prudence, trying now to make as little noise as possible, and leave as little trace of my passage. I met no one, and when I went to ground at dawn in a riverbank cave—some *sheknath*'s winter lair, by the smell of it—there was still no more indication of anyone trailing me than there had been since I began my flight. But I was not fool enough to suppose myself clear of pursuit, not quite. I merely hoped, which was just as bad.

The Queen's Road was farther away than I had supposed: for all the terrible and tempting knowledge that I and others like me acquired in *that place*, practical geography was unheard of. I kept moving, trailing after the hard stars through the marshes as intently as the Hunters were surely trailing me. More than once, the bog sucked both shoes off my feet, taking them down so deeply that I would waste a good half-hour fishing for them; again and again, a sudden screen of burly *jukli* vines or some sticky nameless creepers barred my passage, so I must either lower my head and bull on through, or else blunder somehow around the obstacle and pray not to lose the way, which I most often did.

Nearing dawn of the fourth day, I heard the rumble of cartwheels, like a faraway storm, and the piercing squawk, unmistakable, of their *pashidi* drivers' clan-whistles along with them, and realized that I was nearing the Queen's Road.

If the Hunters were following as closely as I feared, was this to be the end of the game—were they poised to cut me down as I raced wildly, recklessly, toward imaginary safety? Did they expect me to abandon all caution and charge forward into daylight and the open, whooping with joy and triumph? They had excellent reason to do so, as idiotic a target as I must have made for them a dozen times over. But even idiots—even terrified young idiots—may learn one or two things in four days of being pursued through a quagmire by silent, invisible hounds. I waited that day out under a leech-bush: few trackers will ever investigate one of those closely; and if you lie *very* still, there is a fairish chance that the serrated, brittle-seeming leaves will not come seeking your blood. At moonset I started on.

Just as the ground began to feel somewhat more solid, just as the first lights of the Queen's Road began to glimmer through the thinning vegetation...there they were, there they were, both of them, each standing away at an angle, making me the third point of a murderous triangle. They simply *appeared*—can you understand?—assembling themselves out of the marsh dawn: weaponless both, their arms hanging at their sides, loose and unthreatening. One was smiling; one was not—there was no other way to tell them apart. In the dimness, I saw laughter in their eyes, and a weariness such as even I have never imagined, and death.

They let me by. They turned their backs to me and let me pass, fading so completely into the gray sunrise that I was almost willing to believe them visions, savage mirages born of my own fear and exhaustion. But with that combination came a weary understanding of my own. They were playing with me, taking pleasure in allowing me to run loose for a bit, but letting me know that whenever they tired of the game I was theirs, in the dark marshes or on the wide white highway, and not a thing I could do about it. At my age, I am entitled to forget what I forget—terror and triumph alike, grief and the wildest joy alike—and so I have, and well rid of every one of them I am. But that instant, that particular recognition, remains indelible. Some memories do come to live with you for good and all, like wives or husbands.

I went forward. There was nothing else to do. The marshes fell away around me, rapidly giving place to nondescript country, half-ragged, halfway domesticated to give a sort of shoulder to the road. Farmers were already opening their fruit and vegetable stands along that border; merchants' boys from towns farther along were bawling their employers' wares to the carters and wagoners; and as I stumbled up, a *shukri*-trainer passed in front of me, holding his arms out, like a scarecrow, for folk to see his sharp-toothed pets scurrying up and down his body, and more of them pouring from each pocket as he strode along. Ragged, scabbed and filthy as I was, not one traveler turned his head as I slipped onto the Queen's Road.

On the one hand, I blessed their unconcern; on the other, that same indifference told me clearly that none of them would raise a finger if they saw me taken, snatched back before their eyes to *that place* and whatever doom might await me there. Only the collectors at their tollgates might be at all likely to mourn the fate of a potential contributor—and I had nothing for them anyway, which was going to be another problem in a couple of miles. But right then was problem enough for me: friendless on a strange road, utterly vulnerable, utterly without resources, flying—well, trudging—from the only home I had known since the age of nine, and from the small, satisfied assassins it had sent after me. And out of *tilgit* as well.

The Queen's Road runs straight all the way from Bitava to Fors na' Shachim, but in those days there was a curious sort of elbow: unleveled, anciently furrowed, a last untamed remnant of the original wagon-road, beginning just before the first tollgate I was to reach. I could see it from a good distance, and made up my mind to dodge away onto it—without any notion of where the path might come out, but with some mad fancy of at once eluding both the killers and the collectors. Sometimes, in those nights when the dreams and memories I cannot always tell apart anymore keep me awake, I try to imagine what my life would have been if I had actually carried my plan through. Different, most likely. Shorter, surely.

Even this early, the road was steadily growing more crowded with traffic, wheeled and afoot, slowing my pace to that of my closest neighbor—which, in this case, happened to be a bullock-cart loaded higher than my head with *jejebhai* manure. Absolutely the only thing the creatures are good for; we had a pair on the farm where I was a boy—if I ever was, if any of that ever happened. Ignoring the smell, I kept as close to the cart as I could, hoping that it would hide me from the toll-collectors' sight when I struck off onto that odd little bend. My legs were tensing for the first swift, desperate stride, when I heard the voice at my ear, saying only one word, *"No."*

A slightly muffled voice, but distinctive—there was a sharpness to it, and a hint of a strange cold amusement, all in a single word. I whirled, saw nothing but the manure cart, determined that I had misheard a driver's grunt, or even a wheel-squeak, and set myself a second time to make my move.

Once again the voice, more insistent now, almost a bark: *"No, fool!"*

It was not the driver; he never looked at me. I was being addressed—commanded—by the manure pile.

It shifted slightly as I gaped, and I saw the eyes then. They were gray and very bright, with a suggestion of pale yellow far under the grayness. All I could make out of the face in which they were set was a thick white mustache below and brows nearly as heavy above. The man—for it was a human face, I was practically sure—was burrowed as deeply into the *jejebhai* dung as though he were lolling under the most luxurious of quilts and bolsters on a winter's night. He beckoned me to join him.

I stopped where I was, letting the cart jolt past me. The sharp voice from the manure was clearer this time, and that much more annoyed with me. "Boy, if you have any visions of a life beyond the next five minutes, you will do as I tell you. *Now.*" The last word was no louder than the others, but it brought me scrambling into that cartload of muck faster than ever I have since lunged into a warm bed, with a woman waiting. The man made room for me with a low, harsh chuckle.

"Lie still, so," he told me. "Lie still, make no smallest row, and we will pass the gate like royalty. And those who follow will watch you pass, and never take your scent. Thank me later—" I had opened my mouth to speak, but he put a rough palm over it, shaking his white head. "Down, down," he whispered, and to my disgust he pushed himself even farther into the manure pile, all but vanishing into the darkness and the stench. And I did the same.

He saved my life, in every likelihood, for we left that gate and half a dozen like it behind as we continued our malodorous excursion, while the driver, all unwitting, paid our toll each time. Only with the last barrier safely past did we slide from the cart, tumble to the roadside and such cover as there was, and rise to face each other in daylight. We reeked beyond the telling of it—in honesty, almost beyond the smelling of it, so inured to the odor had our nostrils become. We stank beyond anything but laughter, and that was what we did then, grimacing and howling and falling down on the dry grass, pointing helplessly at each other and going off again into great, ridiculous whoops of mirth and relief, until we wore ourselves out and could barcly brcathc, lct alonc laugh. Thc old man's laughter was as shrill and cold as the mating cries of *shukris*, but it was laughter even so.

He was old indeed, now I saw him in daylight, even under a crust of filth and all that still stuck to the filth—straw, twigs, dead spiders, bullock-hair. His own hair and brows were as white as his mustache, and the gray eyes streaked with rheum; yet his cheeks were absurdly pink, like a young girl's cheeks, and he carried himself as straight as any young man. Young as I was myself, and unwise as I was, when I first looked into his eyes, I already knew far better than to trust him. And nonetheless, knowing, I wanted to. He can do that.

"I think we bathe," he said to me. "Before anything else, I do think we bathe."

"I think so too," I said. "Yes." He jerked his white head, and we walked away from the Queen's Road, off back into the wild woods.

"I am Soukyan," I offered, but to that he made no response. He clearly knew the country, for he led me directly to a fast-flowing stream, and then to a pool lower down, where the water gathered and swirled. We cleaned ourselves there, though it took us a long time, so mucky we were; and afterward, naked-new as raw carrots, we lay in the Sun and talked for a while. I told truth, for the most part, leaving out only some minor details of *that place*—things I had good reason not to think about just then—and he...ah, well, what he told me of his life, of how he came to hail me from that dungheap, was such a stew of lies and the odd honesty that I've never studied out the right of it yet, no more than I have ever learned his own name. The truth is not in him, and I would be dearly disappointed if it should show its poor face now. He was there—leave it at that. He was there at the particular moment when I needed a friend, however fraudulent. It has happened so since.

"So," he said at last, stretching himself in the Sun. "And what's to be done with you now?"—for all the world as though he had all the disposing of me and my future. "If you fancy that your followers have forsaken you, merely because we once stank our way past them, I'd greatly enjoy to have the writing of your will. They will run behind you until you die—they will never return to their masters without you, or whatever's left of you. On that you have my word."

"I know that well enough," said I, trying my best to appear as knowledgeable as he. "But perhaps I am not to be taken so easily." The old man snorted with as much contempt as I have ever heard in a single exhalation of breath, and rolled to his feet, deceptively, alarmingly graceful. He crouched naked on his haunches, facing me, studying me, smiling with pointed teeth.

"Without me, you die," he said, quite quietly. "You know it and I know it. Say it back to me." I only stared, and he snapped, *"Say it back.* Without me?"

And I said it, because I knew it was true. "Without you, I would be dead." The old man nodded approvingly. The yellow glint was stronger in the gray eyes.

"Now," he said. "I have my own purposes, my own small annoyance to manage. I could deal with it myself, as I've done many a time—never think otherwise—but it suits me to share roads with you for a little. It suits me." He was studying me as closely as I have ever been considered, even by those at *that place,* and I could not guess what he saw. "It suits me," he said for a third time. "We may yet prove of some use to each other."

"We may, or we may not," I said, more than a bit sharply, for I was annoyed at the condescension in his glance. "I may seem a gormless boy to you, but I know this country, and I know how to handle myself." The first claim was a lie; of the second, all I can say is that I believed it then. I went on, probably more belligerent for my fear: "Indeed, I may well owe you my life, and I will repay you as I can, my word on it. But as to whether we should ally ourselves...sir, I hope only to put the width of the world between myself and those who seek me—I have no plans beyond that. Of what your own plans, your own desires may be, you will have to inform me, for I have no notion at all."

He seemed to approve my boldness; at any rate, he laughed that short, yapping laugh of his and said, "For the moment, my plans run with yours. We're dried enough—dress yourself, so, and we'll be off and gone while our little friends are still puzzling over how we could have slipped their grasp. They'll riddle it out quickly enough, but we'll have the heels of them a while yet." And I could not help finding comfort in noticing that "your followers" had now become "our little friends."

So we ourselves were allies of a sort, united by common interests, whatever they were. Having no goal, nor any vision of a life beyond flight, I had no real choice but to go where he led, since on my own the only question would have been whether I should be caught before I stumbled into a swamp and got eaten by a *lourijakh*. For all his age, he marched along with an air of absolute serenity, no matter if we were beating our way through some near-impenetrable thornwood or crossing high barrens in the deepest night. Wherever he was bound—which was only one of the things he did not share with me—we encountered few other travelers on our way to it. An old lone wizard making his *lamisetha*; a couple of deserters from someone's army, who wanted to sell us their uniforms; a little band of prospectors, too busy quarreling over the exact location of a legendary hidden *drast* mine to pay overmuch attention to us. I think there was a water witch as well, but at this reach it is hard to be entirely sure.

By now I would not have trusted my woodcraft for half a minute, but it was obvious from our first day together that my new friend had enough of that for the pair of us. Every night, before we slept—turn and turn about, always one on watch—and every morning, before anything at all, he prowled the area in a wide, constantly shifting radius, clearly going by his nose as much as his sight and hearing. Most of the time he was out of my view, but on occasion I would hear a kind of whuffling snort, usually followed by a low, disdainful grunt. In his own time he'd come trotting jauntily up from the brushy hollow or the dry ravine, shaking his dusty white hair in the moonlight, to say, "Two weeks, near enough, and not up with us yet? Not taking advantage of my years and your inexperience to pounce on us in the dark hours and pull us apart like a couple of boiled chickens? Indeed, I begin to lose respect for our legendary entourage—as stupid as the rest, they are, after all." And what he meant by *the rest*, I could not imagine then.

Respect the Hunters or no, he never slackened our pace, nor ever grew careless in covering our tracks. We were angling eastward, into the first folds of the Skagats—the Burnt Hills, your people call them, I believe. At the time I had no name at all for them, nor for any other feature of this new landscape. For all the teachings I had absorbed at *that place*, for all the sly secret knowledge that was the true foundation of the great house, for all the wicked wisdom that I would shed even today, if I could, as a snake scours itself free of its skin against a stone...nevertheless, then I knew next to nothing of the actual world in which that knowledge moved. We were deliberately kept quite ignorant, you see, in certain ways.

He ridiculed me constantly about that. I see him still, cross-legged across the night's fire from me, jabbing out with a long-nailed forefinger, demanding, "And you mean to sit there and tell me that you've never heard of the Mildasi people, or the Achali? You know the lineage, the lovers and the true fate of every queen who ever ruled in Fors—you know the deep cause of the Fishermen's Rebellion, and what really came of it—you know the entire history of the Old Arrangement, which cannot be written—but you have absolutely no inkling where Byrnarik Bay's to be found, nor the Northern Barrens, nor can you so much as guess at the course of the Susathi. Well, you've had such an education as never was, that's all I can say. And it's worthless to us, all of it worthless, nothing but a waste of head-space, taking up room that could have been better occupied if you'd been taught to read track, steal a horse, or shoot a bow. *Worthless.*"

"I can shoot a bow," I told him once. "My father taught me."

"Oh, indeed? I must remember to stand behind you when you loose off." There was a deal more of that as we journeyed on. I found it tedious most often, and sometimes hurtful; but there was a benefit, too, because he began taking it on himself to instruct me in the nature and fabric of this new world—and this new life, as well—as though I were visiting from the most foreign of far-off lands. Which, in ways even he could not have known, I was.

One thing I did understand from the first day was that he was plainly a fugitive himself, no whit different from me, for all his conceit. Why else would he have been hiding in a dung-cart, eager to commandeer the company of such a bumpkin as I? Kindly concern for my survival in a dangerous world might be part of it, but he was hardly combing our backtrail every night on my behalf. I knew that much from the way he slept—when he slept—most often on his back, his arms and legs curled close and scrabbling in the air, running and running behind his closed eyes, just as a hound will do. I knew it from the way he would cry out, not in any tongue I knew, but in strange yelps and whimpers and near-growls that seemed sometimes to border on language, so close to real words that I was sure I almost caught them, and that if he only kept on a bit longer, or if I dared bend a bit closer, I'd understand who—or what—was pursuing him through his dreams. Once he woke, and saw me there, studying him; and though his entire body tensed like a crossbow, he never moved. The gray eyes had gone full yellow, the pupils slitted almost to invisibility. They held me until he closed them again, and I crept away to my blanket. In the morning, he made no mention of my spying on his sleep, but I never imagined that he had forgotten.

So young I was then, all that way back, and so much I knew, and he was quite right—none of it was to prove the smallest use in the world I entered on our journey. That nameless, tireless, endlessly scornful old man showed me the way to prepare and cook *aidallah*, which looks like a dungball itself, which is more nourishing than *tilgit*, and tastes far better, and which is poisonous if you don't strip every last bit of the inner rind. He taught me to carry my silly little knife out of sight in a secret place; he taught me how to sense a *sheknath*'s presence a good mile before winding it, and—when we were sneaking through green, steamy Taritaja country—how to avoid the mantraps those cannibal folk set for travelers. (I was on my way over the lip of two of them before he snatched me back, dancing with scorn, laughing his yap-laugh and informing me that no one would ever eat *my* brain to gain wisdom.) And, in spite of all my efforts, I cannot imagine forgetting my first introduction to the sandslugs of the Oriskany plains. There isn't a wound they can't clean out, nor an infection they can't digest; but it is not a comfortable process, and I prefer not to speak of it any further. Nevertheless, more than once I have come a very long way to find them again.

But cunning and knowing as that old man was, even he could detect no sign of the Hunters from the moment when we joined fortunes on the Queen's Road. Today I'd have the wit to be frightened more every day by their absence; but then I was for once too interested in puzzling out the cause of my companion's night terrors, and the identity of his pursuers to be much concerned with my own. And on the twentieth twilight that we shared, dropping down from the Skagats into high desert country, I finally caught sight of it for a single instant: the cause.

It stalked out of a light evening haze on long bird legs—three of them. The third appeared to be more tail than leg—the creature leaned back on it briefly, regarding us—but it definitely had long toes or claws of its own. As for the head and upper body; I had only a dazed impression of something approaching the human, and more fearsome for that. In another moment, it was gone, soundless for all its size; and the old man was up out of a doze, teeth bared, crouching to launch himself in any direction. When he turned to me, I'd no idea whether I should have seen what I had, or whether it would be wisest to feign distraction. But he never gave me the chance to choose.

I cannot say that I actually saw the change. I never do, not really. Never any more than a sort of sway in the air—you could not even call it a ripple—and there he is: there, like that first time: red-brown mask, the body a deeper red, throat and chest and tail-tip white-gold, bright yellow eyes seeing me—*me*, lost young Soukyan, always the same—seeing me truly and terribly, all the way down. Always. The fox.

One wild glare before he sprang away into the mist, and I did not see him again for a day and another night. Nor the great bird-legged thing either, though I sat up both nights, expecting its return. It was plainly seeking him, not me—whatever it might be, it was no Hunter—but what if it saw me as his partner, his henchman, as liable as he for whatever wrong it might be avenging? And what if I *had* become a shapeshifter's partner, unaware? Not all alliances are written, or spoken, or signed. Oh, I had no trouble staying awake those two nights. I thought it quite likely that I might never sleep again.

Or eat again, either, come to that. As I have told you, I never went back to my room at *that place*, which meant leaving my bow there. I wished now that I had chanced fetching it: not only because I had killed a man with that bow when I was barely tall enough to aim and draw, but because without it, on my own, I was bound to go very hungry indeed. I stayed close to our camp—what point in wandering off into unknown country in search of a half-mad, half-sinister old man?—and merely waited, making

137

do with such scraps and stores as we had, drinking from a nearby waterhole, little more than a muddy footprint. Once, in that second night, something large and silent crossed the Moon; but when I challenged it there was no response, and nothing to see. I sat down again and threw more wood on my fire.

He came back in human form, almost out of nowhere, but not quite—I never saw that change, either, but I did see, far behind him, coming around a thicket beyond the waterhole, the two sets of footprints, man and animal, and the exact place where one supplanted the other. Plainly, he did not care whether I saw it or not. He sat down across from me, as always, took a quick glance at our depleted larder, and said irritably, "You ate every last one of the *sushal* eggs. Greedy."

"Yes. I did." Formal, careful, both of us, just as though we had never shared a dung-cart. We stared at each other in silence for some while, and then I asked him, most politely, "What are you?"

"What I need to be," he answered. "Now this, now that, as necessary. As are we all."

I was surprised by my own sudden fury at his blandly philosophical air. "We do not *all* turn into foxes," I said. "We do not *all* abandon our friends—" I remember that I hesitated over the word, but then came out with it strongly—"leaving them to face monsters alone. Nor do we *all* lie to them from sunup to sundown, as you have done to me. I have no use for you, and we have no future together. Come tomorrow, I go alone."

"Well, now, that would be an extremely foolish mistake, and most probably fatal as well." He was as calmly judicial as any human could have been, but he was *not* human, *not* human. He said, "Consider—did I not keep you from your enemies, when they were as close on your heels as your own dirty skin? Have I not counseled you well during this journey you and I have made together? That *monster*, as you call it, did you no harm—nor even properly frighted you, am I right? Say honestly." I had no fitting answer, though I opened my mouth half a dozen times, while he sat there and smiled at me. "So. Now. Sit still, and I will tell you everything you wish to know."

Which, of course, he did not.

This is what he did tell me:

"What you saw—that was no monster, but something far worse. That was a Goro." He waited only a moment for me to show that I knew the name; quite rightly not expecting this, he went on. "The Goro are the bravest, fiercest folk who walk the Earth. To be killed by a Goro is considered a great honor, for they deign to slay only the bravest and fiercest of their enemies—merely to make an enemy of a Goro is an honor as well. However short-lived."

"Which is what you have done," I said, when he paused. He looked not at all guilty or ashamed, but distinctly embarrassed.

"You could say that, I suppose," he replied. "In a way. It was a mistake—I made a serious mistake, and I'm not too proud to admit it, even to you." I had never heard him sound as he did then: half-defiant, yet very nearly mumbling, like a child caught out in a lie. He said, "I stole a Goro's dream."

I looked at him. I did not laugh—I don't recall that I said anything—but he sneered at me anyway. His eyes were entirely gray now, narrow with disdain, and somewhat more angled than I had noticed before. "Mock me, then—why should you not? Your notion of dreams will have them all gossamer, all insubstantial film and gauze and wispy vapors. I tell you now that the dream of a Goro is as real and solid as your imbecile self, and each one takes solid form in our world, no matter if we recognize it or not for what it is. Understand me, fool!" He had grown notably heated, and there was a long silence between us before he spoke again.

"Understand me. Your life may well depend on it." For just that moment, the eyes were almost pleading. "It happened that I was among the Goro some time ago, traveling in…that *shape* you have seen." In all the time that we have known each other, he has never spoken the word *fox,* not to me. He said, "A Goro's dream, once dreamed, will manifest itself to us as it chooses—a grassblade or a jewel, a weed or a log of wood, who knows why? In my case…in my case—pure chance, mind you—it turned out to be a shiny stone. The *shape* likes shiny things." His voice trailed away, again a guilty child's voice.

"So you took it," I said. "Blame the shape, if you like—no matter to me—but it was you did the stealing. I may be only a fool, but I can follow you that far."

"It is not so simple!" he began angrily, but he caught himself then, and went on more calmly. "Well, well, your morality's no matter to me either. What should matter to you is that a stolen dream cries out to its begetter. No Goro will ever rest until his dream is safe home again, and the thief gathered to his ancestors in very small pieces. Most often, some of the pieces are lacking." He smiled at me.

"A grassblade?" I demanded. "A stone—a stick of wood? To pursue and kill for a discarded stick, no use to anyone? You neglected to mention that your brave, fierce Goro are also quite mad."

The old man sighed, a long and elaborately despairing sigh. "They are no more mad than yourself—a good deal less so, more than likely. And a Goro's dream is of considerable use—to a Goro, no one else. They keep them all, can you follow *that?* A Goro will hoard every physical manifestation of every dream he dreams in his life, even if at the end it seems only to amount to a heap of dead twigs and dried flower petals. Because he is bound to present the whole unsightly clutter to his gods, when he goes to them. And if even one is missing—one single feather, candle-end, teacup, seashell fragment—then the Goro will suffer bitterly after death. So they believe, and they take poorly to having it named nonsense. Which I am very nearly sure it is."

When he was not railing directly at me, his arrogance trickled away swiftly, leaving him plainly uneasy, shapeshifter or no. I found this rather shamefully enjoyable. I said, "So. This one wants his shiny stone back, and it has called him all this way on your trail. It does seem to me—"

"That I might simply return it to him? Apologies—some small token gift, perhaps—and no harm done?" This time his short laugh sounded like a branch snapping in a storm. "Indeed, nothing would suit me better. It is only a useless pebble, as you say—the *shape* lost all interest in it long ago. Unfortunately, for such an offense against a Goro—such a sin, if you like—vengeance is required." Speaking those words silenced him again for a long moment:

his eyes flicked constantly past and beyond me, and his whole body had grown so taut that I half-expected him to turn back into a fox as we sat together. For the first time in our acquaintance, I pitied him.

"Vengeance is required," he repeated presently. "It is a true sacrament among the Goro, much more than a matter of settling tribal scores. Something to do with evening all things out, restoring the proper balance of the world. Smoothing the rumples, you might say. Very philosophical, the Goro, when they have a moment." He was doing his best to appear composed, you see, though he must have known I knew better. He does that.

"All as may be," I said. "What's clear to me is that we now have two different sets of assassins to deal with, each lot unstoppable—"

"The Goro are *not* assassins," he interrupted me. "They are a civilized and honorable people, according to their lights." He was genuinely indignant.

"Splendid," I said. "Then by all means, you must stay where you are and allow yourself to be honorably slaughtered, so as to right the balance of things. For myself, I'll give them a run, in any case," and I was on my feet and groping for my belongings. Wonderful, what weeks of flight can do for a naturally mild temper.

He rose with me, nodding warningly, if such a thing can be. "Aye, we'd best be moving. I can't speak for your lot, but the day's coming on hot, and our Goro will sleep out the worst of it, if I know them at all. Pack and follow."

That brusquely—*pack and follow*. And so I did, for there was no more choice in the matter than there ever had been. The old man set a fierce pace that day, not only demanding greater speed from me than ever, but also doubling back, zigzagging like a hare with a *shukri* one jump behind; then inexplicably going to ground for half an hour at a time, absolutely motionless and silent until we abruptly started on again, with no more explanation than before. During those stretches he often slipped out of sight, each time hissing me to stillness, and I knew that he would take the fox-shape (or would it take him? which was real?) to scout back along the way we had come. But whether we were a trifle safer, or whether death was a little closer on our heels, I could never be sure. He never once said.

The country continued high desert, simmering with mirages, but there were moments in the ever-colder nights when I could smell fresh water; or perhaps I felt its presence in the water composing my own body. The old man did finally reveal that in less than a week, at our current rate, we should strike the Nai, the greatest river in this part of the country, which actually begins in the Skagats. There are always boats, he assured me—scows and barges and little schooners, going up and down with dried fish for this settlement, nails and harness for that one, a full load of lumber for the new town building back of the old port. Paying passengers were quite common on the Nai, as well as the non-paying sort—and here he winked elaborately at me, looking enough like the grandfather I still think I almost remember that I had to look away for a moment. Increasingly, as the years pass, I prefer the fox-shape.

"Not that this will lose our Goro friend," he said, "not for a moment. They're seagoing people—a river is a city street to the Goro. But they dislike rivers, exactly as a countryman dislikes the city, and the farther they are from the sea, the more tense and uneasy they become. Now the Nai will take us all the way to Druchank, which is a hellpit, unless it has changed greatly since I was last there. But from Druchank it's a long, long journey to the smell of salt, yet no more than two days to...."

And here he stopped. It was not a pause for breath or memory, not an instant's halt to find words—no interruption, but an end, as though he had never intended to say more. He only looked at me, not with his usual mockery, nor with any expression that I could read. But he clearly would not speak again until I did, and I had a strong sense that I did not want to ask what I had to ask, and get an answer. I said, at last, "Two days to where?"

"To the place of our stand." The voice had no laughter in it, but no fear either. "To the place where we turn and meet them all. Yours and mine."

It was long ago, that moment. I am reasonably certain that I did not say anything bold or heroic in answer, as I can be fairly sure that I did not shame myself. Beyond that...beyond that, I can only recall a sense that all the skin of my face had suddenly grown too tight for my head. The rest is stories. *He* might remember exactly how it was, but he lies.

I do recollect his response to whatever I finally said. "Yes, it *will* come to that, and we will not be able to avoid facing them. I thought we might, but I always look circumstance in the eye." (And would try to steal both eyes, and then charge poor blind circumstance for his time, but never mind.) He said, "Your Hunters and my Goro—" no more sharing of shadows, apparently—"there's no shaking them, none of them.

I would know if there were a way." I didn't doubt that. "The best we can do is to choose the ground on which we make our stand, and I have long since chosen the Mihanachakali." I blinked at him. That I remember, blinking so stupidly, nothing to say.

The Mihanachakali was deep delta once—rich, bountiful farmland, until the Nai changed course, over a century ago. The word means *black river valley*—I suppose because the Nai used to carry so much sweet silt to the region when it flooded every year or two. You wouldn't know that now, nor could I believe it at the time, trudging away from Druchank (which was just as foul a hole as he remembered, and remains so), into country grown so parched, so entirely dried out, that the soil had forgotten how to hold even the little mist that the river provided now and again. We met no one, but every turn in the road brought us past one more abandoned house, one more ruin of a shed or a byre; eventually the road became one more desiccated furrow crumbling away to the flat, pale horizon. The desert had never been anything but what it was; this waste was far wilder, far lonelier, because of the ghosts. Because of the ghosts that I could feel, even if I couldn't see them—the people who had lived here, tried to live here, who had dug in and hung on as long as they could while the Earth itself turned ghost under their feet, under their splintery wooden ploughs and spades. I hated it as instinctively and deeply and sadly as I have ever hated a place on Earth, but the old man tramped on without ever looking back for me. And as I stumbled after him over the cold, wrinkled land, he talked constantly to himself, so that I could not help but overhear.

"Near, near—they never move, once they...twice

before, twice, and then that other time…listen for it, smell it out, find it, find it, so close…no mistake, it cannot have moved, I *will* not be mistaken, listen for it, reach for it, find it, find it, *find it!*" He crouched lower and lower as we plodded on, until he might as well have taken the fox-form, so increasingly taut, elongated and pointed had his shadow become. To me during those two days crossing the Mihanachakali, he spoke not at all.

Then, nearing sundown on the second day, he abruptly broke off the long mumbled conversation with himself. Between one stride and the next, he froze in place, one foot poised off the ground, exactly as I have seen a stalking fox do when the chosen kill suddenly raises its head and sniffs the air. "Here," he said quietly, and it seemed not so much a word but a single breath that had chosen shape on its own, like a Goro's dream. "Here," he said again. "Here it was. I remembered. I *knew.*"

We had halted in what appeared to me to be the exact middle of anywhere. River off *that* way, give or take; a few shriveled hills lumping up *that* way; no-color evening sky baking above…I could never have imagined surroundings less suitable for a gallant last stand. It wouldn't have taken a Goro and two Hunters to pick us off as we stood there with the sunset at our backs: two small, weary figures, weaponless, exposed to attack on all sides, our only possible shelter a burned-out farmhouse, nothing but four walls, a caved-in roof, a crumbling chimney, and what looked to be a root cellar. A shepherd with a sling could have potted us like sparrows.

"I knew," he repeated, looking much more like his

former superior self. "Not whether it would *be* here, but that it would be *here*." It made no sense, and I told him so, and the yap-laugh sounded more elated than I had yet heard it. "Think for once, idiot! No, no—*don't* think, forget about thinking! Try remembering, try to remember something, anything you didn't learn at that bloody asylum of yours. Something your mother told you about such places—something the old people used to say, something children would whisper in their beds to frighten each other. Something even a fool just might already know—remember! Remember?"

And I did. I remembered half-finished stories of houses that were not quite...that were not there all the time...rumors, quickly hushed by parents, of house-things blooming now and then from haunted soil, springing up like mushrooms in moonlight...I remembered an uncle's absently mumbled account of a friend, journeying, who took advantage of what appeared to be a shepherd's mountain hut and was not seen again—no more than the hut itself—and someone else's tale of bachelor cousins who settled into an empty cottage no one seemed to want, lived there comfortably enough for some years, and then...I did remember.

"Those are fables," I said. "Legends, nothing more. If you mean *that* over there, I see nothing but a gutted hovel that was most likely greatly improved by a proper fire. Let it appear, let it vanish—either way, we are both going to die. Of course, I may once again have missed something."

He could not have been more delighted. "Excellent. I must tell you, I might have felt a trifle anxious if you had actually grasped my plan." The pale yellow glow was rising in his eyes. "The true nature of that house is not important, and in any case would take too long to explain to an oaf. What matters is that if once our pursuers pass its door, they will not ever emerge again—therefore, we two must become bait and deadfall together, luring them on to disaster." Everything obviously depended on our pursuers running us to this Earth at the same time; if they fell upon each other in their lust to slaughter us, so much the better, but he was plainly not counting on this. "Once we've cozened them into that corner," and he gestured toward the thing that looked so like a ruinous farmhouse, "why, then, our troubles are over, and no burying to plague us, either." He kicked disdainfully at the stone-hard soil, and the laugh was far more fox than human.

I said, as calmly and carefully as I could, "This is not going to work. There are too many unknowns, too many possibilities. What if they do *not* arrive together? What if, instead of clashing, they cooperate to hunt us down? Much too likely that we will be the ones trapped in your—your *corner*—with no way out, helpless and doomed. This is absurd."

Oh, but he was furious then! Totally enraged, how he stamped back and forth, glaring at me, even his mustache crouched to spring, every white hair abristle. If he had been in the fox-shape—well, who knows?—perhaps he might indeed have leaped at my throat. "Ignorant, ignorant! *Unknowns, possibilities*—you know nothing, you are *fit* for nothing but my bidding." He stamped a few more times, and then turned to stalk away toward the farmhouse...toward the thing that looked like a farmhouse. When I made to follow, he waved me back without turning his head.

"Stay!" he ordered, as you command a dog. "Keep watch, call when they come in sight. You can do that much."

"And what then?" I shouted after him, as angry as he by now. "Have you any further instructions for the help? When I call to you, what then?"

Still walking, still not looking back, he answered, "Then you run, imbecile! Toward the house—*toward*, but not *into!* Do try to remember that." On the last words, he vanished into the shadow of the farmhouse. And I...why, I took up my ridiculous guard, stolidly patrolling the dead fields in the twilight, just as though I understood what I was to expect, and exactly what I would do when it turned up. The wind was turning steadily colder, and I kept tripping on the ruts and tussocks I paced, even falling on my face once. I am almost certain that he could not have seen me.

In an hour, or two hours, the half-Moon rose: the shape of a broken button, the color of a knife. I am grateful for it still; without it, I would surely never have seen the pair of them flitting across the dark toward me from different directions, dodging my glance, constantly dropping flat themselves, taking advantage of every dimness, every little swell of ground. The sight of them froze me, froze the tongue in my mouth. I could no more have cried out warning than I could have flown up to that Moon by flapping my arms. They knew it, too. I could see their smiles slicing through the moonlight.

I was not altogether without defenses. They had taught us somewhat of *kuj'mai*—the north-coast style—in *that place,* and I was confident that I could take passable care of myself in most situations. But not here, not in this situation, not for a minute, not against those two. My mind wanted to run away, and my body wanted to wet and befoul itself. Somehow I did neither, no more than I made a sound.

The worst moment—my stomach remembers it exactly, if my mind blurs details—was when I suddenly realized that I had lost sight of them, Moon or no. Then panic took me entirely, and I turned and fled toward the farmhouse-thing, as instructed, my eyes clenched almost shut, fully expecting to be effortlessly overtaken at any moment, as a *sheknath* drags down its victim from behind. They would be laughing—were laughing already, I knew it, even if I couldn't hear them. I could feel their laughter pulling me down.

When the first hand clutched at my neck, I did turn to fight them. I like to remember that. I did shriek in terror—yes, I admit that without shame—but only once; then I whirled in that grasp, as I had been taught, and struck out with right hand and left foot, in proper *kuj'mai* style, aiming at once to shatter a kidney and paralyze a breathing center. I connected with neither, but found myself dangling in the air, screaming defiance into a face like no face I knew. It had a lizard's scales, almost purple in color, the round black eyes of some predatory bird—but glaring with a savage philosophy that never burdened the brain of any bird—a nose somewhere between a snout and a beak, and a long narrow muzzle fringed with a great many small, shy fangs. The Goro.

"Where is he?" it demanded in the Common Tongue. Its voice was higher than I had imagined, sounding as though it had scales on it as well, and it spoke with a peculiar near-lisp which would likely have been funny if I had not been hearing it with a

set of three-inch talons very nearly meeting in my throat. The Goro said again, almost whispering, "Where is he? You have exactly three *daks* to tell me."

What measure of time a *dak* might be, I cannot tell you to this day, but it still sounds short. What I can say is that all that kept me from betraying the old man on the instant was the fact that I could barely make a sound, once I had heard that voice and the hissing, murderous wisdom in that voice. I managed to croak out, "Sir, I do not know, honestly"—I did say *sir,* I am sure of that anyway—but the Goro only gripped me the tighter, until I felt my tongue and eyes and even my teeth about to explode from my head. It wanted the shapeshifter's life, not mine; but to the wrath in that clench, what difference. In another moment I would be just as dead as if it had been I who stole a dream. The pure injustice of it would have made me weep, if I could have.

Then the Hunters hit him (or her, I never knew), one from either side. The Goro was so intent on strangling information out of me that it never sensed or saw them until they were upon it. It uttered a kind of soft, wheezing roar, hurled me away into a dry ditch, and turned on them, slashing out with claws at one, striking at the other's throat, all fangs bared to the yellow gums. But they were quicker: they spun away like dancers, lashing back with their weaponless hands—and, amazingly, hurting the creature. Its own attacks drew blood from exposed flesh, but theirs brought grunts of surprised pain from deep in the Goro's belly; and after that first skirmish it halted abruptly, standing quite still to take their measure properly. Still struggling for each breath, I found myself absurdly sympathetic. It knew nothing of Hunters, after all, while I knew a little.

But then again, they had plainly never encountered such an opponent. They seemed no more eager to charge a second time than it was to come at them. One took a few cautious steps forward, pausing immediately when the Goro growled. The Hunter's tone was blithe and merry, as I had always been told their voices were. "We have no dispute with you, friend," and he pointed one deadly forefinger at me as I cowered behind the creature who had so nearly killed me a moment before. The Hunter said, "We seek *him.*"

"Do you so?" Those three slow words, in the Goro's voice, would have made me reconsider the path to paradise. The reply was implicit before the Goro spoke again. "He is mine. I need what he knows."

"Ah, but so do we, you see." The Hunter might have been lightly debating some dainty point of poetry or religion with a fine lady, such as drifted smokily now and then through the chill halls of *that place.* He continued, "What *we* need will come back to where it belongs. He will...stay here."

"Ah," said the Goro in turn, and the little sigh, coming from such a great creature, seemed oddly gentle, even wistful. The Goro said, "I also have no wish to kill you. You should go away now."

"We cannot." The other Hunter spoke for the first time, sounding almost apologetic. "There it is, unfortunately."

I had at that point climbed halfway out of the ditch, moving as cautiously and—I hoped—as inconspicuously as I possibly could, when the Goro turned and saw me. It uttered that same chilling wheeze, feinted a charge, which sent me diving back down to bang my head on stony mud, and then wheeled faster than anything that big should have been able to move, swinging its clawed tail to knock the nearer Hunter a good twenty feet away. He regained his feet swiftly enough, but he was obviously stunned, and only stood shaking his head as the Goro came at him again. The second Hunter leaped on its back, chopping and jabbing at it with those hands that could break bones and lay open flesh, but the Goro paid no more heed than if the Hunter had been pelting it with flowers. It simply shook him off and struck his dazed partner so hard—this time with a paw—that I heard his neck snap from where I stood. It does not, by the way, sound like a dry twig, as some say. Not at all.

I scrambled all the way out of the ditch on my second try, and poised low on the edge, ready to bolt this way or that, according to what the Goro did next. Vaguely I recalled that the old man had ordered me to run for the house once I had gained the attention of all parties; but, what with the situation having altered, I thought that perhaps I might not move much for some while—possibly a year, or even two. The surviving Hunter, mortally bound to avenge his comrade, let out a howl of purest grief and fury and sprang wildly at the Goro—who, amazingly, backed away so fast that the Hunter literally fell short, and very nearly sprawled at the Goro's feet, still crying vengeance. The Goro could have killed him simply by stepping on him, or with a quick slash of its tail, but it did no such thing. Rather, it backed farther, allowing him to rise without any hindrance, and the two of them faced each other under the half-Moon, the Hunter crouched and panting, the Goro studying him thoughtfully out of lidless black eyes.

The Hunter said, his voice still lightly amused, "I am not afraid of you. We have killed—" he caught himself then, and for a single moment, a splinter of a moment, I saw real, rending pain in his own pitiless eyes—"*I* have killed a score greater than you, and each time walked away unscathed. You will not live to say the same."

"Perhaps not," said the Goro, and nothing more than that. It continued to stand where it was, motionless as a long-legged *gantiya* waiting in the marshes for a minnow, while the Hunter, just as immobile, seemed to vibrate with bursting, famished energy. I began to ease away from the ditch, one slow-sliding foot at a time, freezing for what seemed hours between steps and wishing desperately now for the Moon to sink or cloud over. There came no sound or signal from the farmhouse-thing; for all I knew, the old man had taken full advantage of the Goro's distraction to abandon me to its mercy, and that of my own pursuer. Neither of them had yet paid any further heed to me, but each waited with a terrible patience for the other's eyes to make the first move. At the last, the eyes are all you have.

Gradually gaining an idiotic confidence in my chances of slipping off unnoticed, I forgot completely how I had earlier tripped in a rut and sprawled on my face, until I did it again. I made no sound, for all my certainty that I had broken my nose, but they heard me. The Hunter gave a sudden short laugh, far more terrifying than the Goro's strange, strangled roar, and came bounding at me, flying over those same furrows like a dolphin taking the sunset waves. I was paralyzed—I have no memory of reacting, until I found myself on my back, curled into a half-ball, as a *shukri* brought to bay will do, biting and clawing madly at an assailant too vast for the malodorous little beast even to conceive of. The Hunter was over me like nightfall: still perfectly efficient, for all his fury, contemptuously ignoring my flailing attempts at both attack. and defense, while seeking the one place for the one blow he would ever need to strike. He found it.

He found it perhaps half a second after I found the cook's paring knife in the place where the old man had scornfully insisted that I carry it. Thought was not involved—the frantic, scrabbling thing at the end of my arm clutched the worn wooden handle and lunged blindly upward, slanting the blade along the Hunter's rib cage, which turned it like a melting candle. I felt the warm, slow trickle—*ah, they could bleed, then!*—but the Hunter's face never changed; if anything, he smiled with a kind of taunting triumph. *Yes, I can bleed, but that will not help you. Nothing will help you.* Nevertheless, he missed his strike, and I somehow rolled away, momentarily out of range and still, still alive.

The Hunter's hands were open, empty, hanging at his sides. The brown tunic was dark under his left arm, but he never stopped smiling. He said clearly, "There is no hope. No hope for you, no escape. You must know that."

"Yes," I said. "Yes, I know." And I did know, utterly, beyond any delusion. I said, "Come ahead, then."

To do myself some justice, he moved in rather more deliberately this time, as though I might have given him something to consider. I caught a moment's glimpse of the Goro standing off a little way, apparently waiting for us to destroy each other, as the old man had hoped it and the Hunters would do. The Hunter eased toward me, sideways-on, giving my paring knife the smallest target possible, which was certainly a compliment of a sort. I feinted a couple of times, left and right, as I had seen it done. He laughed, saying, "Good—very good. Really." A curious way to hear one's death sentence spoken.

Suddenly I had had enough of being quarry: the one pursued, the one hunted down, dragged down, the one helplessly watching his derisive executioner approach, himself unable to stir hand or foot. Without anything resembling a strategy, let alone a hope, I flung myself at the Hunter like a stone tumbling downhill. He stepped nimbly aside, but surprise slowed him just a trifle, and I hurtled into him, bringing us down together for a second time, and jarring the wind out of his laughter.

For a moment I was actually on top, clutching at the Hunter's throat with one hand, brandishing my little knife over him with the other. Then he smiled teasingly at me, like a father pretending to let a child pin him at wrestling, and he took the knife away from me and snapped it between his fingers. His face and clothes were splotched with blood now, but he seemed no whit weaker as he shrugged me aside and kneeled on my arms. He said kindly, "You gave us a better run than we expected. I will be quick."

Then he made a mistake.

Under the chuckling benignity, contempt, always, for every living soul but Hunters. Under the gracious amusement, contempt, utter sneering contempt. They cannot help it, it is what they are, and it is their only weakness. He tossed the broken handle of the paring knife—with its one remaining jag of blade— lightly into my face, and raised a hand for the killing blow. When he did that, his body weight shifted—only the least bit, but his right knee shifted with it, and slipped in a smear of blood. My half-numb left arm pulled free.

There was no stabbing possible with that fraction of a knife—literally no point to it, as you might say. I thought only to *mark* him, to make him know that he had *not* killed a pitiful child, but a man grown. One last time I slashed feebly at his smiling face, but he turned his head slightly, and I missed my target completely, raking the side of his neck. I remember my disappointment—*well, failed at that, too, my last act in this world.* I remember.

It was no dribble this time, no ooze, but a fierce leap like a living animal over my hand—even Hunters have an artery there—followed immediately by a lover's triumphant blurt of breath into my face. The Hunter's eyes widened, and he started to say something, and he died in my arms.

I might have lain there for a little while—I don't know. It cannot have been long, because the body was abruptly snatched off mine and flung back and away, like a snug blanket on a winter's morning, when your mother wants you out feeding the *jejebhais*. The Goro hauled me to my feet.

"Him," it said, and nothing more. It made no menacing gesture, uttered no horrifying threat; none of that was necessary. Now here is where the foolishness comes in. I had every hysterical intention of crying,

"Lord, lord, please, do not slay me, and I will lead you straight to where he hides, only spare my wretched life." I meant to, I find no disgrace in telling you this, especially since what I actually heard myself say—quite politely, as I recall—was, "You will have to kill me, sir." For that miserable, lying, insulting, shapeshifting old man, I did that, and he jeered at me for it, later on. Ah, well, we begin as we are meant to continue, I suppose.

The Goro regarded me out of those eyes that could neither blink (though I saw a sort of pinkish membrane flick across them from time to time) nor reveal the slightest feeling. It said, "That would serve no useful purpose. You will take me to him."

As I have said, it raised no deadly paw, showed no more teeth than the long muzzle normally showed. But I *felt* the command, and the implacable will behind the command—I *felt* the Goro in my mind and my belly, and to disobey was not possible. Not possible…I can tell you nothing more. Except, perhaps, that I was young. Today, withered relic that I am become, I might yet perhaps hold that will at bay. It was not possible then.

"Yes," I said. "Yes." The Goro came up to me, moving with a curious shuffling grace, if one can say that, wrapping that tail around its haunches as daintily as a lace shawl. It gripped me between neck and shoulder and turned me. I said nothing further, but started slowly toward the farmhouse that was not a farmhouse—or perhaps it was? what did I know of anything's reality anymore? My ribs were so badly bruised that I could not draw a full breath, and there was something wrong with the arm that had killed the Hunter. The half-Moon was setting now, silvering the shadows and filling the hard ruts with shivering, deceiving light, and it was cold, and I was a child in a man's body, wishing I were safe back in *that place*.

Nearing the farmhouse, the Goro halted, tightening its clutch on my shoulder. Weary and bewildered as I was—no, more than bewildered, half-mad, surely—I studied the house, *looked* at it for the first time, and could not imagine anyone ever having taken it for anybody's home. The dark waiting beyond the sagging door sprang out to greet us with a stench far beyond stench: not the smell that anciently abandoned places have, of wood rotted into black slush, blankets moldering on the skeleton of a bed, but of an unhuman awareness having nothing to do with our notions of life or shelter, or even ordinary fear. The thing's camouflage—how long in evolving? how can it have begun to pass itself off as something belonging to this world?—might serve well enough from a distance, on a dark night, but surely close to…? Then I glanced back at the Goro.

The Goro had forgotten me completely, though its paw remembered. Its eyes continued to tell me nothing, but it was staring at the farmhouse-thing with an intensity that would have been rapture in a human expression. It lisped, much more to itself than to me, "He is in there. I have run him to earth at last."

"No," I said, once more to my own astonishment. "No. It is a trap. Believe me."

"I honor your loyalty," the Goro said. It bent its awful head and made a curious gesture with its free paw which I have never seen again, and which may have meant blessing, or merely a compliment. I try not to think about it. It said, "But you cannot know him as I do. He is here because what he stole from

159

me is here. Because his honor demands that he face me to keep it, as mine demands that he pay the price of a stolen dream. We understand each other, we two."

"Nonsense," I said. I felt oddly lightheaded, and even bold, in the midst of my leg-caving, bladder-squeezing terror. "He has no honor, and he cares nothing for your dream, or for anything but his continual falsehearted existence. And that is no house, but a horror from somewhere more alien to you than you are to me. Please—I am trying to save *you*, not him. Believe me, please."

The Goro looked at me. I have no more idea now than I did then of what it could have been thinking, nor of what it made of my warning. Did it take me seriously and begin silently altering its plans? Had it assumed from the first that, as some sort of partner of its old enemy, nothing I said must ever be trusted for a moment? All I know is what happened—which is that out of the side of my eye I saw the fox burst from the shadows that the farmhouse was real enough to cast in this world, under this Moon, and come racing straight toward the Goro and me. In the moonlight, he shone red as the Hunter's blood.

He halted halfway, cocking his head to one side and grinning to show the small stone held in his jaws. I did not notice it immediately: it was barely more than a pebble, less bright than the sharp teeth that gripped it, or the mocking yellow eyes above it. The Goro's crystallized dream, the cause of the unending flight and pursuit that had called to me from a wagonload of manure. The fox tilted his head back, tossed the stone up at the sinking Moon, and caught it again.

And the Goro went mad. Nothing I had seen of its

raging power, even when it was battling the two Hunters, could possibly have prepared me for what I saw in the next moment. The eyes, the lidless eyes that I had thought could never express any emotion...I was in a midnight fire at sea once, off Cape Dylee, when the waves themselves seemed alight to the horizon, all leaping and dancing with an air of blazing delight at our doom. The Goro's eyes were like that as it lunged forward, not shambling at all now, but charging like a rock-*targ*, full-speed with the second stride. It was making a sound that it had not made before: if an avalanche had breath, if an entire forest were to fall at once, you might hear something—*something*—like what I heard then. Not a roar, not a bellow, not a howl—no word in any language I know will suit that sound. Flesh never made that sound; it came through the Goro out of the tortured Earth, and that is all there is to that. That is what I believe.

The fox wheeled and raced away, his red brush joyously, insultingly high, and the Goro went after him. I stumbled forward, shouting, *"No!"* but I might as well have been crying out to a forest or an avalanche. Distraught, battered, uncertain of anything at all, it may be that I was deceived, but it seemed to me that the shadow of the farmhouse-thing reared up as they neared it, spreading out to shapelessness and *reaching*...I knew the fox well enough to anticipate his swerving away at the last possible minute, but I miscalculated, and so did he. The shadow's long, long arms cut off his escape on three sides, taking him in mid-leap, as a frog laps a fly out of the air. I thought I heard him utter a single small puppyish yelp, not like a fox at all.

The Goro went straight in after him, never trying

to elude the shadow's grasp—I doubt it saw anything but the little dull pebble in the fox's jaws. It vanished as instantly and completely as he had, without a sound.

Telling you this tale, I notice that I am constantly pausing to marvel at my own stupidity. Each time I offer the same defense: I was young, I was inexperienced, I had been reared in a stranger place than any scoffer can possibly have known…all of it true, and none of it resembling an explanation for what I did next. Which was to plunge my naked hands into the devouring shadow, fumbling to rescue *anything* from its grip—the fox, the Goro, some poor creature consumed before we three ever came within its notice, within range of its desire. Today, I can only say that I pitied the Goro, and that the old man—the fox, as you will—was my guide, occasionally my mentor, and somehow nearly my friend, may the gods pity *me*. Have to do, won't it?

Where was I? Yes, I remember—groping blindly in the shadow on the chance of dragging one or the other of them back into the moonlight of this world. My arms vanished to the wrists, the forearms, past the elbows, into…into the flame of the stars? Into the eternal, unimaginable cold of the gulfs between them? I do not know to this day; for that, you must study my scarred old flesh and form your own opinion. What I know is that my hands closed on something they could not feel, and in turn I hauled them back, though I could not connect them, even in my mind, with a human body, mine or anyone else's. I screamed all the time, of course, but the pain had nothing to do with me—it was far too terrible, too *grand*, to belong to one person alone. I felt almost guilty keeping it for myself.

The shadow fought me. Whatever I had seized between my burning, frozen hands—and I could not tell whether it was as small a thing as the fox or as great as the Goro—the shadow wanted it back, and very nearly took it from me. And why I did not, *would* not, allow that to happen, I cannot put into words for you. I think it was the hands' decision, surely not my own. They were the ones who suffered, they were the ones entitled to choose—*yes, no, hang on, let go*... I was standing far—oh, very far indeed—to one side, looking on.

Did I pull what I held free by means of my pure heart and failing strength, or did the shadow finally give in, for its own reasons? I know what I believe, but none of that matters. What does matter is that when my hands came back to me, they held the fox between them. A seemingly lifeless fox, certainly; a fox without a breath or a heartbeat that I could detect; a fox beyond bedraggled, looking half his normal size, with most of his fur gone, the rest lying limply, and his proud brush as naked as a rat's tail. Indeed, the only indication that he still lived was the fact that he was unconsciously trying to shape-shift in my hands. The shiver of the air around him, the sudden slight smudging of his outline...I jumped back, as I had not recoiled from the house-thing's shadow, letting him fall to the ground.

He landed without the least thump, so insubstantial he was. The transformation simply faded and failed; though whether that means that the fox-shape was his natural form and the other nothing but a garment he was too weak to assume, I have never known. The

Moon was down, and with the approach of false dawn, the shadow was retreating, the house-thing itself withering absurdly, like an overripe vegetable, its sides slumping inward while its insides—or whatever they might have been—seemed to ooze palely into the rising day, out to where the shadow had lain in wait for prey. Only for a moment...then the whole creature collapsed and vanished before my eyes, and the one trace of its passage was a dusty hole in the ground. A small hole, the sort of hole that remains when you have pulled a plant up by its roots. Or think you have.

There was no sign of the Goro. When I looked back at the fox, he was actually shaking himself and trying to get to his feet. It took him some while, for his legs kept splaying out from under him, and even when he managed to balance more or less firmly on all four of them, his yellow eyes were obviously not seeing me, nor much else. Once the fox-shape was finally under control, he promptly abandoned it for that of the old man, who looked just as much of a disaster, if not even more so. The white mustache appeared to have been chewed nearly away; one burly white eyebrow was altogether gone, as were patches of the white mane, and the skin of his face and neck might have been through fire or frostbite. But he turned to stare toward the place where the house that was not a house had stood, and he grinned like a skull.

"Exactly as I planned it," he pronounced. "Rid of the lot of them, we are, for good and all, thanks to my foresight. I *knew* it was surely time for the beast to return to that spot, and I *knew* the Goro would care for nothing else, once it caught sight of me and that stone." Amazingly, he patted my shoulder with a still-shaky hand. "And you dealt with your little friends remarkably well—far better than I expected, truth be told. I may have misjudged you somewhat."

"As you misjudged the thing's reach," I said, and he had the grace to look discomfited. I said, "Before you thank me—" which he had shown no sign of doing "—you should know that I was simply trying to save whomever I could catch hold of. I would have been just as relieved to see the Goro standing where you are."

"Not for long," he replied with that supremely superior air that I have never seen matched in all these years. "The Goro consider needing any sort of assistance—let alone having to be *rescued*—to be dishonorable in its very nature. He'd have quickly removed a witness to his sin, likely enough." I suspected that to be a lie—which it is, for the most part—but said nothing, only watching as he gradually recovered his swagger, if not his mustache. It was fascinating to observe, rather like seeing a newborn butterfly's wings slowly plumping in the Sun. He said then—oddly quietly, I remember—"You are much better off with me. Whatever you think of me."

When he said that, just for that moment, he looked like no crafty shapeshifter but such a senile clown as one sees in the wayside puppet plays where the young wife always runs off with a soldier. He studied my hands and arms, which by now were hurting so much that in a way they did not hurt at all, if you can understand that. "I know something that will help those," he said. "It will not help enough, but you will be glad of it."

Not yet true dawn, and I could feel how hot the

day would be in that barren, utterly used-up land that is called the Mihanachakali. There was dust on my lips already, and sweat beginning to rise on my scalp. A few scrawny *rukshi* birds were beginning to circle high over the Hunters' bodies. I turned away and began to walk—inevitably back the way we had come, there being no other real road in any direction. The old man kept pace with me, pattering brightly at my side, cheerfully informing me, "The coast's what we want—salt water always straightens the mind and clears the spirit. We'll have to go back to Druchank—no help for that, alas—but three days farther down the Nai—"

I halted then and stood facing him. "Listen to me," I said. "Listen closely. I am bound as far from Goros and Hunters, from foxes that are not foxes and houses that are not houses as a young fool can get. I want nothing to do with the lot of you, or with anything that is like you. There must be a human life I am fit to lead, and I will find it out, wherever it hides from me. I will find my life."

"Rather like our recent companions seeking after us," he murmured, and now he sounded like his old taunting self, but somehow subdued also. "Well, so. I will bid you good luck and good-bye in advance, then, for all that we do appear to be traveling the same road—"

"We are *not*," I said, loud enough to make my poor head ache, and my battered ribs cringe. I began walking again, and he followed. I said, "Whichever road you take, land or water, I will go some other way. If I have to climb back into a manure wagon a second time, I will be shut of you."

"I have indeed misjudged you," he continued, as

though I had never spoken. "There is promising stuff to you, and with time and tutelage you may blossom into adequacy yet. It will be interesting to observe."

"I will write you a letter," I said through my teeth. There would plainly be no ridding myself of him until Druchank, but I was determined not to speak further word with him again. And I did not, not until the second night, when we had made early camp close enough to Druchank to smell its xfoulness on a dank little breeze. Hungry and weary, I weakened enough to ask him abruptly, "That house—whatever it was—you called it *the beast*. It was alive, then? Some sort of animal?"

"Say *vegetable*, and you may hit nearer the mark," he answered me. "They come and go, those things—never many, but always where they grew before, and always in the exact guise they wore the last time. I have seen one that you would take for a grand, shady *keema* tree without any question, and another that looks like a sweet little dance pavilion in the woods that no one seems to remember building. I cannot say where they are from, nor what exactly becomes of their victims—only that it is a short blooming season, and if they take no prey they rot and die back before your eyes. As that one did." He yawned as the fox yawned, showing all his teeth, and added, "A pity, really. I have…made use of that one before."

"And you led me there," I said. "You told me nothing, and you led me there."

He shrugged cheerfully. "I tried to tell you—a little, anyway—but you did not care to hear. My fault?" I did not answer him. A breeze had come up, carrying with it the smell of the Nai—somewhat fresher than that of the town—and the bray of a boat horn.

"It had already taken the Goro," I said finally, "and still it died."

"Ah, well, a Goro's not to everybody's taste." He yawned again, and suddenly barked with laughter. "Probably gave the poor old thing a bellyache—no wonder!" He literally fell over on his back at the thought, laughing, waving his arms and legs in the air, purely delighted at the image, and more so with himself for creating it. I watched him from where I lay, feeling a curious mixture of ironic admiration, genuine revulsion, and something uncomfortably like affection, which shocked me when I made myself name it to myself. As it occasionally does even now.

"I tried to stop the Goro," I said. "I told him that it was a trick, that you were deceiving him. I begged him not to fall into your trap."

The old man did not seem even slightly perturbed. "Didn't listen, did he? They never do. That's the nature of a Goro. Just as not wanting to know things is the nature of humans."

"And your nature?" I challenged him. "What is the nature of whatever you are?"

He considered this for some time, still lying on his back with his arms folded on his chest in the formal manner of a corpse. But his eyes were wide open, and in the twilight they were more gray than fox-yellow just then.

"Deceptive," he offered at last. "That's fair enough—deceptive. Misleading, too, and altogether unreliable." But he seemed not quite satisfied with any of the words, and thought about it for a while longer. At last he said, "Illusory. Good as any, *illusory*. That will do."

I lay long awake that night, reflecting on all that I had passed through—and all that had passed through and over me—since I fled across another night from *that place*, with the Hunters behind me. Deceptive, misleading, illusory, even so he had done me no real ill, when you thought about it. Led me into peril, true, but preserved me from it more than once. And he had certainly taught me much that I needed to know, if I were to make my way forward to wherever I was making my way to in this world. I could have had worse counselors, and doubtless would yet, on my journey.

My hands and arms pained me still, but far less than they had, as I leaned to nudge him out of his usual twitchy fox-sleep. He had searched out a couple of fat-leaved weeds that morning, pounded them for a good hour, mixed the resulting mash with what I tried not to suspect was his own urine, and spread it from my palms to my shoulders, where it crusted cool and stiff. I had barely touched his own shoulder before his eyes opened, yellow as they always are when he first wakes. I wonder what his dreams would look like, if they were to take daylight substance, as a Goro's do.

"Three more days on the Nai brings us where?" I asked him.

The Enchanted Trousseau
Deborah Roggie

Deborah Roggie lives in New Jersey. Her fiction has appeared in Lady Churchill's Rosebud Wristlet, *and she has read her stories on the NYC radio program, WBAI's "Hour of the Wolf," and at the New York Review of Science Fiction Reading Series at Dixon Place. She is currently working on a novel.*

Her story here considers the lengths to which a mother will go to protect a willful child.

Mothers worry about their daughters. There are so many things that can go wrong before a young woman comes into her own. And you can't be there for everything, much as you'd like to. Still, when your daughter announces her intention to marry a powerful wizard—about whom you know next to nothing—what's a mother to do?

Get sewing.

After all, a girl needs a trousseau.

Our daughter Gerinet had grown up a little wild, a little spoiled. The only girl among three brothers

(Dran and Jerret still lived at home; my eldest was married with a small farm of his own down the road), she loved the outdoors, looked after our horses, and helped on the farm. But Gerinet had no interest in the domestic arts, and in this her father backed her. Why make her learn to scrub and sew and cook when his pretty girl would make a fine marriage someday, and need never lift a finger? Didn't I already have a hired girl to help with the work? Many's the angry word Owit and I had on the subject. And Gerinet would take advantage of her father's weakness for her, peck him on the cheek, and skip off, laughing at having bested me again.

Just wait and she'll come around, I told myself. Mothers and daughters are often at odds during the growing-up years. Some day she'll have a household of her own and want to learn how to run it. There was time. So I never got a fair chance to teach her housekeeping, nor the secret art beneath—the spells and recipes that were her heritage.

On market days Owit took her with him, especially if I wasn't of a mind to endure six jouncing miles over rutted roads. Gerinet fair danced to go to town, as any girl would. Upper Tiswick was really just a little country village with a weekly market, an inn, and less than a dozen shops. There she could giggle and whisper with the other girls, and mock and moon over the boys, and sigh over pretty ribbons and bolts of cloth and bits of lace. I sympathized: I was the same at her age.

But it was there the wizard saw her, this Carac Frye, from somewhere up north in Mosria, Owit told me later. This wizard watched Gerinet, and liked what he saw (as who would not?): a round, fair face, a little brown from working in the sun, a graceful figure, sparkling green eyes. Once Carac Frye decided he wanted her, he cozied up to Owit over a mug of ale and flattered him this way and that, seasoning his words with a bit of magic, no doubt, until my poor husband came to feel like a brother to him.

This Carac had another advantage, good as a knife in one's boot: he was handsome Oh, there's no denying he was fine to look at!—with thick, dark hair and soulful eyes, and a lopsided, boyish grin. He gazed at Gerinet with those dark eyes, and before long she felt him watching her.

Not a word did they tell me, Owit and Gerinet, about the tall young wizard coming to the market three weeks in a row. Not a word about Owit looking the other way while the two young ones courted among the market stalls. Not a word, until the young man offered, and Gerinet accepted, and Owit put his hand on the bargain, fool that he was.

"But, Alrea, he's a wealthy man, a wizard, with land up north," pleaded Owit.

"And do you have more than his word on that?"

"They all know him at the market. He comes there regular. Cy Reskit will vouch for him."

"Cy Reskit would vouch for any man who buys his beer," I said.

"Besides, it's obvious he loves our daughter."

I faced him, my hands on my hips. "You know nothing about this man," I said. "Who are his kin? What kind of people are they?"

"Mother, I'm not marrying his kin," Gerinet said.

"That shows how little you know about marriage."

"Mother!"

"Girl," said Owit heavily, "let me talk to your mother alone."

We argued back and forth: I got nowhere with him. Finally, Owit pounded the wall with his fist and bellowed, "Woman, that's enough! I've given my word, and there will be no more argument!"

He left a hole in the plaster.

I could see all my words and warnings were wasted on them both: especially on Gerinet, who was far gone with imagining herself a wizard's wife, with a house of her own and no mother's interfering ways. No one to tell her to mend her skirt, nor to make up the beds, nor when she could come or go. And Carac Frye's dark eyes and lopsided grin and boyish hair all her own.

It was bitter medicine to me, to see how little power I had in my own household. I wondered what hold this wizard had over my husband and daughter. It was time to meet him. I bit my tongue and cleaned my house.

So Carac Frye came to dinner, with his most charming manners reserved for me, the obstacle between him and his desire. "You have a lovely house, Mistress Alrea," he said, glancing at the polished brass and pewter, the trim linens, the spotless floor. My two boys were as well-scrubbed as the hearthstone.

"You are kind to say so," I replied. I could smell magic on him like bitter smoke clinging to clothing. Of course, you'd have to expect that of a wizard, it being his stock in trade. But he would not cloud my judgment so easily.

"Gerinet and I will try to make our home together

173

as much like this as possible, won't we?" Gerinet
nodded as if she had every domestic skill ready to put
into service. The boys managed not to snort.

"I thought you already had a house in Mosria,"
Jerret said.

"I do."

"A fine stone house," said Gerinet, "with a tower
for studying the stars, fit for a wizard."

"That is so," said Carac Frye.

Dinner was more of the same. Compliments over
the fish baked in a salt crust, over the bread, the
sheep's milk cheese, the apple tarts. He wanted me
to like him, and he wanted it too much. The more he
tried, the less I liked him.

Owit drank it all in—the flattery, the admiration
for his taste, the esteem for his foresight, the deference
to his opinions. What trim sheepfold gates, what a
wise choice of breeding stock, what well-thought out
plans for rotating crops! This is what a son-in-law
should be, my husband's expression told me.

My silence made him uncomfortable. With a
nervous eye cast my way, Owit asked, "So, Carac,
this wizardry…. Is it a solid profession?"

"Oh, yes, it can be. Some wizards never settle
down, I'll grant you that. I'm not the wandering type,
though—I'm happiest in my tower, pursuing my
studies."

"What you do, then, is study the stars?"

"Yes."

"And what do they tell you?" demanded Jerret, his
curiosity getting the better of his manners.

"Many things." Frye leaned forward, a lock of dark
hair falling into his eyes. "When to set a cornerstone,
and how far the spring floods will spread. Where to

find the hidden entrance to the Koraltar mines. Who will inherit the duchy of Turing, where the current duke is childless and civil war is brewing. The stars predict the rise and fall of kingdoms, if only one can understand their language. I've studied their movements for years. In fact," he leaned back with a smile, "they told me where to look for Gerinet."

"They did?" she asked, simpering. Owit smiled broadly. I sighed.

My youngest, Dran, spoke up, less interested in romance than in magic. "Do you think you could show us a spell?" he asked. "I mean, is that something you could do here?"

"Dran!" Gerinet was appalled, but Carac Frye grinned.

"Of course." He turned to my husband. "A small demonstration, sir, with your permission."

Owit beamed apprehensively. "Certainly, certainly, of course!"

"If Mistress Alrea does not object."

All eyes turned to me: Dran, pleading; Owit, embarrassed; Jerret, curious to see what I'd do; Gerinet, trembling on the brink of hostility. And as the young wizard looked at me, I had the odd sense that he was measuring me for a small box in his workroom, where he kept the dried and powdered remains of people who got in his way.

I smiled. "I think a small demonstration would be in order," I said.

Carac Frye tilted his head, and suddenly Gerinet started, and exclaimed in a soft voice, "Now, where did you come from?"

She was addressing a spot on the table in front of her.

"What do you see?" said Dran.

"Don't you see it?" She pursed her lips and made a *tck-tck-tck-tck* sound. And it seemed as if a shadowy form did hop on the table—a small, yellow bird, with black and white markings on the head, wings, and tail. Owit could see it, and the boys could, too. I found the more I believed in the bird, the brighter and more colorful it became. But when I reminded myself that it was an illusion, it faded until I could see the table through it.

Gerinet coaxed the bird to hop on her finger. It perched there prettily, tilting its head; then it suddenly bobbed forward and pecked her cheek. Gerinet recoiled with a shriek. Carac Frye snapped his fingers and the bird flew three times around the room, squawking, then crashed headfirst into the mantelpiece. It disappeared with an explosion of feathers. Each feather that fell to the floor turned into a little yellow-and-gray striped snake that slithered across the hearth right into the hot ashes, with a blue sizzle and tiny cries of pain, followed by the smell of scorched flesh.

Gerinet sat there with her hand over her mouth, wide-eyed. "You must remember, my dear, it was only an illusion," the wizard said. A small line of blood trickled down her cheek from where the bird had pecked her. Carac Frye dabbed at the blood with his napkin, then took her hand, smiling his boyish lopsided smile, and she nodded slowly, as if in a dream.

The boys looked sick; Owit was dazed. I found I was shaking. A wizard's illusion is like a signature: it tells you something about the basic nature of the illusionist. This Carac Frye was powerful, inventive, and cruel. I had more than met my match.

That night, I planned Gerinet's trousseau.

There was not much time: the two were to be married in a scant five weeks. Carac Frye needed to travel home, make preparations for his bride, and return after the first hard frost. Then they would marry and make their bridal trip while the ground was hard and traveling easy, before the first snows.

I sewed, day and night, to be in time for the wedding. To everyone's dismay, I put Gerinet in charge of the kitchen. I only had time and energy for my needle.

I fashioned patterns and cut out the pieces for chemises, for aprons, dresses, capes, tablecloths, napkins, linens, petticoats, surcoats, bodices, collars, shawls, skirts, and sleeves. I pinned seams and sewed them, trimmed and tacked and fitted and stitched and hemmed, until I had a substantial pile of linens and clothing.

At the other end of the house, a string of disastrous meals tumbled out of the kitchen, one after the other. The boys complained. Owit looked grim. The bread was burnt, the eggs scorched, the milk gone sour, the roasts tough and stringy.

While I sewed, Gerinet confronted me with flour in her hair and grease on her apron.

"You don't like him."

"I barely know him."

"Mother, don't dodge my question."

"That was a question?"

Gerinet tossed her head. A cloud of flour exploded around her.

"Why don't you like him?"

The needle slipped and stabbed my finger. I grimaced and put it in my mouth and tasted blood. Gerinet waited.

"I don't know him. He shows up and suddenly he's taking my daughter away to who knows where—a house in Mosria somewhere, with a stone tower. Where's that? No one knows him, knows his family. What's his hurry?"

"We're in love!"

I shook my head in disgust. "Another illusion."

Gerinet exclaimed, "I don't believe you were ever in love!" and flounced out.

That hurt. I thought it would be obvious that, after twenty-two years of marriage, four children living and two buried, I still loved my husband. How could Gerinet not see it? Owit was stubborn and generous, tender, taciturn, passionate and teasing. He could be bitter about his failures. But he was my foundation. I saw him whole, and loved him whole.

I set out my embroidery thread. I had thread dyed in shades of green and rose and scarlet, gold and oak-orange, all the colors of sky and sea, and the russet browns of the forest. I took up a linen petticoat, and began to ply my needle.

"Don't you mark the cloth first?" Dran asked, when he came in after his chores were done.

"No need," said I. "The design comes to me as I go."

"I'd make it lopsided."

"Mine will be straight. Check back in a week and tell me what you think," I said with a grin.

"She's cooking another whole week? Ma, you've got to have some pity on us. We're all losing weight."

"So am I. Maybe you could help her."

Dran laughed. Help his sister in the kitchen? "When sows have kittens!"

My needle flew. The weeks were passing too fast. My fingers were sore, my eyes red. I sat up late nights, using my best candles over Owit's protests.

The embroidery grew, a band three hands deep along the length of the hem: tiny leaves and serpents, vines, trees, and birds, in a pattern that only looked regular from a distance. Intricate flowers, stars and sea-creatures, insects and fantastic animals danced almost knee-high.

Owit fingered the petticoat I had finished.

I had no mind to tell him that the petticoat was embroidered with recipes, for someone who had eyes to see it. Recipes like:

A spell to prevent conception.

A spell to ensure conception.

A spell to end conception.

A spell to increase a man's desire.

A spell to decrease a man's desire.

An ointment for the eyes to enable the user to see past illusion.

These I had embroidered on her petticoat, recipes for the life that really matters, where life itself touches a woman's body.

For her shawl, on a rich, wine-red wool, I had chosen less intimate recipes.

A soup that sharpens the senses.

A sweet-cake that dulls the perceptions.

A sleeping potion.

A wakefulness potion.

A cream that encourages healing.

A tea the produces clarity of mind.

If she looked closely at my handiwork, if Gerinet studied them—as I hoped she would—I knew she would recognize it for what it was: a collection of recipes stitched in the language of her childhood. I'd told her these stories as I'd brushed her hair and readied her for bed not so many years ago, as my mother had told me, and as her mother had done before.

For Gerinet's cape, in cloth of deep forest green, I'd embroidered directions:

For opening locked doors.
For finding the way home.
For seeing in the dark.
For telling truth from falsehood.
For sending a message over long distances.
For shape-changing.
For returning to one's true shape.

Owit dropped the petticoat, seeing nothing but colored threads. I could read his expression: *Typical woman's foolishness*, he thought, *to waste all that effort on something that will never show!*

Once he was gone, in the hem of her cloak I dropped a small, white stone, and embroidered it in place with a spell.

At last Gerinet's wedding day came. The clothes and linens were packed for the trip. Carac Frye wed my daughter and prepared to take her away. As he checked the horses' packs, I pulled the heavy green cape around Gerinet's shoulders. "Remember this. If you should find trouble and miss home, look to my needlework and think of her who sewed it."

Gerinet, round-eyed, whispered, "I will, Mama."

Then my son-in-law put a possessive arm around her and drew her away.

One day, about a week after Gerinet and Carac Frye had left, I found a stone in my shoe, a twin to the one I'd sewn into my daughter's cloak. *Already,* I thought. *That's not good.* I put the stone in a cup on the mantle.

As the months went by, I added stones to the cup, once a week or so at first, but then more often. I found them in my shoes, in my teakettle, in my pockets, on my pillow. Most were white, a few troubling pebbles were gray, and, one terrible day, the stone was red. Gerinet was in danger and there was nothing I could do but wait and hope that she would find her way home.

The next day's stone was pink, and the stones on the following days grew paler, which eased my mind somewhat. Still, they kept turning up, in my washbasin, in my mug of tea, in the dough I was shaping into bread. The cup on the mantelpiece overflowed.

It was May, and the first thunderstorm of the season had caught us by surprise. Our best mare was in foal, and Owit and the boys stayed in the barn to look after her. I went back to the house. As I changed out of my wet clothes, I heard a scratching at my bedroom window. It was a starveling gray tabby cat, all spine and legs and green eyes. I opened the casement. "Come in," I said to the poor soaked creature. "It's a bad afternoon to be out."

The cat leaped into the room and settled itself in the middle of the floor, making a puddle. It neither groomed itself nor explored. It simply sat and looked at me, as if waiting.

I reached out to touch its head, and said experimentally, "Gerinet?"

The cat hissed. I pulled back, and ran to my locked cabinet, where I stored my own potions and supplies, those that would keep. With shaking hands, I brought out a small, earthenware jar with a narrow mouth. I removed the stopper and passed it under the cat's nose. It's nostrils flared with distaste, and it sneezed.

And suddenly I was touching my daughter's lank hair, plastered against her shivering body. I pulled the quilt from the bed and wrapped her up and held her while she cried. She was thinner than she should be, and her face was drawn.

She dressed while I slipped downstairs, ladled up some broth from the soup pot and cut her a fresh slice of bread, and brought the meal up to the bedroom. In between bites, Gerinet told me her story:

"Carac wanted so much of me, he was always after me. At first it was flattering, but I could never do enough to please him. He said it was my duty to look after him, and I tried, I really did try. He said I was spoiled. I was to work as hard as the servants, and set them a good example. If I made a mistake and dinner wasn't right, he would lose his temper.

"When he was working on a spell and it didn't succeed, he would blame me. Once I answered sharply, and he grabbed my arm and bent it back and said if I ever spoke that way again to him he would break it."

I laid a hand on Gerinet's arm. It was too thin; I felt even I could snap it with little effort.

"One night, he hit me." She bowed her head, then

looked up at me through her damp hair, newly combed.

"I saw no one else but the servants. Carac said it wasn't fitting for me to make friends with them. I believe he told them stories about me, to make them unfriendly. I was really quite alone. And I wasn't allowed to go out on my own. Oh, Mother, you have no idea how lonely I was.

"And then I found out I was pregnant. I thought Carac would be happy—I thought everything would be all right again. I would have a baby to love and there would be laughter and brightness.

"But one day I put something out of place. Carac accused me of trying to ruin his work. He hit me in the stomach, hard, and left me on the floor. A servant found me there, bleeding, and brought me to bed. I lost the child that night."

Her face was so still, her voice flat. She would not meet my eyes.

"When I could sit up in bed again, I wrapped my shawl around my shoulders, the red shawl that you made for me. It was so warm, and the colors so alive. And I began to notice something in the embroidery. That it had meaning. That I knew the stories it was telling. It all meant something, the colors and the way they were related, the symbols and the patterns. The very stitches, the different weights of thread, had different meanings. And I began to read them.

"Once I understood, I rummaged through my trousseau, through all the things you'd sewn. I found all the recipes. All of them."

I got her under the covers at last and settled her down.

In sleep she seemed younger, her pain smoothed away. I had to make a plan.

I knew he would come looking for her, and soon. Carac Frye was not one to let a wife go. He would come, crackling with angry magic, and Gerinet was no match for him. For that matter, I wasn't sure I could take him on. When your daughter is the target of an angry wizard, what's a mother to do?

Get cooking.

After all, the way to a man's heart is through his stomach. I meant to reach in, hold his heart in my hand, and squeeze it dry.

Owit and the boys were still in the barn. I hoped the mare was not in trouble. Gerinet slept the rest of the afternoon away. I got supper going, then went upstairs to wake her.

I had to check my own trousseau for some of the recipes. Some I had never tried before. Together, Gerinet and I opened the linen press and shook out a creamy embroidered tablecloth, that was a gift from my mother and grandmother both. I remember them working on it in the months before my wedding. The cloth came with twelve matching napkins, each embroidered with a different spell. My trousseau had been quite extensive, unlike my daughter's hastily made-up wardrobe.

"Yes! There it is," I said. I pointed to a section of embroidery featuring a cat and the new moon, orange-flowering herbs, and falling rain. "Can you make it out?"

"A spell to hide a person from all seekers," said Gerinet slowly.

Exactly. It was time to get to work. Carac Frye would soon be upon us, of that I was sure.

Though Gerinet was exhausted, she wanted to help. We hauled out a cast-iron pot that I reserved for such work, and gathered ingredients. I began by dry-toasting the necessary spices until the kitchen was fragrant. Gerinet pounded catweed seeds in a mortar, and added them to the pot. Then I added rainwater, and pickled moonflowers, and false saffron, each according to its nature, and boiled it down into a thin paste. I passed the mixture through a sieve.

With a horsetail brush I painted the soles of my daughter's feet, the palms of her hands, and her lips with the warm mixture, leaving an orange stain on her skin. "Concealment: only I will hear your step; only I will feel your touch; only I will hear your words, until this is washed from your skin," I chanted softly. Gerinet turned her hands and feet to inspect the outcome. "Don't worry—it will wear off in a couple of days if not renewed."

"But then he'll come back," said Gerinet.

"Not if we take care of him properly the first time. But until then you must not wash your hands or face, nor walk in wet grass barefoot."

Dran came clattering in from the barn, his eyes shining, startling us both. "She's born! She's born!," he said. "A little filly! Brown with two white stockings. I helped rub her down."

"Dran, I'm back," said Gerinet.

He took no notice of his sister. "But Dad and Jerret want to stay with her a while, and so do I. They're cleaning out the dirty hay. It's a mess! I'm to bring out some food for all three of us."

"Dran, I'm right here," said Gerinet. She waved her orange palms in front of him. He brushed his nose as if flicking away a fly.

"And how is the mare?" I asked as I cut thick slices of bread and leftover lamb, and filled a pitcher of cider, trying to ignore Gerinet as she danced giddy circles around her brother.

Dran—his mouth already half-crammed with cheese—answered, "She's all right. She's nursing the foal already."

"I'll help you bring supper over," I said, and secretly nodded to Gerinet. "I want to see the foal, too."

There was no way to pretty it up: I wanted the wizard dead. I didn't want to do a killing, but I wanted Carac Frye to be stiff and cold and trouble us no more. How else to keep him from harming my daughter again?

And there was another, more shameful thing, past justice, past reason, past self-protection. He killed my grandchild-to-be, and in doing so nearly killed Gerinet. I wanted him dead.

It was a wretched thing, that hate, that dark thing that crawled out of my soul and sat on my shoulder. I had a good long look at it. Its twin sat on my daughter's shoulder. It had an ugly stench.

That night, when the rest of the household was asleep, my daughter and I desperately searched through my trousseau for the recipe that would end a wizard's life. Napkins, aprons, tea-linens, towels: *a spell for binding, a spell for loosening, a spell for concealment, a spell to reveal that which is hidden....* Pairs of recipes, one to do, the other to undo, but none to create or end the life of a man. Sheets, blankets, shawls, smocks: *a spell to create fear,* and another *to dispel fear, an oil to sharpen hearing,* and one *to cause deafness....* The women of my family were healers, not murderers, I thought. They had not foreseen my need. I pulled a length of blue cloth, embroidered but not finished, from the pile, and studied the patterns closely.

"It might work," I murmured.

"What is it?"

I showed the embroidery to Gerinet. "See here? This is *a spell to enhance memory*. And below it, *a spell to erase memory*. That's how we'll do it."

"I don't understand." Her eyes were swollen and I could see it was an effort for her to hold up her head. I put an arm around her. "Go to sleep," I said, "and don't worry about a thing. I've found the way to deal with Carac Frye."

It was early morning.

I was up, of course—there's no late sleeping on a farm—and Owit and the boys were already out and about, getting the early chores done. I had a little pan of something simmering on a grate over a few coals.

The insects fell quiet—their normal meadow racket gave way to utter silence. I poked my head out the door. A flock of starlings startled and flew away. There grew a waiting sense like before a thunderstorm.

I saw a shimmering disturbance down the lane, like the air above a pot of boiling water, as tall as a man and almost as wide. It disappeared, then, a minute or two later, reappeared, closer this time. And again.

Then it resolved itself into Carac Frye.

He shook himself, like a dog, as if to settle himself into his own skin. He peered up at the house. I grabbed a bucket and clattered out the door in the direction of the well, startling him.

"My goodness, it's Carac! It's so good to see you!" I cried, giving him a big hug. He smelled of dangerous magic: it clung to his skin, to his hair, making the hairs on my arms stand on end. I held him back at arms' length. "But where is Gerinet? Don't tell me you left her at home!"

"She—"

"Just let me get some water and I'll be right with you," I interrupted. "And then I want to hear all about her. And you, of course. But not a letter in all this time, shame on you two. Being newlyweds is not an excuse. Gerinet is my only daughter, after all. She is well, isn't she?"

Then Gerinet stepped out of the door onto the stone step. The door slammed behind her.

"What was that?"

He could neither see her nor hear her footstep, but she'd forgotten that she could still cause noise.

"I don't know. Did one of the cats slip out? I'll have to get Owit to put a weight on that door. I asked him once before but it must have slipped his mind." I could see my chattering was starting to irritate him. So much the better. I wanted him distracted.

But how were we going to get past Gerinet into the house without her stepping into the wet morning grass?

"Do you know, we had a foal last night, out of Willow. Owit and the boys had quite a time of it. But she's a real beauty. Come see!"

"Perhaps later," he said politely, running a hand through his dark hair.

"Do you by chance know a charm to help the foal

grow straight and strong? Or one to help the mare heal quickly, or sweeten her milk? That would be a kindness. Oh, do come, there's something special about a newborn that I wouldn't have you miss."

"Later, mistress, it will still be there," he said, starting toward the house. Gerinet's eyes grew wide as she realized the danger, and she put an orange hand before her orange mouth. Her husband had almost reached the step, and she was readying herself to jump aside when there came a shout.

"Carac Frye, by all that's holy!" Owit rounded the barn and came striding up to his son-in-law.

I grasped my bucket. "I've got to get this inside," I said, and eased Gerinet in before me while Owit gave Carac a hug and an enthusiastic thump on the back.

I glared at Gerinet and hissed, "Go upstairs!" then popped my head out of the door and called, "Breakfast in a half-hour! Owit, Carac doesn't want to see the foal. See how tired he looks? Let the poor man come inside."

He stepped over the threshold, and straightened his spine, and snapped his fingers, then splayed them, palm up, in a gesture that said, *Come—I am waiting* Gerinet silently walked into the room, unable to resist.

"I know you are here," he said.

She made no answer.

"I am not a patient man," said my son-in-law, looking in the wrong direction. "You are my wife, and you are coming home with me. And if I am kept waiting, I will have to make you obey—and so much the worse for you." He turned and faced me where I stood by the hearth. "Alrea, my wife's dear mother, who sees so much and usually says so little, what shall I do about you?"

"Go home, Carac," I said. "There is nothing for you here."

He began to laugh. It was an ugly sound, thick and muddy. If he had not been exhausted from his pursuit of Gerinet in all her forms, I could never have managed to fight him. He was a powerful man.

"I know what you are, mistress, and how you and your kind manipulate every man within your reach—how you've poisoned my wife's heart against honest marriage. Don't think you can touch me with your pathetic spells and potions."

I permitted myself a brief smile. "They brought my daughter home."

He bashed the linen press—the only piece of furniture within his reach—with his fist. The paneled door cracked. "Her home is with me!"

"Never again," said Gerinet. I could hear her, but her husband could not. She wiped the stain from her lips with the back of her hand. "I will never go with you again."

At this, Carac Frye tilted his head, as if to better hear a muffled voice from below the floor. I surreptitiously reached for the little pan, my hand sheathed by my apron, for it was made of thick crockery; the handle was hot.

But Carac caught my movement and growled a few words in an unfamiliar tongue, flicking his hand in my direction. I gasped in pain and brought my free hand to my eyes. My vision blurred and I could not see.

Gerinet cried, "What have you done to her?"

If only she would stay silent, and stay back—in a moment he would have her. I could not see my hand

190

in front of my face: the world had become a many-colored blur. But I flung the pan in his direction.

He screamed and the crock shattered on the slate floor.

Over the sound of Carac's moans, I called, "Gerinet, stay back! Don't go near him. Gerinet, are you all right? Don't touch the liquid, do you hear me? Whatever you do, don't let it touch your skin."

"Mother, what have you done to him?" I could hear she was at the far end of the room. "Mother?"

I reached for the wall and edged away from the hearth. I found I was shaking. Carac was still moaning, in a rhythmic, animal way.

The door burst open, and Owit said "What in blazes is going on here?"

I went straight to the sound of his voice; he held me up by the wrists. It was the only thing keeping me standing, the strength that flowed from my husband to me.

Then came the explanations. The potion was still dangerous, because it was absorbed through the pores, and they must carefully clean the room of every drop, and remove and burn Carac Frye's clothing. The boys must stay in the barn for the time being. All the while, Gerinet's husband crouched on the floor, moaning.

"What are we to do with him?"

"Put him to bed," I said. "I have a sleeping potion upstairs that will help. Where is Gerinet?"

"I'm here," said Gerinet's voice by my ear. "But what about your eyes? Are you blind?"

"Blind enough. I can see light and shadow, that's all."

"You must have a recipe—"

"Not for this."

While Carac Frye slept fitfully upstairs under Owit's watchful eye, Gerinet searched my trousseau for a spell that restored sight.

"Ointment for the eyes to enable the user to see past illusion," Gerinet read. *"Soup that sharpens the senses. A cream that encourages healing. For seeing in the dark.* Mother, none of these are quite right."

"Maybe there is some common ingredient that has to do with sight," I said. "Combined with the healing cream, we might have something useful."

"Or we might have something harmful," said Gerinet.

My eyes constantly burned, as if I had a fever. "I'll take that risk," I said.

When Carac Frye woke, he was confused and slow of speech. He knew nothing of himself: not his name, his past, his talents. I could no longer sense magic clinging to him as it had before. He was empty as a spilled kettle.

But he was Gerinet's husband, and our joint responsibility. And since he was like an unformed child, we took it upon ourselves to raise him right. Oh, there were flashes of the old Carac—the lopsided grin, a gesture, a fit of temper when he was frustrated—but, essentially, the wizard was dead. His replacement, this new man in the old body, seemed oddly flat without the memories that make up a man. He had no opinions but those we gave him.

We kept Carac on as a farm hand, and he slowly learned how to split wood, and make hay, and care for the animals. Learning was difficult for him—especially reading or tasks that exercised one's memory. He never could keep the animals' names straight.

Gerinet bore it all, not patiently, but I give her credit for trying. The man she'd loved and feared was gone. In his place was this hollow fellow who only looked like her husband. For all the world cared or knew, she was still married. She tolerated him, with an absent kindness, but treated him only as a foster-brother, and they slept apart.

In the months that followed, Gerinet set herself to restoring my eyesight: she ransacked my trousseau for the ingredients to sharpen eyesight, and experimented with endless potions, creams, and oils. In the end, my vision mostly healed; although I leave the fine sewing to others now.

One day, some years later, Carac Frye wandered off into a snowstorm after a lost sheep. Owit and the boys searched as best as they could, but the storm developed into the worst blizzard in years, and he was not found for four days. He had frozen to death within a half-mile of the barn. They found him with his arms around the dead sheep, as if he'd been trying to keep it warm, or to warm himself.

"If only he'd not lost his memory, he could have found his way home easy as walking across a room," said Owit, thawing out by the fire that night.

"At last," said Gerinet softly. She had slipped past girlhood and settled into the loveliness of a woman, fierce and sad and knowing.

I shivered, but not from the cold. I knew what she'd meant—in truth, I'd felt the same. I'd killed him partway, stealing his memory; now the storm had done the rest.

There was no potion in my trousseau for forgiveness.

The Sorcerer's Apprentice
Robert Silverberg

Robert Silverberg is one of the most important writers in the history of science fiction and fantasy. He published his first story in 1954 and first novel, Revolt on Alpha C, *in 1955, quickly establishing what has become one of the most successful and sustained careers in science fiction. He wrote prolifically for SF and other pulp markets during the '50s, focused on nonfiction and other work in the early '60s, then returned to SF with greater ambition, publishing stories and novels that pushed genre boundaries and were often dark in tone as they explored themes of human isolation and the quest for transcendence.*

Works from the years 1967-1976, still considered Silverberg's most influential period, include Hugo winner "Nightwings," The Masks of Time, Tower of Glass, *Nebula winner* A Time of Changes, Dying Inside, The Book of Skulls, *and Nebula winners "Good News from the Vatican" and "Born with the Dead," among many others. Silverberg retired in the late '70s before returning with popular SF/fantasy* Lord Valentine's Castle, *first in his ongoing "Majipoor" series, and more novels and stories throughout the '80s and '90s, including Nebula winner "Sailing to Byzantium," Hugo winners "Gilgamesh in the Outback" (1986) and "Enter a Soldier. Later: Enter Another" (1989), and many others.Silverberg's latest novel is* Roma Eterna *and his most recent book is major career retrospective* Phases of the Moon. *Upcoming is new collection* In the Beginning.

The story that follows, originally published in Al Sarrantonio's Flights, *takes us back once again to the world of Majipoor.*

Gannin Thidrich was nearing the age of thirty and had come to Triggoin to study the art of sorcery, a profession for which he thought he had some aptitude, after failing at several for which he had none. He was a native of the Free City of Stee, that splendid metropolis on the slopes of Castle Mount, and at the suggestion of his father, a wealthy merchant of that great city, he had gone first into meat-jobbing, and then, through the good offices of an uncle from Dundilmir, he had become a dealer in used leather. In neither of these occupations had he distinguished himself, nor in the desultory projects he had undertaken afterward. But from childhood on he had pursued sorcery in an amateur way, first as a boyish hobby, and then as a young man's consolation for shortcomings in most of the other aspects of his life—helping out friends even unluckier than he with an uplifting spell or two, conjuring at parties, earning a little by reading palms in the marketplace—and at last, eager to attain more arcane skills, he had taken himself to Triggoin, the capital city of sorcerers, hoping to apprentice himself to some master in that craft.

Triggoin came as a jolt, after Stee. That great city, spreading out magnificently along both banks of the river of the same name, was distinguished for its huge parks and game preserves, its palatial homes, its towering riverfront buildings of reflective gray-pink marble. But Triggoin, far up in the north beyond the grim Valmambra Desert, was a closed, claustrophobic place, dark and unwelcoming, where Gannin Thidrich found himself confronted with a bewildering tangle of winding medieval streets lined by ancient mustard-colored buildings with blank facades and gabled roofs. It was winter here. The trees were leafless and the air was cold. That was a new thing for him, winter: Stee was seasonless, favored all the year round by the eternal springtime of Castle Mount. The sharp-edged air was harsh with the odors of stale cooking-oil and unfamiliar spices; the faces of the few people he encountered in the streets just within the gate were guarded and unfriendly.

He spent his first night there in a public dormitory for wayfarers, where in a smoky, dimly lit room he slept, very poorly, on a tick-infested straw mat among fifty other footsore travelers. In the morning, waiting on a long line for the chance to rinse his face in icy water, he passed the time by scanning the announcements on a bulletin board in the corridor and saw this:

APPRENTICE WANTED

FIFTH-LEVEL ADEPT OFFERS INSTRUCTION FOR SERIOUS
STUDENT, PLUS LODGING. TEN CROWNS PER WEEK FOR
ROOM AND LESSONS. SOME HOUSEHOLD WORK
REQUIRED, AND ASSISTANCE IN PROFESSIONAL TASKS.
APPLY TO V. HALABANT, 7 GAPELIGO BOULEVARD,
WEST TRIGGOIN.

That sounded promising. Gannin Thidrich gathered
up his suit-cases and hired a street-carter to take him
to West Triggoin. The carter made a sour face when
Gannin Thidrich gave him the address, but it was
illegal to refuse a fare, and off they went. Soon Gannin
Thidrich understood the sourness, for West Triggoin
appeared to be very far from the center of the city, a
suburb, in fact, perhaps even a slum, where the
buildings were so old and dilapidated they might well
have dated from Lord Stiamot's time and a cold, dusty
wind blew constantly down out of a row of low,
jagged hills. 7 Gapeligo Boulevard proved to be a
ramshackle lopsided structure, three asymmetrical
floors behind a weatherbeaten stone wall that showed
sad signs of flaking and spalling. The ground floor
housed what seemed to be a tavern, not open at this
early hour; the floor above it greeted him with a
padlocked door; Gannin Thidrich struggled upward
with his luggage and at the topmost landing was met
with folded arms and hostile glance by a tall, slender
woman of about his own age, auburn-haired, dusky-
skinned, with keen unwavering eyes and thin, savage-
looking lips. Evidently she had heard his bumpings
and thumpings on the staircase and had come out to
inspect the source of the commotion. He was struck
at once, despite her chilly and even forbidding aspect,

with the despairing realization that he found her immensely attractive.

"I'm looking for V. Halabant," Gannin Thidrich said, gasping a little for breath after his climb.

"I am V. Halabant."

That stunned him. Sorcery was not a trade commonly practiced by women, though evidently there were some who did go in for it. "The apprenticeship—?" he managed to say.

"Still available," she said. "Give me these." In the manner of a porter she swiftly separated his bags from his grasp, hefting them as though they were weightless, and led him inside.

Her chambers were dark, cheerless, cluttered, and untidy. The small room to the left of the entrance was jammed with the apparatus and paraphernalia of the professional sorcerer: astrolabes and ammatepilas, alembics and crucibles, hexaphores, ambivials, rohillas and verilistias, an armillary sphere, beakers and retorts, trays and metal boxes holding blue powders and pink ointments and strange seeds, a collection of flasks containing mysterious colored fluids, and much more that he was unable to identify. A second room adjacent to it held an overflowing bookcase, a couple of chairs, and a swaybacked couch. No doubt this room was for consultations. There were cobwebs on the window and he saw dust beneath the couch, and even a few sandroaches, those ubiquitous nasty scuttering insects that infested the parched Valmambra and all territories adjacent to it, were roaming about. Down the hallway lay a small dirty kitchen, a tiny room with a toilet and tub in it, storeroom piled high with more books and pamphlets, and beyond it the closed door of what he supposed—correctly, as it turned out—to be her own bedroom. What he did not see was any space for a lodger.

"I can offer one hour of formal instruction per day, every day of the week, plus access to my library for your independent studies, and two hours a week of discussion growing out of your own investigations," V. Halabant announced. "All of this in the morning; I will require you to be out of here for three hours every afternoon, because I have private pupils during that time. How you spend those hours is unimportant to me, except that I will need you to go to the marketplace for me two or three times a week, and you may as well do that then. You'll also do sweeping, washing, and other household chores, which, as you surely have seen, I have very little time to deal with. And you'll help me in my own work as required, assuming, of course, your skills are up to it. Is this agreeable to you?"

"Absolutely," said Gannin Hidrich. He was lost in admiration of her lustrous auburn hair, her finest feature, which fell in a sparkling cascade to her shoulders.

"The fee is payable four weeks in advance. If you leave after the first week the rest is refundable, afterwards not." He knew already that he was not going to leave. She held out her hand. "Sixty crowns, that will be."

"The notice I saw said it was ten crowns a week."

Her eyes were steely. "You must have seen an old notice. I raised my rates last year."

He would not quibble. As he gave her the money he said, "And where am I going to be sleeping?"

She gestured indifferently toward a rolled-up mat in a corner of the room that contained all the apparatus. He realized that that was going to be his bed. "You decide that. The laboratory, the study, the hall-way, even. Wherever you like."

His own choice would have been her bedroom, with her, but he was wise enough not to say that, even as a joke. He told her that he would sleep in the study, as she seemed to call the room with the couch and books. While he was unrolling the mat she asked him what level of instruction in the arts he had attained, and he replied that he was a self-educated sorcerer, strictly a novice, but with some apparent gift for the craft. She appeared untroubled by that. Perhaps all that mattered to her was the rent; she would instruct anyone, even a novice, so long as he paid on time.

"Oh," he said, as she turned away. "I am Gannin Thidrich. And your name is—?"

"Halabant," she said, disappearing down the hall-way.

Her first name, he discovered from a diploma in the study, was Vinala, a lovely name to him, but if she wanted to be called "Halabant," then "Halabant" was what he would call her. He would not take the risk of offending her in any way, not only because he very much craved the instruction that she could offer him, but also because of the troublesome and unwanted physical attraction that she held for him.

He could see right away that that attraction was in no way reciprocated. That disappointed him. One of the few areas of his life where he had generally met with success was in his dealings with women. But he knew that romance was inappropriate, anyway, between master and pupil, even if they were of differing sexes. Nor had he asked for it: it had simply smitten him at first glance, as had happened to him two or three times earlier in his life. Usually such smitings led only to messy difficulties, he had discovered. He wanted no such messes here. If these feelings of his for Halabant became a problem, he supposed, he could go into town and purchase whatever the opposite of a love-charm was called. If they sold love-charms here, and he had no doubt that they did, surely they would sell antidotes for love as well. But he wanted to remain here, and so he would do whatever she asked of him, call her by whatever name she requested, and so forth, obeying her in all things. In this ugly, unfriendly city she was the one spot of brightness and warmth for him, regardless of the complexities of the situation.

But his desire for her did not cause any problems, at first, aside from the effort he had to make in suppressing it, which was considerable but not insuperable.

On the first day he unpacked, spent the afternoon wandering around the unprepossessing streets of West Triggoin during the stipulated three hours for her other pupils, and, finding himself alone in the flat when he returned, he occupied himself by browsing through her extensive collection of texts on sorcery until dinnertime. Halabant had told him that he was free to use her little kitchen, and so he had purchased a few things at the corner market to cook for himself. Afterward, suddenly very weary, he lay down on his mat in the study and fell instantly asleep. He was vaguely aware, sometime later in the night, that she had come home and had gone down the hallway to her room.

In the morning, after they had eaten, she began his course of instruction in the mantic arts.

Briskly she interrogated him about the existing state of his knowledge. He explained what he could and could not do, a little surprised himself at how much he knew, and she did not seem displeased by it either. Still, after ten minutes or so she interrupted him and set about an introductory discourse of the most elementary sort, beginning with a lecture on the three classes of demons, the untamable valisteroi, the frequently useful kalisteroi, and the dangerous and unpredictable irgalisteroi. Gannin Thidrich had long ago encompassed the knowledge of the invisible beings, or at least thought he had; but he listened intently, taking copious notes, exactly as though all this were new to him, and after a while he discovered that what he thought he knew was shallow indeed, that it touched only on the superficialities.

Each day's lesson was different. One day it dealt with amulets and talismans, another with mechanical conjuring devices, another with herbal remedies and the making of potions, another with interpreting the movements of the stars and how to cast spells. His mind was awhirl with new knowledge. Gannin Thidrich drank it all in greedily, memorizing dozens of spells a day. ("To establish a relationship with the demon Ginitiis: *Iimea abrasax iabe iarbatha chramne*"….."To invoke protection against aquatic creatures: *Loma zath aioin acthase balamaon*"…."Request for knowledge of the Red Lamp: *Imantou lantou anchomach*"….) After each hour-long lesson he flung himself into avid exploration of her library, searching out additional aspects of what he had just been taught. He saw, ruefully, that while he had wasted his life in foolish and abortive business ventures, she had devoted her years, approximately the same number as his, to a profound and comprehensive study of the magical arts, and he admired the breadth and depth of her mastery.

On the other hand, Halabant did not have much in the way of a paying practice, skillful though she obviously was. During Gannin Thidrich's first week with her she gave just two brief consultations, one to a shopkeeper who had been put under a geas by a commercial rival, one to an elderly man who lusted after a youthful niece and wished to be cured of his obsession. He assisted her in both instances, fetching equipment from the laboratory as requested. The fees she received in both cases, he noticed, were minimal: a mere handful of coppers. No wonder she lived in such dismal quarters and was reduced to taking in private pupils like himself, and whoever it was who came to see her in the afternoons while he was away. It puzzled him that she remained here in Triggoin, where sorcerers swarmed everywhere by the hundreds or the thousands and competition had to be brutal, when she plainly would be much better off setting up in business for herself in one of the prosperous cities of the Mount where a handsome young sorcereress with skill in the art would quickly build a large clientele.

It was an exciting time for him. Gannin Thidrich felt his mind opening outward day by day, new knowledge flooding in, the mastery of the mysteries beginning to come within his grasp.

His days were so full that it did not bother him at

all to pass his nights on a thin mat on the floor of a room crammed with ancient acrid-smelling books. He needed only to close his eyes and sleep would come up and seize him as though he had been drugged. The winter wind howled outside, and cold drafts broke through into his room, and sandroaches danced all around him, making sandroach music with their little scraping claws, but nothing broke his sleep until dawn's first blast of light came through the library's uncovered window. Halabant was always awake, washed and dressed, when he emerged from his room. It was as if she did not need sleep at all. In these early hours of the morning she would hold her consultations with her clients in the study, if she had any that day, or else retire to her laboratory and putter about with her mechanisms and her potions. He would breakfast alone—Halabant never touched food before noon—and set about his household chores, the dusting and scrubbing and all the rest, and then would come his morning lesson and after that, until lunch, his time to prowl in the library. Often he and she took lunch at the same time, though she maintained silence throughout, and ignored him when he stole the occasional quick glance at her across the table from him.

The afternoons were the worst part, when the private pupils came and he was forced to wander the streets. He begrudged them, whoever they were, the time they had with her, and he hated the grimy taverns and bleak gaming-halls where he spent these winter days when the weather was too grim to allow him simply to walk about. But then he would return to the flat, and if he found her there, which was not always the case, she would allow him an hour or so of free discourse about matters magical, not a lesson but simply a conversation, in which he brought up issues that fascinated or perplexed him and she helped him toward an understanding of them. These were wonderful hours, during which Gannin Thidrich was constantly conscious not just of her knowledge of the arts but of Halabant's physical presence, her strange off-center beauty, the warmth of her body, the oddly pleasing fragrance of it. He kept himself in check, of course. But inwardly he imagined himself taking her in his arms, touching his lips to hers, running his fingertips down her lean, lithe back, drawing her down to his miserable thin mat on the library floor, and all the while some other part of his mind was concentrating on the technical arcana of sorcery that she was offering him.

In the evenings she was usually out again—he had no idea where—and he studied until sleep overtook him, or, if his head was throbbing too fiercely with newly acquired knowledge, he would apply himself to the unending backlog of housekeeping tasks, gathering up what seemed like the dust of decades from under the furniture, beating the rugs, oiling the kitchen pots, tidying the books, scrubbing the stained porcelain of the sink, and on and on, all for her, for her, for love of her.

It was a wonderful time.

But then in the second week came the catastrophic moment when he awoke too early, went out into the hallway, and blundered upon her as she was heading into the bathroom for her morning bath. She was naked. He saw her from the rear, first, the long lean back and the narrow waist and the flat, almost boyish buttocks, and then, as a gasp of shock escaped his lips and she became aware that he was there, she turned and faced him squarely, staring at him as coolly and unconcernedly as though he were a cat, or a piece of furniture. He was overwhelmed by the sight of her breasts, so full and close-set that they almost seemed out of proportion on such a slender frame, and of her flaring sharp-boned hips, and of the startlingly fire-hued triangle between them, tapering down to the slim thighs. She remained that way just long enough for the imprint of her nakedness to burn its way fiercely into Gannin Thidrich's soul, setting loose a conflagration that he knew it would be impossible for him to douse. Hastily he shut his eyes as though he had accidentally stared into the sun; and when he opened them again, a desperate moment later, she was gone and the bathroom door was closed.

The last time Gannin Thidrich had experienced such an impact he had been fourteen. The circumstances had been somewhat similar. Now, dizzied and dazed as a tremendous swirl of adolescent emotion roared through his adult mind, he braced himself against the hallway wall and gulped for breath like a drowning man.

For two days, though neither of them referred to the incident at all, he remained in its grip. He could hardly believe that something as trivial as a momentary glimpse of a naked woman, at his age, could affect him so deeply. But of course there were other factors, the instantaneous attraction to her that had afflicted him at the moment of meeting her, and their proximity in this little flat, where her bedroom door was only twenty paces from his, and the whole potent master-pupil entanglement that had given her such a powerful role in his lonely life here in the city of the sorcerers. He began to wonder whether she had worked some sorcery on him herself as a sort of amusement, capriciously casting a little lust-spell over him so that she could watch him squirm, and then deliberately flaunting her nakedness at him that way. He doubted it, but, then, he knew very little about what she was really like, and perhaps—how could he say?—there was some component of malice in her character, something in her that drew pleasure from tormenting a poor fish like Gannin Thidrich who had been cast up on her shore. He doubted it, but he had encountered such women before, and the possibility always was there.

He was making great progress in his studies. He had learned now how to summon minor demons, how to prepare tinctures that enhanced virility, how to employ the eyebrow of the sun, how to test for the purity of gold and silver by the laying on of hands, how to interpret weather omens, and much more. His head was swimming with his new knowledge. But also he remained dazzled by the curious sort of beauty that he saw in her, by the closeness in which they lived in the little flat, by the memory of that one luminous encounter in the dawn. And when in the fourth week it seemed to him that her usual coolness toward him was softening—she smiled at him once in a while, now, she showed obvious delight at his growing skill in the art, she even asked him a thing or two about his life before coming to Triggoin—he finally mistook diminished indifference for actual warmth and, at the end of one morning's lesson, abruptly blurted out a confession of his love for her.

An ominous red glow appeared on her pale cheeks. Her dark eyes flashed tempestuously. "Don't ruin everything," she warned him. "It is all going very well as it is. I advise you to forget that you ever said such a thing to me."

"How can I? Thoughts of you possess me day and night!"

"Control them, then. I don't want to hear any more about them. And if you try to lay a finger on me I'll turn you into a sandroach, believe me."

He doubted that she really meant that. But he abided by her warning for the next eight days, not wanting to jeopardize the continuation of his course of studies. Then, in the course of carrying out an assignment she had given him in the casting of auguries, Gannin Thidrich inscribed her name and his in the proper places in the spell, inquired as to the likelihood of a satisfactory consummation of desire, and received what he understood to be a positive prognostication. This inflamed him so intensely with joy that when Halabant came into the room a moment later Gannin Thidrich impulsively seized her and pulled her close to him, pressed his cheek against hers, and frantically fondled her from shoulder to thigh.

She muttered six brief, harsh words of a spell unknown to him in his ear and bit his earlobe. In an instant he found himself scrabbling around amidst gigantic dust-grains on the floor. Jagged glittering motes floated about him like planets in the void. His vision had become eerily precise down almost to the microscopic level, but all color had drained from the world. When he put his hand to his cheek in shock he discovered it to be an insect's feathery claw, and the cheek itself was a hard thing of chitin. She had indeed transformed him into a sandroach.

Numb, he considered his situation. From this perspective he could no longer see her—she was somewhere miles above him, in the upper reaches of the atmosphere—nor could he make out the geography of the room, the familiar chairs and the couch, or anything else except the terrifyingly amplified details of the immensely small. Perhaps in another moment her foot would come down on him, and that would be that for Gannin Thidrich. Yet he did not truly believe that he had become a sandroach. He had mastered enough sorcery by this time to understand that that was technically impossible, that one could not pack all the neurons and synapses, the total intelligence of a human mind, into the tiny compass of an insect's head. And all those things were here with him inside the sandroach, his entire human personality, the hopes and fears and memories and fantasies of Gannin Thidrich of the Free City of Stee, who had come to Triggoin to study sorcery and was a pupil of the woman V. Halabant. So this was all an illusion. He was not really a sandroach; she had merely made him *believe* that he was. He was certain of that. That certainty was all that preserved his sanity in those first appalling moments.

Still, on an operational level there was no effective difference between thinking you were a six-legged chitin-covered creature one finger-joint in length and actually *being* such a creature. Either way, it was a horrifying condition. Gannin Thidrich could not speak out to protest against her treatment of him. He could not restore himself to human shape and height. He could not do anything at all except the things that sandroaches did. The best he could manage was to scutter in his new six-legged fashion to the safety to be found underneath the couch, where he discovered other sandroaches already in residence. He glared at them balefully, warning them to keep their distance, but their only response was an incomprehensible twitching of their feelers. Whether that was a gesture of sympathy or one of animosity, he could not tell.

The least she could have done for me, he thought, was to provide me with some way of communicating with the others of my kind, if this is to be my kind from now on.

He had never known such terror and misery. But the transformation was only temporary. Two hours later—it seemed like decades to him, sandroach time, all of it spent hiding under the couch and contemplating how he was going to pursue the purposes of his life as an insect—Gannin Thidrich was swept by a nauseating burst of dizziness and a sense that he was exploding from the thorax outward, and then he found himself restored to his previous form, lying in a clumsy sprawl in the middle of the floor. Halabant was nowhere to be seen. Cautiously he rose and moved about the room, reawakening in himself the technique of two-legged locomotion, holding his outspread fingers up before his eyes for the delight of seeing fingers again, prodding his cheeks and arms and abdomen to confirm that he was once again a creature of flesh. He was. He felt chastened and immensely relieved, even grateful to her for having relented.

They did not discuss the episode the next day, and

all reverted to as it had been between them, distant, formal, a relationship of pure pedagogy and nothing more. He remained wary of her. When, now and then, his hand would brush against hers in the course of handling some piece of apparatus, he would pull it back as if he had touched a glowing coal.

Spring now began to arrive in Triggoin. The air was softer; the trees grew green. Gannin Thidrich's desire for his instructor did not subside, in truth grew more maddeningly acute with the warming of the season, but he permitted himself no expression of it. There were further occasions when he accidentally encountered her going to and fro, naked, in the hall in earliest morning. His response each time was instantly to close his eyes and turn away, but her image lingered on his retinas and burrowed down into his brain. He could not help thinking that there was something intentional about these provocative episodes, something flirtatious, even. But he was too frightened of her to act on that supposition.

A new form of obsession now came over him, that the visitors she received every afternoon while he was away were not private pupils at all, but a lover, rather, or perhaps several lovers. Since she took care not to have her afternoon visitors arrive until he was gone, he had no way of knowing whether this was so, and it plagued him terribly to think that others, in his absence, were caressing her lovely body and enjoying her passionate kisses while he was denied everything on pain of being turned into a sandroach again.

But of course he *did* have a way of knowing what took place during those afternoons of hers. He had progressed far enough in his studies to have acquired some skill with the device known as the Far-Seeing Bowl, which allows an adept to spy from a distance. Over the span of three days he removed from Halabant's flat one of her bowls, a supply of the pink fluid that it required, and a pinch of the grayish activating powder. Also he helped himself to a small undergarment of Halabant's—its fragrance was a torment to him—from the laundry basket. These things he stored in a locker he rented in the nearby marketplace. On the fourth day, after giving himself a refresher course in the five-word spell that operated the bowl, he collected his apparatus from the locker, repaired to a tavern where he knew no one would intrude on him, set the bowl atop the garment, filled it with the pink fluid, sprinkled it with the activating powder, and uttered the five words.

It occurred to him that he might see scenes now that would shatter him forever. No matter: he had to know.

The surface of the fluid in the bowl rippled, stirred, cleared. The image of V. Halabant appeared. Gannin Thidrich caught his breath. A visitor was indeed with her: a young man, a boy, even, no more than twelve or fifteen years old. They sat chastely apart in the study. Together they pored over one of Halabant's books of sorcery. It was an utterly innocent hour. The second student came soon after: a short, squat fellow wearing coarse clothing of a provincial cut. For half an hour Halabant delivered what was probably a lecture—the bowl did not provide Gannin Thidrich with sound—while the pupil, constantly biting his lip, scribbled notes as quickly as he could. Then he left, and after a time was replaced by a sad, dreamy-looking fellow with long shaggy hair, who had brought some sort of essay or thesis for Halabant to examine. She leafed quickly through it, frequently offering what no doubt were pungent comments.

No lovers, then. Legitimate pupils, all three. Gannin Thidrich felt bitterly ashamed of having spied on her, and aghast at the possibility that she might have perceived, by means of some household surveillance spell of whose existence he knew nothing, that he had done so. But she betrayed no sign of that when he returned to the flat.

A week later, desperate once again, he purchased a love-potion in the sorcerers' marketplace—not a spell to free himself from desire, though he knew that was what he should be getting, but one that would deliver her into his arms. Halabant had sent him to the marketplace with a long list of professional supplies to buy for her—such things as elecamp, golden rue, quicksilver, brimstone, goblin-sugar, mastic, and thekka ammoniaca. The last item on the list was maltabar, and the same dealer, he knew, offered potions for the lovelorn. Rashly Gannin Thidrich purchased one. He hid it among his bundles and tried to smuggle it into the flat, but Halabant, under the pretext of offering to help him unpack, went straight to the sack that contained it, and pulled it forth. "This was nothing that I requested," she said.

"True," he said, chagrined.

"Is it what I think it is?"

Hanging his head, he admitted that it was. She tossed it angrily aside. "I'll be merciful and let myself believe that you bought this to use on someone else. But if I was the one you had in mind for it—"

"No. Never."

"Liar. Idiot."

"What can I do, Halabant? Love strikes like a thunderbolt."

"I don't remember advertising for a lover. Only for an apprentice, an assistant, a tenant."

"It's not my fault that I feel this way about you."

"Nor mine," said Halabant. "Put all such thoughts out of your mind, if you want to continue here." Then, softening, obviously moved by the dumbly adoring way in which he was staring at her, she smiled and pulled him toward her and brushed his cheek lightly with her lips. "Idiot," she said again. "Poor hopeless fool." But it seemed to him that she said it with affection.

Matters stayed strictly business between them. He hung upon every word of her lessons as though his continued survival depended on committing every syllable of her teachings to memory, filled notebook after notebook with details of spells, talismans, conjurations, and illusions, and spent endless hours rummaging through her books for amplifying detail, sometimes staying up far into the night to pursue some course of study that an incidental word or two from her had touched off. He was becoming so adept, now, that he was able to be of great service to her with her outside clientele, the perfect assistant, always knowing which devices or potions to bring her for the circumstances at hand; and he noticed that clients were coming to her more frequently now, too. He hoped that Halabant gave him at least a little credit for that too.

He was still aflame with yearning for her, of

course—there was no reason for that to go away—but he tried to burn it off with heroic outpourings of energy in his role as her housekeeper. Before coming to Triggoin, Gannin Thidrich had bothered himself no more about household work than any normal bachelor did, doing simply enough to fend off utter squalor and not going beyond that, but he cared for her little flat as he had never cared for any dwelling of his own, polishing and dusting and sweeping and scrubbing, until the place took on an astonishing glow of charm and comfort. Even the sandroaches were intimidated by his work and fled to some other apartment. It was his goal to exhaust himself so thoroughly between the intensity of his studies and the intensity of his housework that he would have no shred of vitality left over for further lustful fantasies. This did not prove to be so. Often, curling up on his mat at night after a day of virtually unending toil, he would be assailed by dazzling visions of V. Halabant, entering his weary mind like an intruding incubus, capering wantonly in his throbbing brain, gesturing lewdly to him, beckoning, offering herself, and Gannin Thidrich would lie there sobbing, soaked in sweat, praying to every demon whose invocations he knew that he be spared such agonizing visitations.

The pain became so great that he thought of seeking another teacher. He thought occasionally of suicide, too, for he knew that this was the great love of his life, doomed never to be fulfilled, and that if he went away from Halabant he was destined to roam forever celibate through the vastness of the world, finding all other women unsatisfactory after her. Some segment of his mind recognized this to be puerile romantic nonsense, but he was not able to make that the dominant segment, and he began to fear that he might actually be capable of taking his own life in some feverish attack of nonsensical frustration.

The worst of it was that she had become intermittently quite friendly toward him by this time, giving him, intentionally or otherwise, encouragement that he had become too timid to accept as genuine. Perhaps his pathetic gesture of buying that love potion had touched something in her spirit. She smiled at him frequently now, even winked, or poked him playfully in the shoulder with a finger to underscore some point in her lesson. She was shockingly casual, sometimes, about how she dressed, often choosing revealingly flimsy gowns that drove him into paroxysms of throttled desire. And yet at other times she was as cold and aloof as she had been at the beginning, criticizing him cruelly when he bungled a spell or spilled an alembic, skewering him with icy glances when he said something that struck her as foolish, reminding him over and over that he was still just a blundering novice who had years to go before he attained anything like the threshold of mastery.

So there always were limits. He was her prisoner. She could touch him whenever she chose but he feared becoming a sandroach again should he touch her, even accidentally. She could smile and wink at him but he dared not do the same. In no way did she grant him any substantial status. When he asked her to instruct him in the great spell known as the Sublime Arcanum, which held the key to many gates, her reply was simply, "That is not something for fools to play with."

There was one truly miraculous day when, after he had recited an intricate series of spells with complete accuracy and had brought off one of the most difficult effects she had ever asked him to attempt, she seized him in a sudden joyful congratulatory embrace and levitated them both to the rafters of the study. There they hovered, face to face, bosom against bosom, her eyes flashing jubilantly before him. "That was wonderful!" she cried. "How marvelously you did that! How proud I am of you!"

This is it, he thought, the delirious moment of surrender at last, and slipped his hand between their bodies to clasp her firm round breast, and pressed his lips against hers and drove his tongue deep into her mouth. Instantly she voided the spell of levitation and sent him crashing miserably to the floor, where he landed in a crumpled heap with his left leg folded up beneath him in a way that sent the fiercest pain through his entire body.

She floated gently down beside him.

"You will always be an idiot," she said, and spat, and strode out of the room.

Gannin Thidrich was determined now to put an end to his life. He understood completely that to do such a thing would be a preposterous overreaction to his situation, but he was determined not to allow mere rationality to have a voice in the decision. His existence had become unbearable and he saw no other way of winning his freedom from this impossible woman.

He brooded for days about how to go about it, whether to swallow some potion from her storeroom or to split himself open with one of the kitchen knives or simply to fling himself from the study window, but all of these seemed disagreeable to him on the esthetic level and fraught with drawbacks besides. Mainly what troubled him was the possibility that he might not fully succeed in his aim with any of them, which seemed even worse than succeeding would be.

In the end he decided to cast himself into the dark, turbulent river that ran past the edge of West Triggoin on its northern flank. He had often explored it, now that winter was over, in the course of his afternoon walks. It was wide and probably fairly deep, its flow during this period of springtime spate was rapid, and an examination of a map revealed that it would carry his body northward and westward into the grim uninhabited lands that sloped toward the distant sea. Since he was unable to swim—one did not swim in the gigantic River Stee of his native city, whose swift current swept everything and everyone willy-nilly downstream along the mighty slopes of Castle Mount—Gannin Thidrich supposed that he would sink quickly and could expect a relatively painless death.

Just to be certain, he borrowed a rope from Halabant's storeroom to tie around his legs before he threw himself in. Slinging it over his shoulder, he set out along the footpath that bordered the river's course, searching for a likely place from which to jump. The day was warm, the air sweet, the new leaves yellowish-green on every tree, springtime at its finest: what better season for saying farewell to the world?

He came to an overlook where no one else seemed to be around, knotted the rope about his ankles, and without a moment's pause for regret, sentimental

219

thoughts, or final statements of any sort, hurled himself down headlong into the water.

It was colder than he expected it to be, even on this mild day. His plummeting body cut sharply below the surface, so that his mouth and nostrils filled with water and he felt himself in the imminent presence of death, but then the natural buoyancy of the body asserted itself and despite his wishes Gannin Thidrich turned upward again, breaching the surface, emerging into the air, spluttering and gagging. An instant later he heard a splashing sound close beside him and realized that someone else had jumped in, a would-be rescuer, perhaps.

"Lunatic! Moron! What do you think you're doing?"

He knew that voice, of course. Apparently V. Halabant had followed him as he made his doleful way along the riverbank and was determined not to let him die. That realization filled him with a confused mixture of ecstasy and fury.

She was bobbing beside him. She caught him by the shoulder, spun him around to face her. There was a kind of madness in her eyes, Gannin Thidrich thought. The woman leaned close and in a tone of voice that stung like vitriol she said, *"Iaho ariaha.... aho ariaha.... bakaksikhekh! Ianian! Thatlat! Hish!"*

Gannin Thidrich felt a sense of sudden forward movement and became aware that he was swimming, actually swimming, moving downstream with powerful strokes of his entire body. Of course that was impossible. Not only were his legs tied together, but he had no idea of how to swim. And yet he was definitely in motion: he could see the riverbank changing from moment to moment, the trees lining the footpath traveling upstream as he went the other way.

There was a river otter swimming beside him, a smooth sleek beautiful creature, graceful and sinuous and strong. It took Gannin Thidrich another moment to realize that the animal was V. Halabant, and that in fact he was an otter also, that she had worked a spell on them both when she had jumped in beside them, and had turned them into a pair of magnificent aquatic beasts. His legs were gone—he had only flippers down there now, culminating in small webbed feet—and gone too was the rope with which he had hobbled himself. And he could swim. He could swim like an otter.

Ask no questions, Gannin Thidrich told himself. Swim! Swim!

Side by side they swam for what must have been miles, spurting along splendidly on the breast of the current. He had never known such joy. As a human he would have drowned long ago, but as an otter he was a superb swimmer, tireless, wondrously strong. And with Halabant next to him he was willing to swim forever: to the sea itself, even. Head down, nose foremost, narrow body fully extended, he drilled his way through the water like some animate projectile. And the otter who had been V. Halabant kept pace with him as he moved along.

Time passed and he lost all sense of who or what he was, or where, or what he was doing. He even ceased to perceive the presence of his companion. His universe was only motion, constant forward motion. He was truly a river otter now, nothing but a river otter, joyously hurling himself through the cosmos.

But then his otter senses detected a sound to his

left that no otter would be concerned with, and whatever was still human in him registered the fact that it was a cry of panic, a sharp little gasp of fear, coming from a member of his former species. He pivoted to look and saw that V. Halabant had reverted to human form and was thrashing about in what seemed to be the last stages of exhaustion. Her arms beat the air, her head tossed wildly, her eyes were rolled back in her head. She was trying to make her way to the riverbank, but she did not appear to have the strength to do it. Gannin Thidrich understood that in his jubilant onward progress he had led her too far down the river, pulling her along beyond her endurance, that as an otter he was far stronger than she and by following him she had exceeded her otter abilities and could go no farther. Perhaps she was in danger of drowning, even. Could an otter drown? But she was no longer an otter. He knew that he had to get her ashore. He swam to her side and pushed futilely against her with his river-otter nose, trying in vain to clasp her with the tiny otter flippers that had replaced his arms. Her eyes fluttered open and she stared into his, and smiled, and spoke two words, the counterspell, and Gannin Thidrich discovered that he too was in human form again. They were both naked. He found that they were close enough now to the shore that his feet were able to touch the bottom. Slipping his arm around her, just below her breasts, he tugged her along, steadily, easily, toward the nearby riverbank. He scrambled ashore, pulling her with him, and they dropped down gasping for breath at the river's edge under the warm spring sunshine.

They were far out of town, he realized, all alone in the empty but not desolate countryside. The bank was soft with mosses. Gannin Thidrich recovered his breath almost at once; Halabant took longer, but before long she too was breathing normally. Her face was flushed and mottled with signs of strain, though, and she was biting down on her lip as though trying to hold something back, something which Gannin Thidrich understood, a moment later, to be tears. Abruptly she was furiously sobbing. He held her, tried to comfort her, but she shook him off. She would not or could not look at him.

"To be so weak—" she muttered. "I was going under. I almost drowned. And to have you see it—you—*you*—"

So she was angry with herself for having shown herself, at least in this, to be inferior to him. That was ridiculous, he thought. She might be a master sorcerer and he only a novice, yes, but he was a man, nevertheless, and she a woman, and men tended to be physically stronger than women, on the average, and probably that was true among otters too. If she had displayed weakness during their wild swim, it was a forgivable weakness, which only exacerbated his love for her. He murmured words of comfort to her, and was so bold to put his arm about her shoulders, and then, suddenly, astonishingly, everything changed, she pressed her bare body against him, she clung to him, she sought his lips with a hunger that was almost frightening, she opened her legs to him, she opened everything to him, she drew him down into her body and her soul.

Afterward, when it seemed appropriate to return to the city, it was necessary to call on her resources of sorcery once more. They both were naked, and many miles downstream from where they needed to be. She seemed not to want to risk returning to the otter form again, but there were other spells of transportation at her command, and she used one that brought them instantly back to West Triggoin, where their clothing and even the rope with which Gannin Thidrich had bound himself were lying in damp heaps near the place where he had thrown himself into the river. They dressed in silence and in silence they made their way, walking several feet apart, back to her flat.

He had no idea what would happen now. Already she appeared to be retreating behind that wall of untouchability that had surrounded her since the beginning. What had taken place between them on the riverbank was irreversible, but it would not transform their strange relationship unless she permitted it to, Gannin Thidrich knew, and he wondered whether she would. He did not intend to make any new aggressive moves without some sort of guidance from her.

And indeed it appeared that she intended to pretend that nothing had occurred at all, neither his absurd suicide attempt nor her foiling of it by following him to the river and turning them into otters nor the frenzied, frenetic, almost insane coupling that had been the unexpected climax of their long swim. All was back to normal between them as soon as they were at the flat: she was the master, he was the drudge, they slept in their separate rooms, and when during the following day's lessons he bungled a spell, as even now he still sometimes did, she berated him in the usual cruel, cutting way that was the verbal equivalent of transforming him once again into a sandroach. What, then, was he left with? The taste of her on his lips, the sound of her passionate outcries in his ears, the feel of the firm ripe swells of her breasts against the palms of his hands?

On occasions over the next few days, though, he caught sight of her studying him surreptitiously out of the corner of her eye, and he was the recipient of a few not so surreptitious smiles that struck him as having genuine warmth in them, and when he ventured a smile of his own in her direction it was met with another smile instead of a scowl. But he hesitated to try any sort of follow-up maneuver. Matters still struck him as too precariously balanced between them.

Then, a week later, during their morning lesson, she said briskly, "Take down these words: *Psakerba enphnoun orgogorgoniotrian phorbai.* Do you recognize them?"

"No," said Gannin Thidrich, baffled.

"They are the opening incantation of the spell known as the Sublime Arcanum," said Halabant.

A thrill rocketed down his spine. The Sublime Arcanum at last! So she had decided to trust him with the master spell, finally, the great opener of so many gates! She no longer thought of him as a fool who could not be permitted knowledge of it.

It was a good sign, he thought. Something was changing.

Perhaps she was still trying to pretend even now that none of it had ever happened, the event by the riverbank. But it had, it had, and it was having its effect on her, however hard she might be battling against it, and he knew now that he would go on searching, forever if necessary, for the key that would unlock her a second time.

The Annals of the Eelin-Ok
Jeffrey Ford

*Jeffrey Ford is the author of five novels—Vanitas,
World Fantasy Award winner* The Physiognomy,
Memoranda, The Beyond *(the Well-Built City trilogy),
and* The Portrait of Mrs Charbuque—*and World
Fantasy Award winning short story collection* The
Fantasy Writer's Assistant and Other Stories. *His short
fiction—which has appeared in* The Magazine of
Fantasy & Science Fiction, SciFiction, Black Gate,
The Green Man, Leviathan 3, The Dark, *and a number
of year's best anthologies—has won the World Fantasy
Award and been nominated for the Hugo and Nebula
Awards. Ford's story "Creation" was reprinted in*
Fantasy: The Best of 2002. *He lives in South Jersey
with his wife and two sons, and teaches Writing and
Literature at Brookdale Community College in Mon-
mouth County, New Jersey. Upcoming are a new novel,*
The Girl in the Glass, *novella,* The Cosmology of the
Wider World, *and collection,* The Empire of Ice Cream
and Other Stories.

*The touching story of life in the margins that follows
comes from Ellen Datlow and Terri Windling's* The
Faery Reel.

When I was a child someone once told me that gnats, those miniscule winged specs that swarm in clouds about your head on summer evenings, are born, live out their entire lives, and die all in the space of a single day. A brief existence, no doubt, but briefer still are the allotted hours of that denizen of the faerie world, a Twilmish, for its life is dependent upon one of the most tenuous creations of mankind, namely, the sand castle. When a Twilmish takes up residence in one of these fanciful structures, its span of time is determined by the durability and duration of its chosen home.

Prior to the appearance of a sand castle on the beach, Twilmish exist merely as a notion; an invisible potentiality of faerie presence. In their insubstantial form, they will haunt a shoreline for centuries, biding their time, like an idea waiting to be imagined. If you've ever been to the beach in the winter after it has snowed and seen the glittering white powder rise up for a moment in a miniature twister, that's an indication of Twilmish presence. The phenomenon has something to do with the power they draw from the meeting of the earth and the sea; attraction and repulsion in a circular fashion like a dog chasing its tail. If on a perfectly sunny summer afternoon, you are walking along the shoreline during the time of the outgoing tide and suddenly enter a zone of frigid cold air no more than a few feet in breadth, again, it indicates that your beach has a Twilmish. The drop in degrees is a result of their envy of your physical form. It means one is definitely about, searching for the handy-work of industrious children.

No matter how long a Twilmish has waited for a home, no matter the degree of desire to step into the world, not just any sand castle will do. They are as shrewd and judicious in their search as your grandmother choosing a melon at the grocery, for whatever place one does decide on will, to a large extent, define its life. Once the tide has turned and the breakers roar in and destroy the castle, its inhabitant is also washed away, not returning to the form of energy to await another castle, but gone, returned physically and spiritually to Nature, as we are at the end of our long lives. So the most important prerequisite of a good castle is that it must have been created by a child or children. Too often with adults, they transfer their penchants for worry about the future and their reliance on their watches into the architecture, and the spirit of these frustrations sunders the effect of *Twilmish Time*; the phenomenon that allows those few hours between the outgoing and incoming tide to seem to this special breed of faerie folk to last as long as all our long years seem to us.

Here are a few of the other things they look for in a residence: a place wrought by children's hands and not plastic molds or metal shovels, so that there are no right angles and each inch of living space resembles the unique contours of the human imagination; a complex structure with as many rooms and tunnels, parapets, bridges, dungeons, and moats as possible; a place decorated with beautiful shells and sea glass (they prize most highly the use of blue bottle glass tumbled smooth as butter by the surf, but green is also welcome); the use of driftwood to line the roads or a pole made from a sea horse's spike flying a sea weed flag; the absence of sand crabs, those burrowing, armored nuisances that can undermine a wall or infest a dungeon; a retaining wall of modest height, encircling the entire design, to stave off the sea's hungry high-tide advances as long as possible but not block the ocean view; and a name for the place, already bestowed and carefully written with the quill of a fallen gull feather above the main gate, something like *Heart's Desire* or *Sandland* or *Castle of Dreams*, so that precious seconds of the inhabitant's life might not be taken up with this decision.

Even many of those whose life work it is to study the lineage and ways of the faerie folk are unfamiliar with the Twilmish, and no one is absolutely certain of their origin. I suppose they have been around at least as long as sand castles, and probably before, inhabiting the sand caves of Neanderthal children way back at the dawn of human history. Perhaps, in their spirit form, they had come into existence with the universe and had simply been waiting eons for sand castles to finally appear, or perhaps they are a later development in the evolution of the faerie phylum. Some believe them to be part of that special line of enchanted creatures that associate themselves with the creativity of humans, like the *monkey of the ink pot*, attracted to the work of writers, or the *painter's demon*, which plays in the bright mix of colors on an artist's pallet, resulting in never before seen hues.

Whichever and whatever the case may be, there is only one way to truly understand the nature of the Twilmish, and that is to meet one of them. So here, I will relate for you the biography of an individual of their kind. All of what follows will have taken place on the evening of a perfect summer day after you had left the beach, and will occupy the time between tides—from when you had sat down to dinner and five hours later when you laid your head upon the pillow to sleep. There seemed to you to be barely enough time to eat your chicken and potatoes, sneak your carrots to the dog beneath the table, clean up, watch your favorite TV show, draw a picture of a pirate with an eye patch and a parrot upon her shoulder, brush your teeth and kiss your parents goodnight. To understand the Twilmish, though, is to understand that in a mere moment, all can be saved or lost, an ingenious idea can be born, a kingdom can fall, love can grow, and life can discover its meaning.

Now, if I wasn't an honest fellow, I would, at this juncture, merely make up a bunch of hogwash concerning the biography of a particular Twilmish, for it is fine to note the existence of a race, but one can never really know anything of substance about a group until one has met some of its individuals. The more one meets, the deeper the understanding. There is a problem, though, in knowing anything definitive about any particular Twilmish, and that is because they are no bigger than a human thumbnail. In addition, they move more quickly than an eye-blink in order to stretch each second into a minute, each minute into an hour.

I've never been a very good liar, and as luck and circumstance would have it, there is no need for it in this situation, for out of the surf one day in 1999, on the beach at Barnegat Light, in New Jersey, a five year old girl, Chieko Quigley, found a conch shell at the shore line, whose spiral form enchanted her. She took it home and used it as a decoration on the windowsill of her room. Three years later, her cat, Madelain, knocked the shell onto the floor and from within the winding labyrinth, the opening to which she would place her ear from time to time to listen to the surf, fell an exceedingly tiny book, no bigger than ten grains of sand stuck together; its cover made of sea horse hide, its pages, dune grass. Since I am an expert on faeries and faerie lore, it was brought to me to discern whether it was a genuine artifact or a prank. The diminutive volume was subjected to electron microscopy, and what was discovered was that it was an actual journal that had once belonged to a Twilmish named Eelin-Ok.

Eelin-Ok must have had artistic aspirations as well, for on the first page is a self-portrait, a line drawing done in squid ink. He stands, perhaps on the tallest turret of his castle, obviously in an ocean breeze that lifts the long dark hair of his topknot and causes his full-length cape to billow out behind him. He is stocky, with broad shoulders, calf muscles and biceps as large around as his head. His face, homely-handsome, with its thick brow and smudge of a nose, might win no beauty contests but could inspire comfort with its look of simple honesty. The eyes are intense and seem to be intently staring at something in the distance. I can not help but think that this portrait represents the moment when Eelin-Ok realized that the chaotic force of the ocean would at some point consume himself and his castle, *While Away*.

The existence of the journal is a kind of miracle in its own right, and the writing within is priceless to the Twilmish historian. It seems our subject was a

Twilmish of few words, for between each entry it is evident that some good portion of time has passed, but taken all together they represent, as the title page suggests: *The Annals of Eelin-Ok*. So here they are, newly translated from the Twilmish by the ingenious decoding software called *Faerie-Speak* (a product of Fen & Dale Inc.), presented for the first time to the reading public.

How I Happened

I became aware of It, a place for me to be, when I was no more than a cloud, drifting like a notion in the breaker's mist. It's a frightening thing to make the decision to be born. Very little ever is what it seems until you get up close and touch it. But this castle that the giant, laughing architects created and named While Away (I do not understand their language but those are the symbols the way they were carved) with a word scratched driftwood plaque set in among the scalloped maroon cobbles of the courtyard, was like a dream come true. The two turrets, the bridge and moat, the counting room paneled with nautilus amber, the damp dungeon and secret passage, the strong retaining wall that encircled it, every sturdy inch bejeweled by beautiful blue and green and clear glass, decorated with the most delicate white shells, seemed to have leaped right out of my imagination and onto the beach in much the same way that I leaped into my body and life as Eelin-Ok. Sometimes caution must be thrown to the wind, and in this instance it was. Those first few moments were confusing what with the new feel of being, the act of breathing, the wind in my face. Some things I was born knowing, as I was born full grown, and others I only remember that I have forgotten them. The enormous red orb, sitting atop the horizon, and the immensity of the ocean, struck me deeply; their powerful beauty causing my emotions to boil over. I staggered to the edge of the lookout post on the taller turret, leaned upon the battlement and wept. "I've done it," I thought, and then a few moments later after I had dried my eyes, "Now what?"

Phargo

Upon returning from a food expedition, weighed down with a bit of crab meat dug out from a severed claw dropped by a gull and a goodly portion of jelly fish curd, I discovered a visitor in the castle. He waited for me at the front entrance, hopping around impatiently; a lively little sand flea, black as a fish eye, and hairy all over. I put down my larder and called him to me, patting his notched little head. He was full of high spirits and circled round me, barking in whispers. His antics made me smile. When I finally lifted my goods and trudged toward the entrance to the turret that held the dining hall, he followed, so I let him in and gave him a name, Phargo. He is my companion, and although he doesn't understand a word of Twilmish, I tell him everything.

Faerie Fire

Out of nowhere, came my memory of the spell to make fire—three simple words and a snapping of the fingers. I realize I have innate powers of magic and enchantment, but they are meager, and I have decided to not rely on them too often as this is a world in which one must learn to trust mainly in muscle and brain in order to survive.

Making Things

The castle is a wondrous structure, but it is my responsibility to fill it with items both useful and decorative. There is no luckier place to be left with nothing than the sea shore, for with every wave useful treasures are tossed onto the beach, and before you can collect them, another wave carries more. I made my tools from sharp shards of glass and shell, not yet worried smooth by the action of the waters. These I attached to pieces of reed and quills from bird feathers and tied tight with tough lanyards of dune grass. With these tools I made a table for the dining hall from a choice piece of driftwood, carved out a fireplace for my bedroom, created chairs and sofas from the cartilage of blue fish carcasses. I have taught Phargo the names of these tools, and the ones he can lift, he drags to me when I call for them. My bed is a mussel shell, my wash basin a metal thing discarded by the giant, laughing architects, on the back of which are the characters "Root Beer," and smaller, "twist off," along with an arrow following the circular curve of it (very curious), my weapon is an axe of reed handle and shark's tooth head. Making things is my joy.

The Fishing Expedition

Up the beach, the ocean has left a lake in its retreat, and it is swarming with silver fish as long as my leg. Phargo and I set sail in a small craft I burned out of a block of driftwood and rigged with a sail made from the fin of a dead Sea Robin. I took a spear and a lantern; a chip of quartz that catches the rays of the red orb and magnifies them. The glow of the prism stone drew my prey from the depths. Good thing I tied a generous length of seaweed round the spear, for my aim needed practice. Eventually, I hit the mark, and dragged aboard fish after fish, which I then bludgeoned with my axe. The boat was loaded. As we headed back to shore, a strong gust of wind caught the sail and tipped the low riding craft perilously to one side. I lost my grip on the tiller and fell overboard into the deep water. This is how I learned to swim. After much struggling and many deep, spluttering draughts of brine, Phargo whisper barking frantically from on board, I made it to safety and climbed back aboard. This, though, my friend is also how I learned to die. The feeling of the water rising around my ears, the ache in the lungs, the frantic racing of my mind, the approaching blackness, I know I will meet again on my final day.

Dune Rat

The dunes lie due north of While Away, a range of tall hills, sparsely covered with a sharp forbidding grass I use to tie up my tools. I have been to them on expeditions to cut blades of the stuff, but never ventured into their recesses, as they are vast and their winding paths like a maze. From out of this wilderness came a shaggy behemoth with needle teeth and a tail like an eel. I heard it squeal as it tried to clear the outer wall. Grabbing my spear I ran to the front gate and out along the bridge that crosses the moat. There I was able to take the shell staircase to the top of the wall. I knew that if the rat breached the wall the castle would be destroyed. As it tried to climb over, though, its back feet displaced the sand the battlement was made of and it kept slipping back. I charged headlong and drove the tip of my spear into its right eye. It screeched in agony and retreated, my weapon jutting from the oozing wound. There was no question that it was after me, a morsel of Twilmish meat, or that others would eventually come.

The Red Orb Has Drowned

The red orb has sunk into the ocean, leaving only pink and orange streaks behind in its wake. Its drowning has been gradual and it has struggled valiantly, but now darkness reigns upon the beach. Way above there are points of light that hypnotize me when I stare too long at them and reveal themselves in patterns of—a sea gull, a wave, a crab. I must be sure to gather more driftwood in order to keep the fires going, for the temperature has also slowly dropped. Some little time ago, a huge swath of pink material washed ashore. On it was a symbol belonging, I am sure, to the giant, laughing architects, a round yellow circle made into a face with eyes and a strange, unnerving smile. From this I will cut pieces and make warmer garments. Phargo sleeps more often now, but

when he is awake he still bounds about senselessly
and makes me laugh often enough. We swim like fish
through the dark.

In My Bed

I lay in my bed writing. From beyond the walls of my
castle I hear the waves coming and going in their
steady assuring rhythm, and the sound is lulling me
toward sleep. I have been wondering what the name
assigned to my home by the architects means. While
Away—if only I could understand their symbols, I
might understand more the point of my life. Yes, the
point of life is to fish and work and make things and
explore, but there are times, especially now since the
red orb has been swallowed, that I suspect there is
some secret reason for my being here. There are
moments when I wish I knew and others when I
couldn't care less. Oh, to be like Phargo, for whom
a drop of fish blood and a hopping run along the
beach is all the secret necessary. Perhaps I think too
much. There is the squeal of a bat, the call of a plover,
the sound of the wind, and they mix with the salt air
to bring me closer to sleep. When I wake, I will.........

What's This?

Something is rising out of the ocean in the east, being
born into the sky. I think it is going to be round like
the red orb, but it is creamy white. Whatever it is, I
welcome it, for it seems to cast light, not bright
enough to banish the darkness, but an enchanted light
that reflects off the water and gracefully illuminates

the beach where the shadows are not too harsh. We rode atop a giant brown armored crab with a sharp spine of a tail as it dragged itself up the beach. We dined on bass. Discovered a strange fellow on the shore of the lake. A kind of statue but not made of stone. He bobbed on the surface, composed of a slick and somewhat pliable substance. He is green from head to toe. He carries in his hands what appears to be a weapon and wears a helmet, both also green. I have dragged him back to the castle and set him up on the tall turret to act as a sentinel. Getting him up the winding staircase put my back out. I'm not as young as I used to be. With faerie magic I will give him the power of sight and speech, so that although he does not move, he can be vigilant and call out. I wish I had the power to cast a spell that would bring him fully to life, but alas, I'm only Twilmish. I have positioned him facing the north, in order to watch for rats. I call him Greenly, just to give him a name.

200 Steps

I now record the number of steps it is at this point in time from the outer wall of the castle to where the breakers flood the beach. I was spied upon in my work, for the huge white disk on the horizon has just recently shown two eyes over the brim of the ocean. Its light is dream-like, and it makes me wonder if I have really taken form or if I am still a spirit, dreaming I am not.

A Momentous Discovery

Phargo and I discovered a corked bottle upon the beach. As has become my practice, I took out my hatchet and smashed a hole in its side near the neck. Often, I have found that these vessels are filled with an intoxicating liquor that, in small doses warms the innards when the wind blows and in large doses makes me sing and dance upon the turret. Before I could venture inside, I heard a voice call out, "Help us." I was frozen in my tracks, thinking I had opened a ship of ghosts. Then, from out of the dark, back of the bottle, came a figure. Imagine my relief when I saw it was a female faerie. I am not exactly sure which branch of the folk she is from, but she is my height, dressed in a short gown woven from spider thread, and has alluring, long orange hair. She staggered forward and collapsed in my arms. Hiding behind her was a small faerie child: a boy, I think. He was frightened and sickly-looking, and said nothing but followed me when I put the woman over my shoulder and carried her home. They now rest peacefully down the hall in a makeshift bed I put together from a common clamshell and a few folds of that pink material. I am filled with questions.

The Moon

Meiwa told me the name of the white circle in the sky, which has now revealed itself completely. She said it was called the Moon, the bright specks are Stars, and the red orb was the Sun. I live in a time of darkness called the Night, and amazingly, there exists a time of brightness when the sun rules a blue sky and one can see a mile or more. All these things, I think I knew at one time before I was born into this life. She knows many things and some secrets of the giant architects. The two of them, she and her son, are Willnits, sea faring people apparently who live aboard the ships of the giants. They had fallen asleep in an empty rum bottle, thinking it was safe, but when they awoke, they found the top stopped with a cork and their haven adrift upon the ocean. Sadly enough, her husband had been killed by one of the giants, called humans, who mistook him for an insect and crushed him. I can vouch that she is expert with a fishing spear and was quite fierce in helping turn back an infestation of burrowing sand crabs in the dungeon. The boy, Magtel, is quiet but polite and seems a little worse for wear from their harrowing adventures. Only Phargo can bring a smile to him. I made him his own axe to lift his spirits.

A Small Night Bird

Meiwa has enchanted a small night bird, by attracting it with crumbs of a special bread she bakes from thin air and sea foam and then using her lovely singing voice to train it. When she mounted the back of the delicate creature and called me to join her, I will admit I was skeptical. Once upon the bird, my arms around her waist, she made a kissing noise with her lips, and we took off into the sky. My head swam as we went higher and higher and then swept along the shoreline in the light of the moon. She laughed wildly at my fear, and when we did not fall, I laughed too. She took me to a place where the giants live, in giant houscs. Through a glass pane, we saw a giant girl, drawing a colorful picture of a bird sitting upon a one eyed woman's shoulder. Then we were off, traveling miles, soaring and diving, and eventually coming to rest on the bridge moat of While Away. The bird is not the only creature who has been enchanted by Meiwa.

150 Steps

Magtel regularly accompanies me on the search for food now. When we came upon a blue claw in the throes of death, he stepped up next to me and put his hand in mine. We waited until the creature stopped moving, and then took our axes to the shell. Quite a harvest. It is now only 150 steps from the wall to the water.

Greenly Speaks

I did not hear him at first as I was sleeping so soundly, but Meiwa, lying next to me, did and pinched my nose to wake me. We ran to the top of the turret, where Greenly was still sounding the alarm, and looked north. There three shadows moved ever closer across the sand. I went and fetched my bow and arrows, my latest weapon, devised from something Meiwa had said she'd seen the humans use. I was waiting to fire until they drew closer. Meiwa had a plan, though. She called for her night bird, and we mounted its back. We attacked from the air, and the monsters never got within 50 steps of the castle. My arrows could not kill them but effectively turned them away. I would have perished without her.

While Meiwa Slept

While Meiwa slept, Magtel and I took torches, slings for carrying large objects upon the back, and our axes, and quietly left the castle. Phargo trailed after us, of course. There was a far place I had been to only one other time before. Heading west, I set a brisk pace and the boy kept up, sometimes running to stay next to me. Suddenly he started talking, telling me about a creature he had seen while living aboard the ship. "A whale," he called it. "Bigger than a hundred humans, with a mouth like a cavern." I laughed and asked him if he was certain of this. "I swear to you," he said. "It blows water from a hole on its back, a fountain that reaches to the sky." He told me the humans hunted them with spears from small boats and made from their insides lamp oil and perfume. What an imagination the child has, for it did not end with the whale, but he continued to relate to me so many unbelievable wonders as we walked along I lost track of where we were and, though I watched for danger and the path through the sand ahead, it was really inward that my vision was trained, picturing his fantastic ideas. Before this he had not said but a few words to me. After turning north at the shark skeleton, we traveled a while more and then entered the forest. Our torches pushed back the gloom, but it was mightily dark in there among the brambles and stickers. A short way in, I spotted what we had come for. Giant berries, like clusters of beads, indigo in color and sweating their sweetness. I hacked one off its vine and showed Magtel how to chop one down. We loaded them into our slings and then started back. There were a few tense moments before leaving the forest, for a long yellow snake slithered by as we stood stiller than Greenly, holding our breath. I had to keep one foot lightly on Phargo's neck to keep him from barking or hopping and giving us away. On the way home, the boy asked if I had ever been married, and then a few minutes later if I had any children. We presented the berries to Meiwa upon her waking. I will never forget the taste of them.

The Boy Has A Plan

Maglet joined Meiwa and me as we sat on the tall turret enjoying a sip of liquor from a bottle I had recently discovered on the beach. He said he knew how to protect the castle against the rats. This was his plan. Gather as much dried seaweed that has blown into clumps upon the beach, encircle the outer wall of the castle with it. When Greenly sounds the alarm, we will shoot flaming arrows into it, north, south, east and west, creating a ring of fire around us that the rats can not pass through. I thought it ingenious. Meiwa kissed him and clapped her hands. We will forthwith begin collecting the necessary seaweed. It will be a big job. My boy is gifted.

100 Steps

I don't know why I checked how far the ocean's flood could reach. 100 is a lot of steps.

We Are Ready

After a long span of hard work, we have completed the seaweed defense of the castle. The rats are nowhere in sight. I found a large round contrivance, one side metal, one glass, buried in the sand. It had a heartbeat that sounded like a tiny hammer tapping glass. With each beat, an arrow inside the glass moved ever so slightly in a course describing a circle. Meiwa told me it was called a watch, and the humans use them to mark the passage of time. Later, I returned to it and struck it with my axe until its heart stopped beating. The longer of the metal arrows, I have put in my quiver.

The Truth, Like A Wave

Magtel has fallen ill. He is too tired to get out of bed. Meiwa told me the truth. They must leave soon and find another ship, for they can not exist for too long away from one. She told me that she had used a spell to keep them alive for the duration they have been with me, but now it is weakening. I asked her why she had never told me. "Because we wanted to stay with you, at While Away, forever," she said. There were no more words. We held each other for a very long time, and I realized that my heart was a castle made of sand.

They Are Gone

In order to get Magtel well enough to take the flight out to sea on the night bird, I built a bed for him in the shape of a ship, and this simple ruse worked to get him back upon his feet. We made preparations for their departure, packing food and making warm blankets to wrap around them as they flew out across the ocean. "We will need some luck to find a ship," Meiwa told me. "The night bird is not the strongest of fliers and she will be carrying two. We may have to journey far before we can set down." "I will worry about your safety until the day I die," I told her. "No," she said, "when we find a home on the sea, I will have the bird return to you, and you will know we have survived the journey. Then write a note to me and tie it to the bird's leg and it will bring us word of you." This idea lightened my heart a little. Then it was time to say goodbye. Magtel, shark-tooth axe in hand, put his arms around my neck. "Keep me in your imagination," I told him and he said he always would. Meiwa and I kissed for the last time. They mounted the night bird. Then with that sound she made, Meiwa called the wonderful creature to action, and it lit into the sky. I ran up the steps to the top of the tall turret in time to see them circle once and call back to me. I reached for them, but they were gone, out above the ocean, crossing in front of the watchful moon.

50 Steps

It has been so long, I can't remember the last time I sat down to record things. I guess I knew this book contained memories I have worked so hard to overcome. It is just Phargo and me now, fishing, gathering food, combing the shore. The Moon has climbed high to its tallest turret and looks down now with a distant stare as if in judgment upon me. 50 steps remain between the outer wall and the tide. I record this number without trepidation or relief. I have grown somewhat slower, a little dimmer, I think. In my dreams, when I sleep, I am forever heading out across the ocean upon the night bird.

Greenly Speaks

I was just about to go fishing when I heard Greenly pipe up and call, "Intruders." I did not even go up to the turret to look first, but fetched my bow and arrows and an armful of driftwood sticks with which to build a fire. When I reached my lookout, I turned north, and sure enough, in the pale moonlight I saw the beach crawling with rats, more than a dozen.

I lit a fire right on the floor of the turret, armed my bow, and dipped the end of the arrow into the flames until it caught. One, two, three, four, I launched my flaming missiles at the ring of dry seaweed. The fire grew into a perfect circle, and some of the rats were caught in it. I could hear them scream from where I stood. Most of the rest turned back, but to the west, where one had fallen in the fire, it smothered the flame, and I saw another climb upon its carcass and keep coming for the castle. I left the taller turret and ran to the smaller one to get a better shot at the attacker. Once atop it, I fired arrow after arrow at the monster, which had cleared the retaining wall and was within the grounds of While Away. With shafts sticking out of it, blood dripping, it came ever forward, intent upon devouring me. Upon reaching the turret on which I stood, it reared back on its haunches and scrabbled at the side of the structure which started to crumble. In one last attempt to fell it, I reached for the metal arrow I had taken from the watch and loaded my bow. I was sweating profusely, out of breath, but I felt more alive in that moment than I had in a long while. My aim was true, the shaft entered its bared chest, and dug into its heart. It toppled forward, smashed the side of the turret, and then the whole structure began to fall. My last thought was, "If the fall does not kill me, I will be buried alive." That is when I lost my footing and dropped into thin air. But I did not fall, for something caught me, like a soft hand, and eased me down to safety upon the ground. It was a miracle I suppose, or maybe a bit of Meiwa's magic, but the night bird had returned. The smaller turret was completely destroyed, part of it having fallen into the courtyard. I dug that out, but the entire structure of the place was weakened by the attack and since then pieces of wall crumble off every so often and the bridge is tenuous. It took me forever to get rid of the rat carcass. I cut it up and dragged the pieces outside what remained of the retaining wall and burned them.

A Letter

The night bird stayed with me while I repaired, as best I could, the damage to the castle, but as soon as I had the chance, I sat down and wrote a note to Meiwa and Maglet, trying desperately and, in the end, ultimately failing, to tell them how much I missed them. Standing on the turret with Phargo by my side, watching the bird take off again brought back all the old feelings even stronger and I felt lost.

The Moon, The Sea, The Dark

The water laps only ten steps from the outer wall of the castle. Many things have happened since I last wrote. Once, while lying in bed, I saw, through my bedroom window, two humans, a giant female and male, walk by hand in hand. They stopped at the outer wall of the castle and spoke in booming voices. From the sound of their words, I know they were admiring my home, even in its dilapidated state. I took back the enchantment from Greenly, so he would not have the burden of sight and speech any longer; his job was finished and he had done it well. I dragged him to the lake and set him in my boat and pushed it off. Oh, how my back ached after that. If the rats come now, I will not fight them. The dungeon has been over run by sand crabs, and when I am quiet in my thoughts, I hear their constant scuttling about down below, undermining the foundation of While Away. A piece of the battlement fell away from the turret, which is not a good sign, but gives me an unobstructed view of the sea. Washed up on the beach, due east of the castle, I found the letter I had sent so long ago with the night bird. The ink had run and it was barely legible, but I knew it was the one I had written. I am tired.

The Stars Fall

I have just come in from watching the stars fall.

Dozens of them came streaking down. I smiled at the beauty of it. What does it mean?

A Visitor

I saw the lights of a ship out on the ocean and then I saw something large and white descending out of the darkness. Phargo was barking like mad, hopping every which way. I cleared my eyes to see it was a bird, a tern, and a small figure rode upon its back. It was Maglet, but no longer a boy. He was grown. I ran down from the turret, nearly tripping as I went. He met me by the bridge of the moat and we hugged for a very long time. He is now taller than I. He could only stay a little while, as that was his ship passing out at sea. I made us clam broth and we had jellyfish curd on slices of spearing. When I asked him, "Where is Mciwa?" he shook his head. "She took ill some time ago and did not recover," he said. "But she asked me to bring this to you if I should ever get the chance." I held back my tears not to ruin the reunion with the boy. "She stole it from one of the humans aboard ship and saved it for you." Here he produced a little square of paper that he began to unfold. When it was completely undone, and spread across the table, he smoothed it with his hands. "A picture of the Day," he said. There it was, the sun, bright yellow, the sky blue, a beach of pure white sand lapped by a crystal clear, turquoise ocean. When it came time for Maglet to leave, he told me he still had his axe and it had come in handy many times. He told me that there were many other Willnits aboard the big ship and it was a good community. We did not say goodbye. He patted Phargo on the head and got upon the back of the large white bird. "Thank you, Eelin-Ok," he said and then was gone. If it wasn't for the picture of Day, I'd have thought it all a dream.

The Tide Comes In

The waves have breached the outer wall and the sea floods in around the base of the castle. I have folded up the picture of Day and have it now in a pouch on a string around my neck. Phargo waits for me on the turret, from where we will watch the last seconds of While Away. Just a few more thoughts, though, before I go up to join him. When first I stepped into myself as Eelin-Ok, I worried if I had chosen well my home, but I don't think there can be any question that While Away was everything I could have asked for. So too, many times I questioned my life, but now, in this final moment, memories of Phargo's whisper bark, the thrill of battle against the rats, fishing on the lake, the face of the moon, the taste of blackberries, the wind, Greenly's earnest nature, the boy, holding my hand, flying on the night bird, lying with Meiwa in the mussel shell bed, come flooding in like the rising tide. "What does it all mean?" I have always asked. "It means you've lived a life, Eelin-Ok." I hear now the walls begin to give way. I have to hurry. I don't want to miss this.

Pat Moore
Tim Powers

*Tim Powers was born in Buffalo, New York in 1952
and graduated from California State University,
Fullerton, in 1976 where he had met fellow writers
James P. Blaylock and K.W. Jeter. Powers published
two early novels,* The Skies Discrowned *and* Epitaph
in Rust, *that year, but his first novel of interest was
an Arthurian fantasy,* The Drawing of the Dark *in
1979. It was followed by one of his best known novels,*
The Anubis Gates, *which introduced recurring character William Ashbless and won the Philip K. Dick
Award. Powers won the Dick Award again the following year for his SF novel* Dinner at Deviants Palace.
He followed this with the Mythopoeic Award-winner
The Stress of Her Regard, *the first of his major novels
to incorporate the supernatural, magic, mythology and
the "secret histories" of historical figures—in this case
Byron, Keats and Shelley.*

Powers' next novel, Last Call, *was published in 1992
and won the World Fantasy Award for Best Novel. And
was the first in a loose trilogy with* Expiration Date
and Earthquake Weather *(both Locus Award winners).
His most recent novel is* Declare, *a supernatural "secret*

history" of post-WWII British and Soviet spies, won both the World Fantasy Award and the International Horror Guild Award.

Powers has only written a handful of short stories, most of which have been collected in Night Moves and Other Stories *and* The Devils in the Details *(with James P. Blaylock). Upcoming is* Strange Itineraries, *a collection of his complete short fiction. Powers and his wife Serena live in San Bernardino, California.*

The story that follows is classic Powers, taking a skewed look at the world, the afterlife, and the likelihood of happenstance.

"Is it okay if you're one of the ten people I send the letter to," said the voice on the telephone, "or is that redundant? I don't want to screw this up. 'Ear repair' sounds horrible."

Moore exhaled smoke and put out his Marlboro in the half-inch of cold coffee in his cup. "No, Rick, don't send it to me. In fact, you're screwed—it says you have to have ten friends."

He picked up the copy he had got in the mail yesterday, spread the single sheet out flat on the kitchen table and weighted two corners with the dusty salt and pepper shakers. It had clearly been photocopied from a photocopy, and originally composed on a typewriter.

THIS HAS BEEN SENT TO YOU FOR GOOD LUCK, it read. THE ORIGINAL IS IN SAN FRANSISCO. YOU MUST SEND IT ON TO TEN FRIEND'S, WHO, YOU THINK NEED GOOD LUCK, WITHIN 24 HRS OF RECIEVING IT.

"I could use some luck," Rick went on. "Can you loan me a couple of thousand? My wife's in the hospital and we've got no insurance."

Moore paused for a moment before going on with the old joke; then, "Sure," he said, "so we won't see you at the lowball game tomorrow?"

"Oh, I've got money for *that*." Rick might have caught Moore's hesitation, for he went on quickly, without waiting for a dutiful laugh, "Mark 'n' Howard mentioned the chain-letter this morning on the radio. You're famous."

THE LUCK IS NOW SENT TO YOU—YOU WILL RECIEVE GOOD LUCK WITHIN THREE DAYS OF RECIEVING THIS, PROVIDED YOU SEND IT ON.. DO NOT SEND MONEY, SINCE LUCK HAS NO PRICE.

On a Wednesday dawn five months ago now, Moore had poured a tumbler of Popov Vodka at this table, after sitting most of the night in the emergency room at—what had been the name of the hospital in San Mateo? Not St. Lazarus, for sure—and then he had carefully lit a Virginia Slims from the orphaned pack on the counter and laid the smoldering cigarette in an ashtray beside the glass. When the untouched cigarette had burned down to the filter and gone out, he had carried the full glass and the ashtray to the back door and set them in the trash can, and then washed his hands in the kitchen sink, wondering if the little ritual had been a sufficient goodbye. Later he had thrown out the bottle of vodka and the pack of Virginia Slims too.

A YOUNG MAN IN FLORIDA GOT THE LETTER, IT WAS VERY FADED, AND HE RESOLVED TO TYPE IT AGAIN, BUT HE FORGOT. HE HAD MANY TROUBLES, INCLUDING EXPENSIVE EAR REPAIR. BUT THEN HE TYPED TEN COPY'S AND MAILED THEM, AND HE GOT A BETTER JOB.

"Where you playing today?" Rick asked.

"The Garden City in San Jose, probably," Moore said, "the six-and-twelve dollar Hold-'Em. I was just about to leave when you called."

"For sure? I could meet you there. I was going to play at the Bay on Bering, but if we were going to meet there you'd have to shave—"

"And find a clean shirt, I know. But I'll see you at Larry's game tomorrow, and we shouldn't play at the same table anyway. Go to the Bay."

"Naw, I wanted to ask you about something. So you'll be at the Garden City. You take the 280, right?"

PAT MOORE PUT OFF MAILING THE LETTER AND DIED, BUT LATER FOUND IT AGAIN AND PASSED IT ON, AND RECEIVED THREESCORE AND TEN.

"Right."

"If that crapped-out Dodge of yours can get up to freeway speed."

"It'll still be cranking along when your Saturn is a planter somewhere."

"Great, so I'll see you there," Rick said. "Hey," he added with forced joviality, "you're famous!"

DO NOT IGNORE THIS LETTER
ST LAZARUS

"Type up ten copies with your name in it, you can be famous too," Moore said, standing up and crumpling the letter. "Send one to Mark 'n' Howard. See you."

He hung up the phone and fetched his car-keys from the cluttered table by the front door. The chilly sea breeze outside was a reproach after the musty staleness of the apartment, and he was glad he'd brought his denim jacket.

He combed his hair in the rear-view mirror while the old slant-six engine of the Dodge idled in the carport, and he wondered if he would see the day when his brown hair might turn gray. He was still thirty years short of threescore and ten, and he wasn't envying the Pat Moore in the chain letter.

The first half hour of the drive down the 280 was quiet, with a Gershwin CD playing the *Concerto in F* and the pines and green meadows of the Fish and Game Refuge wheeling past on his left under the gray sky, while the pastel houses of Hillsborough and Redwood City marched across the eastern hills. The car smelled familiarly of Marlboros and Doublemint gum and engine exhaust.

Just over those hills, on the 101 overlooking the Bay, Trish had driven her Ford Grenada over an unrailed embankment at midnight, after a St. Patrick's Day party at the Bayshore Meadows. Moore was objectively sure he would drive on the 101 some day, but not yet.

Traffic was light on the 280 this morning, and in his rear-view mirror he saw the little white car surging from side to side in the lanes as it passed other vehicles. Like most modern cars, it looked to Moore like an oversized a computer mouse. He clicked up his turn signal lever and drifted over the lane-divider bumps into the right lane.

The white car—he could see the blue Chevy cross on its hood now—swooped up in the lane Moore had just left, but instead of rocketing on past him, it slowed, pacing Moore's old Dodge at sixty miles an hour.

Moore glanced to his left, wondering if he knew the driver of the Chevy—but it was a lean-faced stranger in sunglasses, looking straight at him. In the moment before Moore recognized the thing as a shotgun viewed muzzle-on, he thought the man was holding up a microphone; but instantly another person in the white car had blocked the driver—Moore glimpsed only a purple shirt and long dark hair—and then with squealing tires the White Chevy veered sharply away to the left.

Moore gripped the hard green plastic of his steering wheel and looked straight ahead; he was braced for the sound of the Chevy hitting the center-divider fence, and so he didn't jump when he heard the crash—even though the seat rocked under him and someone was now sitting in the car with him, on the passenger side against the door. For one unthinking moment he thought someone had been thrown from the Chevrolet and had landed in his car.

He focussed on the lane ahead and on holding the Dodge Dart steady between the white lines. Nobody could have come through the roof; nor the windows; nor the doors. Must have been hiding in the back seat all this time, he thought, and only now jumped over into the front. What timing. He was panting shallowly, and his ribs tingled, and he made himself take a deep breath and let it out.

He looked to his right. A dark-haired woman in a purple dress was grinning at him. Her hair hung in a neat pageboy cut, and she wasn't panting.

"I'm your guardian angel," she said. "And guess what my name is."

Moore carefully lifted his foot from the accelerator—he didn't trust himself with the brake yet—and steered the Dodge onto the dirt shoulder. When it had slowed to the point where he could hear gravel popping under the tires, he pressed the brake; the abrupt stop rocked him forward, though the woman beside him didn't shift on the old green upholstery.

"And guess what my name is," she said again.

The sweat rolling down his chest under his shirt was a sharp tang in his nostrils. "Hmm," he said, to test his voice, then he said, "You can get out of the car now."

In the front pocket of his jeans was a roll of hundred dollar bills, but his left hand was only inches away from the .38 revolver tucked into the open seam at the side of the seat. But both the woman's hands were visible on her lap, and empty.

She didn't move.

The engine was still running, shaking the car, and he could smell the hot exhaust fumes seeping up through the floor. He sighed, then reluctantly reached forward and switched off the ignition.

"I shouldn't be talking to you," the woman said in the sudden silence. "*She* told me not to. But I just now saved your life. So don't tell me to get out of the car."

It had been a purple shirt or something, and dark hair. But this was obviously not the person he'd glimpsed in the Chevy. A team, twins?

"What's your name," he asked absently. A van

whipped past on the left, and the car rocked on its shock absorbers.

"Pat Moore, same as yours," she said with evident satisfaction. He noticed that every time he glanced at her she looked away from something else to meet his eyes; as if whenever he wasn't watching her she was studying the interior of the car, or his shirt, or the freeway lanes.

"Did you—get threescore and ten?" he asked. Something more like a nervous tic than a smile was twitching his lips. "When you sent out the letter?"

"That wasn't me, that was *her*. And she hasn't got it yet. And she won't, either, if her students kill all the available Pat Moores. You're in trouble every which way, but I like you."

"Listen, when did you get into my car?"

"About ten seconds ago. What if he had backup, another car following him? You should get moving again."

Moore called up the instant's glimpse he had got of the thing in front of the driver's hand—the ring had definitely been the muzzle of a shotgun, twelve-gauge, probably a pistol-grip. And he seized on her remark about a back-up car because the thought was manageable and complete. He clanked the gearshift into PARK, and the Dodge started at the first twist of the key, and he levered it into Drive and gunned along the shoulder in a cloud of dust until he had got up enough speed to swing into the right lane between two yellow Stater Bros trucks.

He concentrated on working his way over to the fast lane, and then when he had got there, his engine roaring, he just watched the rearview mirror and the oncoming exit signs until he found a chance to make a sharp right turn across all the lanes and straight into the exit lane that swept toward the southbound 85. A couple of cars behind him honked.

He was going too fast for the curving interchange lane, his tires chirruping on the pavement, and he wrestled with the wheel and stroked the brake.

"Who's getting off behind us?" he asked sharply.

"I can't see," she said.

He darted a glance at the rearview mirror, and was pleased to see only a slow-moving old station wagon, far back.

"A station wagon," she said, though she still hadn't looked around. Maybe she had looked in the passenger-side door mirror.

He had got the car back under control by the time he merged with the southbound lanes, and then he braked, for the 85 was ending ahead, at a traffic signal by the grounds of some college.

"Is your neck hurt?" he asked. "Can't twist your head around?"

"It's not that. I can't see anything you don't see."

He tried to frame an answer to that, or a question about it, and finally just said, "I bet we could find a bar fairly readily. Around here."

"I can't drink, I don't have any ID."

"You can have a Virgin Mary," he said absently, catching a green light and turning right just short of the college. "Celery stick to stir it with." Raindrops began spotting the dust on the windshield.

"I'm not so good at touching things," she said. "I'm not actually a living person."

"Okay, see, that means what? You're a *dead* person, a ghost?"

"Yes."

Already disoriented, Moore flexed his mind to see if anything in his experience or philosophies might let him believe this; and there was nothing that did. This woman, probably a neighbor, simply knew who he was, and she had hidden in the back of his car back at the apartment parking lot. She was probably insane. It would be a mistake to get further involved with her.

"Here's a place," he said, swinging the car into a strip-mall parking lot to the right. "Pirate's Cove. We can see how well you handle peanuts or something, before you try a drink."

He parked around behind the row of stores, and the back door of the Pirate's Cove led them down a hallway stacked with boxes before they stepped through an arch into the dim bar. There were no other customers in the place at this early hour, and the long room smelled more like bleach than beer; the teenaged-looking bartender barely gave them a glance and a nod as Moore led the woman across the worn carpet and the parquet square to a table under a football poster. There were four low stools instead of chairs.

The woman couldn't remember any movies she'd ever seen, and claimed not to have heard about the war in Iraq, so when Moore walked to the bar and came back with a glass of Budweiser and a bowl of popcorn, he sat down and just stared at her. She was easier to see in the dim light from the jukebox and the neon bar-signs than she had been out in the gray daylight. He would guess that she was about thirty—though her face had no wrinkles at all, as if she had never laughed or frowned.

"You want to try the popcorn?" he asked as he unsnapped the front of his denim jacket.

"Look at it so I know where it is."

He glanced down at the bowl, and then back at her. As always, her eyes fixed on his as soon as he was looking at her. Either her pupils were fully dilated, or else her irises were black.

But he glanced down again when something thumped the table and a puff of hot salty air flicked his hair, and some popcorn kernels spun away through the air.

The popcorn still in the bowl had been flattened into little white jigsaw-puzzle pieces. The orange plastic bowl was cracked.

Her hands were still in her lap, and she was still looking at him. "I guess not, thanks."

Slowly he lifted his glass of beer and took a sip. That was a powerful raise, he thought, forcing himself not to show any astonishment—though you should have suspected a strong hand. Play carefully here.

He glanced toward the bar; but the bartender, if he had looked toward their table at all, had returned his attention to his newspaper.

"Tom Cruise," the woman said.

Moore looked back at her and after a moment raised his eyebrows.

She said, "That was a movie, wasn't it?"

"In a way." *Play carefully here.* "What did you—is something wrong with your vision?"

"I don't have any vision. No retinas. I have to use yours. I'm a ghost."

"Ah. I've never met a ghost before." He remembered a line from a Robert Frost poem: *The dead are holding something back.*

"Well, not that you could see. You can only see me because…I'm like the stamp you get on the back of your hand at Disneyland; you can't see me unless there's a black light shining on me. *She's* the black light."

"You're in her field of influence, like."

"Sure. There's probably dozens of Pat Moore ghosts in the outfield, and *she's* the whole infield. I'm the shortstop."

"Why doesn't…*she* want you to talk to me?" He never drank on days he intended to play, but he lifted his glass again.

"She doesn't want me to tell you what's going to happen." She smiled, and the smile stayed on her smooth face like the expression on a porcelain doll. "If it was up to me, I'd tell you."

He swallowed a mouthful of beer. "But."

She nodded, and at last let her smile relax. "It's not up to me. She'd kill me if I told you."

He opened his mouth to point out a logic problem with that, then sighed and said instead, "Would she know?" She just blinked at him, so he went on, "Would she know it, if you told me?"

"*Oh* yeah."

"How would she know?"

"You'd be doing things. You wouldn't be sitting here drinking a beer, for sure."

"What would I be doing?"

"I think you'd be driving to San Francisco. If I told you—if you asked—" For an instant she was gone, and then he could see her again; but she seemed two-dimensional now, like a projection on a screen—he had the feeling that if he moved to the side he would

262

just see this image of her get narrower, not see the other side of her.

"What's in San Francisco?" he asked quickly.

"Well if you asked me about Maxwell's Demon-n-n-n—"

She was perfectly motionless, and the drone of the last consonant slowly deepened in pitch to silence. Then the popcorn in the cracked bowl rattled in the same instant that she silently disappeared like the picture on a switched-off television set, leaving Moore alone at the table, his face suddenly chilly in the bar's air-conditioning. For a moment "air-conditioning" seemed to remind him of something, but he forgot it when he looked down at the popcorn—the bowl was full of brown BBs, unpopped dried corn. As he watched, each kernel slowly opened in white curls and blobs until all the popcorn was as fresh-looking and uncrushed as it had been when he had carried it to the table. There hadn't been a sound, though he caught a strong whiff of gasoline. The bowl wasn't cracked anymore.

He stood up and kicked his stool aside as he backed away from the table. She was definitely gone.

The bartender was looking at him now, but Moore hurried past him and back through the hallway to the stormy gray daylight.

What if she had backup? he thought as he fumbled the keys out of his pocket; and, *She doesn't want me to tell you what's going to happen.*

He only realized that he'd been sprinting when he scuffed to a halt on the wet asphalt beside the old white Dodge, and he was panting as he unlocked the door and yanked it open. Rain on the pavement was a steady textured hiss. He climbed in and pulled the door closed, and had rammed the key into the ignition—

—when the drumming of rain on the car roof abruptly went silent, and a voice spoke in his head: *Relax. I'm you. You're me.*

And then his mouth had opened and the words were coming out of his mouth: "We're Pat Moore, there's nothing to be afraid of." His voice belonged to someone else in this muffled silence.

His eyes were watering with the useless effort to breathe more quickly.

He knew this wasn't the Pat Moore he had been in the bar with. This was the *her* she had spoken of. A moment later the thoughts had been wiped away, leaving nothing but an insistent pressure of *all-is-well.*

Though nothing grabbed him, he found that his head was turning to the right, and with dimming vision he saw that his right hand was moving toward his face.

But *all-is-well* had for some time been a feeling that was alien to him, and he managed to resist it long enough to make his infiltrated mind form a thought —*she's crowding me out.*

And he managed to think, too, *Alive or dead, stay whole.* He reached down to the open seam in the seat before he could lose his left arm too, and he snatched up the revolver and stabbed the barrel into his open mouth. A moment later he felt the click through the steel against his teeth when he cocked the hammer back. His belly coiled icily, as if he were standing on the coping of a very high wall and looking up.

The intrusion in his mind paused, and he sensed confusion, and so he threw at it the thought, *One more step and I blow my head off.* He added, *Go ahead and call this bet, please. I've been meaning to drive the 101 for a while now.*

His throat was working to form words that he could only guess at, and then he was in control of his own breathing again, panting and huffing spit into the gun barrel. Beyond the hammer of the gun he could see the rapid distortions of rain hitting the windshield, but he still couldn't hear anything from outside the car.

The voice in his head was muted now: *I mean to help you.*

He let himself pull the gun away from his mouth, though he kept it pointed at his face, and he spoke into the wet barrel as if it were a microphone. "I don't want help," he said hoarsely.

I'm Pat Moore, and I want help.

"You want to…take over, possess me."

I want to protect you. A man tried to kill you.

"That's your pals," he said, remembering what the ghost woman had told him in the car. "Your students, trying to kill all the Pat Moores—to keep you from taking one over, I bet. Don't joggle me now." Staring down the rifled barrel, he cautiously hooked his thumb over the hammer and then pulled the trigger and eased the hammer down. "I can still do it with one pull of the trigger," he told her as he lifted his thumb away. "So you—what, you put off mailing the letter, and died?"

The letter is just my chain-mail. The only important thing about it is my name in it, and the likelihood that people will reproduce it and pass it on. Bombers evade radar by throwing clouds of tinfoil. The chain-mail is my name, scattered everywhere so that any blow directed at me is dissipated.

"So you're a ghost too."

A prepared ghost. I know how to get outside of time.

"Fine, get outside of time. What do you need me for?"

You're alive, and your name is mine, which is to say your identity is mine. I've used too much of my energy saving you, holding you. And you're the most compatible of them all—you're a Pat Moore identity squared, by marriage.

"Squared by—" He closed his eyes, and nearly lowered the gun. "Everybody called her Trish," he whispered. "Only her mother called her Pat." He couldn't feel the seat under him, and he was afraid that if he let go of the gun it would fall to the car's roof.

Her mother called her Pat.

"You can't have me." He was holding his voice steady with an effort. "I'm driving away now."

You're Pat Moore's only hope.

"You need an exorcist, not a Poker player." He could move his right arm again, and he started the engine and then switched on the windshield wipers.

Abruptly the drumming of the rain came back on, sounding loud after the long silence. She was gone.

His hands were shaking as he tucked the gun back into its pocket, but he was confident that he could get back onto the 280, even with his worn-out windshield-wipers blurring everything, and he had no intention of getting on the 101 any time soon; he had been almost entirely bluffing when he told her, *I've been meaning to drive the 101 for a while now.* But like an alcoholic who tries one drink after long abstinence, he was remembering the taste of the gun barrel in his mouth: *That was easier than I thought it would be,* he thought.

He fumbled a pack of Marlboros out of his jacket pocket and shook one out.

As soon as he had got onto the northbound 85 he became aware that the purple dress and the dark hair were blocking the passenger-side window again, and he didn't jump at all. He had wondered which way to turn on the 280, and now he steered the car into the lane that would take him back north, toward San Francisco. The grooved interchange lane gleamed with fresh rain, and he kept his speed down to forty.

"One big U-turn," he said finally, speaking around his lit cigarette. He glanced at her; she looked three-dimensional again, and she was smiling at him as cheerfully as ever.

"I'm your guardian angel," she said.

"Right, I remember. And your name's Pat Moore, same as mine. Same as everybody's, lately." He realized that he was optimistic, which surprised him; it was something like the happy confidence he had felt in dreams in which he had discovered that he could fly, and leave behind all earthbound reproaches. "I met *her,* you know. She's dead too, and she needs a living body, and so she tried to possess me."

"Yes," said Pat Moore. "That's what's going to happen. I couldn't tell you before."

He frowned. "I scared her off, by threatening to shoot myself." Reluctantly he asked, "Will she try again, do you think?"

"Sure. When you're asleep, probably, since this didn't work. She can wait a few hours; a few days, even, in a pinch. It was just because I talked to you that she switched me off and tried to do it right away, while you were still awake. *Jumped the gun*," she added, with the first laugh he had heard from her—it sounded as if she were trying to chant in a language she didn't understand.

"Ah," he said softly. "That raises the ante." He took a deep breath and let it out. "When did you…die?"

"I don't know. Some time besides now. Could you put out the cigarette? The smoke messes up my reception, I'm still partly seeing that bar, and partly a hilltop in a park somewhere."

He rolled the window down an inch and flicked the cigarette out. "Is this how you looked, when you were alive?"

She touched her hair as he glanced at her. "I don't know."

"When you were alive—did you know about movies, and current news? I mean, you don't seem to know about them now."

"I suppose I did. Don't most people?"

He was gripping the wheel hard now. "Did your mother call you Pat?"

"I suppose she did. It's my name."

Did your…friends, call you Trish?"

"I suppose they did."

I suppose, I suppose! He forced himself not to shout at her. She's dead, he reminded himself, she's probably doing the best she can.

But again he thought of the Frost line: *The dead are holding something back.*

They had passed under two gray concrete bridges,

and now he switched on his left turn signal to merge with the northbound 280. The pavement ahead of him glittered with reflected red brake lights.

"See, my wife's name was Patricia Moore," he said, trying to sound reasonable. "She died in a car crash five months ago. Well, a single-car accident. Drove off a freeway embankment. She was drunk." He remembered that the popcorn in the Pirate's Cove had momentarily smelled like spilled gasoline.

"I've been drunk."

"So has everybody. But—you might be her."

"Who?"

"My wife. Trish."

"I might be your wife."

"Tell me about Maxwell's Demon."

"I would have been married to you, you mean. We'd *really* have been Pat Moore then. Like mirrors reflecting each other."

"That's why *she* wants me, right. So what's Maxwell's Demon?"

"It's...she's dead, so she's like a smoke-ring somebody puffed out in the air, if they were smoking. Maxwell's Demon keeps her from disappearing like a smoke-ring would, it keeps her..."

"Distinct," Moore said when she didn't go on. "Even though she's got no right to be distinct anymore."

"And me. Through her."

"Can I kill him? Or make him stop sustaining her?" And you, he thought; it would stop him sustaining you. Did I stop sustaining you before? Well obviously.

Earthbound reproaches.

"It's not a him, really. It looks like a sprinkler you'd screw onto a hose, to water your yard, if it would

269

spin. It's in her house, hooked up to the air-conditioning."

"A sprinkler." He was nodding repeatedly, and he made himself stop. "Okay. Can you show me where her house is? I'm going to have to sleep sometime."

"She'd kill me."

"Pat—Trish—" Instantly he despised himself for calling her by that name. "—you're already dead."

"She can get outside of time. Ghosts aren't really in time anyway, I'm wrecking the popcorn in that bar in the future as much as in the past, it's all just cards in a circle on a table, none in front. None of it's really now or not-now. She could make me not ever—she could take my thread out of the carpet—you'd never have met me, even like this."

"Make you never have existed."

"Right. Never was any me at all."

"She wouldn't dare—Pat." Just from self-respect he couldn't bring himself to call her Trish again. "Think about it. If you never existed, then I wouldn't have married you, and so I wouldn't be the Pat Moore squared that she needs."

"If you *did* marry me. *Me,* I mean. I can't remember. Do you think you did?"

She'll take me there, if I say yes, he thought. She'll believe me if I say it. And what's to become of me, if she doesn't? That woman very nearly crowded me right out of the world five minutes ago, and I was wide awake.

The memory nauseated him.

What becomes of a soul that's pushed out of its body, he thought, as *she* means to do to me? Would there be *anything* left of *me,* even a half-wit ghost like poor Pat here?

Against his will came the thought, You always did lie to her.

"I don't know," he said finally. "The odds are against it."

There's always the 101, he told himself, and somehow the thought wasn't entirely bleak. Six chambers of it, hollow-point .38s. Fly away.

"It's possible, though, isn't it?"

He exhaled, and nodded. "It's possible, yes."

"I think I owe it to you. Some Pat Moore does. We left you alone."

"It was my fault." In a rush he added, "I was even glad you didn't leave a note." It's true, he thought. I was grateful.

"I'm glad she didn't leave a note," this Pat Moore said.

He needed to change the subject. *"You're* a ghost," he said. "Can't you make *her* never have existed?"

"No. I can't get far from real places or I'd blur away, out of focus, but she can go way up high, where you can look down on the whole carpet, and—twist out strands of it; bend somebody at right angles to *everything,* which means you're gone without a trace. And anyway, she and her students are all blocked against that kind of attack, they've got ConfigSafe."

He laughed at the analogy. "You know about computers?"

"No," she said emptily. "Did I?"

He sighed. "No, not a lot." He thought of the revolver in the seat, and then thought of something better. "You mentioned a park. You used to like Buena Vista Park. Let's stop there on the way."

Moore drove clockwise around the tall, darkly-wooded hill that was the park, while the peaked roofs and cylindrical towers of the old Victorian houses were teeth on a saw passing across the gray sky on his left. He found a parking space on the eastern curve of Buena Vista Avenue, and he got out of the car quickly to keep the Pat Moore ghost from having to open the door on her side; he remembered what she had done to the bowl of popcorn.

But she was already standing on the splashing pavement in he rain, without having opened the door. In the ashy daylight her purple dress seemed to have lost all its color, and her face was indistinct and pale; he peered at her, and he was sure the heavy raindrops were falling right through her.

He could imagine her simply dissolving on the hike up to the meadow. "Would you rather wait in the car?" he said. "I won't be long."

"Do you have a pair of binoculars?" she asked. Her voice too was frail out here in the cold.

"Yes, in the glove compartment." Cold rain was soaking his hair and leaking down inside his jacket collar, and he wanted to get moving. "Can you...*hold* them?"

"I can't hold anything. But if you take out the lens in the middle you can catch me in it, and carry me."

He stepped past her to open the passenger side door, and bent over to pop open the glove compartment, and then he knelt on the seat and dragged out his old leather-sleeved binoculars and turned them this way and that in the wobbly gray light that filtered through the windshield.

"How do I get the lens out?" he called over his shoulder.

"A screwdriver, I guess," came her voice, barely audible above the thrashing of the rain. "See the tiny screw by the eyepiece?"

"Oh. Right." He used the small blade from his pocketknife on the screw in the back of the left barrel, and then had to do the same with a similar screw on the forward side of it. The eyepiece stayed where it was, but the big forward lens fell out, exposing a metal cross on the inside; it was held down with a screw that he managed to rotate with the knife-tip—and then a triangular block of polished glass fell out into his palm.

"That's it, that's the lens," she called from outside the car.

Moore's cell phone buzzed as he was stepping backward to the pavement, and he fumbled it out of his jacket pocket and flipped it open. "Moore here," he said. He pushed the car door closed and leaned over the phone to keep the rain off it.

"Hey Pat," came Rick's voice, "I'm sitting here in your Garden City Club in San Jose, and I could be at the Bay. Where are you, man?"

The Pat Moore ghost was moving her head, and Moore looked up at her. With evident effort she was making her head swivel back and forth in a clear *no* gesture.

The warning chilled Moore. Into the phone he said, "I'm—not far, I'm at a bar off the 85. Place called the Pirate's Cove."

"Well, don't chug your beer on my account. But come over here when you can."

"You bet. I'll be out of here in five minutes." He closed the phone and dropped it back into his pocket.

"They made him call again," said the ghost. "They

273

lost track of your car after I killed the guy with the shotgun." She smiled, and her teeth seemed to be gone. "That was good, saying you were at that bar. They can tell truth from lies, and that's only twenty minutes from being true."

Guardian angel, he thought. "You killed him?"

"I think so." Her image faded, then solidified again. "Yes."

"Ah. Well—good." With his free hand he pushed the wet hair back from his forehead. "So what do I do with this?" he asked, holding up the lens.

"Hold it by the frosted sides, with the long edge of the triangle pointed at me; then look at me through the two other edges."

The glass thing was a blocky right-triangle, frosted on the sides but polished smooth and clear on the thick edges; obediently he held it up to his eye and peered through the two slanted faces of clear glass.

He could see her clearly through the lens—possibly more clearly than when he looked at her directly—but this was a mirror-image: the dark slope of the park appeared to be to the left of her.

"Now roll it over a quarter turn, like from noon to three," she said.

He rotated the lens ninety degrees—but her image in it rotated a full hundred-and-eighty degrees, so that instead of seeing her horizontal he saw her upside down.

He jumped then, for her voice was right in his ear. "Close your eyes and put the lens in your pocket."

He did as she said, and when he opened his eyes again she was gone—the wet pavement stretched empty to the curbstones and green lawns of the old houses.

"You've got me in your pocket," her voice said in his ear. "When you want me, look through the lens again and turn it back the other way."

It occurred to him that he believed her. "Okay," he said, and sprinted across the street to the narrow stone stairs that led up into the park.

His leather shoes tapped the ascending steps, and then splashed in the mud as he took the uphill path to the left. The city was gone now, hidden behind the dense overhanging boughs of pine and eucalyptus, and the rain echoed under the canopy of green leaves. The cold air was musky with the smells of mulch and pine and wet loam.

Up at the level playground lawn the swingsets were of course empty, and in fact he seemed to be the only living soul in the park today. Through gaps between the trees he could see San Francisco spread out below him on all sides, as still as a photograph under the heavy clouds.

He splashed through the gutters that were made of fragments of old marble headstones—keeping his head down, he glimpsed an incised cross filled with mud in the face of one stone, and the lone phrase "in loving memory" on another—and then he had come to the meadow with the big old oak trees he remembered.

He looked around, but there was still nobody to be seen in the cathedral space, and he hurried to the side and crouched to step in under the shaggy foliage and catch his breath.

"It's beautiful," said the voice in his ear.

"Yes," he said, and he took the lens out of his pocket. He held it up and squinted through the right-angle panels, and there was the image of her, upside-down. He rotated it counter-clockwise ninety-degrees and the image was upright, and when he moved the lens away from his eye she was standing out in the clearing.

"Look at the city some more," she said, and her voice now seemed to come from several yards away. "So I can see it again."

One last time, he thought. Maybe for both of us; it's nice that we can do it together.

"Sure." He stepped out from under the oak tree and walked back out into the rain to the middle of the clearing and looked around.

A line of trees to the north was the panhandle of Golden Gate Park, and past that he could see the stepped levels of Alta Vista Park; more distantly to the left he could just make out the green band that was the hills of the Presidio, though the two big piers of the Golden Gate Bridge were lost behind miles of rain; he turned to look southwest, where the Twin Peaks and the TV tower on Mount Sutro were vivid above the misty streets; and then far away to the east the white spike of the Transamerica Pyramid stood up from the skyline at the very edge of visibility.

"It's beautiful," she said again. "Did you come here to look at it?"

"No," he said, and he lowered his gaze to the dark mulch under the trees. Cypress, eucalyptus, pine, oak—even from out here he could see that mushrooms were clustered in patches and rings on the carpet of wet black leaves, and he walked back to the trees and then shuffled in a crouch into the aromatic dimness under the boughs.

After a couple of minutes, "Here's one," he said, stooping to pick a mushroom. Its tan cap was about two inches across, covered with a patch of white veil.

He unsnapped his denim jacket and tucked the mushroom carefully into his shirt pocket.

"What is it?" asked Pat Moore.

"I don't know," he said. "My wife was never able to tell, so she never picked it. It's either *Amanita lanei,* which is edible, or it's *Amanita phalloides,* which is fatally poisonous. You'd need a real expert to know which this is."

"What are you going to do with it?"

"I think I'm going to sandbag *her.* You want to hop back into the lens for the hike down the hill?"

He had parked the old Dodge at an alarming slant on Jones Street on the south slope of Russian Hill, and then the two of them had walked steeply uphill past close-set gates and balconies under tall sidewalk trees that grew straight up from the slanted pavements. Headlights of cars descending Jones Street reflected in white glitter on the wet trunks and curbstones, and in the wakes of the cars the tire-tracks blurred away slowly in the continuing rain.

"How are we going to get into her house?" he asked quietly.

"It'll be unlocked," said the ghost. "She's expecting you now."

He shivered. "Is she. Well I hope I'm playing a better hand than she guesses."

"Down here," said Pat, pointing at a brick-paved alley that led away to the right between the Victorian-gingerbread porches of two narrow houses.

They were in a little alley now, overhung with rose bushes and rosemary, with white-painted fences on either side. Columns of fog billowed in the breeze, and then he noticed that they were human forms—female torsos twisting transparently in the air, blank-faced children running in slow motion, hunched figures swaying heads that changed shape like water balloons.

"The outfielders," said the Pat Moore ghost.

Now Moore could hear their voices: *Goddam car—I got yer unconditional right here—excuse me, you got a problem?—He was never there for me—So I told him, you want it you come over here and take it—bless me father, I have died—*

The acid smell of wet stone was lost in the scents of tobacco and jasmine perfume and liquor and old, old sweat.

Moore bit his lip and tried to focus on the solid pavement and the fences. "Where the hell's her place?" he asked tightly.

"This gate," she said. "Maybe you'd better—"

He nodded and stepped past her; the gate latch had no padlock, and he flipped up the catch. The hinges squeaked as he swung the gate inward over flagstones and low-cut grass.

He looked up at the house the path led to. It was a one-story 1920s bungalow, painted white or gray, with green wicker chairs on the narrow porch. Lights were on behind stained glass panels in the two windows and the porch door.

"It's unlocked," said the ghost.

He turned back toward her. "Stand over by the roses there," he told her, "away from the…the outfielders. I want to take you in my pocket, okay?"

"Okay."

She drifted to the roses, and he fished the lens out of his pocket and found her image through the right-angle faces, then twisted the lens and put it back into his pocket.

He walked slowly up the path, stepping on the grass rather than on the flagstones, and stepped up to the porch.

"It's not locked, Patrick," came a woman's loud voice from inside.

He turned the glass knob and walked several paces into a high-ceilinged kitchen with a black and white tiled floor; a blonde woman in jeans and a sweatshirt sat at a Formica table by the big old refrigerator. From the next room, beyond an arch in the white-painted plaster, a steady whistling hiss provided an irritating background-noise, as if a teakettle were boiling.

The woman at the table was much more clearly visible than his guardian angel had been, almost aggressively three-dimensional—her breasts under the sweatshirt were prominent and pointed, and her nose and chin stood out perceptibly too far from her high cheekbones, and her lips were so full that they looked distinctly swollen.

A bottle of Wild Turkey bourbon stood beside three Flintstones glasses on the table, and she took it in one hand and twisted out the cork with the other. "Have a drink," she said, speaking loudly, perhaps in order to be heard over the hiss in the next room.

"I don't think I will, thanks," he said. "You're good with your hands." His jacket was dripping on the tiles, but he didn't take it off.

"I'm the solidest ghost you'll ever see."

Abruptly she stood up, knocking her chair against the refrigerator, and then she rushed past him, her Reeboks beating on the floor; and her body seemed to rotate as she went by him, as if she were swerving away from him; though her course to the door was straight. She reached out one lumpy hand and slammed the door.

She faced him again and held out her right hand. "I'm Pat Moore," she said, "and I want help."

He flexed his fingers, then cautiously held out his own hand. "I'm Pat Moore too," he said.

Her palm touched his, and though it was moving very slowly his own hand was slapped away when they touched.

"I want us to become partners," she said. Her thick lips moved in ostentatious synchronization with her words.

"Okay," he said.

Her outlines blurred for just an instant; then she said, in the same booming tone, "I want us to become one person. You'll be immortal, and—"

"Let's do it," he said.

She blinked her black eyes. "You're—agreeing to it," she said. "You're accepting it, now?"

"Yes." He cleared his throat. "That's correct."

He looked away from her and noticed a figure sitting at the table—a transparent old man in an overcoat, hardly more visible than a puff of smoke.

"Is he Maxwell's Demon?" Moore asked.

The woman smiled, baring huge teeth. "No, that's...a soliton. A poor little soliton who's lost its way. I'll show you Maxwell's Demon."

She lunged and clattered into the next room, and Moore followed her, trying simultaneously not to slip on the floor and to keep an eye on her and on the misty old man.

He stepped into a parlor, and the hissing noise was louder in here. Carved dark wood tables and chairs and a modern exercise bicycle had been pushed against a curtained bay window in the far wall, and a vast carpet had been rolled back from the dusty hardwood floor and humped against the chair-legs. In the high corners of the room and along the fluted top of the window frame, things like translucent cheerleaders' pom-poms grimaced and waved tentacles or locks of hair in the agitated air. Moore warily took a step away from them.

"Look over here," said the alarming woman.

In the near wall an air-conditioning panel had been taken apart, and a red rubber hose hung from its machinery and was connected into the side of a length of steel pipe that lay on a TV table. Nozzles on either end of the pipe were making the loud whistling sound.

Moore looked more closely at it. It was apparently two sections of pipe, one about eight inches long and the other about four, connected together by a blocky fitting where the hose was attached, and a stove stopcock stood half-open near the end of the longer pipe.

"Feel the air," the woman said.

Moore cupped a hand near the end of the longer pipe, and then yanked it back—the air blasting out of it felt hot enough to light a cigar. More cautiously he waved his fingers over the nozzle at the end of the short pipe; and then he rolled his hand in the air-jet, for it was icy cold.

"*It's* not supernatural," she boomed, "even though the air-conditioner's pumping room-temperature air. A spiral washer in the connector housing sends air spinning up the long pipe; the hot molecules spin out to the sides of the little whirlwind in there, and it's them that the stopcock lets out. The cold molecules fall into a smaller whirlwind inside the big one, and they move the opposite way and come out at the end of the short pipe. Room-temperature air is a mix of hot and cold molecules, and this device separates them out."

"Okay," said Moore. He spoke levelly, but he was wishing he had brought his gun along from the car. It occurred to him that it was a rifled pipe that things usually come spinning out of, but which he had been ready to dive into. He wondered if the gills under the cap of the mushroom in his pocket were curved in a spiral.

"But this is counter-entropy," she said, smiling again. "A Scottish physicist named Maxwell p-postu-lay-postul—guessed that a Demon would be needed to sort the hot molecules from the cold ones. If the Demon is present, the effect occurs, and vice versa—if you can make the effect occur you've summoned the Demon. Get the effect, and the cause has no choice but to be present." She thumped her chest, though her peculiar breasts didn't move at all. "And once the Demon is present, he—he—"

She paused, so Moore said, "Maintains distinctions that wouldn't ordinarily stay distinct." His heart was pounding, but he was pleased with how steady his voice was.

Something like an invisible hand struck him solidly in the chest, and he stepped back.

"You don't touch it," she said. Again there was an invisible thump against his chest. "Back to the kitchen."

The soliton old man, hardly visible in the bright overhead light, was still nodding in one of the chairs at the table.

The blonde woman was slapping the wall, and then a white-painted cabinet, but when Moore looked toward her she grabbed the knob on one of the cabinet drawers and yanked it open.

"You need to come over here," she said, "and look in the drawer."

After the things he'd seen in the high corners of the parlor, Moore was cautious; he leaned over and peered into the drawer—but it contained only a stack of typing paper, a felt-tip laundry-marking pen, and half a dozen yo-yos.

As he watched, she reached past him and snatched out a sheet of paper and the laundry-marker; and it occurred to him that she hadn't been able to see the contents of the drawer until he was looking at them.

I don't have any vision, his guardian angel had said. *No retinas. I have to use yours.*

The woman had stepped away from the cabinet now. "I was prepared, see," she said, loudly enough to be heard out on Jones Street, "for my stupid students killing me. I knew they might. We were all working to learn how to transcend time, but I got there first, and they were afraid of what I would do. So *boom-boom-boom* for Mistress Moore. But I had already set up the Demon, and I had Xeroxed my chain-mail and put it in addressed envelopes. Bales of them, the stamps cost me a fortune. I came back strong. And I'm going to merge with you now and get a real body again. You accepted the proposal—you said 'Yes, that's correct'—you didn't put out another bet this time to chase me away."

The cap flew off the laundry-marker, and then she had slapped the paper down on the table next to the Wild Turkey bottle. "Watch me!" she said, and when he looked at the piece of paper, she began vigorously writing on it. Soon she had written PAT in big sprawling letters and was embarked on MOORE.

She straightened up when it was finished. "Now," she said, her black eyes glittering with hunger, "you cut your hand and write with your blood, tracing over the letters. Our name is us, and we'll merge. Smooth as silk through a goose."

Moore slowly dug the pocketknife out of his pants pocket. "This is new," he said. "you didn't do this name-in-blood business when you tried to take me in the car."

She waved one big hand dismissively. "I thought I could sneak up on you. You resisted me, though—you'd probably have tried to resist me even in your sleep. But since you're accepting the inevitable now, we can do a proper contract, in ink and blood. Cut, cut!"

"Okay," he said, and unfolded the short blade and cut a nick in his right forefinger. *"You've* made a new bet now, though, and it's to me." Blood was dripping from the cut, and he dragged his finger over the *P* in her crude signature.

He had to pause halfway through and probe again with the blade-tip to get more freely-flowing blood; and as he was painfully tracing the R in *Moore,* he began to feel another will helping his hand to push his finger along, and he heard a faint drone like a radio carrier-wave starting up in his head. Somewhere he was crouched on his toes on a narrow, outward-tilting ledge with no handholds anywhere, with vast volumes of emptiness below him—and his toes were sliding—

So he added quickly, "And I raise back at you."

By touch alone, looking up at the high ceiling, he pulled the mushroom out of his shirt pocket and popped it into his mouth and bit down on it. Check-and-raise, he thought. Sandbagged. Then he lowered his eyes, and in an instant her gaze was locked onto his.

"What happened?" she demanded, and Moore could hear the three syllables of it chug in his own throat. "What did you do?"

"Amanita," said the smoky old man at the table. His voice sounded like nothing organic—more like sandpaper on metal. "It was time to eat the mushroom."

Moore had resolutely chewed the thing up, his teeth grating on bits of dirt. It had the cold-water taste of ordinary mushrooms, and as he forced himself to swallow it he forlornly hoped, in spite of all his bravura thoughts about the 101 freeway, that it might be the *lanei* rather than the deadly *phalloides*.

"He ate a mushroom?" the woman demanded of the old man. "You never told me about any mushroom! Is it a poisonous mushroom?"

"I don't know," came the rasping voice again. "It's either poisonous or not, though, I remember that much."

Moore was dizzy with the first twinges of comprehension of what he had done. "Fifty-fifty chance," he said tightly. "The Death-Cap Amanita looks just like another one that's harmless, both grow locally. I picked this one today, and I don't know which it was. If it's the poison one, we won't know for about twenty-four hours, maybe longer."

The drone in Moore's head grew suddenly louder, then faded until it was imperceptible. "You're telling the truth," she said. She flung out an arm toward the back porch, and for a moment her bony forefinger was a foot long. "Go vomit it up, now!"

He twitched, like someone mistaking the green left-turn arrow for the green light. No, he told himself, clenching his fists to conceal any trembling. Fifty-fifty is better than zero. You've clocked the odds and placed your bet. Trust yourself.

"No good," he said. "The smallest particle will do the job, if it's the poisonous one. Enough's probably been absorbed already. That's why I chose it." This was a bluff, or a guess, anyway, but this time she didn't scan his mind.

He was tense, but a grin was twitching at his lips. He nodded toward the old man and asked her, "Who *is* the lost Sultan, anyway?"

"Soliton," she snapped. "He's you, you—dumb-brain." She stamped one foot, shaking the house. "How can I take you now? And I can't wait twenty-four hours just to see if I *can* take you!"

"Me? How is he me?"

"My name's Pat Moore," said the gray silhouette at the table.

"Ghosts are solitons," she said impatiently, "waves that keep moving all-in-a-piece after the living push has stopped. Forward or backward doesn't matter to them."

"I'm from the *future*," said the soliton, perhaps grinning.

Moore stared at the indistinct thing, and he had to repress an urge to run over there and tear it apart, try to set fire to it, stuff it in a drawer. And he realized that the sudden chill on his forehead wasn't from fright, as he had at first assumed, but from profound embarrassment at the thing's presence here.

"I've blown it all on you," the blonde woman said, perhaps to herself even though her voice boomed in the tall kitchen. "I don't have the...sounds like 'courses'...I don't have the energy reserves to go after another living Pat Moore *now*. You were perfect, Pat Moore squared—why did you have to be a die-hard suicide fan?"

Moore actually laughed at that—and she glared at him in the same instant that he was punched backward off his feet by the hardest invisible blow yet.

He sat down hard and slid, and his back collided with the stove; and then, though he could still see the walls and the old man's smoky legs under the table across the room and the glittering rippled glass of the windows, he was somewhere else. He could feel the square tiles under his palms, but in this other place he had no body.

In the now-remote kitchen, the blonde woman said "Drape him," and the soliton got up and drifted across the floor toward Moore, shrinking as it came so that its face was on a level with Moore's.

Its face was indistinct—pouches under the empty eyes, drink-wrinkles spilling diagonally across the cheekbones, petulant lines around the mouth—and Moore did not try to recognize himself in it.

The force that had knocked Moore down was holding him pressed against the floor and the stove, unable to crawl away, and all he could do was hold his breath as the soliton ghost swept over him like a spiderweb.

You've got a girl in your pocket, came the thing's raspy old voice in his ear.

Get away from me, Moore thought, nearly gagging.
Who get away from who?

"I can get another living Pat Moore," the blonde
woman was saying, "if I never wasted any effort on
you in the first place, if there was never a *you* for me
to notice." He heard her take a deep breath. "I can do
this."

Her knee touched his cheek, slamming his head
against the oven door. She was leaning over the top
of the stove, banging blindly at the burners and the
knobs, and then Moore heard the triple click of one
of the knobs turning, and the faint thump of the flame
coming on. He peered up and saw that she was
holding the sheet of paper with the ink and blood on
it, and then he could smell the paper burning.

Moore became aware that there was still the faintest
drone in his head only a moment before it ceased.

"Up," she said, and the ghost was a net surrounding
Moore, lifting him up off the floor and through the
intangible roof and far away from the rainy shadowed
hills of San Francisco.

He was aware that his body was still in the house,
still slumped against the stove in the kitchen, but his
soul, indistinguishable now from his ghost, was in
some vast region where *in front* and *behind* had no
meaning, where the once- apparent dichotomy
between *here* and *there* was a discarded optical illusion, where comprehension was total but didn't
depend on light or sight or perspective, and where
even *ago* and *to come* were just compass points;
everything was in stasis, for motion had been left far
behind with sequential time.

He knew that the long braids or vapor-trails that

he encompassed and which surrounded him were life-lines, stretching from births in that direction to deaths in the other—some linked to others for varying intervals, some curving alone through the non-sky—but they were more like long electrical arcs than anything substantial even by analogy; they were stretched across time and space, but at the same time they were coils too infinitesimally small to be perceived, if his perception had been by means of sight; and they were electrons in standing waves surrounding an unimaginable nucleus, which also surrounded them—the universe, apprehended here in its full volume of past and future, was one enormous and eternal atom.

But he could feel the tiles of the kitchen floor beneath his fingertips. He dragged one hand up his hip to the side-pocket of his jacket, and his fingers slipped inside and touched the triangular lens.

No, said the soliton ghost, a separate thing again.

Moore was still huddled on the floor, still touching the lens—but now he and his ghost were sitting on the other side of the room at the kitchen table, too, and the ghost was holding a deck of cards in one hand and spinning cards out with the other. It stopped when two cards lay in front of each of them. The Wild Turkey bottle was gone, and the glow from the ceiling lamp was a dimmer yellow than it had been.

"Hold 'Em," the ghost rasped. "Your whole life-line is the buy-in, and I'm going to take it away from you. You've got a tall stack there, birth to now, but I won't go all-in on you right away. I bet our first seven years—fudgsicles, our dad flying kites in the spring sunsets, the star decals in constellations on our bedroom ceiling, our mom reading the Narnia books out loud to us. Push 'em out." The air in the kitchen was summery with the pink candy smell of Bazooka gum.

Hold 'Em, thought Moore. I'll raise.

Trish killed herself, he projected at his ghost, *rather than live with us anymore. Drove her Granada over the embankment off the 101. The police said she was doing ninety, with no touch of the brake.* Again he smelled spilled gasoline—

—and so, apparently did his opponent; the pouchy-faced old ghost flickered, but came back into focus. "I make it more," said the ghost; "the next seven. Bicycles, the Albert Payson Terhune books, hiking with Joe and Ken in the oil fields, the Valentine from Teresa Thompson. Push 'em out, or forfeit."

Neither of them had looked at their cards, and Moore hoped the game wouldn't proceed to the eventual arbitrary showdown—he hoped that the frail ghost wouldn't be able to keep sustaining raises.

I can't hold anything, his guardian angel had said.

It hurt Moore, but he projected another raise at the ghost: *When we admitted we had deleted her poetry files deliberately, she said, "You're not a nice man." She was drunk, and we laughed at her when she said it, but one day after she was gone we remembered it, and then we had to pull over to the side of the road because we couldn't see through the tears to drive.*

The ghost was just a smoky sketch of a midget or a monkey now, and Moore doubted it had enough substance even to deal cards. In a faint birdlike voice it said, "The next seven. College, and our old motor-cycle, and—"

And Trish at twenty, Moore finished, grinding his teeth and thinking about the mushroom dissolving in his stomach. *We talked her into taking her first drink. Pink gin, Tanqueray with Angostura bitters. And we were pleased when she said "Where has this been all my life?"*

"All my life," whispered the ghost, and then it flicked away like a reflection in a dropped mirror.

The blonde woman was sitting there instead. "What did you have?" she boomed, nodding toward his cards.

"The winning hand," said Moore. He touched his two face-down cards. "The pot's mine—the raises got too high for him." The cards blurred away like fragments left over from a dream.

Then he hunched forward and gripped the edge of the table, for the timeless vertiginous gulf, the infinite atom of the lifelines, was a sudden pressure from outside the world, and this artificial scene had momentarily lost its depth of field.

"I can twist your thread out, even without his help," she told him. She frowned, and a vein stood out on her curved forehead, and the kitchen table resumed its cubic dimensions and the light brightened. "Even dead, I'm more potent than you are."

She whirled her massive right arm up from below the table and clanked down her elbow, with her forearm upright; her hand was open.

Put me behind her, Pat, said the Pat Moore ghost's remembered voice in his ear.

He made himself feel the floor tiles under his hand and the stove at his back, and then he pulled the triangular lens out of his pocket; and when he held it up to his eye he was able to see himself and the blonde woman at the table across the room, and the Pat Moore ghost was visible upside down behind the woman. He rotated the glass a quarter turn, and she was now upright.

He moved the lens away and blinked, and then he was gripping the edge of the table and looking across it at the blonde woman, and at her hand only a foot away from his face. The fingerprints were like comb-tracks in clay. Peripherally he could see the slim Pat Moore ghost, still in the purple dress, standing behind her.

"Arm-wrestling?" he said, raising his eyebrows. He didn't want to let go of the table, or even move—this localized perspective seemed very frail.

The woman only glared at him out of her irisless eyes. At last he leaned back in the chair and unclamped the fingers of his right hand from the table-edge; and then he shrugged and raised his right arm and set his elbow beside hers. With her free hand she picked up his pocketknife and hefted it. "When this thing hits the floor, we start." She clasped his hand, and his fingers were numbed as if with a hard impact.

Her free hand jerked, and the knife was glittering in a fantastic parabola through the air, and though he was braced all the way through his torso from his firmly planted feet, when the knife clanged against the tiles the massive power of her arm hit his palm like a falling tree.

Sweat sprang out on his forehead, and his arm was steadily bending backward—and the whole world was rotating too, narrowing, tilting away from him to spill him, all the bets he and his ghost had made, into zero.

In the car the Pat Moore ghost had told him, *She can bend somebody at right angles to everything, which means you're gone without a trace.*

We're not sitting at the kitchen table, he told himself; we're still dispersed in that vaster comprehension of the universe.

And if she rotates me ninety degrees, he was suddenly certain, I'm gone.

And then the frail Pat Moore ghost leaned in from behind the woman, and clasped her diaphanous hand around Moore's; and together they were Pat Moore squared, their lifelines linked still by their marriage, and he could feel her strong pulse in supporting counterpoint to his own.

His forearm moved like a counter-clockwise secondhand in front of his squinting eyes as the opposing pressure steadily weakened. The woman's face seemed in his straining sight to be a rubber mask with a frantic animal trapped inside it, and when only inches separated the back of her hand from the Formica tabletop, the resistance faded to nothing, and his hand was left poised empty in the air.

The world rocked back to solidity with such abruptness that he would have fallen down if he hadn't been sitting on the floor against the stove.

Over the sudden pressure-release ringing in his ears, he heard a scurrying across the tiles on the other side of the room, and a thumping on the hardwood planks in the parlor.

The Pat Moore ghost still stood across the room, beside the table; and the Wild Turkey bottle was on the table, and he was sure it had been there all along.

He reached out slowly and picked up his pocketknife. It was so cold that it stung his hand.

"Cut it," said the ghost of his wife.

"I can't cut it," he said. Barring hallucinations, his

body had hardly moved for the past five or ten minutes, but he was panting. "You'll die."

"I'm dead already, Pat. This—" She waved a hand from her shoulder to her knee, "—isn't any good. I should be gone." She smiled. "I think that was the *lanei* mushroom."

He knew she was guessing. "I'll know tomorrow."

He got to his feet, still holding the knife. The blade, he saw, was still folded out.

"Forgive me," he said awkwardly. "For everything."

She smiled, and it was almost a familiar smile. "I forgave you in mid-air. And you forgive me too."

"If you ever did anything wrong, yes."

"Oh, I did. I don't think you noticed. Cut it."

He walked back across the room to the arch that led into the parlor, and he paused when he was beside her.

"I won't come in with you," she said, "if you don't mind."

"No," he said. "I love you, Pat."

"Loved. I loved you too. That counts. Go."

He nodded and turned away from her.

Maxwell's Demon was still hissing on the TV table by the disassembled air-conditioner, and he walked to it one step at a time, not looking at the forms that twisted and whispered urgently in the high corners of the room. One seemed to be perceptibly more solid than the rest, but all of them flinched away from him.

He had to blink tears out of his eyes to see the air-hose clearly, and when he did he noticed a plain on/off toggle switch hanging from wires that were still connected to the air-conditioning unit. He cut the hose and switched off the air-conditioner, and the silence that fell then seemed to spill out of the house and across San Francisco and into the sky.

He was alone in the house.

He tried to remember the expanded, timeless perspective he had participated in, but his memory had already simplified it to a three-dimensional picture, with himself floating like a bubble in one particular place.

Which of the...jet-trails or arcs or coils was mine? he wondered now. How long is it?

I'll be better able to guess tomorrow, he thought. At least I know it's there, forever—and even though I didn't see which one it was, I know it's linked to another.

The Angel's Daughter
Jay Lake

Prolific new author Jay Lake has published over seventy short stories since his first story "The Courtesy of Guests" appeared in late 2001. His short fiction has been published in Asimov's, Realms of Fantasy, Interzone, The Third Alternative, *and* Postscripts, *and in the anthologies* Album Zutique, Leviathan 4, *and* The Mammoth Book of Best New Horror. *His first collection,* Greetings from Lake Wu, *was published in 2003, followed by* Green Grow the Rushes-Oh, American Sorrows, *and* Dogs in the Moonlight, *all in 2004.*

Lake's story "Into the Gardens of Sweet Night" won first prize in the L. Ron Hubbard's Writers of the Future contest in 2003 and was short-listed for the Hugo Award. He won the John W. Campbell, Jr. Award for Best New Writer in 2004. With Deborah Layne he is co-editor of the World Fantasy Award-nominated "Polyphony" anthology series and is working on the anthologies All-Star Zeppelin Adventure Stories *and* TEL: Stories. *He lives in Portland, Oregon with his family and their books.*

Listen, everyone understands that an angel's merest fingernail paring is more beautiful than the fairest princess. Even the camels know that the hairs caught in an angel's brush are more lovely than all the Queens of Air and Darkness. Imagine then how exquisite the angel's daughter was, born of that holy beauty to live upon this earth. If you can imagine it, so could every prince and satrap from here to Samarkand and back again.

Far away in the Western Desert, hidden among the high crests of the Dune Sea, there lies a city encircled by an alabaster wall. That wall goes down to bedrock, and rises high to the sky, so smooth not even a fly could land upon it. There is only one gate in the wall—so small that a grown man must bend nearly double to pass through it—of ebony wood secured with a great, golden lock. Inside the city there is a palace of crystal towers. In the tallest tower there lives the angel's daughter. Hidden deep inside her heart is the golden key to the lock. The prophets have declared the man who could pass the gate would have her heart, and the man who had her heart could pass the gate.

Suitors both great and powerful came to the alabaster city. They marched with armies and flew on the backs of rocs. Their elephants carried teak battering rams, their soldiers drove gangs of condemned prisoners to build high ramps of sand and stone.

But the prophecies are not so easily cheated. The elephants died of thirst, and the prisoners revolted.

Teak split in the heat and the rocs came down with bird mites the size of badgers. Armies wandered under the brassy sun until the sands swallowed them up.

Clever men brought thieves, but the walls were too smooth to climb. Determined men brought miners, but the walls were too deep to delve. Wise men brought kites, but the walls were too high to overfly. One crafty prince even brought bundles of reeds on the back of a thousand porters, intending to join them with linen rags infused with gum arabic. It was his plan to pipe in water from the distant sea and make the desert around the City of the Angel's Daughter a sparkling lake, and sail onward to capture her heart. Sadly, he drowned in a rain barrel upon the back of one of his camels—the only man to die so in a desert—and his porters were eaten by lions.

One lad alone from that caravan righteously observed the daily prayers of Fajr, Maghrib, and Isha, even while being stalked. The great cats of the desert spared the lad because of his piety, and he finally reached the alabaster city with a bundle of reeds on his back and a goatskin of wine at his belt. He had seven figs and a date in his wallet, and some of his wits about him. He was small, so the gate seemed of a size to him. He was poor, and thus was used to making do. His only ambitions were to live another day and be free of foolish, prideful princes. He had achieved the latter ambition, apparently at the expense of the former.

The resourceful lad knelt at the little gate and peered through the keyhole in the golden lock. Inside the city he saw the crystal towers, small djinns of dust dancing before them. As he stared, the angel's daughter chanced to pass higher up in the towers, casting her shadow within his sight. The lad was struck dumb with the beauty of her mere silhouette on the sand. With the practicality of the poor, he also reasoned that such an exquisite creature living here in the desert must have food and water and shelter, which he might share after making a guest-offering of his mite of food and wine. Many men had tried to pass the gate, but had any man first touched her heart?

The lad took the narrow reeds from his bundle, and fitted them together with some of the late prince's gum-infused linen rags. He built a long, thin pipe of the reeds, which he carefully pushed through the golden keyhole until the first reed came to rest against the crystal tower.

Now the keyhole was shaped like a harem door, with a rounded head that the reed slipped through and a narrow slot beneath. The lad bent the reed upward, met it with his lips, and tilted his head so that with one eye he might peer through the little slot below.

He thought for a while, then began to sing. It was a simple song, beloved by his people on their stony hilltops overlooking a shallow sea. He and his sisters had sung it to their goats of the mornings. The song had no words, just sweet syllables that recalled the rising of the sun and the waking of the birds and the day's first sip of cool water. The tower began to hum in time with his song, as fine bowls will chime together on the shelf when the earth shakes. Keeping the reed pipe pressed against the crystal tower, the lad sang his song until the glass palace was filled with it, and the song multiplied a thousand-fold to echo across the Dune Sea.

And the beloved shadow again passed before his eye, which he kept trained on the keyhole slot below his reed pipe. The lad then changed his tune, singing instead a love song of his people, of assignations among the olive groves and gods like bulls chasing swan maidens, and the sweet dew of a lover's kiss. The beloved shadow withdrew at the new music, but soon came back, and seemed closer, stronger, waiting, hanging on his words. The lad changed his tune yet again, a funeral hymn that recalled the joy of living, the honeyed wine of marriage, children growing like barley in the field, and a life of sunsets shared hand-inhand.

The reed pressed hard against the crystal tower, and the Dune Sea echoed with memories of a life not yet lived, until the angel's daughter came to the ebon gate, reached inside her heart, and withdrew the key. I would like to say they lived happily forever, but who am I to know such things? Truth be told, blinding beauty can be a curse, and a clever lad might grow to be a frustrated man. But if angels can shed their feathers, perhaps an angel's daughter can step out of her beauty's shadow like a dropped cloak and walk hand-in-hand through life with her lover. With her heavenly advice, a clever lad might prosper in the shipping trade, selecting only the purest spices and the finest silks.

Sometimes, if you walk south from our little port city into the first shifting sands of the Western Desert and listen on a quiet evening, those crystal towers still echo with music. And if the wind were to blow you a bundle of reeds, or a mangy roc feather, what could you do but smile and wish the lovers well? And that is the truth.

If you don't believe me, go ask your mother why she has no shadow.

The Silver Dragon
Elizabeth A. Lynn

Elizabeth A. Lynn was born in New York in 1946. She published her first story, "We All Have to Go," in 1976. It was followed by a handful of other stories, including World Fantasy Award winner "The Woman Who Loved the Moon," most of which appear in her two short story collections, The Woman Who Loved the Moon and Other Stories *and* Tales from a Vanished Country. *Lynn's first novel,* A Different Light, *was published in 1978 and her second, fantasy* Watchtower, *was published in 1979. It was the opening volume in her best known work, "The Chronicles of Tornor," and won the World Fantasy Award for Best Novel. It was followed by* The Dancers of Arun *and* The Northern Girl. *Lynn wrote a second SF novel,* The Sardonyx Net, *in 1981 and young adult fantasy* The Silver Horse *in 1984, before stopping writing for a lengthy period. Her first novel in thirteen years,* Dragon's Winter, *was published in 1997 and began "The Crimson Dragon" series. Her latest novel is* Dragon's Treasure. *She lives in the San Francisco Bay area, teaches martial arts, and is at work on a new novel.*

The story that follows, part of Lynn's "Crimson

Dragon" series and her first story in a decade, is a deceptively simple and direct epic fantasy that proves you don't need a thousand pages to tell a wonderful tale.

This is a story of Iyadur Atani, who was master of Dragon Keep and lord of Dragon's Country a long, long time ago.

At this time, Ryoka was both the same and different than it is today. In Issho, in the west, there was peace, for the mages of Ryoka had built the great wall, the Wizards' Wall, and defended it with spells. Though the wizards were long gone, the power of their magic lingered in the towers and ramparts of the wall. The Isojai feared it, and would not storm it.

In the east, there was no peace. Chuyo was not part of Ryoka, but a separate country. The Chuyokai lords were masters of the sea. They sailed the eastern seas in black-sailed ships, landing to plunder and loot and carry off the young boys and girls to make them slaves. All along the coast of Kameni, men feared the Chuyokai pirates.

In the north, the lords of Ippa prospered. Yet, having no enemies from beyond their borders to fight, they grew bored, and impatient, and quarrelsome. They quarreled with the lords of Issho, with the Talvelai, and the Nyo, and they fought among themselves. Most quarrelsome among them was Martun Hal, lord of Serrenhold. Serrenhold, as all men know, is the smallest and most isolated of the domains of Ippa. For nothing is it praised: not for its tasty beer or its excellence of horseflesh, nor for the beauty of its women, nor the prowess of its men. Indeed, Serrenhold is notable for only one thing: its inhospitable climate. *Bitter as the winds of Serrenhold,* the folk of Ippa say.

No one knew what made Martun Hal so contentious. Perhaps it was the wind, or the will of the gods, or perhaps it was just his nature. In the ten years since he had inherited the lordship from his father Owen, he had killed one brother, exiled another, and picked fights with all his neighbors.

His greatest enmity was reserved for Roderico diCorsini of Derrenhold. There had not always been enmity between them. Indeed, he had once asked Olivia diCorsini, daughter of Roderico diCorsini, lord of Derrenhold, to marry him. But Olivia diCorsini turned him down.

"He is old. Besides, I do not love him," she told her father. "I will not wed a man I do not love."

"Love? What does love have to do with marriage?" Roderico glared at his child. She glared back. They were very alike: stubborn, and proud of it. "Pah. I suppose you *love* someone else."

"I do," said Olivia.

"And who might that be, missy?"

"Jon Torneo of Galva."

"Jon Torneo?" Roderico scowled a formidable scowl. "Jon Torneo? He's a shepherd's son! He smells of sheep fat and hay!" This, as it happened, was not true. Jon Torneo's father, Federico Torneo of Galva, did own sheep. But he could hardly be called a shepherd: he was a wool merchant, and one of the wealthiest men in the domain, who had often come to Derrenhold as Roderico diCorsini's guest.

"I don't care. I love him," Olivia said.

And the very next night she ran away from her father's house, and rode east across the countryside to Galva. To tell you what happened then would be a whole other story. But since the wedding of Olivia diCorsini and Jon Torneo, while of great import to them, is a small part of this story, suffice it to say that Olivia married Jon Torneo, and went to live with him in Galva. Do I need to tell you they were happy? They were. They had four children. The eldest—a boy, called Federico after his grandfather—was a friendly, sturdy, biddable lad. The next two were girls. They were also charming and biddable children, like their brother.

The fourth was Joanna. She was very lovely, having inherited her mother's olive skin and black, thick hair. But she was in no way biddable. She fought with her nurses, and bullied her brother. She preferred trousers to skirts, archery to sewing, and hunting dogs to dolls.

"I want to ride. I want to fight," she said.

"Women do not fight," her sisters said.

"I do," said Joanna.

And her mother, recognizing in her youngest daughter the indomitable stubbornness of her own nature, said, "Let her do as she will."

So Joanna learned to ride, and shoot, and wield a sword. By fourteen she could ride as well as any horseman in her grandfather's army. By fifteen she could outshoot all but his best archers.

"She has not the weight to make a swordsman," her father's arms-master said, "but she'll best anyone her own size in a fair fight."

"She's a hellion. No man will ever want to wed her," Roderico diCorsini said, so gloomily that it made his daughter smile. But Joanna Torneo laughed. She knew very well whom she would marry. She had seen him, shining brighter than the moon, soaring across the sky on his way to his castle in the mountains, and had vowed—this was a fifteen year old girl, remember—that Iyadur Atani, the Silver Dragon, would be her husband. That he was a changeling, older than she by twelve years, and that they had never met disturbed her not a whit.

Despite his age—he was nearly sixty—the rancor of the lord of Serrenhold toward his neighbors did not cool. The year Joanna turned five, his war band attacked and burned Ragnar Castle. The year she turned nine he stormed Voiana, the eyrie of the Red Hawks, hoping for plunder. But he found there only empty chambers, and the rushing of wind through stone.

The autumn Joanna turned fourteen, Roderico diCorsini died: shot through the heart by one of Martun Hal's archers as he led his soldiers along the crest of the western hills. His son, Ege, inherited the domain. Ege diCorsini, though not the warrior his father had been, was a capable man. His first act as lord was to send a large company of troops to patrol his western border. His next act was to invite his neighbors to a council. "For," he said, "it is past time to end this madness." Couriers were sent to Mirrinhold and Ragnar, to Voiana and to far Mako. A courier was even sent to Dragon Keep.

His councilors wondered at this. "Martun Hal has never attacked the Atani," they pointed out. "The Silver Dragon will not join us."

"I hope you are wrong," said Ege diCorsini. "We need him." He penned that invitation with his own hand. And, since Galva lay between Derrenhold and Dragon Keep, and because he loved his sister, he told the courier, whose name was Ullin March, to stop overnight at the home of Jon Torneo.

Ullin March did as he was told. He rode to Galva. He ate dinner that night with the family. After dinner, he spoke quietly with his hosts, apprising them of Ege diCorsini's plan.

"This could mean war," said Jon Torneo.

"It will mean war," Olivia diCorsini Torneo said.

The next day, Ullin March took his leave of the Torneo family, and rode east. At dusk he reached the tall stone pillar that marked the border between the diCorsini's domain and Dragon's Country. He was about to pass the marker, when a slender cloaked form leaped from behind the pillar and seized his horse's bridle.

"Dismount," said a fierce young voice, "or I will kill your horse." Steel glinted against the great artery in grey mare's neck.

Ullin March was no coward. But he valued his horse. He dismounted. The hood fell back from his assailant's face, and he saw that it was a young woman. She was lovely, with olive-colored skin and black hair, tied back behind her neck in a club.

"Who are you?" he said.

"Never mind. The letter you carry. Give it to me."

"No."

The sword tip moved from his horse's neck to his own throat. "I will kill you."

"Then kill me," Ullin March said. Then he dropped,

and rolled into her legs. But she had moved. Something hard hit him on the crown of the head.

Dazed and astonished, he drew his sword and lunged at his attacker. She slipped the blow and thrust her blade without hesitation into his arm. He staggered, and slipped to one knee. Again he was hit on the head. The blow stunned him. Blood streamed from his scalp into his eyes. His sword was torn from his grasp. Small hands darted into his shirt, and removed his courier's badge, and the letter.

"I am sorry," the girl said. "I had to do it. I will send someone to help you, I promise." He heard the noise of hoofbeats, two sets of them. Cursing, he staggered upright, knowing there was nothing he could do.

Joanna Torneo, granddaughter of Roderico diCorsini, carried her uncle's invitation to Dragon Keep. As it happened, the dragon-lord was at home when she arrived. He was in his hall when a page came running to tell him that a courier from Ege diCorsini was waiting at the gate.

"Put him in the downstairs chamber, and see to his comfort. I will come," said the lord.

"My lord, it's not a him. It's a girl."

"Indeed?" said Iyadur Atani. "See to her comfort, then." The oddity of the event roused his curiosity. In a very short time he was crossing the courtyard to the little chamber where he was wont to receive guests. Within the chamber he found a well-dressed, slightly grubby, very lovely young woman.

"My lord," she said calmly, "I am Joanna Torneo, Ege diCorsini's sister's daughter. I bear you his greetings, and a letter." She took the letter from the pocket of her shirt, and handed it to him.

Iyadur Atani read her uncle's letter.

"Do you know what this letter says?" he asked.

"It invites you to a council."

"And it assures me that the bearer, a man named Ullin March, can be trusted to answer truthfully any questions I might wish to put to him. You are not Ullin March."

"No. I took the letter from him at the border. Perhaps you would be so kind as to send someone to help him? I had to hit him."

"Why?"

"Had I not, he would not have let me take the letter."

"Why did you take the letter?"

"I wanted to meet you."

"Why?" asked Iyadur Atani.

Joanna took a deep breath. "I am going to marry you."

"Are you?" said Iyadur Atani. "Does your father know this?"

"My mother does," said Joanna. She gazed at him. He was a handsome man, fair, and very tall. His clothes, though rich, were simple; his only adornment a golden ring on the third finger of his right hand. It was fashioned in the shape of a sleeping dragon. His gaze was very direct, and his eyes burned with a blue flame. Resolute men, men of uncompromising courage, feared that fiery gaze.

When they emerged, first the girl, radiant despite her mud-stained clothes, and then the lord of the Keep, it was evident to all his household that their habitually reserved lord was unusually, remarkably happy.

"This is the lady Joanna Torneo of Galva, soon to

be my wife," he said. "Take care of her." He lifted the girl's hand to his lips.

That afternoon he wrote two letters. The first went to Olivia Torneo, assuring her that her beloved daughter was safe in Dragon Keep. The second was to Ege diCorsini. Both letters made their recipients very glad indeed. An exchange of letters followed: from Olivia Torneo to her headstrong daughter, and from Ege diCorsini to the lord of the Keep. Couriers wore ruts in the road from Dragon Keep to Galva, and from Dragon Keep to Derrenhold.

The council was held in the great hall of Derrenhold. Ferris Wulf, lord of Mirrinhold, a doughty warrior, was there, with his captains; so was Aurelio Ragnarin of Ragnar Castle, and Rudolf diMako, whose cavalry was the finest in Ippa. Even Jamis Delamico, matriarch of the Red Hawk clan, had come, accompanied by six dark-haired, dark-eyed women who looked exactly like her. She did not introduce them: no one knew if they were her sisters, or her daughters. Iyadur Atani was not present.

Ege diCorsini spoke first.

"My lords, honored friends," he said, "for nineteen years, since the old lord of Serrenhold died, Martun Hal and his troops have prowled the borders of our territories, snapping and biting like a pack of hungry dogs. His people starve, and groan beneath their taxes. He has attacked Mirrinhold, and Ragnar, and Voiana. Two years ago, my lord of Mirrinhold, his archers killed your son. Last year they killed my father.

My lords and captains, nineteen years is too long. It is time to muzzle the dogs." The lesser captains shouted. Ege diCorsini went on. "Alone, no one of us has been able to prevail against Martun Hal's aggression. I suggest we unite our forces and attack him."

"How?" said Aurelio Ragnarin. "He hides behind his walls, and only attacks when he is sure of victory."

"We must go to him, and attack him where he lives."

The leaders looked at one another, and then at diCorsini as if he had lost his mind. Ferris Wulf said, "Serrenhold is unassailable."

"How do you know?" Ege diCorsini said. "For nineteen years no one has attacked it."

"You have a plan," said Jamis Delamico.

"I do." And Ege diCorsini explained to the lords of Ippa exactly how he planned to defeat Martun Hal.

At the end of his speech, Ferris Wulf said, "You are sure of this?"

"I am."

"I am with you."

"And I," said Aurelio Ragnarin.

"My sisters and my daughters will follow you," Jamis Delamico said.

Rudolf diMako stuck his thumbs in his belt. "Martun Hal has stayed well clear of my domain. But I see that he needs to be taught a lesson. My army is yours to command."

Solitasry in his fortress, Martun Hal heard through his spies of his enemies' machinations. He summoned his captains to his side. "Gather the troops," he ordered. "We must prepare to defend our borders.

Go," he told his spies. "Watch the highways. Tell me when they come."

Sooner than he expected, the spies returned. "My lord, they come."

"What are their forces?"

"They are a hundred mounted men, and six hundred foot."

"Archers?"

"About a hundred."

"Have they brought a ram?"

"Yes, my lord."

"Ladders? Ropes? Catapults?"

"They have ladders and ropes. No catapults, my lord."

"Pah. They are fools, and over-confident. Their horses will do them no good here. Do they think to leap over Serrenhold's walls? We have three hundred archers, and a thousand foot soldiers," Martun Hal said. His spirits rose. "Let them come. They will lose."

The morning of the battle was clear and cold. Frost hardened the ground. A bitter wind blew across the mountain peaks. The forces of the lords of Ippa advanced steadily upon Serrenhold Castle. On the ramparts of the castle, archers strung their bows. They were unafraid, for their forces outnumbered the attackers, and besides, no one had ever besieged Serrenhold, and won. Behind the castle gates, the Serrenhold army waited. The swordsmen drew their swords and taunted their foes: "Run, dogs! Run, rabbits! Run, little boys! Go home to your mothers!"

The attackers advanced. Ege diCorsini called to the defenders, "Surrender, and you will live. Fight, and you will die."

"We will not surrender," the guard captain said.

"As you wish," diCorsini said. He signaled to his trumpeter. The trumpeter lifted his horn to his lips and blew a sharp trill. Yelling, the attackers charged. Despite the rain of arrows coming from the castle walls, a valiant band of men from Ragnar Castle scaled the walls, and leaped into the courtyard. Back to back, they fought their way slowly toward the gates. Screaming out of the sky, a flock of hawks flew at the faces of the amazed archers. The rain of arrows faltered.

A second group of men smashed its way through a postern gate, and battled in the courtyard with Martun Hal's men. Ferris Wulf said to Ege diCorsini, "They weaken. But still they outnumber us. We are losing too many men. Call him."

"Not yet," Ege diCorsini said. He signaled. Men brought the ram up. Again and again they hurled it at the gates. But the gates held. The men in the courtyard fought, and died. The hawks attacked the archers, and the archers turned their bows against the birds, and shot them out of the sky. A huge red hawk swooped to earth and became Jamis Delamico.

"They are killing my sisters," she said, and her eyes glittered with rage. "Why do you wait? Call him."

"Not yet," said Ege diCorsini. "Look. We are through." The ram broke through the gate. Shouting, the attackers flung themselves at the breach, clawing at the gate with their hands. Fighting with tremendous courage, the attackers moved them back from the gates, inch by inch.

But there were indeed many more defenders. They drove the diCorsini army back, and closed the gate, and braced it with barrels and wagons and lengths of wood.

313

"Now," said Ege diCorsini. He signaled the trumpeter. The trumpeter blew again.

Then the dragon came. Huge, silver, deadly, he swooped upon the men of Serrenhold. His silver claws cut the air like scythes. He stooped his head, and his eyes glowed like fire. Fire trickled from his nostrils. He breathed upon the castle walls, and the stone hissed, and melted like snow in the sun. He roared. The sound filled the day, louder and more terrible than thunder. The archers' fingers opened, and their bows clattered to the ground. The swordsmen trembled, and their legs turned to jelly. Shouting, the men of Ippa stormed over the broken gates, and into Serrenhold. They found the lord of the castle sitting in his hall, with his sword across his lap.

"Come on," he said, rising. "I am an old man. Come and kill me."

He charged them then, hoping to force them to kill him. But though he fought fiercely, killing two of them, and wounding three more, they finally disarmed him. Bruised and bloody, but whole, Martun Hal was bound, and marched at swordpoint out of his hall to the courtyard where the lords of Ippa stood. He bowed mockingly into their unyielding faces.

"Well, my lords. I hope you are pleased with your victory. All of you together, and still it took dragonfire to defeat me."

Ferris Wulf scowled. But Ege diCorsini said, "Why should more men of Ippa die for you? Even your own people are glad the war is over."

"Is it over?"

"It is," diCorsini said firmly.

Martun Hal smiled bleakly. "Yet I live."

"Not for long," someone cried. And Ferris Wulf's

chief captain, whose home Martun Hal's men had burned, stepped forward, and set the tip of his sword against the old man's breast.

"No," said Ege diCorsini.

"Why not?" said Ferris Wulf. "He killed your father."

"Whom would you put in his place?" Ege diCorsini said. "He is Serrenhold's rightful lord. His father had three sons, but one is dead, and the other gone, who knows where. He has no children to succeed him. *I* would not reign in Serrenhold. It is a dismal place. Let him keep it. We will set a guard about his border, and restrict the number of soldiers he may have, and watch him."

"And when he dies?" said Aurelio Ragnarin.

"Then we will name his successor."

Glaring, Ferris Wulf fingered the hilt of his sword. "He should die *now*. Then we could appoint a regent. One of our own captains, someone honorable, and deserving of trust."

Ege diCorsini said, "We could do that. But that man would never have a moment's peace. *I* say, let us set a watch upon this land, so that Martun Hal may never trouble our towns and people again, and let him rot in this lifeless place."

"The Red Hawk clan will watch him," Jamis Delamico said.

And so it came to pass. Martun Hal lived. His weapons were destroyed; his war band, all but thirty men, was disbanded and scattered. He was forbidden to travel more than two miles from his castle. The lords of Ippa, feeling reasonably secure in their victory, went home to their castles, to rest and rebuild and prepare for winter.

Ege diCorsini, riding east amid his rejoicing troops, made ready to attend a wedding. He was fond of his niece. His sister had assured him that the girl was absolutely determined to wed Iyadur Atani, and as for the flame-haired, flame-eyed dragon-lord, he seemed equally anxious for the match. Remembering stories he had heard, Ege diCorsini admitted, though only to himself, that Joanna's husband was not the one he would have chosen for her. But no one had asked his opinion.

The wedding was held at Derrenhold, and attended by all the lords of Ippa, except, of course Martun Hal. Rudolf diMako attended, despite the distance, but no one was surprised; there was strong friendship between the diMako and the Atani. Jamis Delamico came. The bride was pronounced to be astonishingly beautiful, and the bride's mother almost as beautiful. The dragon-lord presented the parents of his bride with gifts: a tapestry, a mettlesome stallion and a breeding mare from the Atani stables, a sapphire pendant, a cup of beaten gold. The couple drank the wine. The priestess said the blessings.

The following morning, Olivia diCorsini Torneo said farewell to her daughter. "I will miss you. Your father will miss you. You must visit often. He is older than he was, you know."

"I will," Joanna promised. Olivia watched the last of her children ride away into the bright autumnal day. The two older girls were both wed, and Federico was not only wed but twice a father.

I don't feel like a grandmother, Olivia Torneo thought. Then she laughed at herself, and went inside to find her husband.

And so there was peace in Ippa. The folk of Derrenhold and Mirrinhold and Ragnar ceased to look over their shoulders. They left their daggers sheathed and hung their battleaxes on the walls. Men who had most of their lives fighting put aside their shields and went home, to towns and farms and wives they barely remembered. More babies were born the following summer than had been born in the previous three years put together. The midwives were run ragged trying to attend the births. Many of the boys, even in Ragnar and Mirrinhold, were named Ege, or Roderico. A few of the girls were even named Joanna.

Martun Hal heard the tidings of his enemies' good fortune, and his hatred of them deepened. Penned in his dreary fortress, he took count of his gold. Discreetly, he let it be known that the lord of Serrenhold, although beaten, was not without resources. Slowly, cautiously, some of those who had served him before his defeat crept across the border to his castle. He paid them, and sent them out again to Derrenhold and Mirrinhold, and even—cautiously—into Iyadur Atani's country.

"Watch," he said, "and when something happens, send me word."

As for Joanna Torneo Atani, she was as happy as she had known she would be. She adored her husband, and was unafraid of his changeling nature. The people of his domain had welcomed her. Her only disappointment, as the year moved from spring to summer and to the crisp cold nights of autumn again, was that she was childless.

"Every other woman in the world is having a baby," she complained to her husband. "Why can't I?"

He smiled, and drew her into the warmth of his arms. "You will."

Nearly three years after the surrender of Martun Hal, with the Hunter's Moon waning in the autumn sky, Joanna Atani received a message from her mother.

Come, it said. *Your father needs you.* She left the next morning for Galva, accompanied by her maid, and escorted by six of Dragon Keep's most experienced and competent soldiers.

"Send word if you need me," her husband said.

"I will."

The journey took two days. Outside the Galva gates, a beggar warming his hands over a scrap of fire told Joanna what she most wanted to know.

"Your father still lives, my lady. I heard it from Viksa the fruit seller an hour ago."

"Give him gold," Joanna said to her captain as she urged her horse through the gate. Word of her coming hurried before her. By the time Joanna reached her parents' home, the gate was open. Her brother stood before it.

She said, "Is he dead?"

"Not yet." He drew her inside.

Olivia diCorsini Torneo sat at her dying husband's bedside, in the chamber they had shared for twenty-nine years. She still looked young; nearly as young as the day she had left her father's house behind for good. Her dark eyes were clear, and her skin smooth. Only her lustrous thick hair was no longer dark; it was shot through with white, like lace.

She smiled at her youngest daughter, and put up her face to be kissed. "I am glad you could come," she said. "Your sisters are here." She turned back to her husband.

Joanna bent over the bed. "Papa?" she whispered. But the man in the bed, so flat and still, did not respond. A plain white cloth wound around Jon Torneo's head was the only sign of injury: otherwise, he appeared to be asleep.

"What happened?"

"An accident, a week ago. He was bringing the herd down from the high pasture when something frightened the sheep: they ran. He fell among them and was trampled. His head was hurt. He has not woken since. Phylla says there is nothing she can do." Phylla was the Torneo family physician.

Joanna said tremulously, "He always said sheep were stupid. Is he in pain?"

"Phylla says not."

That afternoon, Joanna wrote a letter to her husband, telling him what had happened. She gave it to a courier to take to Dragon Keep.

Do not come, she wrote. *There is nothing you can do. I will stay until he dies.*

One by one his children took their turns at Jon Torneo's bedside. Olivia ate her meals in the chamber, and slept in a pallet laid by the bed. Once each day she walked outside the gates, to talk to the people who thronged day and night outside the house, for Jon Torneo was much beloved. Solemn strangers came up to her weeping. Olivia, despite her own grief, spoke kindly to them all.

Joanna marveled at her mother's strength. She could not match it: she found herself weeping at night, and snapping by day at her sisters. She was even, to her shame, sick one morning.

319

A week after Joanna's arrival, Jon Torneo died. He was buried, as was proper, within three days. Ege diCorsini was there, as were the husbands of Joanna's sisters, and all of Jon Torneo's family, and half Galva, or so it seemed.

The next morning, in the privacy of the garden, Olivia Torneo said quietly to her youngest daughter, "You should go home."

"Why?" Joanna said. She was dumbstruck. "Have I offended you?" Tears rose to her eyes. "Oh Mother, I'm so sorry..."

"Idiot child," Olivia said, and put her arms around her daughter. "My treasure, you and your sisters have been a great comfort to me. But you should be with your husband at this time." Her gaze narrowed. "Joanna? Do you not know that you are pregnant?"

Joanna blinked. "What makes you—I feel fine," she said.

"Of course you do," said Olivia. "DiCorsini women never have trouble with babies."

Phylla confirmed that Joanna was indeed pregnant. "You are sure?"

"Yes. Your baby will be born in the spring."

"Is it a boy or a girl?" Joanna asked.

But Phylla could not tell her that.

So Joanna Atani said farewell to her family, and, with her escort about her, departed Galva for the journey to Dragon Keep. As they rode toward the hills, she marked the drifts of leaves on the ground, and the dull color on the hills, and rejoiced. The year was turning. Slipping a hand beneath her clothes, she laid her palm across her belly, hoping to feel the quickening of life in her womb. It seemed strange to be so happy, so soon after her father's untimely death.

Twenty-one days after the departure of his wife from Dragon Keep, Iyadur Atani called one of his men to his side.

"Go to Galva, to the house of Jon Torneo," he said. "Find out what is happening there."

The courier rode to Galva. A light snow fell as he rode through the gates. The steward of the house escorted him to Olivia Torneo's chamber.

"My lady," he said, "I am sent from Dragon Keep to inquire after the well-being of the lady Joanna. May I speak with her?"

Olivia Torneo's face slowly lost its color. She said, "My daughter Joanna left a week ago to return to Dragon Keep. Soldiers from Dragon Keep were with her."

The courier stared. Then he said, "Get me fresh horses."

He burst through the Galva gates as though the demons of hell were on his horse's heels. He rode through the night. He reached Dragon Keep at dawn.

"He's asleep," the page warned.

"Wake him," the courier said. But the page would not. So the courier himself pushed open the door. "My lord? I am back from Galva."

The torches lit in the bedchamber.

"Come," said Iyadur Atani from the curtained bed. He drew back the curtains. The courier knelt on the rug beside the bed. He was shaking with weariness, and hunger, and also with dread,

"My lord, I bear ill news. Your lady left Galva to return home twenty days ago. Since then, no one has seen her."

Fire came into Iyadur Atani's eyes. The courier

turned his head. Rising from the bed, the dragon-lord said, "Call my captains."

The captains came. Crisply their lord told them that their lady was missing somewhere between Galva and Dragon Keep, and that it was their task, their only task, to find her. "You *will* find her," he said, and his words seemed to burn the air like flames.

"Aye, my lord," they said.

They searched across the countryside, hunting through hamlet and hut and barn, through valley and cave and ravine. They did not find Joanna Atani.

But midway between Galva and the border between the diCorsini land and Dragon's Country, they found, piled in a ditch and rudely concealed with branches, the bodies of nine men and one woman.

"Six of them we know," Bran, second-in-command of Dragon Keep's archers, reported to his lord. He named them: they were the six men who had comprised Joanna Atani's escort. "The woman is my lady Joanna's maid. My lord, we have found the tracks of many men and horses, riding hard and fast. The trail leads west."

"We shall follow it," Iyadur Atani said. "Four of you shall ride with me. The rest shall return to Dragon Keep, to await my orders."

They followed that trail for nine long days across Ippa, through bleak and stony hills, through the high reaches of Derrenhold, into Serrenhold's wild, windswept country. As they crossed the borders, a redwinged hawk swept down upon them. It landed in the snow, and became a dark-haired, dark-eyed woman in a grey cloak.

She said, "I am Madelene of the Red Hawk sisters.

I watch this land. Who are you, and what is your business here?"

The dragon-lord said, "I am Iyadur Atani. I am looking for my wife. I believe she came this way, accompanied by many men, perhaps a dozen of them, and their remounts. We have been tracking them for nine days."

"A band of ten men rode across the border from Derrenhold into Serrenhold twelve days ago," the watcher said. "They led ten spare horses. I saw no women among them."

Bran said, "Could she have been disguised? A woman with her hair cropped might look like a boy, and the lady Joanna rides as well as any man."

Madelene shrugged. "I did not see their faces."

"Then you see ill," Bran said angrily. "Is this how the Red Hawk sisters keep watch?" Hawk-changeling and archer glared at one another.

"Enough," Iyadur Atani said. He led them onto the path to the fortress. It wound upward through the rocks. Suddenly they heard the clop of horses' hooves against the stone. Four horsemen appeared on the path ahead of them.

Bran cupped his hands to his lips. "What do you want?" he shouted.

The lead rider shouted back, "It is for us to ask that! You are on our land!"

"Then speak," Bran said.

"Your badges proclaim that you come from Dragon Keep. I bear a message to Iyadur Atani from Martun Hal."

Bran waited for the dragon-lord to declare himself. When he did not, the captain said, "Tell me, and I will carry it to him."

323

"Tell Iyadur Atani," the lead rider said, "that his wife will be staying in Serrenhold for a time. If any attempt is made to find her, then she will die, slowly and in great pain. That is all." He and his fellows turned their horses, and bolted up the path.

Iyadur Atani said not a word, but the dragon rage burned white-hot upon his face. The men from Dragon Keep looked at him, once. Then they looked away, holding their breath.

Finally he said, "Let us go."

When they reached the border, they found Ege diCorsini, with a large company of well-armed men, waiting for them.

"Olivia sent to me," he said to Iyadur Atani. "Have you found her?"

"Martun Hal has her," the dragon-lord said. "He says he will kill her if we try to get her back." His face was set. "He may kill her anyway."

"He won't kill her," Ege diCorsini said. "He'll use her to bargain with. He will want his weapons and his army back, and freedom to move about his land."

"Give it to him," Iyadur Atani said. "I want my wife."

So Ege diCorsini sent a delegation of his men to Martun Hal, offering to modify the terms of Serrenhold's surrender, if he would release Joanna Atani unharmed.

But Martun Hal did not release Joanna. As diCorsini had said, he used her welfare to bargain with, demanding first the freedom to move about his own country, and then the restoration of his war band, first to one hundred, then to three hundred men.

"We must know where she is. When we know

where she is we can rescue her," diCorsini said. And he sent spies into Serrenhold, with instructions to discover where in that bleak and barren country the lady of Ippa was. But Martun Hal, ever crafty, had anticipated this. He sent a message to Iyadur Atani, warning that payment for the trespass of strangers would be exacted upon Joanna's body. He detailed, with blunt and horrific cruelty, what that payment would be.

In truth, despite the threats, he did nothing to hurt his captive. For though years of war had scoured from him almost all human feeling save pride, ambition, and spite, he understood quite well that if Joanna died, and word of that death reached Dragon Keep, no power in or out of Ryoka could protect him.

As for Joanna, she had refused even to speak to him from the day his men had brought her, hair chopped like a boy's, wrapped in a soldier's cloak, into his castle. She did not weep. They put her in an inner chamber, and placed guards on the door, and assigned two women to care for her. They were both named Kate, and since one was large and one not, they were known as Big Kate and Small Kate. She did not rage, either. She ate the meals the women brought her, and slept in the bed they gave her.

Winter came early, as it does in Serrenhold. The wind moaned about the castle walls, and snow covered the mountains. Weeks passed, and Joanna's belly swelled. When it became clear beyond any doubt that she was indeed pregnant, the women who served her went swiftly to tell their lord.

"Are you sure?" he demanded. "If this is a trick, I will have you both flayed!"

"We are sure," they told him. "Send a physician to her, if you question it."

So Martun Hal sent a physician to Joanna's room. But Joanna refused to let him touch her. "I am Iyadur Atani's wife," she said. "I will allow no other man to lay his hands on me."

"Pray that it is a changeling, a dragon-child," Martun Hal said to his captains. And he told the two Kates to give Joanna whatever she needed for her comfort, save freedom.

The women went to Joanna and asked what she wanted.

"I should like a window," Joanna said. The rooms in which they housed her had all been windowless. They moved her to a chamber in a tower. It was smaller than the room in which they had been keeping her, but it had a narrow window, through which she could see sky and clouds, and on clear nights, stars.

When her idleness began to weigh upon her, she said, "Bring me books." They brought her books. But reading soon bored her.

"Bring me a loom."

"A loom? Can you weave?" Big Kate asked.

No," Joanna said. "Can you?"

"Of course."

"Then you can teach me." The women brought her the loom, and with it, a dozen skeins of bright wool. "Show me what to do." Big Kate showed her how to set up the threads, and how to cast the shuttle. The first thing she made was a yellow blanket, a small one.

Small Kate asked, "Who shall that be for?"

326

"For the babe," Joanna said.

Then she began another: a scarlet cloak, a large one, with a fine gold border.

"Who shall that be for?" Big Kate asked.

"For my lord, when he comes."

One grey afternoon, as Joanna sat at her loom, a red-winged hawk alighted on her windowsill.

"Good day," Joanna said to it. It cocked its head and stared at her sideways out of its left eye. "There is bread on the table." She pointed to the little table where she ate her food. She had left a slice of bread untouched from her midday meal, intending to eat it later. The hawk turned its beak, and stared at her out of its right eye. Hopping to the table, it pecked at the bread.

Then it fluttered to the floor, and became a dark-eyed, dark-haired woman wearing a grey cloak. Crossing swiftly to Joanna's seat, she whispered, "Leave the shutter ajar. I will come again tonight." Before Joanna could answer, she turned into a bird, and was gone.

That evening Joanna could barely eat. Concerned, Big Kate fussed at her. "You have to eat. The babe grows swiftly now; it needs all the nourishment you can give it. Look, here is the cream you wanted, and here is soft ripe cheese, come all the way from Merigny in the south, where they say it snows once every hundred years."

"I don't want it." Big Kate reached to close the window shutter. "Leave it!"

"It's freezing."

"I am warm."

"You might be feverish." Small Kate reached to feel her forehead.

"I am not. I'm fine."

At last they left her. She heard the bar slide across the door. She lay down on her bed. As was their custom, they had left her but a single candle, but light came from the hearth log. The babe moved in her belly. "Little one, I feel you," she whispered. "Be patient. We shall not always be in this loathsome place."

Then she heard the rustle of wings. A human shadow sprang across the walls of the chamber. A woman's voice said softly, "My lady, do you know me? I am Madelene of the Red Hawk sisters. I was at your wedding."

"I remember." Tears—the first she had shed since the start of her captivity—welled into Joanna's eyes. She knuckled them away. "I am glad to see you."

"And I you," Madelene said. "Since first I knew you were here, I have looked for you. I feared you were in torment, or locked away in some dark dungeon, where I might never find you."

"Can you help me to escape this place?"

Madelene said sadly, "No, my lady. I have no power to do that."

"I thought not." She reached beneath her pillow, and brought out a golden brooch shaped like a full-blown rose. It had been a gift from her husband on their wedding night. "Never mind. Here. Take this to my husband."

In Dragon Keep, Iyadur Atani's mood grew grimmer, and more remote. Martun Hal's threats obsessed him:

he imagined his wife alone, cold, hungry, confined to darkness, perhaps hurt. His appetite vanished; he ceased to eat, or nearly so.

At night he paced the castle corridors, silent as a ghost, cloakless despite the winter cold, his eyes like white flame. His soldiers and his servants began to fear him. One by one, they vanished from the castle.

But some, more resolute or more loyal, remained. Among them was Bran the archer, now captain of the archery wing, since Jarko, the former captain, had disappeared one moonless December night. When a strange woman appeared among them, claiming to bear a message to Iyadur Atani from his captive wife, it was to Bran the guards brought her.

He recognized her. Leading her to Iyadur Atani's chamber, he pounded on the closed door. It door opened. Iyadur Atani stood framed in the doorway. His face was gaunt.

Madelene held out the golden brooch.

Iyadur Atani knew it at once. The grief and rage and fear that had filled him for four months eased a little. Lifting the brooch from Madelene's palm, he touched it to his lips.

"Be welcome," he said. "Tell me how Joanna is. Is she well?"

"She bade me say that she is, my lord."

"And—the babe?"

"It thrives. It is your child, my lord. Your lady charged me to say that, and to tell you that no matter what rumors you might have heard, neither Martun Hal nor any of his men has touched her. Indeed, no torment has been offered her at all. Only she begs you to please, come quickly to succor her, for she is desperate to be home."

329

"Can you visit her easily?"

"I can."

"Then return to her, of your kindness. Tell her I love her. Tell her not to despair."

"She will not despair," Madelene said. "Despair is not in her nature. But I have a second message for you. This one is from my queen." She meant the matriarch of the Red Hawks, Jamis Delamico. "She said to tell you, where force will not prevail, seek magic. She says, go west, to Lake Urai. Find the sorcerer who lives beside the lake, and ask him how to get your wife back."

Iyadur Atani said, "I did not know there were still sorcerers in the west."

"There is one. The common folk know him as Viksa. But that is not his true name, my queen says."

"And does your queen know the true name of this reclusive wizard?" For everyone knows that unless you know a sorcerer's true name, he or she will not even speak with you.

"She does. And she told me to tell it to you," said Madelene. She leaned toward the dragon-lord, and whispered in his ear. "And she also told me to tell you, be careful when you deal with him. For he is sly, and what he intends he to do, he does not always reveal. But what he says he will do, he will do."

"Thank you," Iyadur Atani said, and he smiled, for the first time in a long time. "Cousin, I am in your debt." He told Bran to see to her comfort, and to provide her with whatever she needed, food, a bath, a place to sleep. Summoning his servants, he asked them to bring him a meal, and wine.

Then he called his officers together. "I am leaving," he said. "You must defend my people, and hold the borders against outlaws and incursions. If you need help, ask for aid from Mako or Derrenhold."

"How long will you be gone, my lord?" they asked him.

"I do not know."

Then he flew to Galva.

"I should have come before," he said. "I am sorry." He assured Olivia that despite her captivity, Joanna was well, and unharmed. "I go now to get her," he said. "When I return, I shall bring her with me. I swear it."

Issho, the southeastern province of Ryoka, is a rugged place. Though not so grim as Ippa, it has none of the gentle domesticated peace of Nakase. Its plains are colder than those of Nakase, and its rivers are wilder. The greatest of those rivers is the Endor. It starts in the north, beneath that peak which men call the Lookout, Mirrin, and pours ceaselessly south, cutting like a knife through Issho's open spaces to the border where Chuyo and Issho and Nakase meet.

It ends in Lake Urai. Lake Urai is vast, and even on a fair day, the water is not blue, but pewter-grey. In winter, it does not freeze. Contrary winds swirl about it; at dawn and at twilight grey mist obscures its contours, and at all times the chill bright water lies quiescent, untroubled by even the most violent wind. The land about it is sparsely inhabited. Its people are a hardy, silent folk, not particularly friendly to strangers. They respect the lake, and do not willingly discuss its secrets. When the tall, fair-haired stranger appeared among them, having come, so he said, from Ippa, they were happy to prepare his food and take his money, but were inclined to answer his questions evasively, or not at all.

The lake is as you see it. The wizard of the lake? Never heard of him.

But the stranger was persistent. He took a room at The Red Deer in Jen, hired a horse—oddly, he seemed to have arrived without one—and roamed about the lake. The weather did not seem to trouble him. "We have winter in my country." His clothes were plain, but clearly of the highest quality, and beneath his quiet manner there was iron.

"His eyes are different," the innkeeper's wife said. "He's looking for a wizard. Maybe he's one himself, in disguise."

One grey March afternoon, when the lake lay shrouded in mist, Iyadur Atani came upon a figure sitting on a rock beside a small fire. It was dressed in rags, and held what appeared to be a fishing pole.

The dragon-lord's heart quickened. He dismounted. Tying his horse to a tall reed, he walked toward the fisherman. As he approached, the hunched figure turned. Beneath the ragged hood he glimpsed white hair, and a visage so old and wrinkled that he could not tell if he was facing a man or a woman.

"Good day," he said. The ancient being nodded. "My name is Iyadur Atani. Men call me the Silver Dragon. I am looking for a wizard."

The ancient one shook its head, and gestured, as if to say, Leave me alone. Iyadur Atani crouched.

"Old One, I don't believe you are as you appear," he said in a conversational tone. "I believe you are the one I seek. If you are indeed—" and then he said the name that Madelene of the Red Hawks had whispered in his ear—"I beg you to help me. For I have come a long way to look for you."

An aged hand swept the hood aside. Dark grey eyes stared out of a withered, wrinkled face.

A feeble voice said, "Who told you my name?"

"A friend."

"Huh. Whoever it was is no friend of *mine*. What does the Silver Dragon need a wizard for?"

"If you are truly wise," Iyadur Atani said, "you know."

The sorcerer laughed softly. The hunched figure straightened. The rags became a silken gown with glittering jewels at its hem and throat. Instead of an old man, the dragon-lord faced a man in his prime, of princely bearing, with luminous chestnut hair and eyes the color of a summer storm. The fishing pole became a tall staff. Its crook was carved like a serpent's head. The sorcerer pointed the staff at the ground, and said three words.

A doorway seemed to open in the stony hillside. Joanna Torneo Atani stood within it. She wore furs, and was visibly pregnant.

"Joanna!" The dragon-lord reached for her. But his hands gripped empty air.

"Illusion," said the sorcerer known as Viksa. "A simple spell, but effective, don't you think? You are correct, my lord. I know you lost your wife. I assume you want her back. Tell me, why do you not lead your war band to Serrenhold and rescue her?"

"Martun Hal will kill her if I do that."

"I see."

"Will you help me?"

"Perhaps," said the sorcerer. The serpent in his staff

turned its head to stare at the dragon-lord. Its eyes were rubies. "What will you pay me if I help you?"

"I have gold."

Viksa yawned. "I have no interest in gold."

"Jewels," said the dragon-lord, "fine clothing, a horse to bear you wherever you might choose to go, a castle of your own to dwell in..."

"I have no use for those."

"Name your price, and I will pay it," Iyadur Atani said steadily. "I reserve only the life of my wife and my child."

"But not your own?" Viksa cocked his head. "You intrigue me. Indeed, you move me. I accept your offer, my lord. I will help you rescue your wife from Serrenhold. I shall teach you a spell, a very simple spell, I assure you. When you speak it, you will be able to hide within a shadow. In that way you may pass into Serrenhold unseen."

"And its price?"

Viksa smiled. "In payment, I will take—*you*. Not your life, but your service. It has been many years since I had someone to hunt for me, cook for me, build my fire, and launder my clothes. It will amuse me to have a dragon as my servant."

"For how long would I owe you service?"

"As long as I wish it."

"That seems unfair."

The wizard shrugged.

"When would this service start?"

The wizard shrugged again. "It may be next month, or next year. Or it may be twenty years from now. Do we have an agreement?"

Iyadur Atani considered. He did not like this wizard. But he could see no other way to get his wife back.

"We do," he said. "Teach me the spell."

So Viksa the sorcerer taught Iyadur Atani the spell which would enable him to hide in a shadow. It was not a difficult spell. Iyadur Atani rode his hired horse back to The Red Deer and paid the innkeeper what remained on his bill. Then he walked into the bare field beside the inn, and became the Silver Dragon. As the innkeeper and his wife watched open-mouthed, he circled the inn once, and then sped north.

"A dragon!" the innkeeper's wife said, with intense satisfaction. "I wonder if he found the sorcerer. See, I told you his eyes were odd." The innkeeper agreed. Then he went up to the room Iyadur Atani had occupied, and searched carefully in every cranny, in case the dragon-lord had chanced to leave some gold behind.

Now it was in Iyadur Atani's mind to fly immediately to Serrenhold Castle. But, remembering Martun Hal's threats, he did not. He flew to a point just south of Serrenhold's southern border. And there, in a nondescript village, he bought a horse, a shaggy brown gelding. From there he proceeded to Serrenhold Castle. It was not so tedious a journey as he had thought it would be. The prickly stunted pine trees that grew along the slopes of the wind-swept hills showed new green along their branches. Birds sang. Foxes loped across the hills, hunting mice and quail and the occasional stray chicken. The journey took six days. At dawn on the seventh day, Iyadur Atani fed the brown gelding and left him in a farmer's yard.

335

It was a fine spring morning. The sky was cloudless; the sun brilliant; the shadows sharp-edged as steel. Thorn-crowned hawthorn bushes lined the road to Serrenhold Castle. Their shadows webbed the ground. A wagon filled with lumber lumbered toward the castle. Its shadow rolled beneath it.

"Wizard," the dragon-lord said to the empty sky, "if you have played me false, I will find you wherever you try to hide, and eat your heart."

In her prison in the tower, Joanna Torneo Atani walked from one side of her chamber to the other. Her hair had grown long again: it fell around her shoulders. Her belly was round and high under the soft thick drape of her gown. The coming of spring had made her restless. She had asked to be allowed to walk on the ramparts, but this Martun Hal had refused.

Below her window, the castle seethed like a cauldron. The place was never still; the smells and sounds of war continued day and night. The air was thick with soot. Soldiers drilled in the courtyard. Martun Hal was planning an attack on Ege diCorsini. He had told her all about it, including his intention to destroy Galva. *I will burn it to the ground. I will kill your uncle and take your mother prisoner,* he had said. *Or perhaps not. Perhaps I will just have her killed.*

She glanced toward the patch of sky that was her window. If Madelene would only come, she could get word to Galva, or to her uncle in Derrenhold...But Madelene would not come in daylight, it was too dangerous.

She heard a hinge creak. The door to the outer chamber opened. "My lady," Big Kate called. She bustled in, bearing a tray. It held soup, bread, and a dish of thin sour pickles. "I brought your lunch."

"I'm not hungry."

Kate said, troubled, "My lady, you have to eat. For the baby."

"Leave it," Joanna said. "I will eat." Kate set the tray on the table, and left.

Joanna nibbled at a pickle. She rubbed her back, which ached. The baby's heel thudded against the inside of her womb. "My precious, my little one, be still," she said. For it was her greatest fear that her babe, Iyadur Atani's child, might in its haste to be born arrive early, before her husband arrived to rescue them. That he would come, despite Martun Hal's threats, she had no doubt. "Be still."

Silently, Iyadur Atani materialized from the shadows.

"Joanna," he said. He put his arms about her. She reached her hands up. Her fingertips brushed his face. She leaned against him, trembling.

She whispered into his shirt, "How did you...?"

"Magic." He touched the high mound of her belly. "Are you well? Have they mistreated you?"

"I am very well. The babe is well." She seized his hand and pressed his palm over the mound. The baby kicked strongly. "Do you feel?"

"Yes." Iyadur Atani stroked her hair. A scarlet cloak with an ornate gold border hung on a peg. He reached for it, and wrapped it about her. "Now, my love, we go. Shut your eyes, and keep them shut until I tell you to open them." He bent, and lifted her into his arms. Her heart thundered against his chest.

She breathed into his ear, "I am sorry. I am heavy."

"You weigh nothing," he said. His human shape

337

dissolved. The walls of the tower shuddered and burst apart. Blocks of stone and splintered planks of wood toppled into the courtyard. Women screamed. Arching his great neck, the Silver Dragon spread his wings and rose into the sky. The soldiers on the ramparts threw their spears at him, and fled. Joanna heard the screaming and felt the hot wind. The scent of burning filled her nostrils. She knew what must have happened. But the arms about her were her husband's, and human. She did not know how this could be, yet it was. Eyes tight shut, she buried her face against her husband's shoulder.

Martun Hal stood with a courier in the castle hall. The crash of stone and the screaming interrupted him. A violent gust of heat swept through the room. The windows of the hall shattered. Racing from the hall, he looked up, and saw the dragon circling. His men crouched, sobbing in fear. Consumed with rage, he looked about for a bow, a spear, a rock...Finally he drew his sword.

"Damn you!" he shouted impotently at his adversary.

Then the walls of his castle melted beneath a white-hot rain.

In Derrenhold, Ege diCorsini was, wearily, reluctantly, preparing for war. He did not want to fight Martun Hal, but he would, of course, if troops from Serrenhold took one step across his border. That an attack would be mounted he had no doubt. His spies had told him to expect it. Jamis of the Hawks had sent her daughters to warn him.

Part of his weariness was a fatigue of the spirit. *This*

is all my fault. I should have killed him when I had the opportunity. Ferris was right. The other part of his weariness was physical. He was tired much of the time, and none of the tonics or herbal concoctions that the physicians prescribed seemed to help. His heart raced oddly. He could not sleep. Sometimes in the night he wondered if the Old One sleeping underground had dreamed of him. When the Old One dreams of you, you die. But he did not want to die and leave his domain and its people in danger, and so he planned a war, knowing all the while that he might die in the middle of it.

"My lord," a servant said, "you have visitors."

"Send them in," Ege diCorsini said. "No, wait." The physicians had said he needed to move about. Rising wearily, he went into the hall.

He found there his niece Joanna, big with child, and with her, her flame-haired, flame-eyed husband. A strong smell of burning hung about their clothes.

Ege diCorsini drew a long breath. He kissed Joanna on both cheeks. "I will let your mother know that you are safe."

"She needs to rest," Iyadur Atani said.

"I do not need to rest. I have been doing absolutely nothing for the last six months. I need to go home," Joanna said astringently. "Only I do not wish to ride. Uncle, would you lend us a litter, and some steady beasts to draw it?"

"You may have anything I have," Ege diCorsini said. And for a moment he was not tired at all.

Couriers galloped throughout Ippa, bearing the news: Martun Hal was dead; Serrenhold Castle was ash, or nearly so. The threat of war was—after twenty years—truly over. Martun Hal's captains—most of them—had died with him. Those still alive hid, hoping to save their skins.

Two weeks after the rescue and the burning of Serrenhold, Ege diCorsini died.

In May, with her mother and sisters at her side, Joanna gave birth to a son. The baby had flame-colored hair and eyes like his father's. He was named Avahir. A year and a half later, a second son was born to Joanna Torneo Atani. He had dark hair, and eyes like his mother's. He was named Jon. Like the man whose name he bore, Jon Atani had a sweet disposition and a loving heart. He adored his brother, and Avahir loved his younger brother fiercely. Their loyalty to each other made their parents very happy.

Thirteen years almost to the day from the burning of Serrenhold, on a bright spring morning, a man dressed richly as a prince, carrying a white birch staff, appeared at the front gate of Atani Castle and requested audience with the dragon-lord. He refused to enter, or even to give his name, saying only, "Tell him the fisherman has come for his catch."

His servants found Iyadur Atani in the great hall of his castle.

"My lord, " they said, "a stranger stands at the front gate, who will not give his name. He says, *The fisherman has come for his catch.*"

"I know who it is," their lord replied. He walked to the gate of his castle. The sorcerer stood there, leaning on his serpent headed staff, entirely at ease.

"Good day," he said cheerfully. "Are you ready to travel?"

And so Iyadur Atani left his children and his kingdom to serve Viksa the wizard. I do not know—no one ever asked her, not even their sons—what Iyadur

Atani and his wife said to one another that day. Avahir Atani, who at twelve was already full-grown, as changeling children are wont to be, inherited the lordship of Atani Castle. Like his father, he gained the reputation of being fierce, but just.

Jon Atani married a granddaughter of Rudolf diMako, and went to live in that city.

Joanna Atani remained in Dragon Keep. As time passed, and Iyadur Atani did not return, her sisters and her brother, even her sons, urged her to remarry. She told them all not to be fools; she was wife to the Silver Dragon. Her husband was alive, and might return at any time, and how would he feel to find another man warming her bed? She became her son's chief minister, and in that capacity could often be found riding across Dragon's country, and elsewhere in Ippa, to Derrenhold and Mirrinhold and Ragnar, and even to far Voiana, where the Red Hawk sisters, one in particular, always welcomed her. She would not go to Serrenhold.

But always she returned to Dragon Keep.

As for Iyadur Atani: he traveled with the wizard throughout Ryoka, carrying his bags, preparing his oatcakes and his bath water, scraping mud from his boots. Viksa's boots were often muddy, for he was a great traveler, who walked, rather than rode, to his many destinations. In the morning, when Iyadur Atani brought the sorcerer his breakfast, Viksa would say, "Today we go to Rotsa"—or Ruggio, or Rowena. "They have need of magic." He never said how he knew this. And off they would go to Vipurri or Rotsa or Talvela, to Sorvino, Ruggio or Rowena.

Sometimes the need to which he was responding had to do directly with magic, as when a curse needed to be lifted. Often it had to do with common disasters. A river had swollen in its banks and needed to be restrained. A landslide had fallen on a house or barn. Sometimes the one who needed them was noble, or rich. Sometimes not. It did not matter to Viksa. He could enchant a cornerstone, so that the wall it anchored would rise straight and true; he could spell a field, so that its crop would thrust from the soil no matter what the rainfall.

His greatest skill was with water. Some sorcerers draw a portion of their power from an element: wind, water, fire or stone. Viksa could coax a spring out of earth that had known only drought for a hundred years. He could turn stagnant water sweet. He knew the names of every river, stream, brook and waterfall in Issho.

In the first years of his servitude Iyadur Atani thought often of his sons, and especially Avahir, and of Joanna, but after a while his anxiety for them faded. After a longer while, he found he did not think of them so often—rarely at all, in fact. He even forgot their names. He had already relinquished his own. *Iyadur is too grand a name for a servant,* the sorcerer had remarked. *You need a different name.*

And so the tall, fair-haired man became known as Shadow. He carried the sorcerer's pack, and cooked his food. He rarely spoke.

"Why is he so silent?" women, bolder and more curious than their men, asked the sorcerer.

Sometimes the sorcerer answered, "No reason. It's his nature." And sometimes he told a tale, a long, elaborate fantasy of spells and dragons and sorcerers, a gallant tale in which Shadow had been the hero, but from which he had emerged changed—broken. Shadow, listening, wondered if perhaps this tale was true. It might have been. It explained why his memory was so erratic, and so vague.

His dreams, by contrast, were vivid and intense. He dreamed often of a dark-walled castle flanked by white-capped mountains. Sometimes he dreamed that he was a bird, flying over the castle. The most adventurous of the women, attracted by Shadow's looks, and, sometimes, by his silence, tried to talk with him. But their smiles and allusive glances only made him shy. He thought that he had had a wife, once. Maybe she had left him. He thought perhaps she had. But maybe not. Maybe she had died.

He had no interest in the women they met, though as far as he could tell, his body still worked as it should. He was a powerful man, well-formed. Shadow wondered sometimes what his life had been before he had come to serve the wizard. He had skills: he could hunt and shoot a bow, and use a sword. Perhaps he had served in some noble's war band. He bore a knife now, a good one, with a bone hilt, but no sword. He did not need a sword. Viksa's reputation, and his magic, shielded them both.

Every night, before they slept, wherever they were, half-speaking, half-chanting in a language Shadow did not know, the sorcerer wove spells of protection about them and their dwelling. The spells were very powerful. They made Shadow's ears hurt.

Once, early in their association, he asked the sorcerer what the spell was for.

"Protection," Viksa replied. Shadow had been surprised. He had not realized Viksa had enemies.

343

But now, having traveled with the sorcerer as long as he had, he knew that even the lightest magic can have consequences, and Viksa's magic was not always light. He could make rain, but he could also make drought. He could lift curses or lay them. He was a man of power, and he had his vanity. He enjoyed being obeyed. Sometimes he enjoyed being feared.

Through spring, summer, and autumn, the wizard traveled wherever he was called to go. But in winter they returned to Lake Urai. He had a house beside the lake, a simple place, furnished with simple things: a pallet, a table, a chair, a shelf for books. But Viksa rarely looked at the books; it seemed he had no real love for study. Indeed, he seemed to have no passion for anything, save sorcery itself—and fishing. All through the Issho winter, despite the bitter winds, he took his little coracle out upon the lake, and sat there with a pole. Sometimes he caught a fish, or two, or half a dozen. Sometimes he caught none.

"Enchant them," Shadow said to him one grey afternoon, when he returned to the house empty-handed. "Call them to your hook with magic."

The wizard shook his head. "I can't."

"Why not?"

"I was one of them once." Shadow looked at him, uncertain. "Before I was a sorcerer, I was a fish."

It was impossible to tell if he was joking or serious. It might have been true. It explained, at least, his affinity for water.

While he fished, Shadow hunted. The country around the lake was rich with game; despite the winter, they did not lack for meat. Shadow hunted deer and badger and beaver. He saw wolves, but did not kill them. Nor would he kill birds, though birds there were; even in winter, geese came often to the lake. Their presence woke in him a wild, formless longing.

One day he saw a white bird, with wings as wide as he was tall, circling over the lake. It had a beak like a raptor. It called to him, an eerie sound. Something about it made his heart beat faster. When Viksa returned from his sojourn at the lake, Shadow described the stranger bird to him, and asked what it was.

"A condor," the wizard said.

"Where does it come from?"

"From the north," the wizard said, frowning.

"It called to me. It looked—noble."

"It is not. It is scavenger, not predator." He continued to frown. That night he spent a long time over his nightly spells.

In spring, the kingfishers and guillemots returned to the lake. And one April morning, when Shadow laid breakfast upon the table, Viksa said, "Today we go to Dale."

"Where is that?"

"In the White Mountains, in Kameni, far to the north." And so they went to Dale, where a petty lordling needed Viksa's help in deciphering the terms and conditions of an ancient prophecy, for within it lay the future of his kingdom.

From Dale they traveled to Secca, where a youthful hedge-witch, hoping to shatter a boulder, had used a spell too complex for her powers, and had managed to summon a stone demon, which promptly ate her. It was an old, powerful demon. It took a day, a night, and another whole day until Viksa, using the strongest spells he knew, was able to send it back into the Void.

345

They rested that night at a roadside inn, south of Secca. Viksa, exhausted from his battle with the demon, went to bed right after his meal, so worn that he fell asleep without taking the time to make his customary incantations.

Shadow considered waking him to remind him of it, and decided not to. Instead, he, too, slept.

And there, in an inn south of Secca, Iyadur Atani woke.

He was not, he realized, in his bed, or even in his bedroom. He lay on the floor. The coverlet around his shoulders was rough, coarse wool, not the soft quilt he was used to. Also, he was wearing his boots.

He said, "Joanna?" No one answered. A candle sat on a plate at his elbow. He lit it without touching it.

Sitting up soundlessly, he gazed about the chamber, at the bed and its snoring occupant, at the packs he had packed himself, the birchwood staff athwart the doorway...Memory flooded through him. The staff was Viksa's. The man sleeping in the bed was Viksa. And he—*he* was Iyadur Atani, lord of Dragon Keep.

His heart thundered. His skin coursed with heat. The ring on his hand glowed, but he could not feel the burning. Fire coursed beneath his skin. He rose.

How long had Viksa's magic kept him in thrall—five years? Ten years? More?

He took a step toward the bed. The serpent in the wizard's staff opened its eyes. Raising its carved head, it hissed at him.

The sound woke Viksa. Gazing up from his bed at the bright shimmering shape looming over him, he knew immediately what had happened. He had made a mistake. *Fool*, he thought, *O you fool.*

It was too late now.

The guards on the walls of Secca saw a pillar of fire rise into the night. Out of it—so they swore, with such fervor that even the most skeptical did not doubt them—flew a silver dragon. It circled the flames, bellowing with such power and ferocity that all who heard it trembled.

Then it beat the air with its great wings, and leaped north.

In Dragon Keep, a light powdery snow covered the garden. It did not deter the rhubarb shoots breaking through the soil, or the fireweed, or the buds on the birches. A sparrow swung in the birch branches, singing. The clouds that had brought the snow had dissipated; the day was bright and fair, the shadows sharp as the angle of the sparrow's wing against the light.

Joanna Atani walked along the garden path. Her face was lined, and her hair, though still lustrous and thick, was streaked with silver. But her step was as vigorous, and her eyes as bright, as they had been when first she came to Atani Castle, over thirty years before.

Bending, she brushed a snowdrop free of snow. By midday, she judged, the snow would be gone. A clatter of pans arose in the kitchen. A clear voice, imperious and young, called from within. She smiled. It was Hikaru, Avahir's first-born and heir. He was only two, but had the height and grace of a lad twice that age.

A woman answered him, her voice soft and firm. That was Geneva Tuolinnen, Hikaru's mother. She was an excellent mother, calm and unexcitable. She was a good seamstress, too, and a superb manager; far better at running the castle than Joanna had ever been. She could scarcely handle a bow, though, and thought swordplay was entirely man's work.

She and Joanna were as friendly as two strong-willed women can be.

A black, floppy-eared puppy bounded across Joanna's feet, nearly knocking her down. Rup the dog-boy scampered after it. They tore through the garden and raced past the kitchen door into the yard.

A man walked into the garden. Joanna shaded her eyes. He was quite tall. She did not recognize him. His hair was nearly white, but he did not move like an old man. Indeed, the height of him and the breadth of his shoulder reminded her of Avahir, but she knew it was not Avahir. He was hundred of miles away, in Kameni.

She said, "Sir, who are you?"

The man came closer. "Joanna?"

She knew that voice. For a moment she ceased to breathe. Then she walked toward him.

It was her husband.

He looked exactly as he had the morning he had left with the wizard, sixteen years before. His eyes were the same, and his scent, and the heat of his body against hers. She slid her palms beneath his shirt. His skin was warm. Their lips met.

I do not know what Iyadur Atani and his wife said to one another that day. Surely there were questions, and answers. Surely there were tears, of sorrow, and of joy.

He told her of his travels, of his captivity, and of his freedom. She told him of their sons, particularly of his heir, Avahir, who ruled Dragon's Country.

"He is a good lord, respected throughout Ryoka. His people fear him and love him. He is called the Azure Dragon. He married a girl from Issho. She is cousin to the Talvela; we are at peace with them, and with the Nyo. She and Avahir have a son, Hikaru. Jon, too, is wed. He and his wife live in Mako. They have three children, two boys and a girl. You are a grandfather."

He smiled at that. Then he said, "Where is my son?"

"In Kameni, at a council called by Rowan Imorin, the king's war leader, who wished to lead an army against the Chuyo pirates." She stroked his face. It was not true, as she had first thought, that he was unchanged. The years had marked him. Still, he looked astonishingly young. She wondered if she seemed old to him.

"Never leave me again," she said.

A shadow crossed his face. He lifted her hands to his lips and kissed them, front and back. Then he said, "My love, I would not. But I must go. I cannot stay here."

"What are you saying?"

"Avahir is lord of this land now. You know the dragon-nature. We are jealous of power, we dragons. It would go ill were I to stay."

Joanna's blood chilled. She did know. The history of the dragon-folk is filled with tales of rage and rivalry: sons strive against fathers, brothers against brothers, mothers against their children. They are bloody tales. For this reason, among others, the dragon-kindred do not live very long.

She said steadily, "You cannot hurt your son."

"I would not," said Iyadur Atani. "Therefore I must leave."

"Where will you go?"

"I don't know. Will you come with me?"

She locked her fingers through his huge ones, and smiled through tears. "I will go wherever you wish. Only give me time to kiss my grandchild, and write a letter to my son. For he must know that I have gone of my own accord."

And so, Iyadur Atani and Joanna Torneo Atani left Atani Castle. They went quietly, without fuss, accompanied by neither man nor maidservant. They went first to Mako, where Iyadur Atani greeted his younger son, and met his son's wife, and their children.

From there they went to Derrenhold, and from Derrenhold, west, to Voiana, the home of the Red Hawk sisters. From Voiana, letters came to Avahir Atani and to Jon Atani from their mother, assuring them, and particularly Avahir, that she was with her husband, and that she was well.

Avahir Atani, who truly loved his mother, flew to Voiana. But he arrived to find them gone.

"Where are they?" he asked Jamis Delamico, who was still matriarch of the Red Hawk clan. For the Red Hawk sisters live long.

"They left."

"Where did they go?"

Jamis Delamico shrugged. "They did not tell me their destination and I did not ask."

There were no more letters. Over time, word trickled back to Dragon Keep that they had been seen in Rowena, or Sorvino, or Secca, or the mountains north of Dale.

"Where were they going?" Avahir Atani asked, when his servants came to him to tell him these stories. But no one could tell him that.

Time passed; Ippa prospered. In Dragon Keep, a daughter was born to Avanir and Geneva Atani. They named her Lucia. She was small and dark-haired and feisty. In Derrenhold, and Mako and Mirrinhold, memories of conflict faded. In the windswept west, the folk of Serrenhold rebuilt their lord's tower.

In the east, Rowan Imorin, the war leader of Kameni, summoned the lords of all the provinces to unite against the Chuyo pirates. The lords of Ippa, instead of quarreling with each other, joined the lords of Nakase and Kameni. They fought many battles. They gained many victories.

But in one battle, not the greatest, an arrow shot by a Chuyo archer sliced into the throat of Avanir Atani, and killed him. Grimly, his mourning soldiers made a pyre, and burned his body. For the dragon-kindred do not lie in earth.

Hikaru, the Shining Dragon, became lord of Dragon Keep. Like his father and his grandfather before him, he was feared and respected throughout Ippa.

One foggy autumn, a stranger arrived at the gates of Dragon Keep, requesting to see the lord. He was an old man, with silver hair. His back was stooped, but they could see that he had once been powerful. He bore no sword, but only a knife with a bone hilt.

"Who are you?" the servants asked him.

"My name doesn't matter," he answered. "Tell him I have a gift for him."

They brought him to Hikaru. Hikaru said, "Old man, I am told you have a gift for me."

"It is so," the old man said. He extended his palm. On it sat a golden brooch, fashioned in the shape of a rose. "It is an heirloom of your house. It was given by your grandfather, Iyadur, to his wife Joanna, on their wedding night. She is dead now, and so it comes to you. You should give it to your wife, when you wed."

Frowning, Hikaru said, "How do you come by this thing? Who are you? Are you a sorcerer?"

"I am no one," the old man replied; "a shadow."

"That is not an answer," Hikaru said, and he signaled to his soldiers to seize the stranger.

But the men who stepped forward to hold the old man found their hands passing through empty air. They hunted through the castle for him, but he was gone. They decided that he was a sorcerer, or perhaps the sending of a sorcerer. Eventually they forgot him. When the shadow of the dragon first appeared in Atani Castle, rising like smoke out of the castle walls, few thought of the old man who had vanished into shadow one autumnal morning. Those who did kept it to themselves. But Hikaru Atani remembered. He kept the brooch, and gave it to his wife upon their wedding night. And he told his soldiers to honor the shadow-dragon when it came, and not to speak lightly of it.

"For clearly," he said, "it belongs here."

The shadow of the dragon still lives in the walls of Atani Castle. It comes as it chooses, unsummoned. And still, in Dragon's Country, and throughout Ippa and Issho, and even into the east, the singers tell the story of Iyadur Atani, of his wife Joanna, and of the burning of Serrenhold.

Individual Story Copyrights